NECROPHENIA

NECROPHENIA

ROBERT RANKIN

The right of Robert Rankin to be identified as the author
of this work has been asserted by him in accordance
with the Copyright, Designs and Patents Act 1988.

First published in Great Britain in 2008 by
Gollancz
An imprint of the Orion Publishing Group
Orion House, 5 Upper St Martin's Lane,
London WC2H 9EA
An Hachette UK Company

This edition published in Great Britain in 2009 by
Gollancz

3 5 7 9 10 8 6 4

A CIP catalogue record for this book
is available from the British Library

ISBN: 978 0575 08242 7

Typeset at The Spartan Press Ltd,
Lymington, Hants

Printed and bound in the UK by
CPI Mackays, Chatham ME5 8TD

The Orion Publishing Group's policy is to use papers that
are natural, renewable and recyclable products and made
from wood grown in sustainable forests. The logging and
manufacturing processes are expected to conform to the
environmental regulations of the country of origin.

THIS BOOK IS DEDICATED,

WITH LOVE,

TO MY GRANDSON

TYLER

THE MAGIC BOY

It was about a
week after I'd
almost saved
mankind.

And I was having a lie-in.

It had been a late one, the night before, I so remember.

A reunion of old school buddies. The class of 63. Of course, there are fewer of us every year now. Not, I think, because we are dying off. No, I suspect that it is because we have, over the years and through the many past reunions, learned just how much we all truly hate each other. How little we ever had in common when we were at school together and how, with the passing of the years, that little has become less and less.

And less.

So fewer turn up every year.

There were just the three of us last night.

And we didn't really have a lot to say to each other.

There was Rob, who is always jolly, come what may, and who is responsible for putting these get-togethers together. Rob is of medium height and about as broad as he is long. He *is* always jolly. Although last night he was less jolly than usual. This lack of jollity probably occasioned by the less-than-impressive turnout.

Rob is in advertising. He is a copywriter and he has, over the years, worked on some quite famous campaigns.

You can earn big money in advertising as a copywriter if you have the ability to come up with snappy catchphrases that touch the public's imagination, and through so doing subtly influence the public to purchase whatever product it happens to be that is having a snappy catchphrase applied to it.

You will no doubt recall the 'Get Some Cheese' campaign a few years back, with that bloke out of that series on the telly saying, 'Get some cheese' to all kinds of famous people in unusual situations.

That was one of Rob's. I never quite got it myself. But, like almost everyone else at the time, I would say, 'Get some cheese' to some stranger on a bus, or the lady behind the dry-cleaner's counter. To much mirth.

In fact, now that I come to think about it, I really miss saying, 'Get some cheese' to complete strangers. I might take it up again today and see how it works out.

So that's Rob, really.

And then there's Neil.

Neil did really well. He went into radio, started as a sound engineer, became a DJ, then a producer. Started with the wireless, but later moved onwards and upwards.

As they say.

Neil is now a film producer.

And he's promised me a part in the next film he produces. Not that I'm altogether keen.

There is something decidedly odd about the films that Neil produces. They aren't ever shown at regular cinemas. They receive 'special showings' in art houses and the DVDs cannot be purchased legally in this country.

I have one of Neil's DVDs. And I hope very much that what is shown on the screen is actually acting.

And so that is Neil.

And that is Rob.

Which leaves only me.

The Third Man, as it were. A bit like Michael Rennie, or indeed Orson Welles, depending upon which version you prefer.

And I am a bit like the Third Man. A bit. I'm enigmatic, me. I move in the shadows. I'm a sort of private investigator. A rather *strange* sort. You see, I developed this technique that I call the Tyler Technique, because my name is Tyler and it is *my* technique. If I take up just a moment to explain it here, it will save time later, when something will occur that will need an explanation, but in all the excitement of whatever is going on (and there will be excitement, lots of it, because in my business there always is) won't get one and therefore may be found worrying by those who worry about such things.

Put simply (and there's a lot more to it than this, let me tell you, but this will suffice for now), the Tyler Technique involves letting things happen naturally. Not pushing things. Not being the *cause and effect* of things. For I've found that things tend to work out for the best, eventually. If you leave them alone.

And so, with all that said by way of a brief introduction to myself – with a brief aside regarding my two ex-school chums Rob and Neil, for more will be spoken of them later – let us take ourselves back, back to where this story began and the events that led me to become the greatest detective that ever was. And how I almost saved Mankind as well.

2

I was a very musical youth.

I harmonised with hairdryers. And whistled along with the rhythm of life. There seems to be music everywhere when you're young. And there certainly was a lot of it about back in the nineteen-sixties, when I was growing up. I know they say a lot of silly things about the nineteen-sixties now, such as all that rot that 'if you can remember the nineteen-sixties, you weren't part of them, *man*'. A lot of tosh and toot, that is. They were very intense and colourful, though. And very musical, too, and when it is said that 'The Beatles' tunes were the background music for an entire generation', this is not without some truth.

But there was a lot more music about than just what you heard coming out of a dolly-bird's transistor radio.

For instance, there were The Sumerian Kynges, who were my favourites. Still are, really. But then, I know where the bodies are buried, so I can have The Sumerian Kynges come and play at my house for free whenever I want them to.

Which isn't often, because they've never really added much to their nineteen-sixties repertoire.

I was the lead singer with The Kynges for a while back in nineteen sixty-three, which is why I mention them here. I was in the original line-up when they formed. And not a lot of people know that.

The Kynges were a school band then. Because we were all at the same school together and the only instruments that there were to be played belonged to the school.

We couldn't afford to purchase our own instruments because we were poor. And poor people cannot afford expensive musical instruments. You will note that whilst you may see many a drunken down-and-out jigging from one foot to another and engaging in a bit of the old unaccompanied singing, you will rarely, if ever, see a drunken down-and-out sitting in the gutter playing either the harp or a Bechstein concert grand. It's a monetary thing. A fiscal thing.

The Kynges began as a ukulele band.

There were five ukuleles in the school's 'band room'. The band room was a large cupboard with a skylight. As far as I can recall, the sole purpose of the skylight was to admit the midnight entry of disgruntled scholars hell-bent on destruction.

Have you noticed that whenever schoolboys break into their schools at night they *always* destroy the musical instruments?

They *always do*. I wonder why that is.

My therapist says it is due to frustration caused by a lack of wish-fulfilment. I tell her that it is more likely a tradition, or an old charter, or something.

Mr Jenner, the music teacher, was evidently a student of human nature who well understood the schoolboy psyche. He kept the sur-viving ukuleles (once there had been a full brass section and two bass drums) under lock and key. Which is to say that they were locked in the 'band room' (the one with the skylight). But they were also locked inside a Cameo Mason Celebrated Percussion Safe. You don't see many of *those* any more, but then they were all but impregnable.

As far as I know, only one boy in the long history of the school ever penetrated the band-room safe without Mr Jenner opening it up for him.

That schoolboy's name was Otto. And there will be *no* more about *him* later.

So, five ukuleles and the dawn of The Sumerian Kynges.

If I recall correctly, and I *do*, it took a great deal of persuading on my part to convince the other members of The Sumerian Kynges that playing the ukulele could be *cool*.

Being cool was essential. It was almost a matter of life and death back then. And in my opinion it still is, even today.

It's a given thing, really. An instinctive thing. If you are cool enough simply to know, then you simply know whether something is cool or whether it is not. And come on now, don't we all, deep, deep down in our very souls, *want* to be cool?

Of course we do.

So, as to those ukuleles.

I knew that being up on stage and playing in a rock 'n' roll band was cool. But then pretty much everyone knows that. And I *did* want to be cool. And I *did* want to play in a rock 'n' roll band. But I was poor and the other guys in the band (notice that I use the word 'guys' here rather than, say, 'schoolboys', and also the word 'band' rather than the words 'teenage combo', which might not necessarily be *cool*) were also poor and we had no way of raising sufficient money to purchase guitars and a drum kit. Nor indeed a Marshall amp and stack system. But as Jim Marshall was only perfecting these things in the garage behind his shop in Hanwell at the time, that is neither here nor there.

So, regarding those ukuleles.

There were four Sumerian Kynges back then. The original Fad Four.* There was Rob, who would later become an advertising copy-writer. Neil, who would later movie-produce. Myself, who would go on to find fame and misfortune in oh so many fields.

And then there was Toby.

And Toby was the odd one.

It was many years later that the rest of The Sumerian Kynges came to realise just how odd Toby really was. But by then the original line-up was no more. And it was all too late.

But more of that anon.

So back to those ukuleles.

'Ukes are *not* cool,' said Rob. 'Harps are cool, but not ukes.'

'*Harps?*' This raised voice belonged to Neil. 'We cannot afford a jews harp, let alone a *real* harp.'

'Harp as in harmonica,' said Rob. 'Do try to be cool, Neil, really.'

Neil did grindings of his teeth. I came to recognise these grindings as 'the grindings of discontent'.

'We can afford nothing,' said Neil. 'We are poor.'

'Tea chests and broom handles,' said Toby. 'They cost next to nothing. We could be a skiffle band.'

'There is a steel band called The Skiffle Bunch,' said Neil, who knew about all kinds of what was then called 'ethnic' music. 'Steel pan maestros. Genius.'

'Get some cheese!' said Rob, as it was what he used to say when he had nothing to say. So to speak.

This conversation was being held in Toby's dad's shed, at the bottom of Toby's dad's and mum's and Toby's too back garden.

It was where we went for band practise.

For lack of instrumentation, it was presently where we went for a cappella vocal practise.

I entered this shed at this very moment.

A veritable Duke of Cool.

* This term was originally coined by a reporter from the *Daily Mirror* who toured with the band during the 1970s, when eating disorders first became fashionable. And the Kynges were at the forefront of this trend.

My hair was all 'gassed back' with Brylcreem. My school shirt was untucked from my school trousers (well, shorts) and its shirt tail protruded from the lower rear of my grey school jumper. This jumper's breast being adorned with many beer-bottle-top badges.*

My socks were rolled down. My shoes were unpolished.

And my armpits *really* smelled.

'Hi, guys,' I said, raising an arm in a parody of the Nazi salute. The guys fell to cringing and covering their noses.

Cool.

'We need instruments,' said Toby, as I lowered my arm and then lowered myself onto the half-bag of solid cement that in those days was to be found in every garden shed.

Not the *same* half-bag, obviously, although it was hard at first glance to tell.

'Ukuleles,' said I.

'Uncool,' quoth one and all. 'We have discussed ukuleles. Ukuleles are *not* cool.'

'On the contrary,' said I. (In fact I said, 'Ooh contraire,' which was French and pretty cool in its way.)

'Ukuleles are *cool*?' said Rob. 'How so, cheesy boy?'

'Robert Johnson,' I said. And I enjoyed the desired effect that the enunciation of this name produced.

There was an awed silence.

And then Toby spoke.

'Robert Johnson did *not* play a ukulele,' said Toby. 'Robert Johnson played a Gibson L-1.'

'Of course,' said I. 'But we also know what Robert Johnson did down at the crossroads at midnight.'

'Sold his soul to the Devil,' said Neil, a-crossing at himself, 'in exchange for musical immortality. And his day is coming soon, believe you me. All will know the name of Robert Johnson.'†

'Yes,' said I, comfying myself upon the half-bag of solid cement, which was no easy thing, but yet I achieved it. 'Well, one week after Robert Johnson went down to the crossroads at midnight, there was a fella over here who went down there too. Well, not the same cross-roads actually. Johnson went down to where Highway Forty-Two crossed Highway Sixty-One. This fella didn't go there.

---

* The technique for adapting the beer-bottle top to badge-wear is now lost in the Mists of Time. Those who remember it, remember it, and these few souls remain cool.
† And they would.

'He went down South (like Johnson), but down just south of Birmingham. He went to the Crossroads Motel. And there he met the Devil and he sold *his* soul to the Devil.

'Right there and then.'

'Who he?' asked Toby.

'George Formby,' I said.

And then they beat me up.

Which was unfair. I was outnumbered. In a fair fight I could have taken any of them. Still can. I keep myself fit. And, as I mentioned, I'm well hard, me. Tough as old boots. And torn trousers. And naked knees on broken glass. And spacemen fighting for a drink at the bar. And so on and so forth and suchlike.

When they had tired of beating me up, I suppose they felt a bit guilty. What with all the blood and the broken bits of me and stuff. And so they let me go on with my talk of George Formby.

'After Johnson sold his soul to the Devil,' I said, in as steady a voice as I could muster, 'it was said that he always played guitar with his back to the audience. But those who managed a glance over his shoulder swore that he played so good because he now had an extra finger on his left hand.'

Heads went nod. That was such a good story, it just *had* to be true.

'Well, it was almost the same with Formby, according to those who have seen him play live. And he doesn't play live in the movies, he mimes to pre-recorded studio tracks.' (I knew so much stuff back then. Still do, really. More, probably. Mind you, back then Neil told me most of it.)

'Well, those who looked over Formby's shoulder while he was re-cording swear that he had an extra string on his little ukulele. And the name George Formby is an anagram of the words "orgy of Begrem", which was something that went on near Sodom and Gomorrah, in the Old Testament.' (I knew this without Neil's help because I went to Sunday School a lot when I was younger.)

And then they beat me up again.

But I *did* talk them into making the most of the available ukuleles in the school-band safe. Because without them we would never be able to play on stage at the school dance and be cool in front of the girls. And so The Sumerian Kynges became vocal *and* instrumental.

Although at that time *unplugged*.

Nowadays, when I hear the word *unplugged* I reach for my pistol. But back then there was Bob Dylan and he was still acoustic.

And so we all took up the ukulele.

And we played on stage in the school hall at the school dance. And we were cool and we became famous. Eventually.

And the school dance is probably as good a place as any other to truly begin this tale (after a brief but necessary digression regarding the origins of our oh-so-cool band name).

This tale that tick-tock-ticks away with the tick-tock-ticking of the clock.

It was, in its way, the beginning of the end.

And if I am honest, and I truly try to be, I do believe that the very end of which I speak was partially my fault.

3

We were called The Sumerian Kynges not because it was cool, although indeed it was, but because it was a meaningful name. I was sixteen in nineteen sixty-three, and I knew the meaning of meaningful.

I was studying, you see, studying all kinds of stuff. Extracurricular stuff. Stuff you were not taught at school.

It was all down to my mother, really. My mother was a fundamentalist Christian, a name in itself that I found at that time most amusing for I had, through my readings of the Bible, encountered the word 'fundament' and looked up its meaning.

My mother attended Northfields Pentecostal Church, a church whose minister was the later-to-become-a-major-influence-in-my-life Captain Lynch. I liked Captain Lynch *a lot* because he was one of those adults who took everything *very seriously*. He would listen *very carefully* to any question that you asked him, and then he would give you a *very serious answer*.

'Why are witches an abomination unto the Lord?' I asked Captain Lynch one Saturday afternoon, when I found myself unexpectedly home, suffering from the mumps, and he had come around to offer consolation to my mother and to solicit funds for a ministry that he hoped to establish in the Orinoco Basin. I would ask him many questions regarding the nakedness of the savages in the Orinoco Basin, because I had seen photographs of them in a copy of *National Geographic* at the dentist's. And Captain Lynch would grow most verbose regarding these naked savages.

'Witches?' said the good captain, removing his Church Army cap and laying it upon his lap. 'Witches, is it, eh?'

'Do you think they should still be burned?' I asked him.

'Yes,' said the captain, in a voice of much graveness. 'I do believe they should.'

'You don't think that's somewhat cruel?' I occupied the Persian pouffe beside the fire. And as it was winter and the fire was lit, I took the opportunity to spit into the flames. 'Those flames would hurt,' I observed.

'The fires of Hell burn hotter,' said the captain – intoned, indeed, in his deepest Sunday-pulpit voice – 'for those who take the name of the Lord in vain. For those who raise divers demons. For those who spit upon the cross as you have spat into the fire. For those who enter into unholy congress with incubi. And for those who engage in the Obscene Kiss.'

'The *Obscene Kiss*?' I enquired. In all of my innocence.

The captain took an increasingly firm hold upon his cap. 'They kiss the Devil's Fundament,' he said.

'What's a fun—' But my mother now entered the front room, bearing a tray. Which in its turn bore tea in a teapot and biscuits on a plate. And cups, and sugar in a bowl and milk in a jug, and napkins and sundry other necessary prerequisites for a successful afternoon tea. Amusing and erudite conversation was not included.

'The captain was telling me all about witches,' I told my mother as she lowered the tray onto the occasional table. Which no doubt rejoiced in its own special way that its occasion had finally arrived.

My mother gave me a bitter look – it was her 'you wait till your father gets home' look, and believe you me, back in *those* days, *those* words carried considerable clout – and so I hastily changed the subject.

'You mentioned the Sumerian Kings a while ago,' I said, as I offered Captain Lynch the run of the biscuits.

'Kynges,' corrected the captain. 'There's a tale to be told there and no mistake.'

'Is it an Old Testament tale?' I enquired. 'Involving the twin cities of the plain?' I had recently come across the word 'sodomite' and had been looking for an opportunity to introduce it into a conversation.

'Not as such,' the captain said. 'This is more to do with Legend and Myth, although I suspect there is more to it than that. And I intend to prove same, as soon as I have mustered up sufficient funds.'

'I thought you were raising funds for your mission to the Orinoco Basin.'

'The Orinoco Basin is merely the tip of the iceberg,' said the captain, which I found somewhat confusing.

'Sumeria is where it all began.' And the captain was doing his pulpit voice once more.

'The Cradle of Civilisation?' I said. 'I've read about that. Would that be where the Garden of Eden was located?'

'Correct, young man, correct.' Captain Lynch did laughings and then did munchings on the biscuit of his choice.

'Is the Garden still there, then?' I asked. 'Could an explorer redis-cover it?' I, like all boys of my age born into the time that was mine, had certain loves. For steam trains and fag cards, Meccano and yo-yos, footballers, pirates and highwaymen.

And explorers.

Very much for explorers.

There was a great deal of exploring still left to do back in those days. Much of the world had yet to be mapped. There were certainly still dragons out there somewhere. And an English explorer could find them.

There were French explorers, too, I believe. I know that certain foreigners were always racing each other towards the North Pole. But there wasn't really much point in them doing so, for an English explorer named Hugo Rune had got there first. Back in Victorian times. He'd flown there in a steam-driven ornithopter.

'Are you an explorer?' I asked Captain Lynch. I did not know exactly, and still do not, how one gains a rank in the Church Army.

'Not yet,' the captain said. And he munched on his garibaldi, which had been the biscuit of his choice. 'But I intend to be. And when I am, then I will find the fabled Lost City of Begrem and I will recover the riches. To distribute amongst the poor. Of course.'

'Of course,' I agreed. 'Riches?' I queried.

'The Sumerian Kynges, boy – their treasure. Would you like to hear all about it?'

And I agreed that I would.

'The Cradle of Civilisation,' said the captain, settling back in the visitors' chair and making an all-inclusive gesture with his biccy. 'From the Garden of Eden, Adam and Eve never walked far. They never had to because all was in abundance back then. When the World was young and Man was younger still, the tribes increased and learning increased and great were the cities that were built. Thus it is written of Babel's tower and of those twin evil cities on the plain. But also it is written that a great city called Begrem* existed. And this city was under the dominion of one of the Sumerian Kynges – Georgius, his name was.'

I chewed upon a custard crème. And I nodded as I chewed.

'In those early times,' Captain Lynch continued, 'those first times, before there were clocks to tick the world away, Man knew God as he

* You see? The George Formby anagram, Orgy of Begrem.

knew his fellow Man. For God walked upon the face of the Earth and did come unto Man and speak unto him thusly:

' "Hello, Man, there," ' saith God.

' "And hello, God, sir," ' saith Man, in return.

'But strange as it is, and I do find this exceedingly strange, even though Man knew God as he knew his fellow Man, there were those Men who fell from the Grace of God, who moved away from His presence. Who even plotted against Him.'

'Why?' I asked, though I probably should not have.

'I'll tell you why,' said the captain. 'The power of Evil. The power of the Devil. The Fallen One. Old Clootie. He That Doth Backwards Walk. The Hornéd. The King of the Shadow World. Man will never know the true nature of the Evil One, just as Man can never truly know the true nature of God. But he exists as God exists and he led the Kynge of Begrem astray.

'He appealed, so they say, to the vanity of the Kynge and to his longing for power, more power. He offered the Kynge of Begrem the wealth of all the ages if he would perform a task for him.'

As I had finished the biscuit of my choice, I helped myself to another one.

'He besought the Kynge to create a Homunculus,' said Captain Lynch. And I had no choice but to ask what one of those was. And I did spit some crumbs onto the captain as I asked.

The captain dusted these lightly from his sleeve. 'The Devil's children, born of Man.'

'Conceived by witches?' I said, quite glad to be back on a subject I really liked. Although still eager for more talk of explorers.

'Allow me to explain,' said Captain Lynch. 'The Devil can tempt. The Devil can lie and cheat. But the Devil cannot have congress with a woman, be she witch or otherwise, that will lead to the birth of the Devil's child. This cannot be done. God decreed that this shall not be done and cannot be done. And it cannot.'

'Hence the Homunculus?' said I.

'Precisely,' said the captain.

And I felt quite pleased with myself.

'It is now understood by clerics and physicians alike,' the captain continued, 'that the soul of a new human being does not enter the body of the foetus until the third month of gestation. Before that, the unborn baby is by all accounts soulless. This is the *real* reason why it is acceptable to abort a child during this period. The child has no soul.'

I said nothing in response to this remark. Although it made me feel somewhat uncomfortable.

'And it is during this period that the unborn child is in the greatest danger.'

'From abortionists?' I asked.

'From alchemists,' said Captain Lynch. 'From the Devil's alchemists. At the behest of their master they attempt to inflict upon the unborn child an alternative soul, to invest it with a soul of an ungodly alchemist's creation. One that he has conjured with the Devil's magic.'

'To what purpose?' I enquired.

'To be a vessel of Satan. To be as near to the Devil's child as the Devil can make him (or her) without transgressing God's law concerning that kind of behaviour. It is a great feat of magic to perform this operation. One of the greatest, in fact. So great, indeed, that it can only be performed once every hundred years.'

I just nodded to all of this. I felt that we had lost the plot somewhere along the line. Because the plot *had* originally been to do with the Sumerian Kynges, riches and explorers. I wasn't altogether certain where all this talk of Homunculi was leading. (You will note that I used the plural correctly. This would be because I had encountered the word a week earlier in a copy of *Alchemist Today*, at the dentist's.)

'About the Sumerian Kynges and the riches and the exploring—' I said.

'The Sumerian Kynge Georgius, Kynge of Begrem, performed the conjuration and the Homunculus was created. And God was very angry as to this, as He was in those early days. He was roused to anger sometimes even through the slightest things back then. But the creation of the Homunculus really got His holy dander up.'

Captain Lynch made a facial expression that I knew not the meaning of.

'And so,' said he, 'there was mighty trouble. The Devil was delighted by the evil progeny that was created. And upon this one occasion – the first, and the *last* – he honoured his side of the bargain and rewarded Georgius with massive wealth. Tons of gold and jewels and precious stones. A Kynge's ransom, if you will.'

'And all this wealth appeared in Begrem?' I asked.

'All. In fact, the Devil turned the entire city into gold.'

'The Golden City of Begrem,' I said. With wonder in my voice.

'Only for a moment. And then God's wrath fell upon it. And it was swallowed into the sand.'

I paused here. Just for a moment. Because I had one of those feelings that you sometimes have. One of those feelings that *something* is coming. Something pertinent. Something important.

'You wouldn't . . .' I said. Hesitatingly. 'Have a map of where Begrem once was, I suppose.'

And Captain Lynch nodded.

'I would,' said he. 'I would.'

4

Captain Lynch didn't show me his map. But I have no doubt whatsoever that he *did* possess it. In fact, I know absolutely that he did. Because, as it is now in *my* possession, I can speak of this particular matter with some degree of authority.

Upon that particular day, our conversation continued just a little longer. The captain had a few final remarks to make upon the subject of the Homunculus.

'Since the creation of the first, each century a powerful magician, aided in his dark magic by the Evil One himself, attempts the conjuration. And throughout history, one has been born each century, the product of pure, unadulterated Evil.'

And he continued. And he finished with, 'The Victorian era bore one who came of age in the twentieth century – Adolf Hitler was his name. And the twentieth century has yielded up his successor.'

'And his name?' I asked.

'Elvis Presley,' said the captain.

5

I recall that, at the time, I found the captain's remark rather un-imaginative. He could have said anyone. He could have said George Formby. But he didn't. He said Elvis Presley.

And I also recall that, at the time, I wasn't convinced.

But I did like the idea of a city of gold, buried probably in a desert somewhere, Sumeria, most likely. And the exploring, and the digging up of the city, and the availing oneself of all the wealth.

None of which, if I am altogether honest – and I might as well be, as this, I suppose, is ultimately *my* story – none of which wealth would I be handing over to the poor.

'Let them steal their own treasure maps,' was my comment on the matter.

But I did like the story and I did like the sound of the Sumerian Kynges. I thought it sounded like a jolly meaningful name for a rock band. Although rock hadn't really been invented then, so I suppose I meant a pop band.

And the other guys who comprised the embryonic entity that was The Sumerian Kynges Phase 1 liked the sound of it, too.

There were two other members back then that I haven't mentioned – Michael and Keithy. They were Sumerian Kynges too at the time. But only for about five minutes. Because they had their own ideas of a name for the band. And when the rest of us didn't agree with their suggestion, they got all huffy and left. I understand that they did get their own band together and gave it the name they wanted. But whatever happened to the foolishly named 'Rolling Stones', I have no idea.*

Which brings me to the night of the school dance.

And the launch of The Sumerian Kynges.

We had been doing a lot of practice. And I do mean *a lot*. Well, you could, you see, in those days. It must have been something to do with it being the nineteen-sixties. If you took up a musical instrument at

---

* I don't think this is altogether true, is it? (Ed.)

school, you could take time off regular lessons to have tuition. And that, as I soon discovered, meant time off *all* lessons. I agree now that perhaps I cannot string words together as well as others of my age and literary persuasion, the Johnny Quinns and Mavis Cheeses who win all the book prizes and inspire the young. But, man, can I play the ukulele!

We'd start our musical tuition at nine-thirty on Monday morning after assembly and prayers and conclude it at three p.m. on Friday. With breaks for lunch, and going home at tea time, of course.

My fingers got a bit sore, I can tell you.

But it got the job jobbed and by the time the school dance came around, we were masters of the finger-pick, the cross-strum and the scale-run. Not to mention the chromatic.

Which I never did. Because I did not believe it to be necessary.

Now, there is a lot to performance. A *good* performance, that is.

A lot!

'A great performance is better than life itself,' Iggy Pop once said. But that was many years later. But it is *not* just down to playing well. You have to emote and you have to look good.

You have to have an image. And a *cool* image at that.

I would love to take all the credit for the original image portrayed by the original line-up of The Sumerian Kynges, but as I am trying to be honest here, I cannot and will not.

Rob is to blame.

Now, I use the word 'blame' here not in a derogatory way. Because I personally believe that it *was* a good look. A *cool* look.

A *cool* image.

I think, again in all honesty, that it was simply ahead of its time.

The girls of Southcross Roads School, class of 63, were simply not ready for Glam Rock.

Glam Rock and *cheese*.

It wasn't a great combination.

We had to get changed into our stage clothes in the boys' toilets. This wasn't a big deal at the time, or later. Bands on the way up always have to get changed in the gents' at gigs, until they are big enough to play bigger gigs. Gigs that come with changing rooms. And with changing rooms come groupies and champagne and riders on contracts and all the fun of the fair. And we knew this. Deep in our rock 'n' roll hearts we knew it. That first performance, we were 'paying our dues'. That's what musicians did on the way up. And we knew it.

And so we got changed in the bog.

I recall, oh so well, what a struggle it was to get my lipstick on.

Rob kept nudging my arm and going on and on about a 'pop-cheese fusion' and how we were 'breaking through preconceived boundaries and crossing textual horizons'. That we were in a 'get-some-cheese' situation.

Neil was having some doubt about his outfit. His mother, who was very big on the local ballroom dancing scene, had run it up on her sewing machine and there were a lot of sequins involved. More sequins than the rest of us put together. So that would be at least *five* sequins!

Neil was having some doubts about the twinkliness of these sequins. He'd always thought of himself as going on stage as a kind of Roy Orbison lookalike – black shirt and trews and big on the big black sunspecs.

'It's pink,' said Neil. 'It's all in pink.'

And it was.

Mine was all in green. And, according to Captain Lynch, green was a colour much favoured by the Sumerian Kynge Georgius.

Gold would have made more sense, but my mum didn't have any gold fabric. 'Gold is for toffs,' she informed me. But she did have plenty of green. Because my father had recently taken employment with a company that manufactured billiard tables and was always coming home with a duffle bag stuffed with green baize offcuts.

And billiard balls.

And walking with a strange stiff-legged gait caused by the introduction of billiard cues into his trousers.

Regarding trousers, the flared trouser was only then on the point of becoming fashionable and I like to think that in our way, upon that night, which was the twenty-seventh of June in the year of nineteen sixty-three, that we, The Sumerian Kynges, helped the flared trouser to enter the fashion consciousness of the nation.

And indeed helped the mullet haircut, which we also pioneered, to gain worldwide prominence and acceptance in the days to come.

Mind you, if I'd known then what I know now, I would never have gone on stage that night. Because (and I know, just know, that you are way ahead of me here) that performance, that night, played its part in hastening the oblivion that would eventually lead to me *almost* saving Mankind.

Shall I tell you how it happened?

No?

I'll tell you anyway.

6

The school hall smelled of plimsolls.

In the days of which I write, all school halls smelled of plimsolls. Plimsolls and the armpits of the young. Not that I have a preoccupation with armpits, or with the smells thereof. Don't get me wrong – I mentioned mine in an earlier chapter because they *were* smelly. I mention armpits again now only because the school hall smelled of them.

Nothing sinister. Nothing weird. Please don't get me wrong.

The school hall also smelled of teenage girls. And that is a smell most men of the heterosexual persuasion . . . warm to, as it were.

The Sumerian Kynges were warming to that smell. Which wasn't easy as we were waiting to go on stage in the school kitchen. We had glammed ourselves up in the boys' bog and now we stood, shuffling nervously (but looking cool), scuffing our winged heels (I would describe those but I don't have time) and cradling our instruments.

And warming to the smell of teenage girls.

Whilst having our nostrils assailed by the stench of rotten cabbage. Why all school kitchens always smelled of rotten cabbage is anyone's guess. Our school cook, Mrs Simian, never even served us cabbage, rotten or otherwise.

But I digress.

Well, no I do not. I am setting the scene.

I set this scene because it is important to do so. I really do want you to know just what this was like. It is a long time ago now, but the memory remains fresh, whilst many others have long ago grown rotten.

Like cabbage.

The school kitchen was painted in cream gloss paint, which made the walls look like slabbed butter. The utensils were huge. And this is not due to the fact that we are smaller when young, so everything seems big. These were *big* utensils, seemingly borrowed – or stolen – from a giant's castle. The utensils were huge and the pots, great aluminium jobbies in which the foodstuffs boiled and gurgled over flaming gas, were of similarly gargantuan proportions. You could have got a whole sheep into any one of those great aluminium jobbies. Or a pig. Or a horse. If you sawed the hoofs off.

And then there were the school plates. Thick white china. And you never saw one get chipped, or cracked, or broken. Even when you dropped them – accidentally, of course. As I so regularly did. Just to see, as it were. Just to see.

The plates rose in giddy stacks, in racks to the left of the butlers' sinks. Fine old stoneware butlers' sinks, where Mrs Simian and her harridan horde of dinner ladies (whom I, for one, felt absolutely certain constituted a coven of witches, if ever there was one) lathered up and dug in deep.

The forks were shabby, though.

But then forks always are. It takes great care and attention and dedication, too, to clean scrupulously between the tines. And I have to confess that I have, on numerous occasions over the years, had to send my fork back to the kitchen because it had been insufficiently lathered-up.

So yes, from the kitchen, the grim cream-glossed school kitchen.

Into the brightly lit hall.

That smelled of plimsolls and also of young women.

And no more mention of armpits.

The end-of-term school dance was a major event. *The* major event in the minds of many. These minds belonging in part, if not all, to fifth-year boys who were leaving school that month.

It would be the last opportunity to pull at school.

At a school dance where it was free admission. Unlike dances and discos to come. Naturally there were other major events – sports days, open evenings, exams. But curiously, I for one never had the faintest interest in any of these.

Into the brightly lit hall.

Brightly lit and brightly décored, too. Every year a theme was chosen by a committee formed of prefects. And therefore, in my humble opinion, hardly a representative committee. This sleek elite would sit about in their common room; oh yes, they had a common room, although only a small one, which doubled as the band room. But they would sit about on the Cameo Mason Celebrated Percussion Safe and choose the theme.

This year the theme was Space Travel.

Last year the theme had been Space Travel. As it had been the year before. I was informed that this year the prefects had actually chosen Women of the Orinoco Basin as the theme.

But it had ended up as Space Travel. As it always did.

Because Mr Jenner, the music teacher, who let the prefects use the band room as their common room, always had the casting vote.

And Mr Jenner really loved the subject of Space Travel.

And so it was a brightly lit and lavishly décored Space-Travel-themed school hall that The Sumerian Kynges had now entered, through the door that led to the school kitchen. And it was a full and crowded hall. And there were a lot of teenage girls amongst this crowd. And I knew, just knew, in my rock 'n' roll heart, that they were just dying to get a piece of The Sumerian Kynges.

Although, of course, they were not, as yet, aware of this.

And so the scene is as set as it can be.

And Mr Jenner mounts the steps.

These steps are those that rise to the left-hand side of the stage (looking from the audience, that is). The very top step is quite small. Mr Jenner often commented that this was 'one small step for man', but happily not tonight.

To those who viewed him upon this night, Mr Jenner was not a God amongst Men. He was, in the common parlance of the day, a bit of a short-arse. And, in secondary school terms, one of the very last of his kind – ex-RAF, with medals to prove it, tweedy and ink-stained, given to mortar boards and scholars' gowns. Always with sheaves of music tucked under his arm. A hurler of chalk dusters. The man who conducted the choir. His head was too big and his feet were too small and he smiled when he spoke of Space Travel.

There was a mic up on that stage. The school microphone. It was a Telefunken U Forty-Seven. Every school had one of those. A few years later, *no* school had one, because with the rise of the minicab, the Telefunken U Forty-Seven had a penchant for picking up the signals of the cab offices and broadcasting directions for cabbies, to the great merriment of assembled students.

I was just dying to sing into that mic. We'd had to rehearse micless, and there was to be no amplification other than that mic, which meant that I was going to have to hold it near Toby's uke when he did his big solo.

Fearing as we all did that Mr Jenner would announce us as 'the school pop group' or something equally uncool, Rob had penned an introduction that would introduce, as it were, the term 'Rock God' into popular culture.

That one, I note, lasted. While the other one – 'Cheese God' – apparently did not.

Mr Jenner walked up to that mic and tap-tap-tapped upon it. If something was to be achieved by this tapping, we, cowering (*un*-coolly, if I remember) all beside the stage steps, didn't hear it.

'Ladies and gentlemen,' he began. The crowd went 'boo' and 'hiss'. Not the kind of thing you could get away with on a school day. But this *wasn't* a school day. *This* was the school dance.

'Calm down. Calm down.' Mr Jenner affected a light-hearted mien. 'I know you've all come here to let off a little steam.' We watched Mr Jenner from the side of the stage. He *was* going to read out Rob's introduction, wasn't he? He had stuck it straight into his trouser pocket when Rob had given it to him. He hadn't even read it through. And now—

Mr Jenner did not take the introduction from his trouser pocket. He had words of his own to say.

'These young gentlemen have rehearsed very hard,' said Mr Jenner, 'and I know that you are really going to shake, rattle and roll to their happening sounds. Please give them a really big hep-cat welcome: the school pop group, The Rolling Stones.'

I looked at Neil. And Neil looked at me. And Neil looked at Rob and Rob looked at Toby and Toby in turn looked at me.

'I'll get him for that,' said Toby. 'You just see if I don't.'

7

The Rolling Stones weren't *that* bad, I suppose.

Because, after all, it was their first ever gig.

The one that never gets a mention in biographies, authorised or otherwise. The one with the original line-up. With Wild Man Fosby on tea-chest bass and Mick Jagger's sister on uke.

And Bill Wyman on uke. And Mick Jagger on uke and vocals.

My uke. And *my* microphone.

In case the reader is experiencing some degree of confusion here, allow me to explain, for it *was* my intention to create this confusion in the hope that it would in some way mirror the confusion that I and my fellow members of The Sumerian Kynges found ourselves in at the time.

We thought that Mr Jenner had simply got the name of our band wrong when he was introducing *us*. But not a bit of *that*. He wasn't introducing *us* at all. He was introducing The Rolling Stones. A band that he had himself been coaching in the evenings. With the ukuleles that we rehearsed with during school time.

And Mick and Keith and Brian and Mick's sister pushed right past us on the left-hand stage steps (looking from the audience), snatching our ukes from our hands as they did so.

We were not pleased about this at all.

Toby was in a blue funk!*

'I'll kill one of them,' he said. And he pointed to one of The Stones at random. Brian Jones, I believe it was. 'I'll kill *him*!' said Toby.

Rob made calming gestures with his ukeless fingers. 'It will all be all right,' he told Toby. 'They can be our warm-up act. Get the crowd going. Remember, they're on before us. They are our support band.'

Toby thought about this. And so did Neil and so did I. I don't know exactly what conclusions the others drew, but I was happy enough to have The Rolling Stones as my support act.

---

* Sequined all over. His mum had made it for him.

And so we stood and we waited. In the shadows beside the brightly lit stage. And we watched The Rolling Stones.

They were an R & B band then. In the days when R & B meant R & B. As opposed to whatever it is that R & B means nowadays. Which is *not* the same thing at all. So to speak. So The Rolling Stones did quite a lot of the blues.

They did 'Love in Vain', the Robert Johnson classic. And they did some Chuck Berry. They did 'Johnny B. Goode'. And *that* is a classic.

They didn't do any George Formby at all. Which I personally felt was a shame. I thought they missed a golden opportunity there, what with such an abundance of ukes and everything. But I didn't really care. We had plenty of George Formby numbers in *our* repertoire. In fact, we were almost exclusively a Formby-orientated rock 'n' roll band.

'I notice,' noticed Neil, 'and I notice that I did not notice this before, that Michael has quite long hair. It covers his ears and also his school-shirt collar.'

We nodded.

'Your point is?' Toby asked.

'Long hair is for girlies, surely,' said Rob. 'Long hair, well shampooed, "because you're worth it", so to speak.'

'I think I'll try and grow mine,' said Neil. 'Just to see how it looks.'

'You will look like Guy Fawkes,' said Toby. 'You are already the only schoolboy I know who sports a goatee beard. Do not add to your notoriety by styling your hair like that of an effeminate anti-parliamentarian.'

'I don't wish to look like some Muff Mary Ellen. I'll shave my head tomorrow,' said Neil. 'Just to be on the safe side.'

And he did.

And in so doing unconsciously invented a look that would later find favour with The Village People.

'I do hate to say this,' said Rob, 'but The Rolling Stones are rather cool. Although it is a rubbish name for a band. They're playing a lot of Robert Johnson – they should have some sort of Demonic name, but with a bit of a regal quality to it, like ours.'

'Their Satanic Majesties,' Toby suggested.

'Don't be silly,' said Rob.

And then suddenly The Rolling Stones had finished. We didn't clap them, of course. How uncool would *that* have been? Neither did we cheer. Not that we could have cheered had we wanted to.

You see, we'd had to talk quite loudly while The Rolling Stones had been playing. Shout, really, in order to make ourselves heard. So we had rather sore throats. Which would *not* help *my* performance.

The Rolling Stones came off stage to considerable applause, and we Sumerian Kynges suddenly found ourselves in the midst of a bit of a crush. Most of the teenage schoolgirls of Southcross Roads School's fourth and fifth years seemed rather anxious to make the personal acquaintance of Michael and his band. We found ourselves getting all pushed about. But we did get our ukes thrust back into our hands, so we elbowed our way onstage.

And Mr Jenner wasn't there. He'd gone. Left the stage by some other steps. Steps we knew not of. And that was the last time I saw Mr Jenner. He vanished mysteriously quite soon after that.

I always wondered what became of him. Nothing good, I hope. Some years after that, when The Rolling Stones became famous (and *yes, of course* I know what happened to them), I saw a photo of them standing with their manager Andrew Oldham. And I recall thinking that if Andrew took off the sunglasses that he always wore, he'd look the dead spit of Mr Jenner.

Whatever. Because *we* were now on the stage.

And I 'one-twoed' with vigour into that mic.

And I introduced the band as the Rock Gods that we were. Or soon would be. And I counted in our first number. And we played. *How* we played.

And I'll bet, just *bet*, that if there had been anyone left in the school hall, anyone who had not followed The Rolling Stones out into the playground, where they were apparently signing autographs and deciding which fourth- and fifth-year girls they would be taking on elsewhere, then I bet, just bet, that *had* there been anyone remaining to watch us play, then that someone would have been *really* impressed by our musicianship and stagecraft. Even though my vocal renditions were a tad countertenor-ish.

But there wasn't and we played to an empty hall.

And when we were done, Toby reiterated his intention to kill one of The Rolling Stones. 'Drown his head in a bucket' being the expression that he used.

'I'm thinking,' said Rob as he retuned his ukulele, for he had done some fearsome finger-work, 'I'm thinking that perhaps I am not cut out for the crazy world of rock 'n' roll. I am thinking that I might just go into advertising and become a copywriter.'

'Not quite so fast,' said Toby. 'Playing to an empty hall is part of paying our dues. It will *not* happen again, you have my promise on this.

27

And let's look on the bright side – the fact that the hall was empty means that no one will ever know how truly rubbish we were.'

I looked at Neil and Neil looked at me and Neil looked at Rob and et cetera and et cetera.

'We were pretty rubbish, weren't we?' said Rob.

'We were excruciating,' said Neil.

'I was good,' said I.

'You were the most rubbish of all,' the blighters said. In unison.

'Perhaps I could go into copywriting also,' I said.

'You'd be rubbish at that, too,' said Rob.

'So where does this leave us?' I asked.

'It leaves you, gentlemen, with a most exciting option.'

Now, I never said that, and nor did Neil and nor did Rob and nor did Toby. And nor did Mr Jenner, nor any of The Rolling Stones, nor any of the fourth- or fifth-year girls of Southcross Road. Nor even Mrs Simian the school cook, nor her weird sisters of the kitchen cauldrons.

'Who said that?' asked Rob. 'Or *Who's Next*, as I might put it, if it were an album, or something.'

'Allow me to introduce myself,' said a gentleman. For surely indeed this *was* a gentleman. He stepped from the shadows at the rear of the brightly lit hall. The left-hand side, when looking, as we were, from the stage.

'Looks like a man of wealth and taste,' Rob whispered to me, as I was standing closest to him.

'Who are you, sir?' I asked.

'Call me Ishmael,' said Ishmael. '*Mr* Ishmael,' said Mr Ishmael. 'I liked your performance.'

'You *did*?' I was puzzled by this. To say the very least.

'Perhaps he's a homo,' whispered Rob. 'They'll say anything in order to get a bit of youthful bottom.'

And then Rob said no more. He sort of clutched at his throat and sort of fainted dead away. And all we Sumerian Kynges hastened to ignore Rob's plight and see what Mr Ishmael's 'most exciting option' might be.

'You are not, by any chance, the owner of a vast cheese empire?' Neil asked Mr Ishmael.

'Why do you ask me that?' the other replied.

'Because Rob has fainted. I'm asking on his behalf.'

'Ah,' said Mr Ishmael. 'I see.'

'Glad that someone does,' said I.

'The Sumerian Kynges,' said Mr Ishmael. 'I like the name. It is very – how shall I put this? – meaningful.'

Our young heads went nod-nod-nod. Here, it was clear, was an adult who was on our wavelength.

He had now stepped fully from the shadows, and we were able to have a really good look at Mr Ishmael. The hall being so brightly lit, and everything.

He was very, very smart, was Mr Ishmael.

He was tall. In a way that transcends the way that the famous are tall. Because the famous are, in truth, rarely if ever tall. The famous are mostly short, but *look tall* because they are famous. And one naturally feels that famous folk must somehow be tall, and so we invest them with a quality of tallness, which mostly belies their shorthood.

Such is ever the way.

But Mr Ishmael was naturally tall. He topped the magic six-foot mark with ease. And he had the big barrel chest of an all-in wrestler. And the barrel chest and the rest of his parts were encased (with the obvious exception of head, neck, hands and feet) within a sumptuously expensive blue velvet suit. His hair was black and all slicked back.

His complexion tanned, his cheekbones high, there was an oriental cast to his features, but it was impossible to put a place to the look. He leaned upon a black Malacca cane that had as its head a silver penis and a pair of balls.

It was a notable cane.

'I do *not* like your music,' said Mr Ishmael. 'And believe you me, the ukulele has seen out its days. But I discern potential and I would be prepared to finance you, to the tune of appropriate instrumentation.'

'And new stage clothes?' asked Neil. 'I'm not too sure about these sequins.'

'The sequins *stay*,' said Mr Ishmael. 'I just adore the sequins.'

And he twirled his cane and tapped it thricely on the floor.

'Instrumentation?' said Toby.

'Electric guitars. Amplifiers. A PA. A stack system.'

'A *what*?'

'All in good time. I think – in fact, I *know* – that you have the seeds of greatness. Sown, as it were, and yet to be reaped. A field of gold, as it were, also.'

The us upon stage that were conscious did further lookings at each other.

'Serious?' said Neil.

'Serious,' said Mr Ishmael. 'I will manage you. Promote you. I will make your names household words.'

'I'd like *that*,' said Neil (whose surname was Dishwasher).

'What is your surname?' Mr Ishmael asked of Neil.

'Garden-Partee,' said Neil. (Whose surname was not really Dishwasher.) 'It's hyphenated. We're a hyphenation, but we have no money to go with it.'

'But you will. You will.' And Mr Ishmael approached the stage. And as he did so, a certain coldness approached with him. A certain chill in the air.

'So,' said Mr Ishmael. 'Will you let me take you to fame and fortune? What do you say?'

And what *did* we say?

Well, we said *yes*, didn't we? Because what else were we likely to say? And Mr Ishmael produced a contract for us to sign, didn't he? Well, of course he did. And we all signed it, didn't we? Well, of course we did that also. We even moved Rob's unconscious hand on his behalf. And we signed *in blood*?

Well, that goes without saying, really, doesn't it?

And so, upon that night, the night of our very first gig, we, unwittingly, but greedily and without thought of any potentially disastrous consequences, signed away God alone knows what to Mr Ishmael and played our part in bringing the world and the universe to the point where I would *almost* save Mankind. Almost.

What a carve-up, eh?

8

It was well after midnight when I got home. Which I found somewhat surprising as I was sure that it was hardly ten.

My mother and father were still up. Because mothers and fathers stayed up in those days if schoolboys didn't arrive home until well gone midnight. And mothers and fathers generally had quite definite things to say to the late-returning youth.

They were both in the hall as I entered.

I pushed open the front door, which was never locked, because no one ever locked their doors back in those days. Well, not in our neighbourhood, anyway.

It wasn't that people were more honest in those days. No, it really wasn't that. It was that we, along with our neighbours and most other folk in our neighbourhood, had absolutely nothing whatsoever worth stealing.

Except, of course, for the Sea-Monkeys.

But then, as everyone had Sea-Monkeys in those days, there was really no need to walk into someone else's home through their un-locked front door and steal theirs.

So I pushed open our unlocked front door to find my mother and father waiting in the hall.

'Hello, Mother,' I said. 'Hello, Father. I have some *really exciting* news.' And then I gave the hall the once-over. But for my mother and my father and now myself, it was otherwise empty.

'Where's my bike?' I asked. 'I left it here in the hall.'

'Someone's nicked it,' said my father. 'Probably either that travelling mendicant who specialised in *gutha pertha* dolls, or that gatherer of the pure who popped in earlier to share a joke about beards and baldness.'

'Right,' I said, slowly and definitely. 'Right, I see.'

'You do,' said my father. 'You do.'

And I did. In a manner of speaking.

'And you are late,' said my father, pointing to his wrist, where a wristwatch, had he worn one, would have been and then towards the circular light patch of wallpaper where, until quite recently, our hall clock had hung. 'It's after midnight.'

'Yes,' I said, 'and I am confused about this.'

'How so?' asked my father, already unbuckling his belt.

And, I knew, preparing himself inwardly for the beating he was about to administer, which would be prefaced with the words, 'This is going to hurt me more than it hurts you'.

'Well,' I said, wondering quietly to myself whether *tonight* might be *that* night. *That* night, which I had been assured by my peers would one day come, when I would stand up to my father and, as a result of him now being old and frail and myself young and in the peak of my physical fitness, mete out to him many summary blows to the skull and never again feel that belt of his across my rarely washed bottom. 'Well—'

'Well *what*?'

I shuddered, silently. It was *not* going to be *that* night.

'Well, *sir*,' I said, 'I don't understand two things in particular. One being how come it is now after midnight, because I am absolutely sure it was only a quarter to ten just a few minutes ago.'

'And secondly?' asked my father, his belt now off and his trousers falling to beneath his knees for the lack of its support.

'Secondly,' I said, 'how we actually know that it's after midnight, as we no longer have any means of accurately telling the time in this house.'

'The boy has a point there,' said my mother, who, I must say, in praise of her loving humanity, hated to see my father laying about me with his belt.

She always thought he went far too easy on me and would have much preferred to have done the job herself.

There were some times when I actually wished that we did not live in the enlightened times of the nineteen-sixties, but back in Mediaeval days.

Because in those days I could have denounced my mum as a witch and had the very last laugh.

'I think twelve of the best are in order,' said my father, struggling one-handedly with his trousers.

And then he beckoned to me with his belt hand and I took a trembly step forward in the hall.

And lo.

I felt a certain something. It was something that I had never felt before. And, as such, it was something that I did not entirely understand

32

at first. My initial thought was that it had snowed in the hall, but that someone had painted the snow. And I'll tell you for why this was.

It was because, as I took that trembly and tentative step forward into the hall, I felt something soft beneath my feet. Where before, and for ever before, there had been bare floorboards, now there was a certain softness all in green.

'Carpet,' I said, in the voice of one exalted. 'Praise baby Jesus, Mother, a miracle – we have a fitted carpet.'

'And not just in the hall—' my mother now raised her voice also '—but all through our poor but honest little home.'

'All through . . .' and my voice tailed off. *All through?* Picture *that*! At this time in my life I could not. And so I must have fainted. Dead away.

I awoke to find myself supported by my mother's arms, upon the Persian pouffe beside the fire. I awoke with a start and then with a cough, for thick smoke appeared to fill the room.

'Don't trouble yourself about the smoke,' said my mother, once she had teased me into full consciousness with a Bourbon biscuit dipped in *sal volatile*. 'It's only the offcuts burning in the grate. They haven't proved themselves to be a particularly good substitute for coal. I think I will discontinue their use as soon as I run out of them.'

'Offcuts?' I said. And then, 'carpet offcuts.' And then I felt faint all over again. But I didn't pass out again. Once wasn't cool. Twice would really be taking the Mickey Mouse hat. And I didn't want to do *that*.

I did a little squinting about and, true as true, we did have a carpet, too, right here in the sitting room. Same as the hall. Same green.

'Billiard table green,' I said.

'Billiard table baize offcuts,' said my mother. 'The same as the stage clothes you are wearing. In fact, when you fainted in the hall we had a job finding you. You sort of blended into the carpet. As would a chameleon.'

'Billiard table baize offcuts?' I did a bit of gauging up and mental arithmetic. 'I would say,' I said, 'that surely this front sitting room of ours would have a floor area roughly equivalent to at least *three* billiard tables. Surely these are *very large* offcuts.'

'That is what the foreman said to your father,' said my mother. 'Before he sacked him, this afternoon.'

'Sacked him?' I said. 'Oh dear, not again.'

'No, he only sacked him the once.' My mother was a stickler for detail.

My father was not in the room. For had he been, I very much doubt whether this conversation would have taken place.

'Since you have known my father,' I said to my mother as she now kindly mopped my fevered brow with a rum-soaked copy of *Pirate Today*,* 'how many different jobs do you think he has had?'

'It depends on what you mean by "different",' said my mother. 'Many have been in the same line of business.'

I nodded and I gave the matter thought. 'With different employers, then,' I said.

'Goodness me,' said my mother. 'I have long ago lost count. But forty or so years from now you will be able to "Google" him on the "Internet". You can find out all about him then.'

'Google?' I said. 'Internet?' I said also.

'Sorry,' said my mother. 'I was just having one of my visions. I have been granted the gift of prophecy, you see, from Northfields Pentecostal Church. Captain Lynch is schooling me in the technique.'

'I'll just bet he is,' I said. 'And have you had any visions, or prophetic insights, regarding him? Such as him discovering a lost city of gold, or suchlike?'

My mother shook her head and said that no, she hadn't.

'I suppose Dad'll be at home a lot now,' I said, with a degree of dread, if not in my voice, then probably upon my face. 'It always takes him a long time to find a new job.'

'Research,' said my mother. 'So much research.'

'Right,' I said, recalling my father's research. 'He always researches the various strengths of alcohol in the local public house, but never takes a job there.'

'Not in a *single* public house,' said my mother, once more the stickler for detail. 'He does his research in many different public houses. He'll do *so* much research in one public house that the landlord will urge him to go elsewhere, lest he *over*-researches.'

'Right,' I said. With the same inflection I had put into the previous 'right'.

'But no,' said my mother, now applying vinegar and brown paper to my forehead, for she had read in a nursery rhyme that this was a timeless remedy. 'He won't be researching in public houses because he already has a new job.'

'Already?' I said. 'But he was only sacked this afternoon.'

* Which had arrived through our letter box by mistake, it being meant for Captain Blood, the retired freebooter who lived next door.

'I know,' said my mother. 'What a world we live in today and no mistake. It must be this Space Age that they are all talking about. But a man knocked upon the door earlier this evening and offered your father a new job. And he took it, right there and then.'

'Well,' I said. And, 'Well indeed. No, hang about,' I then said. 'Dad mentioned a travelling salesman and a gatherer of the pure. He hasn't got a job shovelling up dog shi—'

'No, no, no,' said my mother. 'Something quite different – your father has been given a job as a roadie for a rock 'n' roll band.'

'What?' I said. And I said it loudly, too.

'A chap in dark glasses who looks a bit like your music teacher gave him the job. He's going to be the roadie for a band called The Rolling Stones.'

'What?' said I. And even louder now.

'But let's not talk about your father,' said my mother. 'Tell me, Tyler, what was your *really exciting news* that you mentioned just before you fainted?'

9

The Saturday that followed the Friday evening that had been The Sumerian Kynges' very first gig was much the same as any other at that time.

My father was doing some home improvements. He was papering our sitting-room walls with billiard table baize and Captain Lynch had taken my mother to the pictures, because there was a film on about Jesus that my father wasn't particularly keen to see.

I got up, then went without breakfast because my mother had apparently left early for the pictures so as to be first in the queue. Then I watched my father's increasingly abortive attempts to paper the sitting-room walls until I could control my laughter no longer and had to rush to the toilet and be sick.

Which made me feel even hungrier. So I did what all lads of my age did and went off to the Wimpy Bar for lunch.

Wimpy Bars were the latest thing. They were American and therefore cool. They served a variety of foodstuffs that had never before been served upon these shores. And there were ice-cream desserts with names like the Brown Derby and the Jamaican Longboat.

How fondly I remember those.

I once found a pound note blowing down the street, which I considered was surely a gift from God. And myself and Neil Garden-Partee tried to spend the lot at the Wimpy Bar. And we *really* tried. We had as many burgers (with fries, as the Wimpy Bar's chips were called) as we could pack in, then we laid into the desserts. And the milkshakes.

But we only spent fifteen and sixpence, all told.

Which wouldn't, nowadays, even buy you a cup of tea.

As I have lived my long and eventful life and watched the world falling to pieces all around me, I often think back to those more innocent days of the early nineteen-sixties.

A time when two young men, in the full flush of their youth, could *not* eat their way through one pound's worth of Wimpy Bar grub.

And I feel grateful, somehow. Blessed.

That I hadn't been born twenty years earlier and got myself killed in the war.

What goes around comes around, I suppose.

Like diseases.

And whilst we are on the subject of diseases, I have to admit that I caught my first one of the 'social' persuasion in an alleyway at the back of the Wimpy Bar.

But not on this particular day.

Because on this particular day I was still a virgin.

I wasn't too phased about being a virgin. Most of my pals, I knew, were similarly so. Although most bragged otherwise.

Neil, I knew, was a virgin. The girls didn't take to his goatee. And Rob, although a genius with a chat-up line, never seemed to pull. Toby, however, was another matter. Toby was a bit of an enigma and if all was to be believed, and it probably was, he had had his first sex while at junior school.

With the teacher.

And the teacher wasn't a man.

Just in case you were wondering.

I took the 65 Bus from South Ealing to Ealing Broadway. My favourite clippie, the Jamaican lady with the very white teeth, wasn't clippying on the bus upon this morning and so I had to pay the fare. The Jamaican lady with the very white teeth always took pity on the hang-dog expression that I wore and my tales of poverty and child abuse, and let me off without paying.

The evil harridan of an Irish woman who patrolled today's bus cared nothing for my tragic plight and demanded I fork out my penny-halfpenny without further ado.

Which left me no option but to shout, 'Stop that dog!' and leap from the bus at the next traffic lights.

And travel the rest of the way on foot.

So I had worked up a *really* healthy appetite by the time I got to the Wimpy Bar.

I could spend time describing the interior of the Wimpy Bar, but what would be the point? You either know what it looks like, or you don't. So to speak.

Neil was already there. And so was Rob and they were sharing a chocolate-nut sundae, with extra nuts.

I seated myself in my favourite seat, yawned a bit and stretched and gave my young belly a bit of a rub. 'Give us a spoonful of that,' I said.

'No,' both Neil and Rob agreed.

And I had to order my own.

'Why do we always have the dessert first?' I asked as I tucked into it. 'Surely one should have the main course first.'

'I'm sure *one* should,' said Rob. And he chuckled.

'Are you chuckling at me?' I asked him, pointing with my spoon.

'Yes,' said Rob. 'I am. Do you want to make something of it?'

'Do you want a fight?' I asked him. 'And if so, why?'

'Why?' said Rob. '*Why?* You know why.'

'I don't,' I said. And I noticed Neil moving the chocolate-nut sundae that he had been sharing with Rob somewhat closer to himself.

'What is this all about?' I asked of Rob. 'What have I done to you?'

'You signed me up to something with a maniac,' said Rob. 'While I was out cold. And what was *that* about? What happened to me last night?'

'You came over a little queer,' I said, hoping to lighten the situation with a cheeky little double entendre.

'Outside,' said Rob, rising from his chair.

'No,' I said. 'No. My dessert will melt. Or Neil will eat it.'

'Are you having a go at me now?' asked Neil, rising also.

'No,' I said. 'No. I'm not having a go at anyone. And I'm not fighting anyone. We're friends. Aren't we?'

'Something weird happened last night,' said Rob, who was showing no signs of sitting down again. 'It was before ten, then suddenly it was midnight.'

'I noticed that,' I said.

'Shut up!' said Rob.

'But I—'

'There *was* something weird,' said Neil. 'My watch stopped at midnight and my watch never stops. It's an Ingersoll and I wind it religiously.'

'What, in church?' I asked.

'I *will* hit you,' Neil said in ready reply.

'Oh, come on, lads,' I said and I raised calming open hands to them. 'We're friends – we shouldn't be behaving like this. And we'll get thrown out of here. And that won't be cool.'

Rob made serious fists. And he shook them at me. And then he sat down.

'That's better,' I said. And I sat down. '*And* you, Neil,' I said. And Neil sat down and I felt better.

Though they both now glared at me.

'I don't understand this,' I said. 'Why are you so angry? And why are you so angry *at me*? We all signed Mr Ishmael's contract.'

'You moved my hand,' growled Rob.

'We *all* moved it,' I said. 'Not *just me*.'

Rob made a more than furious face. 'And you didn't know anything about this madman. He turns up unannounced, a total stranger, and you sign us all away, *to what*?'

'To fame and fortune,' I said. 'It was the chance of a lifetime. We would have been stupid to have passed it up.'

'And do you have a copy of this contract onto which you forged my signature?'

'Not as such,' I said. Carefully.

'Not at all,' said Neil.

'And do you have this Mr Ishmael's address?'

'I think he said he'd contact *us*,' I said. 'That was what he said, wasn't it, Neil?'

Neil shrugged, and ate as he shrugged.

'It will all be okay,' I said to Rob. 'We will all be famous. We will all be millionaires.'

'We'll never see him again,' said Rob. 'You have signed away our very souls. I just know it. I can feel it. In my water, like my mum says.'

'Don't be so melodramatic,' I said. 'Signed away our very souls. Don't be so silly.'

And then Toby entered the Wimpy Bar. And he looked most chipper, did Toby.

'Morning, chaps,' said Toby, seating himself next to me and drawing my chocolate-nut sundae in his direction. 'All tickety-boo, as it were?'

'No,' said Rob. 'Anything but.'

'Sorry to hear that,' said Toby. 'I've just been with Mr Ishmael. He dropped me here in his limo.'

We all said, 'What?' As one.

'We've been at Jim Marshall's shop in Hanwell, checking out guitars and amps and speakers.'

'There,' I said to Rob. 'I told you there was nothing to worry about.'

'Well, there is for Rob,' said Toby.

'*What?*' said Rob. On his own this time.

'Mr Ishmael doesn't want you in the band. He says that you are a disruptive influence. And as you clearly suffer from stage fright, what with you fainting last night and everything, you'd never be able to handle the strain of a forty-day transcontinental tour. So you're sacked.'

'I'm *what*?'

'So all's well that ends well, eh?' I said to Rob, raising my sundae glass as if in toast.

And Rob punched me hard.

Right in the face.

And we didn't see too much of Rob for a while after that. He kept to himself at school and didn't come to any band practises.

But then he wouldn't have done, would he, because he was not in the band any more.

But then *we* didn't attend any band practises either. Mr Jenner had gone missing and with him the school ukuleles.

And Mr Ishmael seemed to have gone missing also, because we didn't see anything of him, or our promised instruments.

Which was a bit of a shame.

And time passed by.

And then one Monday morning, the first of the summer holidays, there was a tap-tap-tapping at our front door. And my mother went off to answer it. I was eating my breakfast like a good boy and ignoring Andy, my brother, who was under the table pretending to be a tiger (for reasons of his own that I have no wish to go into here). And as my father was off on tour with The Rolling Stones, it was my mum who had to answer the door.

Which explains *that*.

And she hadn't been gone for more than a moment before she returned and said, 'It's for you, Tyler – the postman, and he has a parcel for you.'

'A parcel for me?' And my mind did somersaults. I had over the years, and unbeknown to my parents, or my brother, saved up my pocket money and then sent it off. A bit at a time. Many times, for many things.

Things that I'd read about in American comics. Things that I coveted.

Wonderful things. Such as huge collections of toy soldiers that came complete with a foot-locker. Whatever that was. And the bike that you got free (an American bike with a sort of humpbacked crossbar) when you sold 'Grit'. And a course in Dimac, the deadliest martial art of them all, sent to you personally by Count Dante, the deadliest man on Earth. And there were X-ray spectacles, which enabled you to see beneath girls' clothes. And latex-rubber masks of Famous Monsters of Filmland. And a body-building course taught by a man named Charles Atlas.

I'd sent off for each and every one of these.

And had never received a single one.

And to this day I do not know why.

Perhaps it was because I never filled in my zip code on the order form that you cut from the comic-book page.

But here was the postman.

And he had a package for me!

Beneath the table I crossed my fingers and I hope, hope, hoped that it was the Dimac course. Because I so wished to brutally mutilate and disfigure with little more than a fingertip's application. I withdrew my crossed fingers rapidly as my brother snapped at them with his tigery teeth.

'Well, hurry up,' said my mother. 'The postman won't wait. He'll get behind schedule. And postmen would rather die than do *that*.'*

I hastened from the table, down the greenly carpeted hall and to the front doorway, where stood the postman.

'You have a package,' I told him. 'For me.'

'Do indeed, squire,' said the postman. 'Sign here, if you please.'

And he proffered a paper upon a clipboard and I put his pen to this paper.

'So where do you want it?' the postman asked.

'In my hand,' I said in reply.

'In his hand. He's a caution, isn't he, missus?' These words were addressed to my mother, who was peering over my shoulder.

And not to my brother, who was peering between my legs and growling.

'I don't think I can fit it all in your hand,' said the postman. And now he read from the paper on his clipboard.

'Two Fender Stratocasters, in flight cases.

'One Gibson EB-Three bass in flight case.

'One set of Premier drums, consisting of twenty-inch bass drum, three graduated toms, snare, hi-hat cymbal, a sixteen-inch crash and a twenty-inch ride.

'In flight cases.

'Three Marshall two-hundred-and-fifty-watt amps.

'Twelve Marshall AUT150HX speakers.

'Five Marshall AUT160HX mega speakers . . .'

And the list went on.

And on and on.

---

* So, some things never change.

And on and on some more.

And I came to the conclusion what a very good thing it was that myself and my fellow members of The Sumerian Kynges had done when we signed that contract.

In blood.

Down at the South*cross Roads* School.

At midnight.

10

Prior to the perfection of the Tyler Technique, I made all kinds of silly mistakes. They were good-hearted mistakes, of course, made in service of the common good, not for self-gain or aggrandisement, oh no. But silly mistakes they were, nonetheless, and I suffered for them each and every time.

I just shouldn't have signed the postman's form. It was one of those COD kind of jobbies that you just don't see any more, which went the way of powdered beer and returnable toilet rolls. One of those sixties things.

'I'll take cash,' said the postman, 'as I suppose you do not have recourse to a major credit card?'

'A what?' I said, all wide-eyed and growing legless.

'Nothing to worry yourself about,' said my mother. 'Another of my visions of times-future-to-be. I mentioned it to the postman the other day, when he popped in to offer me consolation.'

'Right,' I said, which was fair enough.

'I see,' I said, but I didn't.

'So I suppose it will have to be cash, then,' the postman said. 'It's a very large amount of cash, so I hope you don't have it all in copper pennies.'

And then he laughed as if he had said something very funny, which in my opinion he had not.

'What are you talking about?' I asked him when he had ceased with his laughter.

'The money,' he said. 'The filthy lucre, the readies.' And he rubbed the forefinger and thumb of his right hand together in a manner that I found faintly suggestive.

Although of what, I was not altogether sure.

'Cough up,' said the postman. 'It's—'

And it is my considered opinion that he was about to name a not inconsiderable sum of money. But he did not. Instead he screamed.

And then he fought somewhat. And then he flung down his postbag and clipboard and took to his heels at the hurry-up.

And his postbag toppled over and a light breeze sprinkled its contents all along our street.

And I turned and looked at my mother.

And she just smiled at me.

But it was one of those sickly smiles that people sometimes do. One of those embarrassed smiles. And the reason for this was my brother.

Who had sprung from between my legs in full tiger persona and affixed his teeth about the ankle of the postman. The postman had managed to shake him off, but not before he had drawn some blood, which now lightly freckled the pavement. Mum and I watched postie's departure.

And so too did my brother.

'Splendid and well done to you,' I said.

But Andy bared his fangs.

So my mother and I retreated inside and slammed the door upon him.

'Whatever are we going to do?' my mother asked of me. 'Your father is out, your brother's gone mad, the postman's all bloodied and we have sufficient musical accoutrements stacked upon the pavement there for the London Philharmonic to perform an impromptu jam session. Something by Haydn would be nice, or Stockhausen at a push.'

I shushed my mother into silence. For after all, my father *was* out, so *I* was the man of the house.

'Don't shush me,' said my mother.

So I gave her a shove and she tripped, banging her head on the mantelpiece and lapsing into unconsciousness.

I felt rather bad about things then, with her lying prone on the green baize carpet of the living room. So I comfied her head by slipping the Persian pouffe under it and straightened her frock to make her look respectable.

'What have I done?' I wailed, to no one but myself. 'Signed away my birthright. Signed away this house. Signed away everything one way or another.'

And then I made myself a cup of tea and having drunk it felt a lot better about things generally. And so, having peeped out through the letter box to assure myself that my brother was not presently prowling about, I hastened outside to unpack one of the Fender Stratocasters.

I mean—

Well—

44

A Strat!

There was just a *little* bit of trouble. Several pirate chums of Captain Blood had ventured out of his house to help themselves to the musical paraphernalia, on the grounds that as it was unattended, it must therefore be considered salvage and fair game.

I wasn't having any of their old nonsense, though, and I sent them packing in no uncertain terms. The one called Ezekiel gestured at me with his hook and made motions with his single hand towards his cutlass. But I said, 'I'll set my brother on you,' and he soon scuttled off.

'Damn pirates,' I said. 'I do not have the gift of visions and prophecy that has been granted to my sleeping mother, but I foresee a day, not too far distant, when there will be no more pirates in this part of town.'

And although that sounded absurd at the time, what with the new blocks of flats having just been erected and filled, literally to the gunwales, with pirates, nevertheless, it is now the case.

I wonder where they all went.

I flipped open one of the packing cases marked 'STRATO-CASTER' and viewed its contents. A real Strat. I took it out and held it close to my face. You could almost taste the sustain.

'Oooh,' went I. And, 'Mmmm,' also. And I stroked the Strat as one might stroke, say, a fresh kitten, or the neck of a much-loved wife, or something made of solid gold that you stood a fair chance of running off with unseen.

Not that I'd ever do such a thing, you understand.

But I stroked that Strat and it was a magical feeling.

'You like that,' said someone and I almost messed in my trousers.

I went, 'Who?' and, 'What?' and also, 'How?' But there stood Mr Ishmael, smiling sweetly.

'Oh,' I now went, and, 'Sorry, you crept up on me. You gave me a shock.'

'I am light on my feet,' said the man in posh velvet, today's colour being maroon. 'And my limo runs on a special preparation of my own devising that makes the engine all but silent.'

'Hello there,' said Toby, as he was now here. And he was smiling also. And then Toby looked up at the mighty stacks of equipment and he whistled loudly.

'You had no trouble paying the postman, then,' said Mr Ishmael. 'I will reimburse you in time, naturally.'

'Naturally,' I said, and I took to whistling, too.

'Then all is as it should be. Where do you intend to store this equipment? You'll want to get it inside quite quickly, I would have thought – it looks a bit like rain.'

And as he said this, the sky clouded over and thunder took to rumbling.

'Quite quickly,' Mr Ishmael said once more. 'As quickly as you can.'

'Your dad has a lock-up garage, doesn't he?' I asked Toby.

And Toby nodded. 'He certainly does.'

'Then we'll store it in there.'

'We certainly won't.'

'Oh, come on,' I said to Toby. 'I know that your daddy does *not* have a car.'

'No one ever keeps a car in a lock-up garage,' said Toby, and he rolled his eyes. 'You say the silliest things sometimes.'

'And I *do* them, *too*,' I said. 'But it's part of my charm, don't you think?'

But Toby shook his head, which led me to believe that he wasn't always as wise as he thought himself to be.

'I'm wiser than you,' Toby said. Thoughtfully.

'Well, if there's no car in the garage, why can't we store all his equipment in there?'

And Toby rolled his eyes *again*. 'Because,' he explained, 'no one keeps a car in a lock-up garage – a lock-up garage is only used for storing stolen goods.'

Mr Ishmael nodded. 'It's true,' he agreed. 'It's a tradition, or an old charter, or something.'

I had a think about this. And I was inclined to think that this equipment probably now constituted stolen goods. And it would be a good idea to get it both out of the coming rain and out of the way of the postman, who must surely return quite soon with a posse of armed policemen and a lion-tamer.

'My dad's lock-up,' said Toby, 'is packed to the rafters with the lost treasure of the Incas. My dad's minding it for the Pope.'

'So we can't use your dad's lock-up?' I said.

And Toby shook his head. 'No,' he said. 'And that's that.'

'Then it will have to be my dad's allotment shed. We can't bring it all into my house. My mum would go spare.'

And so it all went down to my daddy's allotment shed, a bit at a time, in Mr Ishmael's limo. With one of us standing guard over the pile while the other unloaded at the other end. *I*, I recall, did all the unloading. But it proved to be a good idea, as it happened, the right place for it. My daddy rarely visited that shed, which was in fact three sheds knocked together. My father had had the work done because he intended to set up these three sheds as a West London venue. Once the damp had been taken care of, and a green baize carpet laid, my father had opened this venue – The Divine Trinity, as he rather grandly named it – and awaited the arrival of posh people who wanted to hire it out. It never proved particularly popular, though he hosted a couple of World Line Dance Championships there and a Congress of Wandering Bishops, but that was about it.

My father, being at times philosophical, put this down to competition. Competition that came in the form of The Magnificent Four, a venue also on the allotment constructed of *four* sheds knocked together and owned by a young gentleman named Doveston, who later bought out all the other allotment holders and turned the allotments into a tobacco plantation. He also put on a rock festival there in nineteen sixty-seven. Brentstock, it was called, and *we* almost played at that.

So, The Divine Trinity was currently vacant but for one or two folk singers who were living rough there. Toby and I ousted these and moved in the equipment.

And it *did* prove to be a good idea. Once all was inside there was just enough room for The Sumerian Kynges to squeeze in also. And so we could use the place as a rehearsal room.

Thinking back, as I must do if I am to set the record straight about all that went before and then came to pass, which would lead in turn to what was to come and how things would ultimately turn out, I can say, with hand on heart and one foot in the wardrobe, that I had some of the happiest times of my life rehearsing in The Divine Trinity. I pretty much took up residence at The Divine Trinity.

We were just starting out then. Young and eager and carefree. Life was ours for the taking.

And that tick-tock-ticking of history's clock could not be heard for our laughter.

Oh yes, we were happy then. Though not so happy after we had played our first gig.

Let me tell you all about that.

Because it was quite an experience.

11

It was nearing Christmas, in the year of sixty-three.
The nights had all drawn in and it was chilly.
The snow lay deep and all around,
And tramping o'er the frozen ground
There came a postman by the name of Billy.

I liked Billy the postman. He was a great improvement on the previous postman, who had yet to recuperate from the dose of rabies from which he was suffering.

There had been some unpleasantness. My brother had been arrested and questions had been asked regarding the whereabouts of several thousands of pounds' worth of brand-new musical equipment. These questions had *not* been satisfactorily answered, and when the finger of accusation came to point with an unrelenting pointyness towards my brother, who was presently receiving medication, board and lodging at St Bernard's Lunatic Asylum, I felt that I did not want to confuse things by owning up myself. And my brother was himself beyond caring at this time, for he growled at me through the bars of the special padded room where he spent much of his time, 'I'm a tiger – what would I want with a Marshall stack? Tell them, Tyler, I beg you.'

He was clearly beyond my help.

And I had rehearsing to do.

I had not been invited to reattend school classes after the summer holidays. I had apparently outstayed my welcome at Southcross Roads Secondary School. The headmaster had invited me into his office on the first day of the new term to put his and the school's position to me in a manner that I could understand.

'Taylor,' he said to me as he ushered me into the visitors' chair, which stood, with three inches cut from its legs, before his desk.

'Tyler,' I corrected him.

'Tyler,' said the headmaster. 'Yes, that's as good an occupation as any for a lad such as yourself.'

'My *name* is Tyler, sir,' said I.

'Then how apt,' said he. 'And good luck with it, too.'

And then he asked me to sign a special form. Which was for my own good and merely a formality. 'Just a sort of release form,' he said, 'to release you from the shackles of education and let you loose on the world, as it were. And how is your brother getting along?'

'They had to give him some sleeping tablets,' I said, 'because he woke up again.'

'The world we live in today,' said the headmaster. And he passed me his pen. 'Just sign it at the bottom there,' he said. 'You don't need to read it. You can read, I suppose? We did manage to instil that into you, I hope.'

I nodded and that pen hovered.

'Sign it, boy,' the head now shouted, 'or I'll give you six of the best.'

And so I signed his form and was discharged instantly from school. And I had to hand him my satchel and my cap. Even though they were mine and my mother had paid for them herself. And then I was escorted to the school gate and sent away with a flea in my ear.

And the school nurse put that flea there.

And I never did know why she did. Nor did I ever know why I'd been expelled from school. And probably I will never know.

Nor probably ever care.

And I did walk free from that school upon that day, I can tell you that. It was always a strange feeling to walk the streets during term time – if, say, you had to go to the dentist, or help your mum shopping, or some other important reason that stopped you going into school. But to walk out of the school and know that you were never going back, that was *really* odd.

And as for that flea—

Well, I shook it out before it could lay any eggs and I stamped it into the pavement. And I walked tall, because I was no longer a schoolboy.

I was a man.

And so I went down to the local public house for a beer.

But the landlord threw me straight out again because I was underage. So I went down to Cider Island, that little area beside the weir where all the winos spent their days, and I shared cider with them until I was dizzy and sick.

And then I stumbled home, to receive a really epic hammering from my father.

Those were the days, eh?

But now it was nearly Christmas. The snow lay on the ground deep and crisp and even and The Sumerian Kynges had their first professional gig. Professional in that our audience would be paying to get in to see us, even if we weren't actually to be paid for performing. And as the representative from the new nightclub that was employing us told us, we were 'showcasing' ourselves. Great things were expected. And so we were all young and eager and carefree.

And life was ours for the taking.

Our first gig was to be played at the opening of a nightclub in Ealing Broadway, just down the alleyway steps opposite the Underground Station. It was called The Green Carnation Club and we were top of the bill.

I still have one of the posters. Somewhat crumbling about the edges now, but still bright with pre-psychedelic mimeograph red, upon a background of brown.

Below us, second from top of the bill, was Venus Envy.

A male pre-op-transexual band. Who were already pretty famous.

I had read all about them in a copy of *Teenage She-Male Today* magazine that had been popped through our letter box by Billy the postman, who had a sense of fun that I never fully understood.

Venus Envy featured 'Jimbos', which were, apparently, the male equivalent of Bimbos. I learned a lot from that magazine and it was a real pleasure to boast about what I knew to the other guys in the band.

Especially Neil, who always seemed to know so much about everything. He confessed, in fact he fairly *gushed*, that he knew absolutely *nothing* about Jimbos, and eyed me rather strangely.

But I had heard that Venus Envy were pretty good, and they were especially interesting to me because of the Aleister Crowley connection. I had read much about Aleister Crowley, England's last great magician. The self-styled Beast of the Apocalypse, whose number is 666, Crowley probably wrote more on the subject of occult magic than any other person. Oh, and my dad met him once. Honest.

But I digress. Apparently Venus Envy's lead singer, Vain Glory, was a member of the Ordo Templi Orientii and all the band's song titles had been derived from the titles Crowley had given the various murals he painted on the interior walls of his Abbey of Thelema in Cefalu, Sicily. I treasure the memory of those names:

Egyptian Aztecs Arriving from Norway
The Long-Legged Lesbians
Morbid Hermaphrodite from Basutoland
Japanese Devil-Boy Insulting Visitors
Pregnant Swiss Artists Holding Crocodile

They were really meaningful titles for songs and there would have been no point in writing such songs unless those songs had meaningful lyrics to go with their meaningful titles.

Ours were really, *really* meaningful. And I will give you a sample, shortly.

So, on this crisp December night, with the snow laying all around and about and little flakes of it drifting down towards the allotments, which looked particularly beautiful in what moonlight there was to be had, I stood in the doorway of The Divine Trinity, a hand-rolled cigarette travelling up to my mouth and then down again, and watched the arrival of Toby in our van.

Yes, that's just what I said. *A van!* Toby had got us a van. And although strictly he wasn't old enough to be driving it, he explained to anyone who demanded explanation that he was driving through necessity rather than choice and so they should leave it at *that*.

He had acquired the van from Leo Felix, the local used-car salesman (who, even then, referred to his cars as 'previously-owned vehicles') with a sum of money composed of our shared savings.

It was an old-time Bedford van with sliding doors, so you could ride along with the doors open and your leg hanging out, looking cool. And but for the fact that it drank petrol and oil in equal quantities due to some essential piece of engine being unincluded in the price, and the fact that the exhaust pipe was somewhat peppered with holes and dispensed a thick, black, foggy sort of a smoke cloud into the rear of the van to the great distress of anyone unlucky enough to be sitting therein, it was a cracking van!

The suspension was a little 'stiff' and the tyres, which lacked for any discernible tread, also lacked for inner tubes and had been filled with sand by Leo, who assured Toby that all tyres would be similarly filled in the years to come as pneumatic tyres were nothing but a passing fad.

So, it made for an interesting ride.

We didn't have to load up the full monty of equipment. We couldn't have anyway – it would not all have fitted into the Bedford. The Green Carnation owned a house PA and Venus Envy were prepared to let us use their amps and speakers, which was jolly decent of them. They even sent one of their roadies to help us load up at the allotment. Jolly decent, I thought.

And they had let us be top of the bill, even though they were already quite famous. More than just jolly decent, I decided. Really, really decent pre-op trannies.

I was so looking forward to the gig.

I was nervous, of course, with the old butterflies in the stomach. But I wasn't going to let on to the other guys. I would put a brave face on it and set an example. After all, I *was* the lead singer.

The snow was falling most heavily by the time we had loaded up. And frankly I wasn't *that* impressed by Venus Envy's roadie, who spent most of his time attending to his nails and brushing away imaginary smuts from his white satin trousers. He was *very* flattering about our stage clothes, though, so I suppose I shouldn't be too harsh on him.

But, as I say, the snow was falling heavily and the moon was gone, so it was damnedly cold when we set out for that gig. But we were young, and eager and carefree and life *was* ours for the taking. So the fact that we had to push the van to get it started and Neil fell down and took the left knee out of his jumpsuit and Toby laughed at this and Neil hit him and there was some talk about abandoning the gig and indeed music as a career choice before we had even left the allotments, did not bode particularly well for the coming gig.

But that was nothing, and I repeat *nothing*, in comparison to what was yet to come.

I am not going to waste the reader's time, or patience, with any more of that 'if I'd known then what I know now' kind of toot – you've had quite enough of such stuff.

But if I *had* known, then I would at least have known who to kill and why.

But let me waste no more words at all here.

This is how it happened.

12

Mr Ishmael was awaiting us at the club.

He was in his limo, and as we arrived he signalled the chauffeur to wind down his window so that he could speak to us.

'What are *you* doing *here*?' were the words that he chose to employ.

'We're top of the bill,' I said, with joy in my voice. 'But you arranged this, surely.'

Mr Ishmael shook his head and I noticed for the first time that his aftershave smelled like violets. '*I* never booked you,' he said, rather fiercely. 'I'm only here because I received a special invite to the club's opening.'

'Oh,' I said, as it seemed appropriate.

'Well, as you *are* here, I trust that you will be putting on a memorable performance.'

'You're damn tootin',' I said, as I had recently heard this phrase and now seemed the golden opportunity to use it. 'We're top of the bill – surely you've noticed the posters.'

Mr Ishmael shook his head once more, wafting further violet fragrance at my person. 'I haven't seen any such posters,' he said. 'But go on in now – you're beginning to look like a snowman.'

And I was, as now the snow was falling fast.

We struggled to hump our gear from the van to the club. And Venus Envy's roadie didn't help with this humping at all. He just took off for the bar and we never saw him again.

Now, there is something about humping gear out of a van. Something exciting, something almost mystical. You're *right there*, if you know what I mean. And *I* knew what I meant. And I knew that the other guys in the band would know this, too. It was a camaraderie thing. We were all in this magical thing together.

'You don't mind doing this all by yourself, do you?' said Toby to me. 'Neil and I want to have a few words with Mr Ishmael.'

'But—' said I.

'There's something mystical about humping the gear, don't you think?' said Toby.

So I humped the gear by myself.

And I must have made a really good job of it, because once in a while I'd peer across at Mr Ishmael's parked limo and see Toby and Neil and Mr Ishmael quaffing champagne and laughing together. And if one of them caught my eye, they'd grin very broadly and raise their glass and give me the old thumbs-up.

Nice chaps.

But I do have to say that I didn't think much of The Green Carnation. It was a regular dump. It looked like a derelict building. The door was hanging off its hinges and the electricity appeared to be supplied by a mobile generator.

I cast a dubious eye over these insalubrious surroundings and one of the members of Venus Envy caught me at it.

'Chic, isn't it?' said the he/she. A very thin one, scarcely taller than a dwarf. 'Post-holocaust chic, it's called. You wouldn't believe how much it cost to make it look like this.'

I agreed that I probably wouldn't, then asked where exactly the stage might be.

'You're standing on it,' this Glen/Glenda said. 'It's an entirely new concept in concert staging. A "level-header", it's called, level with the audience. One day all stages will be like this.'

But I did *not* agree that they would.

I continued with my humping. And when done, and somewhat breathless, I asked the Venus Envy she-male where exactly the bar was, so I could avail myself of a beer.

'We don't have a bar, as such,' the man-woman told me. 'If you want a beer you'll have to go to the pub next door. I think our roadie is in there already. You can buy him a pint for helping you to shift your gear.'

I settled for a glass of water. Or would have done, if there'd been any. So I sighed and shrugged and went off to the toilet. And then the obvious struck me and I went out to Mr Ishmael's limo, to share in the champagne.

Only to find that Neil and Toby and Mr Ishmael were now entering the club. As they'd run right out of champagne.

'This is *rough*,' said Neil. 'And when I say rough, I mean it. Let's make like a ✶✶✶✶✶✶ and get out of this ruddy hole.'

There was a moment of silence then.

Followed by a longer one, and then a longer one still.

The moon, briefly out, went behind a cloud and a dog howled in the distance.

'Never,' said Toby, finding his voice, 'never, *ever* say anything as evil and revolting as that again.'

And I agreed with Toby. 'That was *rough*,' I said.

'Sorry,' said Neil. 'I thought I was amongst manly men who would be prepared to share a joke about a ******. But apparently not. Which says so much, doesn't it?' And Neil went off to tune his drums. For he was the drummer that week.

I looked at myself and then at Toby and then at Neil.

'Why did I think,' I asked Toby, 'that there were more than just the three of us in this band?'

Toby shrugged. 'Because you are silly?' he suggested.

'I am going next door for a beer,' said Mr Ishmael. 'After you have done your soundcheck, you might care to join me.'

And off went Mr Ishmael, leaving us behind.

And I looked at Toby once again.

And he looked back at me.

'What is a soundcheck?' I asked Toby. 'I'm sure I did know, but I think I must have forgotten.'

'It's a check,' said Toby, authoritatively, 'to see whether all the walls are sound. Whether they are all right to take the vibrations of our instruments. You know nothing, you.'

I bowed to his superior knowledge. 'So I'll leave that to you, then,' I suggested.

'Where do I set up my drums?' Neil asked. 'I can't find the stage.'

So I had to show him and sigh at his amateurism.

And as the ladyboy from Venus Envy was still hanging around, I made certain enquiries of him regarding, in particular, where the PA system, bass and rhythm-guitar amps and speakers that we had been promised happened to be.

And the birdie-bloke just laughed. 'We're all in the same boat here, sweetie,' he/she said. 'It's row like a big boy or bail out like a girl.' And then he/she giggled foolishly, which put my teeth on edge.

Toby, now with his Gibson EB3 bass out and nowhere to plug it in, waggled the jack-plug in my direction. 'I have a really bad feeling about this,' he said.

'Listen,' said I. And I shrugged. 'We're top of the bill. Venus Envy can hardly play without a PA, amps and speakers. We'll bide our time. Play it cool.'

And so Toby played it cool. And Neil played it cool. And I played it cool. And we stood about, playing it cool and waiting for something to happen and for someone to turn up.

And so things came to pass.

It was about ten of the evening clock when the first nightclubbers arrived. I say first, although we didn't see Mr Ishmael again that night. He never came back from the bar next door. And when we did eventually go looking for him, his limo had gone and he had clearly gone with it.

But folk were arriving. Although they didn't look to me to be your typical clubbers, as it were. And certainly not the class of audience I had been hoping for. Nightclubs are known as the haunts of the young and trendy. These clubbers were old and far from trendy and they smelled rather strongly of meths and cider and looked like the sort of folk who would probably appreciate a joke about a ******.

I engaged the guy/gal from Venus Envy once more in conversation. 'Still no amps or speakers,' I said. 'And a bunch of winos have turned up, several of whom I recognise as residents of Cider Island. I'll give it ten more minutes, then if things do not correct themselves, myself and my colleagues will be taking our leave.' Which was quite an eloquent little speech, really.

And it seemed to get the job jobbed.

The blokey-bird fluttered her/his eyelashes and jigged all about in a fluster. 'Oh, *please* don't go,' wailed and whimpered this person. 'It is *so* important to the club that you perform. The equipment will be here shortly. Oh look – here it is.'

And it was.

Giant ladies now entered the club. Ladies with high heels and higher hair. And that is one of the things that I have always liked so much about transsexuals and female impersonators: the sheer scale of them. I mean, your average man is about five-nine, five-ten, but put a pompadour wig on him and a pair of five-inch stiletto heels and he's going to be hitting near to the seven-foot mark.

Pretty impressive.

And so these giant lady-men, the lad/lassies of Venus Envy, hauled their gear into the club. I do have to say that they didn't haul in *much* gear. And what there was of it looked pretty rough.

'You can't imagine how much it cost to make the gear look like that,' I was told.

But I didn't answer at this time as I was fighting off a bag lady who was trying to go through my pockets.

'You won't need to do a soundcheck, will you?' asked a giant lady-fella, who looked to me to be one of Cinderella's ugly sisters from panto. Possibly played by Les Dawson, who would, in a few short years, become the most famous female impersonator in the country.

And certainly one of the most convincing.

'Actually, we did the soundcheck before you got here,' I told this colourful personage, which must have impressed them a lot.

Neil appeared with a troubled face. 'A gigantic woman wants to play my drums,' he said.

'Give and take,' I said philosophically. 'It's swings and roundabouts, live with it.'

'And another of them is retuning your Strat.'

'No she's ruddy *not*.'

But she did. Or rather he/she did. Well, they were fearsome, those Venus Envys. Big high heels and big high hair and great big eyelashes, too. They fair scared the bejabbers out of us and I am not ashamed to say so. Because they *were fearsome*.

'What is the "Key of La"?' Toby asked me.

'There is no such key,' I said.

'That's what I said, but that great Amazon who's got my bass says she's retuning it to the "Key of La".'

'And who's to argue at that?' I said. 'The Key of La it is.'

It must have been around eleven-thirty when Venus Envy took to the area of floor that had been designated 'the stage'. It was lucky, really, that there wasn't a raised stage as they would certainly not have been able to stand upright if there had been. Apart from the short one. And he/she was sitting down anyway. And I couldn't really tell which one, if any of them, was Vain Glory. But I don't think it mattered because whoever was doing what and playing what, they were complete and utter rubbish.

Which somewhat surprised me, I'll tell you.

Neil and Toby were shaking their heads. 'I thought you said that they were famous,' Neil shouted into my ear, 'and that their songs had meaningful lyrics.'

'That's what it said in *Teenage She-Male Today* magazine.'

'But not in the *NME* or *Melody Maker*,' shouted Neil. 'To my knowledge, and my knowledge in these matters is considerable, they have never received even a paragraph in either of these esteemed organs.'

'Organs?' I said, fearing another ****** reference.

'As in organs of public information. Newspapers.'

'No mention at all?' said I.

'Nix,' shouted Neil. 'Zilch. Nothing. Not one bit.'

'How queer.' And I shrugged.

And eventually Venus Envy concluded their set.

And we clapped politely. Because although clapping *is* uncool, getting beaten up by a bunch of giant trannies for *not* clapping would have been uncooler.

Clap-clap-clap, we went.

And Neil even whistled.

'I wish Mr Ishmael was here,' I said to Neil. 'I feel strangely vulnerable, amongst this crowd of weirdos.'

'We could just grab our gear and run.'

'Do you think they would let us?'

Neil eyed up Venus Envy and concluded, 'They do look rather burly and "useful", don't they?'

And I agreed that they did.

But at least they were smiling.

At us.

'I think we're on,' said Neil. And we were.

Toby and I were handed our guitars and did our very best to de-retune the retunings.

Neil worried at this drum kit. 'How can anyone put a drum kit out of tune?' he asked.

But in a whispery voice. And close to my ear.

'We'll show them,' I said. 'We'll rock the house, right?' And I made a soul-fist at Toby, who responded with something resembling a frown. And very resembling it, too!

'Are you ready to rock 'n' roll?' I asked Toby and Neil.

And they made faces at me.

'Are you ready to rock 'n' roll?' I bawled into the microphone. Eliciting some hearty attention-grabbing feedback.

One or two winos gave me the thumbs-up with their sherry bottles and I counted in the first number.

And then we played that rock 'n' roll.

Like the True Rock Gods we were.

13

We played an absolute blinder that night.

Even with the ropy old PA popping away and the ancient amplifiers fizzing and crackling and a variety of distortion coming out of the speakers the likes of which would not be heard again until nineteen sixty-seven, when, in the Summer of Love and hallucinogenics, everyone would be trying to capture that exact sound.

And I was very proud of the lads – they played a professional set. Neil thrashed those drums and Toby did things to his bass guitar that were probably illegal, but certainly got a cheer from the audience.

And it was a *big* audience now.

Packed very tight. And not smelling as sweetly as did Mr Ishmael. But we had a full house for certain. They just kept packing in, brushing the snow from their shoulders and rubbing their mittened mits together.

'We'd like to play a song now that's a bit of a departure for us. Slow the mood down a little with a bit of a ballad.' And they cheered this. Loudly. 'I wrote this number with Frank Sinatra in mind. It is called "The Smell in the Gents' is Still the Same".'

And as I said in the last chapter that I'd give you a sample of my lyrics, here is that sample now. You have to picture it being sung by Ol' Blue Eyes himself, probably on stage at the Stardust casino in Las Vegas. It goes something like this. Oh, and please bear with the spellings of the place names – I was young then and had not perhaps taken the best possible advantage of the education I was offered.

THE SMELL IN THE GENTS'
IS STILL THE SAME

I've been to Shanghai
Pagodas hang high
Upon the Shaolin plain.
But no matter where I roam
Over land or over foam
The smell in the gents' is still the same.

It's quite a mystery
How come can this be?
I've smelled it time and again
In Trinidad and Tobago
Or Tierra del Fuego –
The smell in the gents' is still the same.

[Middle eight]
If you're caught short in Kioto
Rangoon or Minisoto
In Cuba or Toledo
In Mexico or Rio
Hawaiee or Tahiti
New Zealand or Wai-Ke-Kee
You'll sniff this curiosity
This nasal atrocity.

I pose the question
Take all suggestion
To fill this void in my brain.
How can it be
From Irish Sea
To some Tibettan Monastery,
From any pub in Brentford
To the distant shores of Tripoli,
From John o Groats
To God knows where
This frightful perfume
Fills the air.
This sordid stench, this acrid pong
It lingers loud and lewd and long.
This wretched wang, this pooey niff
You really can't but take a sniff.
The smell in the gents' is still the same
Oh baby
The smell in the gents' is still the same.

Fade out.

Applause.

And they really loved us.

In between 'The Smell in the Gents'' and 'What's That On Your Shoe, Young Man, Please Don't Tread It Into the Carpet', I whispered to Toby, who still had not retuned his retuned bass to his personal preference.

'It's tuned to the Key of Doh,' he said.

'They love us,' I whispered to Toby. 'If there were any teenage girls here, clean ones who didn't smell of old kippers, I bet we'd get off with them.'

Toby muttered something. But I didn't hear what.

But we were on our way to greatness, I just knew it. And Toby knew it, too, I knew that he did. Even if he wasn't letting on.

We ran through all our numbers that night.

All six of them.

And when the crowd called out for an encore, we did 'It Will Never Get Well If You Pick At It' once again. Because that involved us each getting an instrumental solo.

And there it was. We were done.

We came off that bit of bare flooring that had served as a stage as the true stars we were. There was no doubt that we had triumphed. That we did have our foot on the ladder. And several rungs up, at least.

We did that thing known as the 'high five' to each other and Neil even threw his drumsticks into the audience.

'You were absolutely brilliant,' said a gigantic womanish creature. 'It has been an honour to have shared the same floorboards as you.'

'Well, thanks very much,' I said. 'I appreciate that.'

'Tell you what,' said the tottering gargantuan, 'me and the other girly-boys of the band would be really honoured if you would join us for a drink. At our expense, of course.'

'Well . . .' I said. And, I confess, with a degree of hesitation.

'It would mean so much to us,' this being continued. 'You wouldn't want to let us down, would you? That wouldn't be very rock 'n' roll, would it?'

And I agreed that it would not.

And I went to tell the guys the good news.

'I'm not leaving my gear in here,' said Neil. 'It will all be gone by the time we get back.'

'Good point,' I said. 'Good point indeed.'

'Pack it into your van,' said the towering travesty of womanhood. 'And perhaps you'd be kind enough to pack in our gear also. I don't think we want to leave it in here. You'd be amazed how much it cost.'

And so we packed all the gear into the Bedford. And the gear that belonged to Venus Envy also. And Toby locked up that van. Very tightly. And we checked the side doors and the rear doors also and assured ourselves that the van was *well locked up*.

'And so,' said I to the nearest she-creature that loomed above us, 'where would we be having this drink?'

'At our private club. It's open all night and it's just around the corner.'

'Should we drive, do you think?' I asked the colossus.

'But we won't all fit in, will we?' it replied.

Which was true. And so we walked.

And it wasn't really just around the corner. It was up the steps, past Ealing Broadway Station and along the Uxbridge Road, over Ealing Common and all the way to Acton Town. And then off a side road and into a rather sleazy-looking neighbourhood that was new to me. We might have all fitted into Mr Ishmael's limo, but as I said, when we looked for him, he'd gone.

'Go down the alleyway there and wait by the gate,' said the largest of the large Venus Envys. 'We have to sign you in at the front entrance. It's a secret drinking club and you have to appear to be members.' And he/she tapped at his/her nose with a mighty finger and Toby, Neil and I scuttled off down the alley, beating frantically at ourselves as we were now damn near frozen to death.

And there we waited. In the falling snow. Up to our knees in the stuff and risking frostbite.

'This is absurd,' Neil said.

'It's rock 'n' roll,' said Toby. 'And we deserve to be bought a drink – we were brilliant tonight.'

And I agreed that we were.

And we had a moment. We three. In that alleyway. A special moment. In our youth, being all young and eager and carefree and life being ours for the taking.

And we even had a bit of a group hug.

In a manly way, of course.

And probably more in the spirit of survival than camaraderie.

And we waited.

And then we waited some more.

And Neil sought to lighten the mood of this waiting by remarking that in my snow-capped green baize flare-trousered jumpsuit, I made for a passable Christmas tree.

And at very great length, when we were all about to keel over and die from the cold, we did what we should have done earlier and beat upon the back gate with our fists and demanded entry.

And presently someone came to answer our beatings.

But not a nightclub bouncer or barman.

A little old lady with a candle.

'What do you want?' quoth she. 'Banging on my gate at this ungodly hour?'

'We want to come into the club, we're freezing.'

'Club?' went the old woman. 'Club? There's no club here. This is a private house.'

And then it all sort of slotted together.

All of it. Like the pieces of a jigsaw.

And we looked at one another.

And reached what is known as a consensus opinion.

And we ran, fairly ran, all the way back to The Green Carnation Club. But there was no one there. No one. Just that door hanging off its hinge.

And outside that door, a sort of patch of road that had less snow on it than the rest. A patch that corresponded exactly in area to that of our Bedford van. Which, dear reader, as you may well have guessed, was no longer there to be seen.

14

We trudged back, freezing and forlorn.

To The Divine Trinity, where we had left our street clothes.

We were glum and we were angry, too.

We had been had, big time. Done up like a kipper. We had fallen prey to a most inspired piece of chicanery, it was true, and we could hardly have been expected to see it coming, but that didn't make things any better. We had lost all of our instruments.

And then we arrived at the allotments.

And the allotment gates were wide open.

And so was the door to The Divine Trinity. For it had been crowbarred from its hinges.

And there were the tyre tracks of what must surely have been a lorry. And all of our amps and speakers and other expensive equipment—

Had gone.

15

And so I became a private detective.

Well, not quite as quickly as that and things are never that easy. I was *very* upset, I will tell you that. The more I thought about it, the more it became clear that this terrible happenstance was really all my fault. I did my best to deny this, of course, because it did seem logical at the time that there had to be someone to blame who *wasn't* me.

Neil and Toby put me straight on this, however, and I was forced to review the entire sad episode part by part and come to the dire conclusion that it *was* all my fault.

It had all started with the copy of *Teenage She-Male Today* that had come through our letter box. This magazine, it now appeared, was a clever fake, run up by some dodgy printers and brimming with *big* news about a non-existent band called Venus Envy.

I determined to track down the printer. But I was immediately thwarted in this enterprise by the discovery that my fundamentalist mother had consigned *Teenage She-Male Today* to the flames of the sitting-room fire.

But I had the poster.

But the poster had obviously been turned out on one of those Roneo machines. There was one at Southcross Road Secondary School. They were everywhere. And there would be no way of telling *which* machine the posters had been printed on.

But did I say poster*s*? Of course, as it turned out, there had been *no* other posters, just the one that had been – and I had to have a little think about it then – how *had* I come by the poster in the first place? Oh yes, it had been posted through our letter box the day after the *Teenage She-Male Today* had arrived.

And then, of course, there had been that roadie. The one who had volunteered to come to The Divine Trinity to help load the equipment.

But why such an elaborate scheme? Why not simply turn up at any time we weren't there and steal all our equipment?

Well, that was sort of obvious, too: because I pretty much lived there and I wouldn't have given up the equipment without a fight. So they would probably have had to kill me.

No, it *was* a masterpiece. They'd even made sure that Mr Ishmael showed up for the gig. There had been no loose ends. And with all the wigs and heavy make-up, there would be no way of identifying the villains.

I could identify the roadie, though. He looked like . . . well, he looked like . . . well, he looked just like a roadie, really, and they all look very much the same. That roadie looked like my dad.

So I was stuffed, good and proper. Just like a turkey. Which was, at least, seasonal.

But I would have them. I would. Somehow. I would track them all down and retrieve our equipment and bring those blighters to justice.

I was lying in bed, planning the terrible revenge that I would take, when the doorbell rang, and this was shortly followed by my mother coming upstairs and beating upon my bedroom door. 'It's a Mr Ishmael to see you,' she shouted through the pine panelling. 'He seems to be rather upset.'

So I rose from my bed of pain, shrugged on my dressing gown and went downstairs to face the music.

My mother had admitted Mr Ishmael to our sitting room and he stood, his turquoise velvet jacket raised at the back, a-warming his bum by the fire.

'This is a very bad business,' he said as I entered the room, which felt somewhat colder than usual. 'All of the equipment, all of it. This is appalling.'

And I agreed that it was.

'Well, come on, then,' said Mr Ishmael. 'Get your clothes on and I will take you down to the police station. You can make a full report and get a "crime number" so that you can claim on your insurance.'

'Ah,' I said. And, 'That.' And I think I said, 'Really?' also.

'Step to it,' said Mr Ishmael. 'These things take time and the legit-imate gig that I have arranged for you is next week.'

'Ah,' I said, once again. And I do believe that I might have said, 'Now there's a thing,' as well.

But I stood and I dithered and I think that must have been what gave the game away.

'You *do* have the equipment insured, don't you?' asked Mr Ishmael. 'The equipment *is* legitimate? You *did* pay for that equipment, didn't you?'

And I don't think I made any reply at all to this. Although I might well have done some mumbling, and I'm reasonably certain that I scuffed my naked heels upon the green baize carpet.

'Calamity!' cried Mr Ishmael. 'Ruination!' And he began to thrash about with his black Malacca cane, the one with the penis-and-balls handle. And he swept the mantel clock from the mantel shelf and over-turned the Peerage fireplace companion set, the one that was made out of brass and resembled a galleon in full sail.

'Disaster!' he cried, and he kicked over the visitors' chair.

And all this shouting and knocking about of things attracted the attention of my mother, who was turning parsnips gently in a bucket by the stove.

'Whatever is going on?' she shrieked, entering our sitting room with the parsnip-turner raised above her hair-netted head. It was a *big* parsnip-turner, made of brass and of the Peerage persuasion, with a handle that was fashioned into the likeness of an Indian chief.

Mr Ishmael glared at my mother. He fairly glared, I can tell you. And my mother turned tail and fled back to her turning of the parsnips (well, Christmas *was* coming, and a well-turned parsnip is better than a badly shuffled sprout*).

'Well,' said Mr Ishmael to me, 'what do *you* intend to do about this aggrievous situation?'

'I think I might go and assist my mother,' I suggested. 'And whilst doing so, give the matter some most intense thought.'

'Oh you do now, do you?' Mr Ishmael rocked upon his heels and, although it must surely have been some trick of the winter light, it looked for all the world as if little sulphurous wisps of smoke issued from his ears.

'I *will* get the equipment back,' I said. 'I really will, I promise.'

'Ah,' said Mr Ishmael, lowering his cane and placing both hands upon its handle. 'You have formulated a plan. Most enterprising. Share this plan with me this minute and I will see whether it needs any necessary adjustments.'

'I have no plan, as such,' I said and I made a sulky face. 'But I *will* get our stuff back. I really, truly will.'

Mr Ishmael leaned his cane against the fireplace. He picked up the larger pieces of the clock and returned them to the mantel shelf, and he righted the Peerage fireplace companion set that was fashioned from

* Traditional.

brass and resembled a galleon in full sail. And he returned the visitors' chair to its legs and sat himself down on it.

And then he sighed. And it was a real deep, heartfelt belter of a sigh.

'I should have been expecting this,' he said. 'I got careless.'

I shook my head and I shrugged a little, too.

'I thought I had it all sussed out this time, picking a bunch of complete no-marks. It all seemed so simple. But that was because it *was* simple. *Too* simple.'

I sat down on the Persian pouffe, which had, at least, avoided attack. 'Pardon me, sir,' I said, 'but I do not believe that I know what you are talking about.'

'Well, of course you do not. The beauty of this was that had it all worked out, you and your companions would have prospered and probably never ever have needed to know what it was all about.'

Which left me none the wiser, I can tell you.

'I will just have to start all over again,' said Mr Ishmael. 'In another country. Probably the Holy Land. I should have set this up there in the first place. There is no other way for it.'

'Now, hold on,' I said. 'Are you saying that you aren't going to manage us any more?'

'What is there to manage?'

'Oh no, hold on, please.'

'I must go,' said Mr Ishmael. 'I have wasted far too much time on this already.'

'No,' I said. 'Stop. You promised to make us rich and famous. And we signed your contract. In blood! And at midnight, and down at the crossroads. And I know what *that* means.'

'No you don't,' said Mr Ishmael. 'You have no idea what it means. And now you will never know.'

'But I *must*,' I said. And I was getting frantic. Clearly something was going on, something big. And for a moment, and unconsciously, we Sumerian Kynges had been part of this something. But now we were about to be discarded. Cast down from being part of this something. And it was all, it appeared, *my* fault.

'No!' I said. And I said it very loudly. 'You can't just leave us. I will get things sorted, I really, really promise. I've been out of work since I left school, you see, because I couldn't make up my mind about what job I wanted. And I *did* think that as I was going to get rich as a musician that I didn't really need a proper job. But *now* I know, I *do* know. I will become a private investigator. And my first case will be to recover The Sumerian Kynges' stolen equipment.'

Mr Ishmael groaned at this. It was a groan combined with a sigh and it was not a pleasant thing to listen to. Plaintive, it was. Heartfelt.

'Don't doubt me,' I said. 'Don't *ever* doubt me.'

'Oh,' said Mr Ishmael. 'Assertiveness. This is somewhat unexpected.'

'Tell me what all this is about,' I said.

Mr Ishmael shook his head. 'I cannot.'

'But perhaps I could help. In fact, I will *definitely* help. I promise that I will.'

'You are making a *lot* of promises.'

'Because I care,' I said. 'Because this matters to me. I want the band to be a success. I accept that this mess is of my making. I'm taking the blame and I will make amends. And I promise that, too.'

And Mr Ishmael smiled. Which I found quite a relief.

'You are a good boy,' said Mr Ishmael. As indeed my mother had said upon many occasions past. 'And I will tell you what – I will make a personal deal with you.'

'Not more blood on the contract,' I said.

'No.' And now Mr Ishmael laughed. 'I will do *this* deal with you: if you can locate the stolen goods – you only have to locate them, that is all, and tell me where they are, and I will recover them – but if you *can* locate them successfully, then I will tell you everything. It will rock your world, as they say. And you might well wish that you had never been told.

'But I have faith in you, Tyler. Yes, I do. And so if you locate the equipment, you will have proved yourself to me, and in return I will divulge a mighty secret. *The* mighty secret, regarding Mankind, its history and its future. And the part you can play in moulding this future.'

And with that said, he rose from the visitors' chair with consummate dignity, extended his right hand for me to shake, which I did, gave me a card with his telephone number on it and then took his leave of our house.

And the pieces of the mantel clock that had been returned to the mantel shelf managed a rather faltering tick-tock-tick, and I took to wondering just what I was getting myself into.

And just as I had come to the conclusion that it was probably something absolutely wonderful and that I was going to be exalted amongst men for involving myself in it—

The clock *stopped*.

Dead.

16

You surely must know of Hugo Rune, and of his acolyte, Rizla.

Rune was a mystic and master of the arts magical who engaged, in the early nineteen-sixties, in an adventure involving twelve 'carriage-way constellations', zodiac figures formed from the layouts of streets in Brighton. These exploits were recorded in a number-one world best-seller, *The Brightonomicon*, which was translated into twenty-seven languages, became an iconic radio series and then a Hollywood movie, notable for the plethora of Academy Awards that were heaped upon the director and cast.

Well, I suppose that I must have thought, when Mr Ishmael spoke of revealing certain mighty secrets to me, that I might be entering into a kind of partnership with him that would resemble the one that Rizla had entered into with Rune.

But no.

Things couldn't possibly have been more different. The more I think about it, the fewer the parallels become. In fact they are less than few, being less than one, which is none.

So to speak.

And, for a start off, I was going to be on my own for my first case. No gurus' guru to inspire me. This was going to be *my* gig. And I felt slightly worried as to this.

I loved the idea of being a private investigator, of course. It was such a glamorous profession. One would be forever rubbing shoulders with supermodels and movie stars and members of the aristocracy.

And then there were the outfits. The snap-brimmed fedora, and the trench coat with the belt that you tied, and never buckled. For to buckle that belt would be *uncool*. And then there was the tweed suit. All professional private eyes owned a tweed suit. Private eyes donned the tweed suit when they wanted to disguise themselves. As newspaper reporters. It was an infallible disguise, and one that the world's greatest fictional nineteen-fifties genre detective, Lazlo Woodbine, had used to great effect upon many notable occasions.

Whilst solving cases that involved rubbing shoulders with super-models and movie stars and members of the aristocracy.

I couldn't wait to get at it. I was inspired.

But I *would* need a trench coat. *And* a fedora.

And a *gun*.

Private eyes always carried a gun: the trusty Smith & Wesson. I would certainly need one of those. For the final rooftop confrontation with the villain that always ended with shots ringing out and him taking the big fall to oblivion.

I just couldn't wait!

'Mum,' I said to my mum at lunchtime that self-same day and over lunch, 'you have a trench coat, don't you?'

My mother balanced a parsnip delicately upon her fork. 'I *did*,' she said, 'but I don't have one now.'

'You haven't given it to Captain Lynch, have you?' I asked, as recently I had noted that the contents of my wardrobe appeared to be lessening. And on quizzing my mother regarding this curious cir-cumstance was rewarded with tales of naked savages of the Orinoco Basin who were greatly in need of *my* clothes.

'I have *not* given it to Captain Lynch,' said my mother. 'I have given it to your brother, Andy.'

'My brother, Andy? But I thought he was banged-up in the loony bin.'

'We do not use the expression "banged-up",' my mother informed me. 'We say "*locked away*" in the loony bin.'

'But he's out?'

'Discharged yesterday. He was hoping to make it along to see your performance at The Green Carnation. How did that go, by the way? You came home ever so late. I think your father might want to have a word with you regarding that lateness.'

'No, please stop,' I told my mother. 'My brother is out of the loony bin and you have given him your trench coat – why is this?'

'Don't be silly,' said my mother. 'Why would anyone want a trench coat?'

'To be—' I said. And then I paused. She was asking, it appeared, a rhetorical question. '*Why would they?*' I asked in return.

'Because they intended to become a private eye, of course.'

'And my brother Andy intends—'

'To become a private eye. Yes, well, he *has* become one. Already. Actually.'

'But he's just come out of the loony bin—'

'And he needed a job. They offered him a counselling job at the loony bin – they always offer that to cured loonies – but he wasn't keen. He said that he'd been reading a lot of Lazlo Woodbine novels while he was in there and fancied trying his hand at being a private eye.'

And I groaned at this. And combined this groan with a plaintive sigh, as had Mr Ishmael. For it was *I* who had given Andy these books, trying to make peace, as it were. Because for some reason or other, beyond my understanding, he had got it into his mad head that it was somehow *my* fault that he'd been *locked up* in that loony bin.

'Oh,' I said to my mother. 'So where is he now?'

'He's off on his first case,' said my mother. 'Apparently some local pop group had all their instruments and equipment stolen last night, and Andy has vowed to find it. And before the day is over. He sounded very confident.'

'No,' I said to my mother. Then, 'No!' and then, '*NO!*'

'Not so loud, dear,' said my mum. 'You'll have your parsnips going on the turn.'

'Where is Andy now?' I asked, suddenly having no care for parsnips.

'He's gone to the crime scene, of course. On the allotments, apparently. He said that any private eye worthy of the name would always check the crime scene first. Criminals always leave clues, no matter how small. They just do.' And then my mother got that vacant look on her face that she always did when she was having one of her prophetic visions.

And I pushed my lunch plate aside and departed.

Hearing only the words '*CSI Miami*' issuing from my mother's lips. And the name 'Horatio Caine'.

With no trench coat or fedora I was hardly going to look the part on my first day on the job. I *did* have my duffle coat, and as it was still snowing out, I donned this, did up the toggles and raised the special hood.

Which made me look like a British seaman serving on a wartime submarine. Which was *not* the look I was hoping for at all.

And as it was very nippy, I wore my mittens, too – the Fair Isle ones that my mother had knitted. And even though I was now totally impervious to the cold in my upper-body regions, this did nothing at all to raise my spirits as I trudged my way to the allotments.

By the time I reached them, there was a definite blizzard going and I was forced to squint through this and tread very warily, too. And when I reached the doorway of The Divine Trinity I suddenly found myself face to face with my brother.

'Andy,' I said.

'Kenneth More,' he said to me.

'I'm *not* Kenneth More,' I said. 'I'm your brother, Tyler.'

'So,' said my brother, 'I suspected something of the kind.'

He looked rather well, did my brother. Very fit. In looks he looked much like myself, although I was a tiny bit taller. He had the better physique, though, always did have. Lithe, it was, lean, pared down. And he kept himself fit. Did aerobics, even before they'd been invented. And he was a vegetarian. When he wasn't being a carnivorous animal. And he always looked good in whatever he wore. He looked just great in that trench coat.

'I like the hat,' I said to him. 'That is a snap-brimmed fedora.'

'It was Dad's, apparently.'

'Hmmm,' I said. 'So how are you doing? Mum said you were up to some private-eyeing. How's it going – have you had any luck with anything?'

'What's it to you?' Andy asked.

'Nothing,' I said and I shrugged. And snow fell from my shoulders.

'You're tainting the crime scene,' said Andy. 'Bog off, will you.'

'I just wanted to help,' I said. 'I could be your sidekick, if you wanted.'

'My *comedy* sidekick?'

'If you wanted.'

Andy made that face that gives the impression to those who see it that the owner of such a face must be giving matters some really serious consideration.

'No,' said Andy. 'Bog off.'

'I'll pay you,' I said, 'to let me help. I'd like the training, in case one day I fancy becoming a private eye myself. You can never have too many strings to your bow, I say.'

'Oh, do you now?' said Andy. 'Well, bog off all the same.'

'Please,' I said. 'You've always been my hero.'

'Really?'

'Positively.' And I crossed my heart and hoped very much *not* to die.

'Well, all right,' said Andy. 'If you pay me. I'm not getting paid for this job because no one has employed me. I only know about it because I overheard two winos talking about it. They said that it had to be the perfect crime, so I thought that if I solved it, then it would prove that I'm a really good private eye and then I'd get lots of work in the future.'

'And there were those who called you mad,' I said. 'Shame upon those fellows.'

'I will get to them all in good time,' said Andy, 'and set things straight with them.'

'Quite so.'

'And then I will eat them. And it will serve them right.'

'Quite so, once more. And quite right, too.' And I shivered, and it wasn't from the cold.

'So what do you think?' I asked Andy. 'About your first case. This one here. Have you found any clues? Have you made any deductions?'

Andy tapped at his nose in that manner known as conspiratorial. 'I've drawn some conclusions,' he said.

'Go on,' I said to him.

'How much *will* you pay me?' he asked.

'How much do you want?'

'I want ten thousand pounds,' said Andy, 'because I would like to build my own zoo. And building zoos costs money.'

'Ten thousand is quite a lot,' I remarked. 'I could, perhaps, run to *ten* pounds. But I would have to owe you, as I don't have it on me.'

'You wouldn't get much of a zoo for a tenner,' said Andy. 'You'd hardly get a cage for a tenner.'

'You'd get a packing case,' I said. 'And you could use it to import animals.'

'Animals?' said Andy. 'Why would I want to import animals?'

And at this point I felt it prudent to change the subject of the conversation. 'So,' I said, 'that's settled, then. What clues do you have?'

'Well,' said Andy. 'And bear in mind that I am new to this game and just starting out and so haven't reached my full capacity, as it were. I deduce that five individuals burgled this shed complex. One, given the evidence, would appear to have been clad in standard roadie attire. No distinguishing features there. The others are most anomalous. They left tracks of high-heeled shoes, but these were not women. Indeed, I have every reason to believe that they were only dressed up as women.'

I sighed, rather more loudly than I might have wished.

'Tell me something I *don't* know,' I muttered to myself.

'Well,' said my brother, whose hearing was clearly more acute than I might have expected, 'that's where it gets rather iffy. You see, I can tell you with complete confidence that they were *not* women.'

'And?' I said, without too much interest.

'They weren't men either,' said Andy. 'In fact, I have no idea what *precisely* they were. Aliens, perhaps.'

I looked at Andy and I shook my head. Sadly was how I shook it.

'No,' said Andy, gazing at me. 'No, I'm not mad. I *mean* it!'

17

Aliens indeed!

My brother's madness wasn't going to help this situation. Not that it ever helped any situation, particularly. In fact, the more I thought about it, perhaps, ultimately, all this mess was *not* my fault after all. It was my brother's. If he hadn't bitten the postman's ankle, then the postman would *not* have run away and I would *not* have been able to take possession of all that musical paraphernalia.

So perhaps I should just blame Andy and have done with it.

But nice as these thoughts were – and they *were* nice, because I was going through a bit of a mental crisis, particularly as *he* had got the trench coat – none of this was going to help in retrieving all the aforesaid musical paraphernalia.

'Still,' said my brother, 'aliens or not, they have left a pretty clear trail. Following them to their hideaway shouldn't present many difficulties.'

And I said, 'What?' As well I might.

'The lorry they used to transport the stolen goods,' said my brother. 'It left a trail.'

'It left tyre marks, perhaps,' I said. 'But the snow has covered them, surely.'

'Don't call me Shirley*,' said my brother.

'Sorry,' I said. 'But the tyre tracks *are* covered by snow.'

'I'm not talking about tyre tracks,' my brother said. 'I'm talking about oil. There's oil all over the place – it must have leaked from the lorry. We can follow the trail of the oil.'

'Ah,' I said. Because it was clear to me, at least, that the oil in question had probably *not* leaked from the lorry, but rather from our leaky old Bedford van. But then, if, by some unlikely means, my

---

* This, it is to be believed, was the first time this joke was ever used.

brother could actually follow the route taken by the Bedford, it would Shirley* lead to the same place as the lorry.

'So how do you propose to follow the trail?' I asked of my brother. 'Employ the services of a bloodhound, would it be?'

'Don't be silly, Tyler.'

'Sorry,' I said. 'But please tell me.'

'I will take up the scent myself.'

'Oh dear.'

'What did you say?'

'All is clear,' I suggested.

'You'll have to assist me, of course.'

'But of course.'

I hadn't noticed that *my* holdall was in The Divine Trinity, but I noticed it now as my brother reached down, unzipped it, rooted about in it and then brought to light something rather furry-looking.

'And what is *that*?' I asked of Andy.

'It is my dog suit, of course.'

'But of course.'

'Are you being sarcastic?' Andy asked. 'Because if you are—' And he left the sentence unfinished, as the suggestion had sufficient power in itself not to require an explicit description of the potential horrors.

'No, no, no,' went I, shaking my head with vigour.

'I will have to ask you a favour, though.' And Andy slipped out of the trench coat and doffed away his fedora. 'Take these, if you will be so kind, and put them on.'

'Right,' I said, without the merest hint of a question.

'I'll need to tog-up in the dog suit to really do the job properly. That's where I messed up with my *tiger-at-oneness* – no suit. I couldn't get the real feel for being a tiger. So I ran this suit up myself.'

And Andy was now climbing into this suit, which had arms and legs and paws, a tail and a zip up the front. And then he put on the dog's-head mask, which looked, I must say, very real.

'That looks most convincing,' I said to Andy.

'Well, it should. It is made from real dog.'

'Right,' I said, and I tried very hard indeed not to be sick on the floor. But I *did* have the trench coat *and* the fedora. And so, without further words being said, I togged-up and felt a very definite *detective-at-oneness* sweeping over me.

'Help me on with the collar,' said Andy, and I did.

* And this was *never* used.

'And take the lead.' And he nodded at the lead, because he couldn't lift it up between his paws. 'And keep a very tight hold on that lead. There's no telling what might happen if I got loose.'

'Right,' I said, hopefully for the last time that day. But probably, I suspected, *not*.

And then we were off!

Andy dropped to all fours and sprang through the open doorway. He sniffed about at all the oil. And there *was* a lot visible as the snow, it appeared, didn't stay upon such oil. And then he was away, with me clinging on to the lead. Away at the hurry-up on four paws went our Andy.

And he was good, for a sniffer-dog.

We reached the allotment gates and Andy leaped into the road. And off we went at considerable speed with Andy now barking enthusiastically.

'Barking,' I said to myself. How apt.

At short length we arrived at the derelict building that had posed as The Green Carnation Club.

Andy straightened up and growled at me.

'What?' I asked him.

'You could have told me I was following your van,' he said.

'*My* van?'

'I picked up your scent at The Divine Trinity. You might have mentioned that this was *your* band.'

I did chewings on my bottom lip. 'You really picked up *my* scent?' I asked him.

'Well, I *am* a dog, aren't I?'

'Oh yes, you certainly are.'

'So let's get on with this tracking.' And he growled loudly once more, took to some further barking and set off again at a goodly pace.

We headed towards West Ealing. Then through West Ealing and out to Hanwell. And then, in Hanwell High Street, Andy stopped and scratched at the ground and howled very loudly indeed.

'Are we there?' I asked. And then noting *where* we were, I groaned. We were right outside Jim Marshall's shop. The shop from which all the equipment had originally come.

'Oh dear,' I said. 'Oh dear, oh dear, oh dear.'

'Oh what?' said Andy, straightening up.

'We're outside Jim Marshall's. He must have paid those lady-men to retrieve his equipment.'

'No,' said Andy. 'That's not it at all.'

'It's not?'

'It's not. I just stopped because I need to take a poo.'

'Oh no, Andy!' I said, and I threw up my hands in alarm.

'In the gents' toilet over there,' said Andy, pointing with his paw. 'You really can be *so* silly at times.'

I apologised to Andy and he went off to have a poo.

I stood and waited, doing little marchings on the spot to keep the circulation going in my toes whilst admiring my reflection in Jim Marshall's window. I was clearly born to this profession (as an adjunct to being a world famous rock 'n' roll star with a sports car and a speed-boat, of course).

I looked really good.

At little length Andy returned and I swear he was wagging his tail.

'That's a very posh bog,' he said. 'They even have a resident bog troll.'

'You mean a toilet attendant,' I corrected him.

'Same thing. He had the nerve to suggest that dogs should do their business in the street—'

And I could feel another 'oh dear' coming on.

'He won't be doing *that* again,' said Andy. 'And now I think we'd best press on.'

And he was down on all fours once more.

And off and away at a run.

'Andy,' I cried as I stumbled after him, hanging on for the dearness of life to the lead. 'Andy, why are you doing this?'

Andy barked and ran on.

'I know you must be angry,' I puffed, 'about being *locked up* in the lunatic asylum and blamed for stealing this equipment. Are you intending to hand it all over to the authorities when you find it and clear your name? Is that it, Andy, is it?'

Andy stopped and turned and sat down in the snow. 'No,' said he. 'It isn't. I'm not angry and I don't want to hand the equipment over to any authorities. I want *you* to have it back.'

'You *do*?' I said. And Andy nodded. And then he scratched at the back of his head. With his foot, as a dog might do, which I found most impressive. If just a tad creepy.

'On one condition,' said Andy.

'Just name it, my brother.'

'I want to be in your band.'

'Oh dear.'

'Oh *what*?'

'Oh, dear *brother*,' I said. 'It would be an honour and a pleasure.'

'You see, I have certain musical ideas of my own that I would like to realise. They're very meaningful and I think that the pop medium might—'

But he didn't say any more just then as we both had to leap out of the road to avoid being run down by a 207 bus.

'I think we'd better press on,' said Andy, rising from the pavement and shaking the snow from his back in a dog-like fashion. 'Before the trail grows cold. Well, colder anyway.'

And we were off once more. And thankfully now for the very last time.

I didn't know Hanwell particularly well. It had a High Street with Jim Marshall's shop in it. And St Bernard's Loony Bin, which was opposite the bus station. And there were the three bridges – a train bridge, a road bridge and a bridge with the Grand Union Canal in it, all crossing each other in the same place.

Although perhaps I just dreamed the last bit about the bridges. It does seem rather unlikely.

Andy stopped and sniffed at oil. 'I'm getting the scent really strongly now,' he said. 'From up ahead there, just past the three bridges.'

'*Is* there anything beyond Hanwell?' I asked of Andy. 'I sort of thought that the world probably ended somewhere about here.'

Andy straightened up and brushed the snow from his paws. 'Is that true?' he asked of me.

And I sort of nodded that it was.

'Silly, silly sod,' said Andy. 'Come on, let's get this finished.'

And he was off once more, but this time at a more sedate pace. A lady in a straw hat watched us mooching by and I could just imagine what she was thinking:

Look at that stylish-looking private eye, taking his pedigree dog for a walk, would be what she was thinking.

So I have no idea why she screamed and ran off the way she did.

Andy stopped and, like a pointer, pointed with a paw. And did a bit of doggy-panting, which more than captured the mood.

'In there?' I asked Andy.

And Andy barked in the affirmative.

'In *there*? Are you sure?'

Andy's head bobbed up and down.

'But that's a cemetery,' I said. 'Dead people live in there.'

Andy's head went bob-bob-bob some more. And I peeped through the cemetery gates. They were big gates, of iron, all gothic traceries and curlicues with much in the way of funerary embellishment. Skulls and crossed bones, angels in flight. And things of that nature, generally. And beyond these a most picturesque-looking graveyard. The snow took the edge off its grimness and painted it up to a nicety.

'In there and you're absolutely sure?'

But Andy was off once more. Not through one of the big iron gates – those were for the hearses to drive through – but through the pedestrians' entrance to the left-hand side (looking from the road, of course). And we were soon into the snow-covered land of the dead.

And Andy padded along, moving this way and that, following the avenues that led between the tombstones before finally stopping at an impressive-looking marble mausoleum. It was one of those grand Victorian affairs, all fluted columns and angelic ornamentation.

'Here?' I said.

And Andy barked that we were.

I looked up at the marvellous structure, then stepped forward and dusted snow from the engraved brass plaque upon it.

I read from this, aloud to my brother.

Here Lies Count Otto Black
Bavarian Nobleman and Philanthropist
Moved On From this Plane of Existence
31.12.1899

'The stolen equipment is in *here*?' I said to Andy. 'Are you absolutely certain?'

'Absolutely,' said Andy, and he removed his dog-mask. 'And it all falls rather neatly into place, as it happens.'

'Does it?' I asked. 'How so?'

'Because, as I told you, those who stole the equipment were dressed as women. But they weren't women. But neither were they men. That's why I couldn't identify the smell, and pondered, in all foolish frivolousness, the possibility that space aliens might be involved. Nothing of the sort, it appears.' And Andy sniffed again and said, 'It's clear as clear and my nose doesn't lie. The gear wasn't stolen by *living* beings. The gear was stolen by the dead.'

18

Well, all right and fair enough, I wasn't expecting *that*!

'*Dead* people?' I said to Andy. 'Dead men stole my Strat?'

Andy did some further sniffings. 'That's how it's smelling,' said he.

'You mean zombies,' I said to Andy. 'The living dead. Slaves to their voodoo master.'

'That is the popular consensus opinion,' agreed Andy. 'Reanimated corpses controlled by evil puppet-master magicians.'

'But *here*? In Hanwell?'

'Zombism was bound to reach here eventually,' reasoned Andy. 'I read recently the term "global village" being used to describe the world.'

'Did you read it in *Teenage She-Male Today*?' I asked.

But Andy said no, he had not.

'So what do we do?' I now asked. 'Get shovels and dig? Fetch a priest? Employ an exorcist? I am a little out of my depth here. And, if I am altogether honest, rather frightened also.'

'Have no fear,' said Andy. 'Your big brother is with you.'

'I'll go to a phone box and call Mr Ishmael,' I said.

'Mr Ishmael?' said Andy. 'Who he?'

'The manager of the band,' I said. 'I'll have to clear it with him about you joining, of course, but I'm sure it will be nothing but a formality.' And I tried to make a convincing face as I said this.

'All right,' said Andy. 'You find a phone box and call him. Tell him to bring a lot of villagers, with flaming torches.'

'Villagers with flaming torches are more your Frankenstein's monster than your zombie,' I said.

'Well, tell him to get them here before dark.'

'And isn't "after dark" for vampires and werewolves? Zombies are all-day-rounders, I think.'

'You appear to know an awful lot about this sort of thing,' said Andy.

'Not really,' I said and I shrugged. 'I just go to a lot of horror movies, don't you—'

And then I cut that line of conversation short. They probably didn't get to watch too many horror movies in the lunatic asylum.

'I'll go and make the phone call,' I said. 'Perhaps you should come with me.'

'No way,' said Andy. 'I'm staying here.'

'Are you sure it's safe?'

Andy shrugged and replaced his mask. 'I'm a dog,' he said. 'It's safe for me. And think of this place from a dog's perspective – all those buried bones.'

And I took off to find a phone box. Fast.

I didn't know exactly what I was going to say to Mr Ishmael. I didn't think I would broach the subject of zombies. It would be better, I considered, simply to pass on the location of the stolen goods, as he had instructed me to do, and leave the actual recovery of them to him.

So, case solved, really.

I walked tall on my way to the phone box. My first case as a private eye and I had breezed through it. I was a natural, there was no mistake about that. I'd rent an office. There was one up for rent above Uncle Ted the greengrocer's. I could almost visualise the name, engraved into the frosted-glass panel of the door: 'PRIVATE-TYLER', like 'Private-Eye-ler', see? Or 'PRIVATYLER' as just one word that sort of rolled off the tongue.

And I felt rather pleased with myself.

I had triumphed here.

I reached the phone box and found to my chagrin that it had been vandalised and was in a non-operative condition. And it was quite a long walk to the next one, which had been similarly disfigured.

After much walking in the cold, I found myself nearly back at Ealing Broadway, with, as it was late December, night now falling around me. But I *did* eventually find a working phone box and I *did* phone the number on Mr Ishmael's card.

And it was engaged.

And I phoned again and I phoned again and eventually after many many such phonings, the phone rang at his end. But no one answered it. And—

Well, *eventually* I did get through. And I spoke to Mr Ishmael and I told him that I had located the stolen equipment and *where* I had located it and I named the mausoleum of Count Otto Black and everything.

82

And then there was a bit of a silence at his end of the line and I thought that perhaps I had been cut off.

But finally he spoke and he said to me, 'Go home, Tyler. You have done very well and I am proud of you. But you must not, under any circumstance, return to that cemetery. There is great danger there and I do not want you to be put into such danger.'

'Oh,' I said. And then I said, 'Oh dear.'

'Just go home,' said Mr Ishmael to me. And he replaced the receiver.

But of course I didn't go home. I could hardly do that. If there was great danger in that cemetery, then I had left Andy in that great danger, and by doing so, any harm that came to him would be *my fault*. And my fault or no, I really did care about my brother and I certainly didn't want any real harm to come to him. So I jumped onto the next 207 bus that was heading towards Hanwell and took to the chewing of my knuckles on the journey.

The bus stop was only a hundred yards or so away from the cemetery gates and I ran the rest of the way.

But it was dark now and once within the gates of the cemetery there was little or no light at all. I almost immediately lost my sense of direction and began to blunder about blindly, tripping over this and that, bumping into this and that and generally making a complete unholy twat of myself.

But even if I *was* lost, I was *not* dumb.

And so I shouted. Loudly. '*Andy*', I shouted. As loudly as I could. 'Andy, where are you? Mr Ishmael is bringing help. We ought to get out of this graveyard. There's danger. Great danger. Andy, where are you?'

I shouted this and permutations of this. Numerous permutations of this, in fact. And I blundered on and I wished, really wished, that Andy and I were not in this god-forsaken boneyard, but back at home, sitting at the dining table, eating parsnips and chatting away with our mum and our dad. But not talking with our mouths full, obviously.

'Andy,' I shouted. 'Where are you?'

And then things got a little complicated.

I had been blundering and shouting in the darkness for a while, when I suddenly saw the light. This wasn't the Light that was seen by New Testament prophets. At least, I didn't think it was. *No*, it definitely was *not that* Light. This was another light entirely. This was a sinister light, a crepuscular glow of a light, a Jack-o'-Lantern unearthly shimmer of a light, and it wafted up from the ground in all directions around me. It was a very queer light, for it rose a foot or two from the ground and then no further, as if it were contained, had its specific parameters illumination-wise, as it were. It fair put the willies up me, I can tell you. I didn't like that light one bit.

But if the light had qualities about it that were outré and un-quantifiable, then this light and its qualities were as nought (very nought) when put in comparison to what occurred next. For what occurred next was most horrid.

They rose, they did, from the ground. Before me and to either side, and, turning to run, behind me, too, I noticed. They rose from the ground as in climbed from it. Mouldy fingers clawed out from the frozen ground. Hands thrashed up from the snow, fought for release, and then up they came, the terrible ones, the ungodly ones, the walking dead, the hideous crew. The zombies.

And I tried to run. But where could I run, for they were all about me? And I cried out for help and I cried out for Andy and I all but poo-pooed myself.

And then the blighters came at me. From all directions, horrible monsters, decaying and rotten. And I could smell them, that stench of the grave, that evil foetor of death.

And my cries turned to screaming and I sought to peace-make with my maker.

And as the monstrous foetid fingers clawed all about me, I saw the light. Another light and a bright one, too. And I heard the noise that came with it.

I was aware of sweeping arcs of light, swishing down from the sky. And that noise, that deafening noise – not the wingbeats of angels, as I had reasonably supposed, but the thrashing of helicopter blades.

And then there were men – *living* men, I supposed – in black uniforms that had that Special Ops look about them, as if they must surely be the SAS, or the Firearms Response Team. And down they came upon lines from the helicopters, and they had guns and they fired these guns.

And there was the light and the copter sounds and the noises of gunfire and hideous things and I sank down and cowered on my knees.

And then someone thrust some kind of hood over my head and things went rather dark.

And then someone hit me hard on the head.

And things went utterly black.

19

Now, you know that feeling you get when you awaken in a bed that is not your own, with absolutely no recollection of how you came to be in it?

No?

Well, how about that one when you awaken to find yourself in a secret underground research establishment that the British Government denies all knowledge of?

No?

Well, I must confess that this one came as a shock to me. Not that my surroundings weren't plush – comfortable, they were. Plush and comfortable and elegant too, and very 'with it' when it came to the furnishings, which were rendered in the style known as contemporary.

The bed I awoke upon was circular. Circular? I ask you. Where would you buy circular sheets? But this bed did have circular sheets and they appeared to be of silk. Not that I was a connoisseur of silk; I wasn't. We had sheets at home, and our sheets were cotton, but these sheets *were* silk. And I knew this because I had beheld silk, for Toby had brought into school a pair of pink silk French knickers that his father had won in the war. And we'd all had a good feel of those!

Beyond the parameters of the circular bed was a similarly circular room, its walls painted orange, this orangyness relieved at intervals by wall lights of the semicircular persuasion, which cast a soft ambient light in an ever upwards direction.

There was a rug, which was circular, and a chair, which was a sphere with a cut-out section for you to plonk almost all of yourself into.

And there was a door that was *not* circular. And there were no windows at all to speak of. Or even to whisper about.

And it was the lack of windows that upset me. The room I was happy enough with – the room was, in itself, quite splendid. Because it *was* plush and comfortable and elegant.

But the lack of windows was worrying. That lack of windows

signalled that there was a certain untowardness about this room. That this was an outré and anomalous room.

And one that I probably should *not* be in.

And so I sought to escape.

And as there were no windows to climb out of, I made a stab at leaving by the doorway, but sadly to no avail as the door, it transpired, was locked.

I would have given that door a kicking if it hadn't been for the fact that my feet were bare. As, in fact, was all of the rest of me. Bare-naked lady, I was, apart from the bit about being a lady. So I retreated to the circular bed, wrapped a circular sheet about my nakedness, stuck a thumb into my mouth and gave that thumb a good old sulky suck.

And I had a fair old grump going and quite a bit of rising fear also when the door opened to admit a beefy-looking fellow bearing a cloth-covered tray.

And at the sight of this tray I panicked.

Because it looked to be one of those trays that they have in psychiatric hospitals. The ones that always have a hypodermic upon them, covered by a cloth.

And when they stick you with that hypo, you're in trouble.

And so I panicked. And I did a little bit of rueing-the-day also. I rued the day that I had sent off my money to America in the hope of receiving the course in Dimac, the deadliest martial art known to man. And had *not* received it by return of post. It was quite a complex piece of rueing-the-day, but it served me well enough at the time.

The beefy-looking fellow placed the tray upon a cylindrical bedside table that had somehow escaped my notice, whipped away the cloth and said, 'Your breakfast, sir.'

'Phew,' I said, 'breakfast.'

'Breakfast indeed, sir,' said he. 'Were you expecting something else?'

I shook my head and said, 'No, nothing else.'

'Well, that's just sweet, isn't it?' said the beefy-looking fellow. 'So eat up your breakfast like a nice gentleman, or I will be forced to stick you with my hypodermic.'

And with that said, he left the room.

And I tucked into my breakfast.

It was a 'Full Welsh', which was new to me but didn't make it any the less delicious. And by the time I was done with it and was wiping my mouth on the cloth provided, the door opened once more and this time in walked Elvis.

Elvis?

I looked up with surprise at Elvis.

And Elvis smiled down at me.

'Ah,' I said. 'Elvis. It's *you*.'

'It is *not* me,' said Elvis. 'It's *me*.'

'Can I go home, please?' I said and got all upset.

Elvis sat down upon the circular bed and he smiled some more at me. And it *really was* Elvis. That was a stone-cold certain, the quiff and the sideburns, the killer cheekbones, the lip curl and that something. That something Elvis had.

'I am *not* Elvis,' said Elvis, kindly. 'My name is Doctor Darren McMahon. I'm Irish/Liverpudlian.'

'Scouse Elvis?' said I.

And the doctor nodded. 'If you like.'

'But you *are* Elvis,' I said. 'No one looks like Elvis. Elvis is a one-off. There is only one King of rock 'n' roll.'

'I hate to disillusion you,' said Scouse Elvis. Because it did have to be said that he *did* have a Liverpool accent. 'But Elvis is *not* a one-off. Elvis was, in fact, part of a six-off. But only the two of us survived.'

'You are the twin brother of Elvis?' I asked. 'But I thought he died at birth.'

'You are not listening quite as carefully as you should be,' said Scouse Elvis. 'But we will speak of such matters at length. How are you feeling? How is your head?'

And then I recalled how I had been bonked on the head.

'My head's fine, as it happens,' I said. 'It doesn't ache at all.'

'Excellent,' said the Scouse One. 'I had the beefy-looking fellow give you a shot of painkiller with his hypo before you woke up.'

'Urgh!' said I. And I felt all violated. As I probably should have done anyway, waking up in a strange bed, *naked* and everything.

'We're all professionals here,' said Dr McMahon (?). 'You have nothing to worry about.'

'I suspect I have a great deal to worry about,' I said. And then another thought struck me. One that really should have struck me earlier. 'Andy?' I said. 'What happened to my brother, Andy?'

'There was only you,' said Dr Elvis (I felt happier with *this*). 'When we purged the area, you were the only resident.'

'Purged?' I said. 'Resident?' I said. 'And where is *here*?' I also said. Also.

'One thing at a time,' said Dr Elvis (yes, I was *very* happy with this description because, looking him up and down, although he *was* Elvis, he *was* dressed as a doctor – white coat, stethoscope in top pocket, that sort of thing).

'As to where you are, you are in the Ministry of Serendipity, which is a secret underground research establishment beneath Mornington Crescent Underground Station.'

'Right,' I said. Very slowly, I said it.

'There was an incident last night – an outbreak of the Taint. We isolated it, purged the area and uplifted the only original resident amongst the reoccupied within the violated zone.'

'Right,' I said once more. Adding, 'Really?' this time.

'You'd best have a little sleep now,' said Dr Elvis.

'I'm not tired,' I told him.

'You will be,' he said, and he took out a pocket watch and perused its face. 'When you awake you will remember nothing of this.'

'What?' I said, adding, 'How?'.

'Hypnogenic narcotiser, in the Welsh breakfast.' And he counted down upon his watch, starting from ten.

And I have no idea how many were the seconds.

That tick-ticked and tick-tocked away.

But—

'And that's how I solved it,' said Andy. 'Although Tyler will probably try to take all the credit for himself.'

'What?' I said, awakening as if from a dream – a daydream, it must have been – to find myself at the lunching table.

And my mother was dishing out the parsnips and my brother was boasting about something.

'Are you all right there?' my brother said to me, breaking off with the boasting for a moment. 'You look a tad queer. You seemed to be off somewhere else then. Away with the fairies, perhaps.'

'No,' I said, 'I was—' But I couldn't recall where I'd been. I was at my lunching table, with my brother and my mother, but before that—

'Well, do try and pay attention,' said my brother. 'I am expecting to get an award.'

'For what, *exactly*?' I asked.

'For the recovery of all that gear. And there was so much of it, all loaded into that mausoleum vault. It was huge in there, like a storehouse.'

'Last night?' I said, and I got all confused.

'Wakey-wakey,' said Andy. 'The night *before* last. And where did *you* take off to? Going to find a phone box and not coming back until yesterday evening.'

'What?' I said. 'Where was I?'

'Where indeed?' Andy looked at me. 'What's up with you?' he asked.

'I'm confused,' I said. 'The last thing I remember is going off to find a phone box. Then, well, *now*, really.'

'Have you been taking drugs?' my mother asked. 'Have you been smoking reefers?'

'No,' I said. 'Absolutely not.'

'Pussy,' said my mother. 'Captain Lynch and I shared a pipe of kiff the other day that nearly took off the top of my head.'

'I am confused,' I said to Andy. 'Tell me what happened. All of it in detail. Tell me, if you will.'

'Oh, all right,' said Andy. 'You went off to find a telephone box, you remember that?'

'I do,' I said. 'Completely. And I remember it took me ages to find one and call Mr Ishmael.'

'Well, I assumed that you must have found one almost at once because you hadn't been gone five minutes before this huge furniture van arrives. And this gent calling himself Mr Ishmael gives me the big hello, says he knows that I'm your brother and tells me well done and says that he'll handle things from then on.'

'That doesn't make any sense,' I said. 'The timing's all wrong. How could that be?' And I shook my head. 'But go on, please,' I said.

'Well, the back door of the van swings down and out leap all these blokes in full camo, like commandos, and they blast their way into the mausoleum and go herding in. Mr Ishmael had sent me off on my way, but I sneaked back because I wanted to look inside, see if there were any dead people looning about in there.'

'Dead people,' I said. And I had a vague recollection of a coloured mist and of rotten corpses.

'But no zombies,' said Andy, 'just all this gear. Tons of the stuff. Not just the gear you had stolen from you – tons of other stuff. Mr Ishmael looked very pleased and ordered it all into the furniture van at the hurry-up. Then he noticed me sneaking a look in and he told me that I would be amply rewarded but that I really must go now because they had to get all this done quickly before the light went.'

'The light,' I said.

'But he said that I *would* be amply rewarded. And I trusted him. So I just pushed off home. I did wonder what had happened to you, though, but it was cold and growing dark, so I caught a bus and that was that. And *this* arrived today.' Andy now waved something at me. And this something was a cheque.

'A cheque,' I said. 'How much?'

'Five hundred pounds,' said Andy. 'And it's made out to me.'

'Five hundred pounds.' I sat back in my chair and let my spoon go slack. And, as I must have been ladling parsnips with it, I ended up with no little parsnip all down my front.

'I think I might buy a speedboat and a sports car,' said Andy. 'And if I have any money left over, I'll show it to you. Oh, and see what's written on the back.' Andy handed me the cheque and I read what was written on the back: 'If you ever want to be in a band, don't hesitate to ask me,' and it was signed 'Mr Ishmael'.

And I groaned softly and did shakings of my head. This was all so wrong. All of it, the timings of things, the way Mr Ishmael *knew* who my brother was.

There was something missing here. Something *big*. An entire day of my life, for one thing, it appeared. Where had I been? What had happened to me? How had I got home? How had I just 'come to' at the luncheon table? And what *was* this all about?

I recalled my brother's talk of zombies.

And the mausoleum that had been packed with other gear. Stolen from other bands? I was going to have a lot of questions to put to Mr Ishmael the next time I saw him.

'I don't know what to say,' I said to Andy, and I handed him back the cheque. 'I am in a state of considerable confusion.'

'So where *did* you go and what did you get up to yesterday?'

I just shrugged and shook my head.

And Andy shook his, too. 'Memory lapses,' said he, and he tut-tut-tutted. 'First sign of going stone-bonkers. And trust me, I know these things. Perhaps you should check yourself into Saint Bernard's for a couple of weeks.'

'No,' I said. 'I'm not mad. But something happened to me.'

'I lost *my* memory once,' said my mother. 'Or at least I think I did – I can't remember.'

I opened my mouth to say something, although now I can't remember what. But I didn't get to say it because there was a sudden urgent knocking at our front door and my mother went off to answer it.

And when she returned, she said, 'Tyler, it's for you.'

And when I asked her who it was, she replied that it was, 'Two enormous women who look like Les Dawson will in a few years time.'

And I weighed up the pros and cons and left the house by a window.

20

Sometimes you have to wait a really, really long time for an explanation for something that is confusing you. Something that you don't understand. Like the Big Question, I suppose. You know the one – it goes, 'What is it all about?' And you have to wait a really, really long time to get that one answered. In fact, you have to wait until all of your life is finished and you are dead to get that explanation. Obviously the fact that you are now reading this book means that you personally are not going to have to wait that long in order to get an answer to that particular question. Because *I* personally know the answer. And *I* will be divulging it to *you* when the time is right.

Which will be a bit later in the narrative. But I will let you know. And it *is* worth waiting for.

Regarding the questions that were troubling me as I sat at the lunching table listening to my brother, I worried that it might be a really, really long time before these questions were answered. But, in fact, it wasn't.

They got answered very soon.

Which was most convenient.

I ran, you see, upped the sash window and leaped into the garden. It was the back garden. And its normal back-garden dullness was presently enlivened by the addition of a snowman of prodigious proportions, which, I reasoned, was probably the work of my brother.

It was a snowman that resembled a zombie playing a guitar. And that is not a thing that is as easy as it might seem to fashion.

I passed the snowman by at the move-along.

I cleared the garden fence and headed off down the alley.

The alley debouched (a good word, that) into Rose Gardens. Which weren't really gardens, and didn't have any roses. It was the road that ran at right angles to the one I lived in. The name of which I withhold for obvious reasons.

And I would have run right across the road and down the alleyway opposite had I not run straight into the side of a long black limousine that was pulling to a halt in Rose Gardens.

And as I fell back, rubbing at my bruised upper parts, which had taken most of the impact, a rear door opened and Mr Ishmael bade me enter in.

'There's trannies after me,' I explained as I clambered inside. 'And I have every reason to believe that they are of the undead brotherhood.'

Mr Ishmael waved at his chauffeur and off we went in the limo.

Mr Ishmael offered me the comfort of a scotch on the rocks. And I took consolation in this comfort.

'Are you feeling yourself?' asked Mr Ishmael.

And although I confess that I was, and still am, a great fan of a *Carry On* movie, I answered Mr Ishmael that although sound in mind and limb, I was somewhat troubled of spirit and had many questions I thought he might care to answer.

Mr Ishmael nodded and raised a glass of his own.

'To the success of your mission. Your first case,' he said, and he toasted me.

I sampled further scotch and found some joy in this sampling.

'You did very well,' said Mr Ishmael. 'Employing the curious talents of your brother was an inspired idea.'

And I nodded. In agreement. That it *would* have been if I had indeed thought of it. But I was prepared to take the credit, if it was being offered.

'Inspired,' said Mr Ishmael. 'I knew I wasn't wrong about you. And I will be faithful to my promise. You recovered the stolen goods and I will now share with you the Big Secret.'

'Thank you,' I said. 'And I hope that details of the Big Secret will include *exactly* what happened to me yesterday, because I appear to have at least twenty-four hours missing out of my life.'

Mr Ishmael nodded. 'Would you care for a cigar?' he asked.

And I said, 'A cigar?'

'To puff upon. You might need it, to stiffen your nerves. Folk generally have a cup of strong sweet tea to administer at moments like this, but I do not. But I *do* have cigars. You can take one, or leave it, as you please.'

'I'll take one,' I said, for I had never before smoked a cigar. And what better place to begin the smoking of one than the inside of a stretch limousine?

Mr Ishmael went through all the preparations then stuck the cigar into my mouth, asked me to suck hard and administered the flame of a match to it.

And I didn't cough. I puffed.

'Nice,' said Mr Ishmael. 'And now to business that I regret is far from nice. But where to start? Where indeed to start?'

'At the beginning?' I suggested, still not coughing at all.

'No,' said Mr Ishmael, going through further preparatory operations prior to lighting a cigar of his own. 'This story is best told and explained beginning with the end. What would you say that the very end of everything would be, young Tyler?'

'A big explosion, probably,' I said. 'The entire universe blowing up. Something like that.'

Mr Ishmael shook his head. 'Care to have another go?' he asked.

'*Not* an explosion?' I said. '*Nothing*, then. I suppose the end of *every-thing* would be nothing.'

'Very close,' said Mr Ishmael. 'Death would be the beginning.'

'I thought you said that it was the end.'

'The end of life. All life. The creation of the Necrosphere.'

And I asked what this was.

'The world of the dead. A spherical universe of the dead.'

'I think I would like you to explain,' I said.

'The name of your band,' said Mr Ishmael, 'The Sumerian Kynges – you had heard the tales of Captain Lynch regarding the creation of the Homunculus, yes?'

'Yes,' I said, 'but how did you know that?'

'It is my business to know. And I know all about Captain Lynch.'

'I think he's carrying on with my mum,' I said. 'And if my dad finds out, he will probably beat Captain Lynch to an ungodly pulp.'

'I consider this altogether probable. But Captain Lynch told you of the theory that the soul does not enter a person until the third month of gestation, yes?'

'Yes,' I said. 'Carry on.'

'Well, something similar occurs at the point of death, but in reverse – the soul of the deceased remains within the body for a period of three months.'

'Oh no,' I said, and I coughed (just a little) upon my cigar. 'You are not saying that you remain aware after death? That you know what's happening to you while you rot away in the grave?'

Mr Ishmael shook his head. 'You are not *aware*,' he said. 'You sleep, as it were. Your soul sleeps, but it remains within the body; then after three months the soul awakens, in paradise, or otherwise.'

'Oh,' I said. 'But why? Why the three-month wait? Is that like the Catholic belief of Purgatory?'

'The misconception of Purgatory. The truth is that the body is vulnerable for three months after death as the foetus is vulnerable in the first three months after conception. If the soul left the body at the moment of death, it would leave a nice fresh, although dead, vehicle that a magician of sufficient power could instill something into, to reanimate that corpse.'

'As a zombie?'

'We use the term "reoccupied". A living person is referred to as an original "resident", because their soul is the original resident, while the dead who have been afflicted with "the Taint" are "reoccupied".'

These terms rang bells somewhere. As if I had heard them before.

'A conspiracy exists,' said Mr Ishmael, 'to reoccupy the entire planet, to turn this into a planet peopled by the dead – a Necrosphere, do you see?'

'I see, I suppose. But why? What would anyone have to gain from this?'

'Not any*one*. A powerful magician could create, at most, a single Homunculus in a single century. Whatever this is plans to annihilate the entire population of Earth, drive the resident souls from the bodies of the newly dead and reoccupy them with spirits, if you will, that will reanimate these dead bodies.'

'It does sound very gruesome,' I said. 'But it also sounds rather pointless, or of a limited point, at least. Dead bodies aren't going to last very long, are they? They will fall to pieces in no time. This Necrosphere of yours is going to smell pretty rank, I'm thinking.'

'Puppets,' said Mr Ishmael. 'They will survive long enough to serve the needs of their puppet-master.'

'And who he? A man, is this, or the Devil?'

'That I do not know. I have only a piece or two of the jigsaw. With your help I will find further pieces, put them all together, complete the picture. And then.'

'And *then*?' I asked.

'We'll cross that bridge when we come to it.'

'I think you'll probably be crossing that bridge on your own,' said I, 'because I have had more than enough of this madness.'

'Really?' And Mr Ishmael sank some scotch. 'So you won't want to know what happened to you yesterday, then.'

'I would like to know that, as it happens.'

'Then so be it. After the furniture van had been loaded up at the cemetery, myself and my associates left the violated zone, for such had the cemetery become. Some time later you returned. You were then attacked by reoccupied beings. A task force from the Ministry of Serendipity, tipped off anonymously, by myself, arrived to sanitise the area.

'The Government has known about this menace for as long as it has existed. They have a special department that deals with such matters – the Ministry of Serendipity. Their crack troops airlifted you out. You would then have been debriefed, reprogrammed and had your memory selectively erased, and then been returned to your family.'

And *then* I coughed on my cigar. And I said, 'What, what, what?'

'I must say,' said Mr Ishmael, 'that the Ministry does not think as I do. I am, how shall I put this, *independent*. The Ministry has a more corporate mentality. Rather than trying to understand and deal with the cause, they blast in and simply eradicate the effect. They are very efficient at that.'

'Not *that* efficient,' I said. 'Two of the blighters survived. They arrived on my doorstep. They were going to get me. I fled through the window and bumped into your limo.'

'Those were not reoccupied beings,' said Mr Ishmael.

'Oh?' said I. 'They weren't?'

'No,' said he, and he drew further smoke. 'That was just a pair of cross-dressing Jehovah's Witnesses. I believe they refer to themselves as, "Jehovah's Wet-Nurses".'

'Most amusing,' said I. 'But I am far from happy about any of this. Things don't add up. There are too many contradictions. Wrong timings. It's all over the place. And, hang about, reprogramming, did you say? These Ministry men have reprogrammed my brain somehow, is that what you're saying?'

'In as many words, yes.'

'Reprogrammed me to do *what*?'

'Who can say?' And Mr Ishmael shrugged. 'They do have some very state-of-the-art techniques of mind control. They will probably have brainwashed you so that at a given signal, known only to themselves, you will perform certain actions without being aware that you are doing it.'

'What?' I said. And, 'WHAT?' I shouted.

'Calm down, please,' said Mr I.

'Calm down? I've had my brain tampered with. What might I do? What?'

'It might be just a surveillance thing. Although it's more likely to be something more. Assassination, probably.'

'They want to assassinate me?'

'Not you. You will be triggered to assassinate someone else.'

'WHAT?' I shouted. Most loudly.

'But don't worry,' said Mr Ishmael. 'If it's me that they are intending you to assassinate, I will deal with it.'

'How?'

'I will kill you,' said Mr Ishmael. 'Now, what else would you like to know?'

21

It's funny how things turn out, isn't it? How things progress, gain momentum, spiral out of control and things of that nature, generally.

I mean, one minute I was strumming happily on a ukulele. Admittedly to an empty school hall. And then, the next minute, suddenly everything was wrong, wrong, wrong.

There was a day missing out of my life, a day during which, it appeared, I had been put through some kind of mind-control programming that had the potential to turn me into a robotised assassin at the push of a pre-programmed button. A killer zombie, perhaps, but alive.

And zombies. The reoccupied. Could any of that actually be true? I don't know whether I would have believed it if it had just been down to my brother's half-mad ramblings. But Mr Ishmael appeared to confirm it. And whatever Mr Ishmael was, he was clearly something. Somebody. He spoke with authority.

And so I considered doing a runner.

I weighed up the pros and cons. Hanging around here meant considerable danger, but would that danger diminish if I fled elsewhere? If this danger was a sort of Universal Danger, then ultimately there would be nowhere to run. But then if I did run and did hide *very well*, I might just be able to avoid the Universal Danger. If I hid *very, very* well.

It was a tricky one.

Of course, if I stayed, I could go on being a private eye. And it was quite clear from the success that I had enjoyed thus far that I was really born to this particular profession. *And* there was the matter of being in The Sumerian Kynges. Because Mr Ishmael had our equipment and he *had* promised to make us successful.

It was every boy's dream, wasn't it? To be a private eye *and* a rock 'n' roll star. All bases covered. How cool would that be? And I hadn't forgotten about being cool. And just how important that was.

'Speak to me,' said Mr Ishmael, for I was still in the back of his limo, and although I couldn't see *him* now as the vehicle was completely fogged up with cigar smoke, he could clearly see me. Because he then said, 'You have a very silly look upon your face.'

'I am cogitating,' I told him. 'Weighing up the pros and cons. Trying to make a considered judgement.'

'Unnecessary,' said the enigmatic Mr I. 'I will make the big decisions for you, thereby saving you the mental energy. The added benefit being that *I* will arrive at the correct decisions.'

I shook my head and made a wary face. 'I can't make any sense out of any of this,' I said. 'It's all too much for my brainbox.'

'Then leave it to me, young man. More scotch?'

'Yes, please.' And more scotch was poured into my glass.

And then Mr Ishmael touched his glass to mine and said 'cheers'. And we drank.

'It is all very complicated,' said Mr Ishmael, 'and it may take years to unravel. All the loose ends must be carefully tied together. If we are to succeed, we must tread a careful path et cetera, et cetera, et cetera.'

'Et cetera?' I queried.

'You know the form,' said Mr Ishmael. 'It would go on in that vein. But you probably don't want to hear any more clichés.'

'I'd appreciate some comforting ones,' I replied, 'such as, "it will all come out in the wash" and "all will be well that ends well".'

'It will all come out in the wash,' said Mr Ishmael.

'That's comforting indeed,' said I.

'But I will have to drop you off here. I have a luncheon engagement at the Wimpy Bar. Important American contact, I want to make an impression. You know how it is.'

'Yes, but—'

'A Double-Decker followed by a Multiple Pile-Up.'

'I don't think I've tried that one, but—'

'And two Coca-Colas with ice *and* straws.'

'Yes, but—'

'So, keep in touch.' And with that I was ushered from the limo.

As in, the door on my side was opened and I was ejected at speed. It *was* done with skill, however, as my glass and my cigar were snatched from my hands as I was flung from the car and into the street.

I rolled to an uncomfortable standstill in a gutter.

I rose unsteadily to my feet and dusted myself down. Where was I? I looked to the left and the right. I was outside my house, which was something at least. I sighed, brushed further snow from my person and trudged, fairly trudged, up my short garden path.

I rang the doorbell and my mother answered this ringing.

My brother was just finishing my lunch. 'It was a shame to let it go to waste,' said he. 'Christmas pudding, mince pies and gay cream.'

'Gay cream?' I queried.

'Why did you run away from those Jehovah's Bed-Wetters?'

'Jehovah's Wet-Nurses,' I corrected my brother.

'So, why did you run?'

'I don't want to talk about it,' I said. 'It was all a misunderstanding. And why are you looking so happy? Aside from the fact that you've managed to eat my lunch as well as your own?' For my brother was grinning fit to burst.

'I have decided to eschew the speedboat and the sports car and invest my money in opening a private detective agency.'

'Oh,' I said. And, 'Really?'

'Yes, really. Would you care to go into partnership with me? We could cover each other's backs, as our colonial cousins will have it.'

'You and me in our own private detective agency?'

'We'd need to take on a young woman, as secretary and receptionist. She'd need to be blonde with very big bosoms.'

'Why?' I asked, and my brother stared at me.

'Right,' I said once more. 'Enough said.'

'So if you want the job, it's yours.'

'It's tempting,' I said, 'but I have only one question. And it is an important question.'

'Ask away, my brother.'

'Which one of us will wear the trench coat?' I asked.

And so it came to be. My brother rented the rooms above Uncle Ted the greengrocer's. These rooms had been empty for a very long time, due, we were told by Uncle Ted, to their evil reputation. They were cursed, some said, and haunted by a headless Druid policeman.

But Uncle Ted held to his own opinions. 'So,' said he, 'a few folk have gone mad in these rooms. There has been a suicide or two. Murders have been committed and folk have gone missing. But what do you expect for three pounds a week and a share in the electricity bill with downstairs?'

'We'll take it,' said my brother.

And Uncle Ted crossed himself.

We didn't have much in the way of furniture. There was a desk included ('It carries with it a terrible reputation,' Uncle Ted told us) *and* a chair. *One* chair that it was rumoured had once belonged to Satan.

But we were going to need a filing cabinet and a water cooler and another desk and another chair for the big-breasted blonde to sit at and on. And Andy was going to need a chair to sit in, because I intended to have the one that was there. For it swivelled. And how cool is a swivel chair?

And we were going to need a calendar. And a telephone and a business diary and have something etched on the glass of the door, if this was going to be a real private eye's office. Something like—

PRIVATYLER

I suggested.

ANDY INVESTIGATIONS

Suggested my brother.

And so we reached a compromise:

LAZLO WOODBINE
PRIVATE EYE

It was a blinding compromise.

'We will do it by turns,' I explained to my brother, for I, as I've said, was a natural at this. 'One week you can play the part of Laz and wear the trench coat and the fedora. And the next week it will be my turn.'

'And what if a case takes more than a week to solve?' asked Andy.

And I raised my eyebrows at *this*. 'Don't you ever watch TV?' I asked him. 'TV cop shows? They always solve the case in a single episode. And that's only an hour. No case could possibly take more than a week to solve.'

'I like the cut of your jib,' said my brother. 'But I am now beginning to wonder whether putting the name of a fictional private eye upon the door might put off potential punters?'

'No no no,' I said. And I raised my ear-brows. 'People still write to Sherlock Holmes, asking him to solve their cases.'

'That is absurd,' said my brother. 'They don't, do they?'

'They do,' I said.*

'Then they must be mad,' my brother said.

'Misled, I think,' said I.

'Misled indeed, writing to Sherlock Holmes to ask him to solve cases.'

* And they do.

And my brother laughed. 'When everybody knows that he retired to the Sussex Downs to keep bees.'

'Right,' I said. 'The Sussex Downs and bees.'

And so that is how we set up. I hadn't heard from either Toby or Neil for a while and we had not been doing any further rehearsing. Mr Ishmael hadn't contacted me about anything either. So, until something did happen on the music front, there would be no harm in pursuing a career in private-eyeing. Everything was working out perfectly.

So I pushed away all those horrible thoughts about zombies and the Necrosphere and all the rest of it and concentrated on the job in hand.

And we got the door glass etched and everything:

LAZLO WOODBINE
PRIVATE EYE

And we sat, me on the chair and my brother on the floor.

Because a toss of the coin had decided that *I* would be Laz for the first week, and we awaited the arrival of our first client. And also the arrival of the blonde lady with the big bosoms who would hopefully be answering the ad upon a postcard in the newsagent's window.

And, in that bizarre and unexplained way that buses never arrive separately but always two or three at a time, it turned out that our first client and our secretary arrived at precisely the same time. And in the person of the same person. So to speak.

And we had the first of our Big Adventures.

And one Big Adventure it was.

22

Her name was Lola.

And she was a showgirl, she assured us. Although not until later.

Andy was the first to see her coming. A single iron staircase led up to our offices from beside Uncle Ted's greengrocery, and light reflected from that staircase and onto the glass panel of our door. And Andy and I were playing hide and seek for want of something better to do, and I was hiding under the desk, which was the only place to hide in the room and made the game rather pointless in my opinion, so Andy, who was counting, saw her first.

Which showed, in my opinion, that he must have been cheating, because you are supposed to cover your eyes when you count.

'A client,' cried Andy.

'We're playing hide and seek,' I told him, 'not I-spy-with-my-little-eye.' And then I explained that you have to spy something that you can actually see with your little eye.

'Someone's coming up the steps,' said Andy. 'It must be a client.'

'It might be a potential big-breasted secretary.'

'I haven't put the card in the newsagent's window yet.'

'A client!' I rose from beneath the desk.

'So *that* was where you were hiding,' said Andy. 'Very clever.'

I didn't say 'right'. I had been trying really, really hard not to say 'right' unless it was absolutely necessary.

A knock came at our office door and we both beheld the silhouette of the knocker. It was curvaceous. It was an hourglass figure.

'It's crumpet,' said Andy. 'Now be on your best behaviour.'

'*Me?*' I said.

'Well, don't go all silly. You know how you are with girls.'

'I'm suave with girls, me,' I said. 'I'm suave and debonair.'

'You're rubbish and silly with girls,' said Andy. 'I'd best do all the talking.'

'Oh no you don't.' And I snatched up the fedora from where it lay on the desk and slotted it onto my head at that angle known and loved as rakish. 'I am Laz this week. You, if I recall, are Andy the Wonder Dog.'

'I've been meaning to have a word with you about *that*,' said Andy. 'I don't want to—'

But there were further knockings. And I called, 'Please come in.'

And in walked Lola.

And it was love at first sight.

She was beautiful, was Lola. A vision. An angel in human form. She didn't have blonde hair and big bosoms though. She had short dark hair and quite small bosoms, but she did have the most stunning green eyes and one of the sweetest noses imaginable. So, no huge bosoms, but curvaceous indeed, with an hourglass figure. She wore a tight white sweater, a tight white miniskirt and tight white kinky boots.

You can ignore Andy's foolish remarks about my way with the ladies. I was a veritable Love God back in those days and very little has changed.

Lola entered and I said, 'Hellllooooo,' in my finest Leslie Phillips.

'Mr Woodbine?' asked Lola.

'That's me,' I said.

'Don't be silly,' said Lola. 'You're a child. Where is Mr Woodbine? Is he your father?'

'I *am* Lazlo Woodbine,' I protested. 'Behold the trench coat, behold the fedora.'

'I am not altogether convinced,' said this goddess, 'but we will see where it leads. My name is Lola Perbright,' and she smiled me a mouth-load of snow-white gnashers.

'What a beautiful name,' I said to Lola. 'Will you marry me?'

My brother winced, but Lola smiled some more. And she was smiling at me!

'I need your help, Mr Woodbine,' she said. And then she eyed my brother with suspicion.

'You can say anything in front of my apprentice,' I told her. 'He is deaf, dumb and blind and only understands Esperanto. And this only when performed in mime.'

'Right,' said Lola.

'And he thinks he's a dog. Please take a seat,' I told Lola.

'Where?'

I made a mental note: . . . and a visitors' chair.

'Take *my* chair,' I said. 'I can stand. And walk. And run also. And I was very good at the high jump at school. Did you ever do the high jump? The scissors? You can get very high with the scissors.'

I saw Andy rolling his eyes.

'Please sit down,' I said to Lola, and she tottered around the desk, because she was wearing *very* high heels, and sat herself down on my seat.

And crossed her legs, *very* slowly.

'I'll never wash that seat again,' I told her.

And she said, 'What?' in response.

'Nothing,' I said. 'So what can I do for you?'

'It is a delicate matter, Mr Woodbine,' said Lola, 'and must be handled with utmost discretion.'

'I am discretion personified, dear lady.'

'Right.'

'Is it an affair of the heart?' I asked. 'Your boyfriend, or your husband?'

'I have no boyfriend and I am not married.'

'Splendid.'

'Pardon?'

'Please continue.'

'Are you aware of the Perbright name, Mr Woodbine?'

I smiled and nodded thoughtfully. 'I don't think so,' I said.

'My family is noted for its heroes. There are certain surnames that you will always find upon war memorials, and certain ones that you will not.'

I nodded at this. Mine was a will-not, I thought.

'The Perbrights have been renowned throughout the history of the realm for their bravery. Name a battle or a military campaign and there will have been a Perbright in the thick of it, dying for King and country. There are many medals in the family collection. Many post-humous VCs.'

I nodded at this. Professionally. 'Where is this leading?' I asked.

'To my brother,' said Lola. 'The very last in the male line of the Perbrights.'

'Well, I suppose that they were going to get a bit thin on the ground,' I said.

Lola eyed me curiously. 'You are a *real* detective, aren't you?' she asked.

'As opposed to *what*?' I replied. 'One made out of chocolate?'

'I think perhaps I have come to the wrong place.'

'Oh no you haven't,' I said. 'This is definitely my office. Please continue – I feel certain that you can consider the case, whatever it might be, all but solved if I am permitted to take it on.'

'Right,' she said once more. And I came to understand just how annoying that word can be when you are on the receiving end of it.

'It is this way, Mr Woodbine. My family was once very wealthy. Many a grateful monarch rewarded the endeavours of their most noble knight. Posthumously, of course. But over the years the family fortune has been slipping away. And now it is all but gone. And so my brother turned to alchemy.'

'Alchemy?' I said, for I was not expecting *that*.

'The transformation of base metal into gold. The creation of the philosophers' stone, the *lapis philosophorum*. My brother said that it was the only way he could possibly restore the family fortune. You see, there are no real wars at the moment, so dying for King and country and being financially compensated by a grateful monarch are presently out of the question. So my brother sent off to America.'

'He was sent off to America?'

'No, he sent off a coupon, cut from a Marvel comic: *Transform base metal into gold for fun and profit*. Five dollars. It arrived by return of post.'

'One question,' I asked of Lola. 'Do you have a zip code?'

'Of course we do. We're posh.'

Curse these working-class roots, I thought. 'I thought as much,' I said.

'Do you think that is significant?' asked Lola.

'Everything is significant when you are a private eye,' I told her. And my brother once more rolled his eyes. Which were *not* private ones, as it was not his week.

'All right,' I said to Lola. 'Let me summarise. Your family is no longer as wealthy as it once was and so your brother sent off to America for a course in alchemy. Am I so far correct?'

'You are,' said Lola.

'So what *exactly* is the problem?'

'It's the dog. It howls and howls in the night.'

'Your dog, or your brother's?'

'My brother's dog. It knows, you see – dogs know, don't they? Dogs can see and sense things that people can't. My brother's dog senses that Pongo is not my brother.'

'Pongo?' I said. 'Now please just run this past me once again, slowly.'

'The dog knows,' said Lola, 'and I know now, too. I'm sure that my brother is *not* my brother. The person who appears to be my brother is a fake, a mockery, a travesty.' And her voice rose somewhat, which I found strangely exciting. 'My brother has been replaced by some doppelgänger. I want you to find out what this monster has done with my real brother.'

'Monster, you say,' said I. 'You are absolutely sure about this? I mean, there can be no mistake? This person who appears to be your brother is definitely *not* your brother?'

'Mr Woodbine,' said Lola, 'I know my own brother. If you had a brother, would you not know him? Do you have a brother, by the way?'

'I am an only child,' I said. And Andy ground his teeth.

'So, will you take the case? Will you discover what has become of my real brother?'

'Madam,' said I, 'I will. I will be honoured to take on a case for such a notable family as the Perbrights. I will need details, many details. Perhaps we might continue this conversation over dinner tonight.'

'If you think it would help,' said Lola.

'Madam, it is essential. I need as much information as I can get. Tell me, have you ever eaten in a Wimpy Bar?'

23

I don't know *exactly* what happened to Lola, or why she did not turn up for dinner at the Wimpy Bar that night, but there must have been a very good reason. Probably to do with her brother, Pongo. But whatever it was, she never mentioned it and I was far too polite to ask.

'Why Pongo?' asked my brother the following morning as he and I found ourselves plodding through the snow, bound for the Perbright residence.

'Why such a foolish name?' I asked of Andy and Andy nodded in reply. 'It's a toff thing. They all have names like that – Pongo and Binky, Berty, Rupert and Rhino.'

'Rhino?'

'Rhino, Wainscott, Trowel.'

'And how come you know so much about toffs?'

'I know a great many things. I read a lot. I subscribe to *Junior Know-All Today* magazine. It is a mine of information. And I know all about alchemy, too. Captain Lynch told me all about it. Anything to do with gold and Captain Lynch is on the case.'

'Perhaps you'll want his advice on *this* case.'

We reached a gate. And a big one, too. Before a great big house.

'We'll solve this case together,' I said to Andy. 'No one else need apply. And I don't think it's a real case anyway. I suspect that Lola is suffering from some mental aberration.'

'She'd have to be if she had dinner with you last night. How did that go, by the way? You came home very early and went straight to bed.'

'It's a big house, isn't it?' I said, looking up at the big house before us. It rose like a hymn in praise of the banker's craft. Victorian Gothic, my all-time favourite. There were even some turrets and a kind of black-dome affair that might very well have been a camera obscura. 'I think I'll be happy here,' I now said to Andy. 'When we marry, I'll probably live here for a while before I get a big house of my own.'

And Andy made laughter-snortings into his gloved hands. And I recognised those gloves as they were mine.

'Come on,' I told him. 'And remember that you're deaf, dumb and blind, so don't say anything unless I ask you to.'

'I've been wanting to talk to you about that, because—'

But I was up the path now and at the front door and I rang the bell. Which was an old-fashioned hand-pull jobbie, which rang a distant brass-bell-on-a-springy-thing jobbie, distantly. In the servants' quarters, most likely.

And at rather a slackened pace, I considered, an underling arrived and opened the front door for us. A doddering manservant he was, somewhat bow-backed and mangy of hair, and dandruff-flaked about the shoulder regions.

'Mr Lazlo Woodbine and associate,' I informed this superannuated wretch. 'Hasten in conveying us to your mistress – we are expected.'

'You're being a lot more Sherlock Holmes than Lazlo Woodbine,' Andy whispered into my ear.

'I'm more comfortable with it,' I said. And then I shushed him and made motions towards the manservant.

'Yes, yes, yes,' said this ancient. 'Miss Lola-Bonsai is awaiting you in the music room.'

'Lola-Bonsai,' I said to Andy. 'How posh is *that*? Double-barrelled Christian name.'

'This manservant smells of cheese,' whispered Andy as he and I were ushered inside. The entrance hall was well hung with what surely were ancestral portraits – noble men all striking noble poses. Many were battlefield poses. And many of the posers lacked for a limb or two. I drew Andy's attention to a name plaque attached beneath one of their likenesses. *Lord Rhino Wainscott Perbright*, it read.

The music room played host to a grand piano and I was sorely tempted to ask whether I might have a little tickle of the ivories. But I considered that it would have been unprofessional to do so. And anyway, I could thrash about on that old Joanna as much as I liked as soon as Lola-Bonsai and I had tied the knot.

There were heavy velvet curtains and these were half-drawn, which lent the room a certain sombreness. A fire blazed well in an ample hearth, though, and an ormolu mantel clock ticked and tocked on the marble mantel shelf. Tick and tock it went, a-ticking our lives away.

Lola was seated at a permanent table.* She was playing noughts and crosses with real noughts and she laid these delicately aside and rose to her feet as my brother and I were guided into the room.

* As opposed to one that is only occasional.

'Thank you, Sacheveral,' she said to the manservant. 'Perhaps you would be kind enough to make some coffee for our guests.'

The manservant made some throat-clearing sounds that had a distinct death-rattle quality to them and then shuffled away, never to return. I'd sack him straight away, the moment I moved in, thought I.

'He's been in the family for several generations,' said Lola, smiling at me once again. 'I'd let him go, but what would become of him?'

I could think of numerous things, all involving a merciful end. 'He looks after you and your brother,' I said, 'Does anyone else live here?'

'Just myself and that something pretending to be my brother.'

I nodded thoughtfully and then said, 'Perhaps I might now meet this impostor.'

'He's at work in his laboratory. But if we beat loud and long enough at the door, he will eventually let us in.'

'Lead on then, fair lady,' said I. And I gestured to Andy that he should stay where he was.

Lola led the way. And I followed Lola. And Andy, in turn, followed me.

Up a broad sweep of carpeted stairs, along a corridor adorned with further ancestral portraits. Up a smaller staircase, along a narrower corridor, up a little itsy-bitsy staircase and into a corridor so narrow that we had to edge along it with our breath held in. And then Lola began beating on a door and shouting for admittance and after a considerable period of this, sounds were heard of bolts being drawn and a narrow door creaked open.

It had about it the narrowness of a floorboard and it required considerable effort to squeeze ourselves into the room that lay beyond. Which thankfully was a spacious room with a high-domed night-dark ceiling.

'Pongo,' said Lola-Bonsai. And the strain was evident upon her face as she spoke the name of her brother. 'Pongo, these gentlemen have come to see you regarding a pressing matter.'

Pongo viewed my brother and me. And I do have to say that I liked the look of Pongo. He looked like an all-right-kind-of-a-cove to me. He was tall and dignified, with dark hair swept back behind his ears and a very natty Clark Gable-style pencil moustache. His features and his person ran to gauntness and this gauntness suited him. His eyes were blue and pale as a dawning sky and these eyes he now fixed upon me. And a slender right hand he extended also.

'Mr Woodbine?' said the possibly ersatz Pongo. 'Mr Lazlo Woodbine?'

'Why, yes,' I replied as I shook on this hand. 'But how did you know? Did your sister tell you we were coming?'

'Not a bit of it. I recognised you immediately – the fedora, the trench coat, the way you carry yourself – you are Woodbine. You could be no other.'

'Well,' I said. And I grinned, fairly grinned. *What an excellent fellow*, I thought.

'And this must be—' And then he put a finger to his lips. 'But he does not speak, for he is enigmatic. He *is* an enigma. He is forever cool.'

And Andy grinned somewhat at this. And then shook the slender right hand.

'And my darling sister, Lola,' the Pongo impersonator (?) continued. 'Looking so beautiful this morning.'

'I have to go,' said Lola, and she squeezed her way from the room. Leaving my brother and me in the company of whoever it was we were with.

'So, gentlemen,' said this fellow, 'what is it that you require of me?'

I looked at Andy. And he looked back at me. And I confess that I was stuck for a reply. I had not actually thought about what I was going to say when I came face to face with the brother-who-might-not-be.

'Well,' I said, 'It's a rather delicate matter.'

'It's Lola, isn't it?' said the fellow. 'Do you mind if I continue working while we talk?'

'Not in the slightest,' I said. And I cast an eye around and about the room. It was a circular room and it didn't have any windows. And that meant something to me, although I didn't know why. This circular room was a very busy room. It owned to a *lot* of stuff. Alchemical stuff. The classic alchemist's paraphernalia.

I ogled the crucibles, the alembics, the cauldrons and retorts.

'You have accumulated a remarkable collection of alchemical ephemera,' I observed.

'You have some knowledge of the philosophical arts?'

'Some,' I said. 'I know which way up you hold an aspersorium.'

'Splendid. Then you can hold mine for a while, if you wish.'

And I smiled at him and he smiled back at me. Nice fellow.

And I watched him as he worked. As he tended to the distilling tubes and the purification thuribles and the anti-oxidisation sprongs and the catalytic cross-transducers.

Not to mention the megatronic tropositors, which I never did, for to have done so would have been impolite. But it was all very state-of-the-art.

'My sister,' said the alchemically inclined one. 'She is the reason for you being here, I suspect.'

He handed me the aspersorium and I held it. The right way up.

'Why do you say that?' I asked. 'Why would your sister ask us to visit you?'

'Ah, you are as subtle as I might have expected, Mr Woodbine. You seek to catch me out with your cunning wordplay.'

'I assure you that I do *not*,' I assured him. And I handed back his transistorised aspersorium.

'She is very highly strung,' said the aspiring alchemist. 'Since the death of our parents there is only her and myself. The last of the Perbrights. My father's will divided the estate equally between us. Should one of us die, or something of a similar nature, the entire fortune would then pass to the other.'

'I understand that the family's fortunes are somewhat depleted,' I said. 'Could I hold the grum-widget now, please?'

And I was handed the grum-widget.

'My sister gets ideas into her head, you see, Mr Woodbine – that I am trying to kill her, or that I am not myself, but some impostor, that I am trying to have her committed to a mental institution so that I might claim the fortune.'

'But I understand that there is no fortune,' I said.

'It is not a monetary fortune. There is no money. There is an inheritance, but nothing I need explain here and now.'

I shook my head. 'I am becoming a little confused,' I said. 'You are saying that if one of you were to be committed to a lunatic asylum, the other would inherit. And your sister's behaviour – and I admit, yes, she did ask us here – her behaviour, not believing that you are the real you, might well be construed as a psychiatric condition that will lead her into a mental institution.'

'Intriguing, isn't it, Mr Woodbine? Her accusations against *me* load the dice against *her*. What do you make of that?' And he now took up a slap-nosed doohickey. And as I had never seen one of those before, I was at a loss to know which way up it was supposed to be held.

'So,' said our host, 'is there anything you wish to ask me? Some personal details of Pongo Perbright's life that only Pongo would know about?'

I gave my fedora a scratching. I rather wished that I'd pre-planned a question or two. I could have asked Lola to tell me some personal details. It would have been pretty conclusive evidence one way or the other.

'There was one thing,' I said, as it now (and this was a flash of inspiration on my part) occurred to me that I could do this the other way round: ask him first, then check his answer with Lola. 'Pongo had a favourite toy when he was very young. What was it and what was his pet name for it?'

'It was a trowel,' said Pongo. 'And it still is. And its pet name is Trowel.'

I looked at Andy, who shrugged.

'I don't think I need take up any more of your time, sir,' I said. 'I think that perhaps this is a family affair that should be kept within the family.'

'You are astuteness personified.' And Pongo Perbright stuck out his hand once more for a shake. And I shook it firmly and Andy and I squeezed from the circular lab.

We returned to the music room and Lola was waiting for us there. I didn't really know what to say to her apart from asking about Pongo's favourite toy and I thought I would hold on to that for a while, so as to come across as really clever when I dropped it into the conversation. So when she offered to make Andy and me some coffee, as Sacheveral had still not returned, I took her up on the offer. And while she was away I spoke to Andy.

'What do you make of all this?' I asked him.

'They're both barking,' was Andy's conclusion. 'But that's toffs for you.'

'He seems like a very nice fellow,' I said. 'But then she seems like a very nice lady and one who is clearly in love with me, but afraid to show her feelings. But if one is out to get the other, then I don't know which one it might be.'

'I bet you'd rather side with her,' said Andy.

'Well . . .' And I shrugged. 'But he *was* a nice fellow, wasn't he? Cool haircut.'

'*Very* cool haircut,' said Andy. 'Just like mine.'

'Just like yours?' And I laughed. 'Yours is a girly haircut, all short on the top and rattails down the sides and back.'

'It is the latest style,' said Andy. 'And I invented it. I call it the mullet. After the fish. Although I don't remember why.'

'Well, Pongo's was nothing like yours. His was all slicked-back behind his ears. Very stylish, as was his moustache.'

'Moustache?' said Andy. 'He didn't have a moustache.'

'He had a Clark Gable,' I said. 'If you are hoping to become a private eye like me, you will have to hone your observational skills. Take in the small details. That's very important.'

'He did *not* have a moustache,' said Andy. 'He had a mullet and no moustache. Little blokes like him can't wear moustaches. It makes them look like Hitler.'

'Little blokes?' I said. 'He was tall, that Pongo. He was easily as tall as me.'

'Get away,' and Andy laughed. 'He was positively dwarf-like. But in a nice way. I really took to him.'

'Tall, short, moustache, no moustache?'

And I looked at Andy and he in turn looked at me.

And then Lola returned with a tray-load of coffee, and this tray-load included biscuits, too.

She set down her tray-load upon the permanent table and then looked at Andy and me, still looking at each other.

'Is something wrong?' she asked of me.

'Oh no,' I said. 'Nothing at all. If I were to ask you to describe the fellow upstairs, who you claim is not your brother, but according to you looks identical to your brother, how would you describe him?'

Lola shrugged, prettily. 'Medium height?' she said.

'Anything else?'

And Lola shrugged again. 'Apart from his huge red beard I can't think of anything particularly striking about him,' she said.

24

'So what do you make of all *that*?' I asked Andy.

We were home now, having travelled back from the Perbright residence upon a number 65 bus, and we were now sitting down in our sitting room. Andy sat in the visitors' chair and I upon the Persian pouffe. And I poked at the fire with a poker that I had removed from the brass companion set that was topped by a fine brass galleon in full sail.

'I think we're dealing with an alien here,' said Andy. 'A shape-changing alien.'

I shook my head at such stuff and nonsense. 'Your answer to every-thing is always, "it's an alien". You said that last time and it wasn't really aliens, was it?'

'No,' said Andy. 'It was zombies last time. But your point is?'

'That it's unlikely to be an alien.'

'We don't have too many other options. He could be one of the fairy-folk, I suppose. They can disguise their true forms. They cast the Glamour upon you.'

'It's a possibility,' I said.

'You think so?' Andy asked.

'No,' I said. 'No, I do *not*! But it's an odd one, isn't it? He appeared differently to each of us. I wonder if you got a hundred people to look at him whether they'd all see someone different.'

'Perhaps there's nothing strange about it at all,' said Andy. Perhaps it's perfectly natural and we're all like that. People see each other dif-ferently. All people. Which is why the unlikeliest people fall in love with each other. Where you might see a big fat munter of a woman, the man in love sees a Raquel Welch lookalike.'

'Heaven forbid,' I said. 'You don't think that can be true, do you?'

'Probably not. But we could try it out. Check passers-by, see if our descriptions of them tally.'

'What about Mum?' I said. 'We could start with her.'

Mother entered the room to top up the coal scuttle. And as she emptied coal from the pockets of her apron into it, Andy and I sized her up and committed her description to memory.

Which, upon her departure, we shared. And it tallied.

'I think it's just him,' I said. 'I think he has a special gift.'

'Perhaps he doesn't even know that he has it.'

'Or perhaps he has *just* acquired it, through his alchemical experiments or something. Which would explain why his sister doesn't think that he's the real him. A family member would have an instinctive intuition thing going, wouldn't they?'

'That's very good,' said Andy. 'I like that. By the by, I don't recall you discussing money with this Lola Perbright. Money, to whit, our fee.'

'We haven't earned it yet,' I said.

'So how do you propose that we do?'

'Well,' I said to Andy, 'I have been thinking about that. And I have come up with a bit of a plan. I think you will like it because it will involve you putting on a disguise. And you do like doing that, don't you?'

And Andy nodded.

'So you and this Pongo character, whoever or whatever he might prove to be, have something in common. Lean over here and I'll whisper my plan.'

'You will whisper?'

'I will.'

And I did.

Now, as this was before I had perfected the Tyler Technique, I was still going in for the proactive, hands-on school of private detection. And if you are hands-on, you are quite likely to find yourself getting your hands dirty.

And this I soon found out, to my cost.

We returned to the Perbright residence. At midnight. I wore my trench coat and fedora, but in order to disguise myself (as I did not have a tweed jacket) I also wore a pair of sunglasses.

Andy, in his turn, had taken a great deal of trouble to get his disguise 'just so'. And 'just so' it most certainly was, and I congratulated him upon it.

There were no number 65s at midnight, so we had to walk. And I recall commenting that it was a very great shame that the Bedford van that was The Sumerian Kynges' gig bus had not been discovered along with all the music gear. And that, as detectives, we really needed a car.

And Andy said that he would take care of the car business. And that he had not forgotten that he was to be the new lead singer of The Sumerian Kynges (although I remain unsure as to how he got *this* idea in his head) and how I should call Mr Ishmael and ask when rehearsals would recommence.

And we trudged on through the night. Although the snow was beginning to melt. Which made the way now slushy.

We trudged and tromped and slopped and when we arrived at the Perbright residence we searched its façade for lights.

But lights were there none. Which we hoped meant that all within had gone to bed. In separate beds, of course.

We entered the front garden with stealth and crept towards the house. Once there, we flattened ourselves against the front door and I instructed my brother as to what should happen next.

'You swarm up the wall and enter by an attic window,' I whispered to him. Then creep down through the house, open this door and let me in.'

'Swarm?' my brother whispered back.

'Swarm,' I agreed and mimed, with my fingers, swarming motions.

'No.' And Andy shook his head. 'We'll both go in by the front door.' And with no further words spoken, he took out a roll of tools and applied himself to the front door's lock. And presently we were inside.

I offered no comment on this. And my brother tucked away his tools and offered, in return, no explanation.

'Now, houses look all different in the darkness, don't they? They lose all their colour, of course, and the everyday becomes untoward and the mundane outré and suchlike. I had to take off my sunglasses because I couldn't really see very much.

I had brought a torch (or flashlight, as our colonial cousins like to call it) and I now switched this on and flashed its beam all about. 'Weren't there portraits on these walls?' I whispered to Andy.

'All down the hall,' he replied. 'We are in the right house, aren't we?'

I tippy-toed along the tiled floor. I felt certain that it had been carpeted earlier.

I flashed the torch upstairs.

'Those stairs look different, too,' said Andy. 'We *are* in the wrong house.'

'We're not. It's the same. But it's changed, somehow, that's all.'

'Changed its staircase?'

I shrugged and followed Andy, who was now heading upstairs.

The stairs didn't creak, which surprised me, and no lights flashed on to reveal some fellow in a nightshirt with a blunderbuss in his hands. But then, perhaps the nightshirt-wearing blunderbuss-toter was now a thing of the past.

I followed Andy along a pleasantly furnished hallway and up another flight of steps. And so we eventually found ourselves on the top floor in a corridor of fair-to-middling widthness, before a door marked *Pongo's Lab. Keep Out.*

'Do your stuff,' I whispered to Andy. And he took out his tool roll.

And after some minutes of twiddling about, he sprang the door's lock and together we entered Pongo's Lab. And with the door closed behind us I switched on the light and we, together, beheld.

And Andy whistled. 'Well,' he said. 'I wasn't expecting *that*.'

The room, though still circular, was otherwise thoroughly unlike the one we had entered but a few short hours before. There was no evidence at all of any alchemical involvement. No cross-threaded nurdlers or electric toggle-flangers or even a bit of litmus paper. Here was only a comfy bedsitting-room kind of affair, with a bed and a chair to sit upon, and a table to sit at it with, and a sink to wash your hands in when you'd tired of sitting.

Andy raised his palms and said, 'Where did everything go?'

'I don't believe it was ever here,' I said. 'I believe that we saw what we were intended to see, but not what was really there to be seen.'

'Oh,' said Andy. 'Really?' said Andy. 'So what does that mean?' said Andy. 'And why?'

'All a charade,' I said, 'designed for one purpose.'

'And that purpose might be . . . ?'

'I intend to find out,' I said. And I sat myself down on the bed. 'I suggest we switch off the light and settle ourselves down to await the return of the room's occupant.'

'And why would we want to do *that*?'

'Well, it might be instructive to find out who he really is.'

Andy gave me the queerest of looks. 'You think you know what's going on here, don't you, Tyler?'

'I do, Andy. I do.'

'And would you care to share this with me?'

'What, and ruin the surprise?'

And then we both heard sounds from outside the door.

And Andy switched off the light.

And we waited there, crouched in the darkness.

Waiting for something to happen.

And suddenly something did.

But, I have to confess, it wasn't quite the something I had been expecting.

25

It is a fact well known to those who know it well that very bright lights presage trouble. The arrival of aliens and booger-men and bogey-beasts from the bottomless pit. Those ghostly things that come out of the television set. And dawn raids by the police.

Bright lights mean trouble, they do. *Very* bright lights, *much* trouble.

And this light was a bright'n. It wasn't helicopters, although it came from above, and it wasn't flying saucers either. Although it might well have been, because it did come to the accompaniment of some stonking great chords of the Albert Hall organ persuasion.

Which might have had this bright light down as a celestial light, a Holy Light, a light sent by God and delivered by favourite angels. And this, I suppose, was the effect it was intended to create here.

Big bright light and stonking great chords.

Andy and I took to shielding our eyes and our ears as well as we could.

I sank down to my knees and assumed the foetal position. Andy, I think, just rocked backwards and forwards on the bed, but as I was now in no shape to either hear or see things clearly, I couldn't say for sure.

And then the light went super-flash and died away and the stonking chords crashed to an end in the Key of La.

And I did blinkings and peered up from beneath the shelter of my fedora's brim. And there was a beautiful lady.

She wore a long twinkly robe that reached right down to her naked feet. Pre-Raphaelite hair tumbled over her shoulders and a silver head-band encircled this hair, and this had a crescent moon on the front that glittered prettily. As for her features, they were soft and delicate, her eyes large, nose small and mouth very wide indeed. And she held in her right hand a great big flower. And nothing at all in her left.

I peeped up at this beautiful vision, for vision indeed was she. She had materialised, it appeared, right out of the empty air and there she stood, her feet touching the floor, but touching only, not supporting her, for she was hovering just a little. Wafting gently.

Captain Lynch had told me all about angels and how they used to come and visit a lot, back in the good old biblical days, but how eventually they lost patience with Man and so didn't come to visit any more. Which was one of the reasons why the New Testament just suddenly ends and there were no further New Testaments, such as *New Testament Two: The Sequel.*

I climbed slowly to my feet, dusted myself down, took off my fedora and bowed my head. My brother, I noticed, was sitting and staring, which I thought rather rude.

'Why are you here?' asked the vision, her voice as sweet as a cuddly kitten peering out of a handbag. 'Why have you violated the sanctum?'

'Ah,' I said. And, 'Um.'

' "Ah" and "um",' said the vision. 'Most articulate.'

'I'm sorry,' I said. 'I don't know how to address you. What is the correct form? Should I call you madam, or holy one, or Angel of the Lord, or should I just shut up?'

'Just shut up,' counselled the vision, and she waved her flower about and little flecks of fairy-dust shimmered in the air.

So I stood with my hat in my hands and said nothing.

The vision drifted towards the bed and then sat down upon it next to my brother. Who shifted along rather rapidly.

'Don't fuss yourself, dear,' said the vision. And then to me she said, 'You have an oily about yourself, do you?'

'An oily?' I queried. 'A what?'

'An oily-rag – a fag.'

'No,' I said. 'I don't. I never really got around to smoking. I had a cigar once, but I wasn't very impressed.'

'So,' said the vision. And she plucked a petal or two from her flower and let them flutter to the floor. 'This is a ripe old kettle of fish, this, ain't it? A right how-d'ya-do and no mistake.'

'Are you a cockney?' I asked the vision. 'Only I've read about cockneys, but I've never actually met one. I thought they were extinct.'

'They are, luvvy. They've all rolled out the barrel and gorn up the apples to the big Pearly Kingdom in the sky, where every boy's a barrow boy and joins in a knees-up at the drop of a second-hand top hat, as worn by the Artful Dodger. Gawd stripe me pink if I'm telling you a porkie, guv'nor.'

And I came so close to saying, 'Right.'

'You have a very posh voice for a cockney,' I did say. 'I thought cockneys dropped their H's and slurred their vowels.'

'Well, did you now, did you? And you never having met a cockney in your life.'

'I've seen *Mary Poppins*,' I said, 'so I've seen and heard Dick Van Dyke.'

'The King of all the cockneys.' And the vision made a respectful genuflective wiggle about with her flower. 'But this won't get the baby bathed. How do you want to go?'

'Go where?' I asked. Which was a reasonable question.

'To wherever you're bound – Heaven, or Hell, or nowhere at all if you're an atheist. Which wouldn't be too much fun, in my opinion. Although it might be better than Hell. Which I'm told is a really bad place, although I've never been there myself.'

'Hold on,' I said. 'What are you saying to me?'

'I'm offering you the choice of how you want to die. I'd go for a quick and certain one, if I was you. Explosions are always very final. And if you are an atheist, well, at least you've got out and about.' And the vision laughed. In cockney, I supposed.

But I didn't laugh. Not at all. 'You are going to kill me?' I said. 'Why would you want to do that?'

'Because you have violated the sanctuary. I offered you an opportunity to make a case for yourself, but the best you could come up with was "Ah" and "Um". Which, unless they are part of some advanced form of Esperanto, fail to convince on so many levels. Knees up, Mother Brown, me old cock-sparra.'

I did a nervous foot-to-foot dance.

'Do you need the bog?' asked the vision.

'Very shortly, I think. But please don't kill us, please.'

'Us?' said the vision. 'It's only you I'm intending to kill. Get off me barrow and things of that nature generally.'

'But . . .' and I pointed to my brother.

'One thing at a time,' said the vision. 'So how do you want to go? Explosion, or grand piano falling from an impossible height? I really love that one.'

'No, please no,' I wailed and I fell to my knees as I did so.

'What a wuss,' roared the vision, laughing near to burst.

'Just tell me why,' I wailed some more. 'Tell me why, I beg you.'

'Tell you why?' The vision drifted up from the bed and hovered in the air. There was a corona of light about her head and I wondered perhaps whether this was in fact none other than the Virgin Mary herself. There were always reports in the papers of her manifesting here and there about the world, usually to not particularly bright people, to whom she would pass on not particularly bright messages. And I had always wondered about *that*. But then it occurred to me that although she might have been the Mother of Christ, that didn't necessarily mean that she was the brightest candle in the Communion candle box.

You don't have to be clever to be a mum, you just have to be loving and kind.

'Your son won't like this,' I said, suddenly emboldened, although not altogether certain from where this sudden emboldenment had sprung. 'He's the big cheese in Heaven now, and he won't take kindly to you killing off one of his flock. My mum's an Evangelical – she talks to Jesus all the time. She'll tell him what you've done, if you do anything to me.'

'Jesus,' said the vision. 'You think I'm Jesus's mum?'

'Well, you are, aren't you?'

'No,' said the vision. 'I'm not. I am something entirely different. In fact quite unrelated to Christianity. Three-bob-a-pound-tomatoes, get 'em while they're 'ot.'

'Then please tell me,' I begged. 'It's only fair. If you're going to kill me and everything.'

'Oh, all right. Sit down on the floor there and I will tell you a little story. It is a true story and it has a moral, and if you listen very carefully you will understand. Do I make myself understood?'

I sat down on the floor before her and nodded that she did.

'Right then. I will drop the cockney patois, as frankly it does not enhance the telling of the tale. The tale goes this-aways. There once and still is a family called Perbright. Every generation gave birth to a noble Perbright who fought for King and country or Queen and country, and always for God and country.'

I was about to open my mouth and say that I'd already heard this story and so could the vision tell me another one. A really, really long one (in the hope that help in one form or another might arrive in the meantime). But I thought better of it and kept my mouth tight shut.

'You see,' the vision continued, 'there is more to this than simply men dying for their monarch and country. These men, these heroes whose names appear upon the war memorials – these men are magical sacrifices made to appease the Gods of War and return peace to our land.

'And this is not a metaphor. This is a fact. The war memorials, you will notice, are nearly always in the form of obelisks. Magico-phallic megaliths erected at key points across the country, inscribed with the magical names of the sacrificial ones. These magico-phallic megaliths channel natural energy through the landscape, fertilising the soil, bringing joy. And bringing forth the next generation of heroes who must do the same. Such is the way it is and such has it been for thousands of years.

'But since the end of the Second World War, when many heroic sacrifices were made and many magico-phallic obelisks raised, there have been ripples in the ether. Signs and portents in the heavens. Omens of the coming of Ragnarok.

'All over the world, the magicians who advise our world leaders are doing what they can to deal with the situation. A dark force is moving over the face of the Earth and many sacrifices must be made to assuage it. In America the Grand Magus has advised the President to purchase the rights to a war in Vietnam to help take care of the problem. But over here we have no such war to engage in. The Pope and the Archbishop of Canterbury have been holding meetings and they hope to get a civil/religious war going in Belfast. Let us hope that they are successful. But on mainland Britain—'

'No, hold on there,' I said. Well, I couldn't help myself. 'Are you telling me that wars are started for magical reasons? Because in order to protect the planet from some immense overwhelming evil force, it is necessary to sacrifice heroic noble victims, so that their names become ritual words upon magico-phallic obelisks, which channel natural energies throughout Great Britain and keep everything hunky-dory?'

The vision nodded. 'You have a better explanation?' she asked.

'No,' I said. 'Not at all.'

'So, do you want to hear the story?'

'Do you mean it hasn't begun yet?'

'Hardly at all. Do you want to hear it, before I destroy you?'

'Yes,' I told her. 'I'd love to hear it. And take your time with the telling.'

26

I watched the vision as she spoke and tried to get some measure of her. If she was not the Mother of God – and it seemed a fair bet that she was not – then what? A demon, perhaps, clothed in false beauty? That sounded reasonable, considering that she promised death. Alien? No, I wasn't going for alien. Nor fairy, although there was much of the fairy about her. I noted that I had not noted any evidence of wings, fairy-like, angelic or demonic. This lack of wings might have been significant. But then again––

'Are you falling asleep?' the vision asked of me. 'Because if I'm keeping you up, as it were, it might be better if I just put you down, as it were, and have done with it.'

'No, no, no,' I said to the vision. 'I'm all ears, me.'

'Then I will continue. As I have said, a dark cloud of something has settled upon the Earth. A choking, lifeless cloud. And those who can sense its presence are doing all they can to engage it in battle and defeat it.'

Mr Ishmael, I thought. But I didn't speak his name.

'Pongo Perbright,' said the vision. 'A hero, a noble man, a magical sacrifice. A man torn, for, as one who knew and understood what was expected of him and what his fate should have been, he became a tortured soul. He roared and raged and would have done harm to himself and others had he not been visited by a powerful magician who offered him a proposition. This powerful magician was an alchemist, and he possessed the method of transforming base metal into gold. And he offered this formula – for it is a formula – to Pongo.'

'Why?' I asked. 'If you possess the secret of transforming base metal into gold, why would you share that secret with anyone else?'

'Only because they might possess something even more valuable that they would be willing to exchange.'

'And what would that be?' I asked.

'A soul,' said the vision. 'A warrior soul, a noble soul – the soul of a magical sacrifice.'

'But surely Pongo wouldn't have traded. He knew what he was and how important his sacrifice was.'

'Indeed, but this alchemist was a most persuasive talker. He spoke in honeyed words to the poor, tortured soul that was Pongo Perbright. He convinced Pongo that he had been forgotten, cast aside, that he was no longer needed.'

'I don't think Pongo would have believed that if he was really noble,' I said.

'Well spoken,' said the vision. 'And indeed he would not. So the alchemist persuaded him that he could do so much good with the gold that he could create that God would take him directly into the Kingdom of Heaven as a reward.'

'But he was to sign away his soul in exchange for this? That doesn't make any sense.'

'Who do you think it really was who spoke these honeyed words?'

'I suspect it was the Devil,' I said.

'And your suspicion is correct. And so Pongo Perbright signed away his soul. And in exchange he was given a magical formula. He set up an alchemical laboratory right here in this very room. The formula is a complicated affair and requires certain ingredients. Ingredients that can only be found within a human being.

'In order to achieve noble ends, he was going to have to force himself to commit evil crimes. Naturally, at first he baulked at this. But the evil alchemist, the Black Alchemist, we shall call him, returned to him again and again, reminding him of the contract that he had signed with his own blood. And reminding him of what great good he could achieve once he had perfected transmutation.'

'And under such pressure, that noble man—'

'He murdered women,' I said. 'Six women. In Acton and Chiswick. I read of these murders – a modern-day Ripper, the press called him. Pongo Perbright committed these murders?'

'Yes,' said the vision and nodded. 'And he ground up the parts required and created the philosopher's stone, that agent which affords the transmutation of the base into the perfect. Alchemy, you see, is a magical principle, a philosophical principle. And this principle is that all things have the capability to achieve perfection. It is a philosophical concept. A man might perhaps achieve perfection by godly acts. As for minerals, the basest of metals, the lowly iron ones, crave in their way to achieve perfection in the shape of becoming that most perfect of metals, gold. The philosopher's stone is the agent of this transmutation from baseness to perfection.'

I nodded thoughtfully. Captain Lynch had explained all this to me, although he had dwelled more on the making-of-gold part of things rather than the philosophical concepts.

'And so,' continued the vision, 'through a great and unholy cere-mony he brought the process to perfection. Within a great crucible he placed a pound of rough iron ore. And onto this he poured a single grain of the powder he had ground from the philosopher's stone he had created. A single grain. That was all that was required. And there was a great flash of light. Because there is always a great flash of light when something terrific is about to (or *is*) occurring. And whoosh!'

'Whoosh?' I said.

'Whoosh,' said the vision. 'The iron ore had become perfect gold. The thing that was base, almost without value, crude, reached perfec-tion. Whoosh.'

'Whoosh,' I said. 'And is that the end of the story?'

'Well, it is in a manner of speaking.'

'And so where is Pongo Perbright now? Did the Devil take him?'

'No,' said the vision. 'The Devil didn't take him.'

'So he bested the Devil,' I said. 'That doesn't happen very often.'

The vision made a doubtful face and shook her head slowly and sadly.

'So what did happen?' I asked.

'Well,' said the vision, 'he's right here. Why don't you ask him yourself?' And she wafted aside with a dramatic flourish to reveal, behind her, the figure of a man who had, for all I knew, been stand-ing there unnoticed all along. And this figure of a man was Pongo Perbright. Or so I assumed it to be.

But Pongo Perbright was not going to answer any of my questions.

He just stood there with a stupefied look of surprise upon his face, saying nothing and moving not at all.

'The base transformed into perfection,' said the vision, 'at the touch of the magical dust from the philosopher's stone. He touched the gold he had created and—'

'He turned into gold,' I said. For there indeed was Pongo Perbright. And he was a statue made of gold.

27

'Whoa,' I said. And, 'Mercy me.' But it was true as true.

And I approached the golden Pongo on what I must confess were rather wobbly legs. And I did not touch Pongo, oh no, because for all I knew that might have turned *me* into a golden statue. 'Whoa,' I said once more and slowly. 'That is mighty weird.'

'Mighty weird?' said the vision, hovering close. 'I tell you a story like that and show you a man who has turned into solid gold and the best you can manage is "mighty weird".'

'Mighty weird is a *lot*,' I said. 'I haven't seen many things in my life that I would describe as mighty weird. Well, I hadn't until recently, anyway. But it is mighty weird. It really is.'

'Would you like those to be recorded as your final words, then?'

'No,' I said, 'I would not. You're not really going to kill me, are you?'

'I have no choice. You have entered the sacred space. You have encountered me in my true form. You must die. There is no other option.'

'There must be another option,' I said. 'Think hard – I bet you could come up with one.'

'Knees up, Mother Brown,' said the vision.

'And I don't think you're a very convincing cockney,' I said. 'You said "knees up, Mother Brown" before.'

'I can say it as often as I like. So, explosion was it, if I recall?'

'No, no, no,' I said. 'No, please. You have told me the tale of Pongo Perbright – and I admit that it is *beyond* mighty weird – but you haven't told me about yourself. Who are you? If you're not the Virgin Mary, then who?'

'It's none of your business,' said the vision.

'Look,' I said, 'what harm can it do? You're clearly a very magical being possessed of wonderful mystical powers. I'll just bet you have lived a fascinating life. Surely it wouldn't hurt to share a little of it with me?'

'Well,' said the vision, 'perhaps not. Perhaps just a little.'

'Thank you,' I said. 'So what are *you* doing here?'

'I'll tell *my* tale *my way*,' said the vision, '*if* you don't mind.' And she stamped her foot. Although it didn't reach the floor.

'Then please do,' I said. 'I am so eager to hear it.'

'It is this-aways,' spake the vision. 'I arrived too late to save Pongo Perbright. I was alerted to the deal he had made and I rushed as fast as I could to aid him, but I was too late. And so I impersonated him, for the sake of his sister, but she was not convinced by my impersonation and she called you in. And of course you had never met Pongo Perbright before, so you didn't know what he looked like. So I gave *you* an impression of what you thought he must look like and I did the same for your brother here.' And she gestured with her thumb over her shoulder, to where my brother still sat upon the bed.

'I thought you would go away and not return. I have set up my headquarters here, you see. I work at night. I am changing things bit by bit: this house, a piece at a time, and then the whole world.'

'Changing it?' I said. 'How and why? Who *are* you?'

'I am the Zeitgeist,' said the Zeitgeist. 'I am the Spirit of the Age. I am the Spirit of the Nineteen-Sixties.'

'Whoa,' I said once more, and in some surprise. 'So there really *is* a Spirit of the Age. It is an actual physical thing.'

'One is born in every decade. Each decade is different from the last, you notice. No two are ever the same.'

'But surely it is down to Man to determine how a decade works out. You're not telling me that Mankind is just a bunch of puppets with beings like you pulling the strings?'

'There are many answers to many questions,' replied the Zeitgeist, 'and no two are the same. If Mankind was allowed full rein over a decade, there is no telling what kind of mess it would get itself into.'

'So you are perfecting this decade the way you feel it should be perfected.'

'Absolutely,' said the Zeitgeist. 'The nineteen-fifties were a terrible mess: all that powdered egg and Jimmy Handley on the wireless set. And rock 'n' roll – the Devil's music. I'll put a stop to all that, I can tell you.'

'Put a stop to rock 'n' roll?'

'There's no telling how it might develop. No, I am going to calm things down considerably. I am going to re-establish the work ethic, hence the cockney persona. Cockneys are hard workers, with hearts of gold and love for their old mothers, everyone knows that. So that is what the sixties will be remembered for. Coming generations will read of the sixties as a sober decade when everyone knuckled down and worked very hard, eschewing loud music, strong ales and strange drugs.'

'Right,' I said, slowly. And I didn't feel wrong about saying it.

'And now you know everything. And so you must die.'

'Not *everything*, surely,' I said.

'How did you know my name is Shirley?' And then the Zeitgeist fell upon me. And there was a really blinding light.

A terrible, terrible, terrible light, it was.

Really terrible.

28

And what a bright light it was.

And the bright light grew brighter still.

Then suddenly it died away.

And I looked up, expecting to see the heavily bearded face of my creator, but to my surprise and considerable relief saw instead the face of my brother, grinning down at me.

'I'm not dead,' I observed. 'Unless you're dead, too.'

'I'm not dead,' said Andy, 'and neither are you.'

'Wow,' I said. 'What happened?'

'I clocked her,' said Andy. 'Right on the head, as hard as I could.'

'You clocked the Zeitgeist? With what?'

'With this clock,' said Andy, displaying same, 'from the bedside table. As hard as I could, wallop.' And he mimed a mighty swinging and clocking with the clock.

'Is she dead?'

'I certainly hope so.'

Andy looked down and I looked down and there lay the Zeitgeist, all prone on the floor.

'You killed her,' I said, in scarce but a whisper. 'You killed the Spirit of the Age. The Spirit of the Sixties.'

'Well, she was going to kill you, and I couldn't have that.'

'No,' I said. 'Well, thanks,' I said. 'Thank you very much for saving my life.' And I climbed to my feet and did dustings down and gazed at the fallen Zeitgeist.

'She was very beautiful,' I said, rather sadly.

'Yes, but she *was* going to kill you. And think about it, Tyler – did you hear what she had in mind for the nineteen-sixties? All that business of eschewing loud music, strong ales and strange drugs? A decade of the cockney work ethic?'

'You do have a point,' I agreed. 'But without her, there's no telling what might happen to the nineteen-sixties.'

'It's a risk we'll have to take.'

'Well,' I said. And I looked down at the lovely figure once more. 'I hope you haven't done something, you know, cosmic, or something. Changed the course of history, or something.'

'Hm,' went Andy, 'you might have a point there.'

And then the Zeitgeist gave a little moan.

'She is not dead,' I cried.

And Andy leaned down. And clocked her again. Repeatedly and hard.

And there was a sort of twinkling of fairy-dust and the Zeitgeist faded all away.

'She is *now*,' said Andy. And he replaced the clock upon the bedside table. 'And without any evidence of a crime, who is to say that one was ever committed?'

I looked long and hard at Andy. For all his madness, he did at times display a great deal of wisdom. And this was one of those times.

'My only regret—' said Andy.

'Oh,' said I. 'You have a regret?'

'I do,' said he, 'and my only regret is this: that I never had the opportunity to employ my disguise, which, you will agree, is a blinder. But now no one will ever know that I had it on, because it was never employed.'

'That is regrettable,' I agreed. 'Do you think we should go home now?'

'Well,' said Andy. And he made a thoughtful face. 'My thoughts are of Lola.'

'Oh yes,' I said. 'We must wake her up and tell her that we have solved the case.'

'Those weren't precisely my thoughts. My thoughts were of the killing-two-birds-with-one-stone persuasion.'

'Go on,' said I, intrigued.

'Well, firstly, I do not think that Lola would really want to see her brother all turned to gold like that. That might really upset her.'

'I don't *really* think she liked her brother *that* much,' I said. 'I think she'll be glad to see the back of him, so she can claim whatever family inheritance there is. I suspect that we were actually called in to prove that the brother was a fake so that she could have the real one declared either missing or dead.'

'Very wise of you,' said Andy. 'These were my thoughts exactly. But I don't think we need to bother her with this golden fellow. Which is where the other bird that we can kill with the single stone comes in. We have not been paid, and she pleads poverty. So why do we not just take away this frightful turned-to-gold brother? Then we can quietly have him melted down and cast into ingots that we will then sell on the gold market. I got the sense that he is now composed of *very* pure gold. So we get paid, and at no expense to Lola.'

'You are wisdom personified,' I said. 'And altruism, also. Let's get this fellow shifted.'

Pongo Perbright was *not* easily shifted. A man made of gold weighs a great deal more than a man made of flesh and blood. And neither of us were particularly keen to touch him with our bare hands in case there was still some alchemical magic lurking about that might just turn us into gold. So we wrapped him up in an eiderdown and dragged him.

It was a hassle bouncing him down the stairs, but once outside the house, amidst all the slush, it was relatively easy to slide him along the pavement.

But it was a long haul and we were both quite tired when we got home. So we left Pongo in the sitting room with the eidey over him and took ourselves to bed.

I had a good lie-in in the morning. I always like a good lie-in after a strenuous or exciting night. And I had earned this good lie-in and this good lie-in would probably have lasted until beyond lunchtime had my brother not rather rudely woken me up.

'Up and at it!' cried my brother loudly into my ear.

I did the, 'What?' and, 'Who?' and, 'Why?' and damn near wet myself.

'We have to get a move on,' said Andy, shaking me all about. 'We have to get Pongo off to Hatton Garden to arrange for the melting down. I'll borrow Captain Blood's wheelbarrow, the one he uses for shifting contraband. But I need you to give me a hand with Pongo. We can take him on the Underground.'

I, now awake, said, 'What?' once more. And, 'On the Underground?'

'I can't afford a taxi – can you?'

No, I couldn't afford a taxi.

'Breakfast first, then,' I said.

So we both went down for breakfast.

And when we got down for breakfast, there was our mother, all cross, with her pinafore on and her hands on her hips. 'Which one of you beastly boys left the sitting-room windows open last night?' she asked of us.

And Andy and I shook our heads.

'Well, one of you did and until that one owns up, there will be no breakfast.'

I had encountered this logic before and so I owned up immediately. 'It was me,' I said, although it certainly was *not*.

'Well, at least you are being honest now and so I will forgive you and you can have an extra sausage with your breakfast.'

Andy looked daggers at me. But that was his tough luck.

'If you leave the window open, you let the cold in and the warm out. And although there's nothing of value in the living room, apart from the Peerage brass companion set, there is an increase in crime nowadays, so we should all be vigilant.'

And at this I looked at my brother once more.

And he looked at me.

And as one, we both dashed into the sitting room.

The window was now closed. And a fire blazed in the grate. And the brass companion set, the one with the galleon in full sail upon it, was where it always was, right there in the hearth. And there was the visitors' chair and there was the Persian pouffe.

But as to the golden statue that was Pongo Perbright? It was *not* to be seen. It was not there at all.

Andy groaned and I groaned with him. We had been robbed in the night. Someone, or someones, had forced open the sitting-room window and made away with our golden booty.

'I don't believe this,' I said. And I fell to my knees, most dramatically. 'This can't be true. It's so unfair. It can't be true. It can't.'

'Calm yourself down,' commanded Andy. 'Are we not detectives? These burglars have chosen the wrong sitting room to break into.'

'You think?'

And now Andy dropped to his knees also. And he began sniffing around. And then he pointed and said, 'There and there and there and there.'

'What's there?' I asked him.

'Footprints,' said Andy. 'Deep, heavy footprints driven into the green baize carpet. And they're not our footprints, nor Dad's, nor Mum's – although they do bear some resemblance to hers.'

'How?'

'Because they are the imprints of women's shoes, but too big, you see, and too heavily imprinted. They are the footprints of—'

'Cross-dressing zombies?' I asked him.

'Got it in one,' he replied.

29

And how unfair was *that*?

And how angry was I? And how determined to get our booty back? Very. Very. And very, are the answers to those.

But I did have Andy. And Andy did have remarkable skills as a tracker-sniffer dog. And though he didn't bother to don the suit, he took off like a greyhound.

And he sniffed his way to next door. Where we discovered Captain Blood's shed broken into and his wheelbarrow gone. And then he sniffed from there to South Ealing Underground Station.

We made enquiries at the ticket booth and were told that yes, two huge women with a wheelbarrow bearing an enigmatic eiderdown-smothered load had passed through the barrier earlier. Their destination? This was unclear. They had purchased Red Rovers, the one-day travel passes of the day, which allowed folk to travel anywhere on the Underground.

'We're stuffed,' said Andy.

'But they will go to Hatton Garden, surely?'

'Please don't call me Shirley.'*

'But Hatton Garden—'

'No,' said Andy. 'They won't go there – it's too obvious. They've beaten us this time. We've lost this round.'

'But it can't be, it just cannot be!' And I took to storming around the station concourse, screaming and stomping my feet.

'Has he escaped from somewhere?' the ticket man asked my brother. 'Should he be out in his pyjamas, and everything?'

'He's in my care,' said Andy. 'He's really quite harmless. I'll take him home now.'

And Andy took me home.

And I was quite disconsolate.

* Positively the last time.

Andy tried rubbing a bit of Vicks on my chest and dabbing rose water onto my wrists, but it just didn't help.

'There's nothing we can do,' said Andy.

And there was not.

I felt all bitter and twisted. But there was *nothing* I could do about it. The frustration of *that* was killing, but there was nothing I could do about *that*, either, which made it even more frustrating, and so on and so forth and suchlike. But there *was* nothing that we could do, so *that* was *that* was *that*.

And winter turned to spring and spring in its fashion turned to summer. And Lazlo Woodbine Investigations prospered. We took on cases and for the most part we solved them.

They weren't always the sort of cases I would have hoped for. They didn't involve much in the way of adventure, or excitement, although some that Andy took on in his sniffer-dog persona did involve him rescuing children from wells. But it wasn't what I'd been hoping for. And what about my career as a rock 'n' roll star? What of The Sumerian Kynges?

The Rolling Stones had won a contract with Decca and were recording top-ten hits. My father, who was still working as their roadie, tried to placate me with Rolling Stones tour T-shirts, but I found these strangely lacking as a pick-me-up.

In March, Andy and I had some degree of satisfaction. We attended a trial at the Old Bailey. And even though we did not volunteer information and were not called to give evidence, we *were* involved in it. It was the trial of two Jehovah's Wet-Nurses, the very ones who had come a-calling at our front door.

Apparently they had been caught in possession of a great deal of unlicensed gold. Unlicensed? I hadn't known that gold needed to be licensed. But they had a lot of it. Sufficient, it appeared, to cast an entire human figure. Say, the size of Pongo Perbright.

They protested in high, shrill voices that they had no case to answer. But they were both sent down for five years apiece.

'There'd be a moral in there, somewhere,' said Andy to me as we walked from the Bailey. 'Think on these things and ponder.'

'I hope they have a really rough time in Strangeways,' I said. 'I hope they have to be bitches of some big fat drug lord.'

'Mercy me,' said Andy. 'Sometimes I wonder about you.'

★

And so time passed. Ticked and tocked away.

And months passed, and years did, too. And suddenly it was nineteen sixty-seven.

Andy and I were still running the detective agency. And we had a secretary now and her name was Lola. And yes, it was the same Lola – she had wandered back into our lives, the family house all gone and the family inheritance, mysterious as it might have been, proving to have no monetary value, and so she needed a job. And she discovered a rather old and faded and doggy-eared postcard in the corner of the newsagent's window and she applied for the job.

So we gave it to her.

And as I still didn't have a girlfriend, I was rather happy to see Lola again and decided that it had to be fate and we probably would be settling down and having children.

But it *was* nineteen sixty-seven, and so marriage wasn't something that anyone spoke about much. Because it was now the Summer of Love and *free* love was the order of the day.

And I was hoping very much to get some of that free love, because I hadn't had any of it at all, thus far.

And as Lola returned to my life someone else did also, and this someone arrived with an invitation to partake in as much free love as I fancied.

And this someone was Mr Ishmael.

I didn't recognise him at first. He wore a kaftan and had grown his hair long. And he now favoured a beard. Not everyone could carry that off convincingly, but Mr Ishmael did. No matter what he wore, he looked perfect in it. He had style, Mr Ishmael, plenty of it.

And in truth I had almost forgotten about him and about The Sumerian Kynges. I felt that I had grown up and put behind me childish things. So Mr Ishmael's return did come as something of a surprise.

And once I recognised him, I said things such as, 'This is a surprise.'

'Not to me,' said Mr Ishmael. 'How is business?'

'Booming,' I said. 'Andy has even now been called away to rescue a child from a well.'

'Nice work if you can get it,' said Mr Ishmael.

'And what of you?' I asked.

'I continue with my quest. My life is ever fraught with danger.'

'Well,' I said, 'don't get me wrong, but mine rarely *is* nowadays and I'd like to keep it that way. This is nineteen sixty-seven, the Summer of Love – sex and drugs and rock 'n' roll.'

'Yes,' said Mr Ishmael, 'and that does come as something of a surprise to me. I had expected the sixties to be more sober, with people eschewing loud music, strong ales and strange drugs. And adopting the cockney work ethic.'

I cleared my throat. 'Well, there's just no telling,' I said. 'So, what can I do for you?'

'The time has come,' said Mr Ishmael. 'Indeed, the time is now.'

'Very interesting,' I said. 'But what do you mean by this?'

'Your time,' said himself. 'Yours and The Sumerian Kynges'.'

'There are no Sumerian Kynges,' I told Mr Ishmael. 'Toby works in an estate agents' now. Rob, who you sacked, is an advertising copywriter, Neil is something or other in radio and I am a full-time private detective.'

'Yes indeed,' said Mr Ishmael, and he nodded. 'But the time *has* come and indeed the time is *now*. And I *must* fulfil my promise to you all – to whit, fame and fortune. It is time for The Sumerian Kynges to once more take to the stage.'

'But what is the point?' I asked Mr Ishmael. 'You are in some kind of battle with the forces of evil. But what does this have to do with rock 'n' roll? I never understood why zombies stole our equipment, nor all that other equipment also. What did they want with it? What was the point? And what is the point of you trying to put the band back together? What is in it for you?'

'So many questions,' said Mr Ishmael.

'I have had plenty of time to compose them.'

'And I will answer them all in time.'

'I'm sure you will,' I said, 'but not to me. Because in all truth, I have no further interest in any of it. I don't want to be in The Sumerian Kynges again. We were rubbish anyway.'

'Oh, I'm so sorry,' said Mr Ishmael.

'No problem, don't worry.'

'No,' said Mr Ishmael. 'I am so sorry that I apparently made it sound like a request. The Sumerian Kynges *will* reform. They *will* reform because *I* say they *will* reform. You signed the contract, in your blood.'

'I really don't give a monkey's about that,' I said. 'Sue me for breach of contract if you wish.'

'There will be fame and fortune in it for you, as I promised.'

'I'm really not interested. I have a good job here. It started out rather weird, but it's all quite normal now and that's the way I like it. If I throw my lot in with you again there's no telling where it might lead.

But I'll just bet that it will lead me into weirdness and trouble. And I don't want any. So, thank you, no.'

'No?' And Mr Ishmael fairly bristled. I never saw him bristle often – it took an extreme situation for him to exhibit even mild bristling, but he fairly bristled right at this moment. Fairly bristled did he.

'I am not impressed by such bristling,' I told him. Although secretly I was most impressed.

'You will telephone your ex-band members and arrange a meeting,' Mr Ishmael told me.

I shook my head. 'I won't.'

'You will and you will do it now.'

'Or what?'

And thinking back I really wish I hadn't said *that*. Because in a flash, Mr Ishmael showed me what. And it involved a flash. A flash of very bright light. *Again*.

And what happened within the glare of this very bright light I have no wish to go into here. Nor anywhere.

But suffice it to say, I made that telephone call.

And I arranged a meeting of the former members of The Sumerian Kynges. And there must have been something about the degree of urgency and desperation in my voice that made those former members agree to attend that meeting.

And that meeting truly sealed our fates.

And changed our lives for ever.

30

Nothing is ever straightforward.

And even the simplest things have a habit of becoming complicated.

For instance, I thought at the time, when I was running the private detective agency with my brother, that I was, at least, master of my own destiny. That I was making my own rules and living by them. And then Mr Ishmael returned to my life, bringing complications to my simplicity. It was only later that I came to realise that the period of my life spent working with Andy was nothing more than a rehearsal. A honing of techniques. That Mr Ishmael had been watching me all along, monitoring my progress until he felt I was ready to serve him once again. To aid him in his Quest.

So I had not been master of my own destiny at all, rather a pawn in a game I did not understand. And I have to tell you that Mr Ishmael had frightened me badly and could no longer be seen as a benevolent figure. He was a tyrant and he was someone to be feared.

But what he had in store for The Sumerian Kynges I could only guess. And when I met up with the former members and thanked them for responding to my telephone calls, they informed me that Mr Ishmael had already contacted them and made it brutally clear that they had no choice in the matter either. So they were expecting my call. Or perhaps a better word was, dreading.

We met up in the Wimpy Bar. Which made it quite like the good old days.

'It's quite like the good old days!' I said to Neil and Rob and Toby, too, and I smiled them some encouragement.

'It is *not* like the good old days,' said Neil. 'In fact I am not altogether sure that there ever were any good old days.' Neil hadn't changed much. He still had the goatee, but he no longer wore a school uniform, preferring instead a rather smart and modish suit.

'I think we should just run,' said Toby. Who wore a suit of equal modishness.

'What?' I asked of him.

'Have it away on our toes and put as much distance between ourselves and Mr Ishmael as possible.'

'I agree with that,' said Rob. Who had grown his hair a bit longer, but also favoured a suit. 'And he sacked me, anyway. I don't know what *I'm* doing here.'

'He told me he wants to put the band back together as a five-piece,' said Neil. 'And he wants me to take charge of the recording sessions, because that is something that I now know all about.'

'And me to handle the promotional side,' added Rob. 'He did mention that to me, now I've been in advertising for three years.'

'And he wants me to find him a new house, one with a recording studio attached,' said Toby.

And it was at *that* moment that I realised Mr Ishmael had been watching all of us. And perhaps guiding our separate movements? Our separate careers? For his own ends?

It seemed entirely probable.

'Hold on a minute,' Rob said. 'What do you mean, Neil, about him wanting a five-piece band? Who is the fifth member? Not Mr Ishmael himself, I hope.'

'Ah,' said I. And this 'Ah' drew their attention.

'You know, don't you, Tyler?' said Neil.

'I like your suit,' I said to Neil. 'Did you get it from Carnaby Street?'

'Who is the fifth member?' Neil asked. 'And do *not* try to change the subject.'

'It's him,' I said, and I pointed.

'This big cocker spaniel?' said Neil.

'Cocker spaniel indeed!' said the great big bloodhound.

And Neil and Toby and Rob fell back in their seats.

But I didn't and I just said, 'Lads, allow me to introduce you to my brother, Andy. He is our new lead singer.'

'A man dressed up as a dog,' said Rob. And he nodded thoughtfully.

'Are you nodding thoughtfully?' Neil asked him.

'Well, I can appreciate the novelty value. I've been working on a concept of an extended family of furry animals who live on a common and pick up litter. Children will love them, and parents will love them loving them because they will instil decent habits into the children: abstemiousness and the cockney work ethic. I'm thinking of naming them after the common.'

'The Ealings?' said Neil.

But Rob shook his head. 'The Wandles of Wandsworth Common. Catchy, eh?'

I looked at those I could look at. And those I could look at looked back at me. And as one we shook our heads. Rather sadly.

'Well, I'm working on it,' said Rob. 'I'll pull it together. But there is potential for a singer dressed as a dog. Think of Howling Wolf.'

'Did *he* dress as a wolf?' I asked.

'No,' said Rob. 'I just said to think of him. Maybe we could do some Howling Wolf numbers.'

'We're *not* going to do any George Formby numbers, I'm telling you *that*,' said Rob. 'I have a few catchy ones of my own that I've recently penned about cheese.'

'We'll do exclusively all our own material,' said Andy, divesting himself of his dog's head. 'Mr Ishmael has commissioned me to write all the new material.'

'This is the first I've heard of *this*,' I said.

Andy just shrugged. 'If you have any problems with it, then I suggest you take them up with Mr Ishmael.'

That was a phrase that would come to be used quite a lot in the near future. And it never lost any of its power.

'I'm fine with it,' said Neil. And his teeth made the 'grindings of discontent'.

'And I suppose running *is* out of the question,' said Toby. 'So I suppose we'd better buckle down and do some rehearsing.'

'Where?' I enquired.

'At my rehearsal studio,' said Toby. 'I acquired it quite cheaply during a big property deal I was doing. I can't quite remember why I decided to buy it now. But it's handy I did, isn't it?'

And we all agreed.

It was *very* handy.

It was not a jolly reunion lunch. In fact, it set a precedent for all reunion get-togethers to come. They would, from now on, always be grim affairs. But at that first lunch, certain lines were drawn. And we knew where we stood. We agreed that we now feared and hated Mr Ishmael. But we also agreed that if we were going to be forced into putting The Sumerian Kynges on the road, then we would become a force to be reckoned with. We would do everything in our power to become the very future and spirit of rock 'n' roll. A Supergroup.

And that when this came about, as we now determined *it would*, we would then enjoy the company of as many young women as our celebrity entitled us to.

So that was rock 'n' roll and sex taken care of. Which only left the drugs. And there were a lot of those about in nineteen sixty-seven, I can tell you.

But not, perhaps, at this moment.

Because at this moment, and for quite a few moments to come, we were rather busy with rehearsals. Andy and I wondered whether we should employ a couple of private eyes to fill in for us whilst we rehearsed, because we wanted to keep the agency open.

And we were just on the point of hiring two when the Cease and Desist Order arrived from Brentford County Court.

It transpired that P. P. Penrose, the author of the Lazlo Woodbine novels, had finally caught word, as it were, that his fictional hero had opened a detective agency within a mile of that eminent author's house. We were served with an order to Cease and Desist using the licensed name of Woodbine. Licences again!

And so we closed the agency and we had to let Lola go.

Which was a shame, because I had grown very fond of her and was on the point of asking her to marry me.

But this was nineteen sixty-seven. And if I was going to be in a Supergroup, I would, of course, have my pick of Supergroupies. So it was probably for the best that I simply forgot about Lola.

Which would, on the face of it, appear to be very simple and uncomplicated. But which was, in fact, anything but.

Toby's rehearsal studio turned out to be a very large industrial complex on Old Brentford Docks. At one time, big business had flourished here, but by the sixties it was a wasteland.

By the eighties it became a very expensive estate of executive homes. And Toby made quite a killing selling up. But that, too, is for the future.

But for the present, which was our present then, there it was: a great big isolated building. Which did, at least, boast significant security. Which was certainly needed, as it happens, because when the equipment arrived, it turned out that there was a great deal of it – all that other equipment that wasn't ours, but had been hidden away in Count Otto Black's mausoleum. And what a lot there was. Sufficient indeed to amplify any band that wanted to play a huge stadium, or a vast festival gig, or whatever.

Gigs of a nature that had not existed in the time when the gear was originally stolen. But now? When such gigs were all the rage?

Well, how handy was that, eh? It was almost as if it had somehow been planned. That this equipment had been stored away just waiting for its moment to come.

And its moment *had* come.

And its moment was *now*.

And so we began our rehearsals. Rehearsing what? Rehearsing Andy's songs, of course. There were a dozen of them. Sufficient for a gig. Sufficient for an album. And although I, as were the other Sumerian Kynges, was prepared to hate Andy's songs, it turned out that they really weren't bad at all. You will, of course, know them all by now, most probably by heart, because each has become a Rock Anthem, covered by many bands, sung at many a karaoke night, considered modern classics.

I think my favourite (and probably yours also) would have to be 'The Land of the Western God'.

And so I print the lyrics below, so that you can enjoy them once more.

> *The king sends me his linen to wash.*
> *Whatever is right, is right whatever.*
> *Life on life downstricken goes*
> *To the Land of the Western God.*
>
> *A wolf in his belly and a fire in the hearth,*
> *Attacking the windmills as we go,*
> *A word to the wise should be sufficient*
> *In the Land of the Western God.*
>
> *You never must shout till you're out of the woods*
> *For the lion doesn't roar until he's eaten*
> *A brain of feathers and a heart of gold*
> *In the Land of the Western God.*
>
> *His face is his fortune, that's understood,*
> *Two faces hidden beneath one hood*
> *As good as gold and as golden as good*
> *In the Land of the Western God.*
>
> *All looks yellow to a jaundiced eye –*
> *They'd skin a flea for his hide and tallow.*
> *An ounce of discretion's worth a pound of wit*
> *In the Land of the Western God.*

> *There's the Devil to pay,*
> *Every dog has his day*
> *And an old dog learns no tricks, they say.*
> *And the dead men tell their tales today*
> *In the Land of the Western God.*
>
> *Here's an eye for the past and one for the present.*
> *The future is dark as a new-dug grave.*
> *Will our children sing any songs tomorrow*
> *In praise of the Western God?*

So uplifting! Pure joy!

You don't get quality lyrics like that any more. And the new Sumerian Kynges are, in my opinion, little more than a pale shadow of their original counterparts. But still right there at the top of the pops, you notice. So some of our class rubbed off on them, and class, as we know, never dates.

And so, without any further words needed, let us get it on, as they say. And for the first time ever, as no biographies of the band have ever been published (for I now knew how to employ a Cease and Desist Order), let me take you on a cosmic journey into the world of the twentieth century's ultimate band. The raunchy rock 'n' roll World that was The Sumerian Kynges.

Let's Rock.

31

The Sumerian Kynges did plenty of rehearsing in Toby's big rehearsal room, and when we had half an hour's worth of material ready, we knew that *we* were ready. Now, I know what you are thinking: *half an hour's worth* of material? That's not very much. But these were the nineteen-sixties, so you do have to allow for the adding in of the guitar solos. Those long and inspired twiddly-widdly guitar solos that were so loved back then, and so missed now by folk who so loved them back then.

So we had ten three-minute songs rehearsed. But if you added in the obligatory twenty-minute guitar solo at the rate of one per song, well – you had a decent performance.

And when we were done with our rehearsals, we took to the road with The Flange Collective.

The Flange Collective was the catch-all title, the banner, as it were, beneath which danced the colourful ladies and dandified gents. Where the jugglers, stilt-walkers, fire-eaters, tumblers, clowns, madmen and fools followed their crafts. Where freaks and freaksters mingled. Where strange music played. Where strange drugs were imbibed. Where the weird and the wonderful were the ways of the everyday. And in the midst of what might be mayhem one moment and revolutionary genius the next, stood a single figure. A grey eminence. A puppet master supreme. What Warhol was to the Factory, The Flange was to The Flange Collective.

There is much that could be said regarding The Flange, all of it fascinating in its own way and books and books could be written about him, but to give you an idea, I'll tell you about a pet theory of The Flange's that he spent the last few years of his life trying to prove. The Flange believed in the Universal Axiom that *things are where they should be because they should be where they are*. The Flange's deepest desire was to facilitate the Second Coming of the Lord, and in his retirement, he worked long and hard to create something that he called The Lounge of the Lord – the perfect sitting room for God. He believed that when the room was completed, correct to the tiniest degree, completely and utterly correct down to the sub-atomic level, then following the Universal Truth that states that *things are where they should be because they should be where they are*, Jesus would come and have a good sit down in that sitting room, and that the Second Coming would come to pass.

Weird and wonderful were the ways of The Flange, and I am truly glad I met him. For had I not, things would have turned out very differently . . .

But I digress, and I will stop that now. Honest.

On the day that we were to begin our tour with The Flange Collective, Mr Ishmael sent a furniture van to pick up all our equipment, then had his own chauffeur (Rapscallion, his name was) come over and pick us up in the limo. Which was pretty fab and raised our spirits no end.

Not that our spirits were down, really. Back together and playing again, we had sort of picked up where we left off. And although we all thought that we'd given up music for good, deep down in those rock 'n' roll hearts of ours I feel certain that we'd all been secretly hoping that we might get the chance to climb back up on a stage again. In front of a genuine and appreciative audience this time, and hopefully composed of teenage girls.

And this time we *were really* ready.

We'd grown into ourselves, as it were. We were no longer foolish boys who would probably, in truth, have gone all to pieces on the road. No, we were older and more sophisticated and mature and better able to cope.

So this was *our time*. And we meant to make the most of it. Take it to the limit and beyond.

So, Rapscallion drove us off to The Flange Collective, which was presently camped upon Ealing Common. And we had the windows of the limo wound down so we could shout out at the girls.

And I think it was Neil who first coined that immortal hailing-of-the-female call, 'Yo, bitches.' Or it might have been Rob, although I think he was mostly calling, 'You cheeses.'

But I cannot be altogether sure, so please don't quote me on it.

What I can be sure of is that I was most impressed when, having stepped from Mr Ishmael's limo, I was greeted by The Flange, who presented to us a most unique appearance. He was wearing the robes of a wizard of myth, all stars and moons and sigils. And he carried a staff of the Gandalf persuasion and wore a mighty wig that reached down almost to his knees.

'This fellow,' I said to myself, 'is a character.'

And The Flange shook me warmly by the hand. 'You,' said he, 'are a character, sir. Dressed up as a billiard table.'

'It's Glam Rock,' I informed The Flange. 'We invented it. But it has yet to come into its own.'

'Well, welcome, friend, to The Flange Collective, the place where dreams come true.'

'I often dream of cheese,' said Rob. 'Do you have any cheese in The Flange Collective?'

'More cheese than you can shake a stick at, should you so choose.' And now The Flange admired Neil's baldy head. Because Neil, having had his head shaved, had decided to stick with that look.

'Superb,' said The Flange. 'Might I stroke it a little?'

But Neil wasn't keen and said, 'No.'

'Never mind, never mind – welcome all.' And The Flange shook Andy's hand and made admiring glances at his mullet, asked why he was dressed up as a postman but did not receive a coherent answer, and led us all into the tent.

A big top, it was, one of those jolly candy-striped affairs with seating all racked up around a central ring. And this ring was covered in sawdust, just as a ring should be. I admired that big top very much, for I was fond of the circus. There was a circus on Ealing Common for one week each year. It would appear as if magically from nowhere, set up and perform and then in a week be gone, leaving nothing but a circle of flattened grass.

I recall, years later, seeing photographs of crop circles and reading the ludicrous theories put forward to explain their existence. I shook my head rather sadly, I also recall, knowing that the mundane but obvious explanation – that of 'travelling circuses' – didn't seem to be making any headlines.

I've seen crop circles myself and there is no doubt in my mind that they are the result of travelling circuses. Travelling *fairy* circuses, I might add.

'Why is this not called The Flange Circus?' I asked The Flange.

'Because it is *not* a circus. It has elements of circus, but it is more a shared experience, an interactive human be-in.'

The Flange had a freak or two in that show. And I'd never encountered a *real* freak before this time. Certainly there were sufficient human oddities living in the Ealing area during the nineteen-sixties to have overstocked P. T. Barnum's American Museum, had he chosen to return from the dead and set up shop once more, but you didn't see them much in the streets. My mother told me that there were con-joined triplets living at number twenty-seven. But other than the family of dwarves who lived at number thirty-two and the Human Blanc-mange who lived at number forty-two, you just didn't see them around. So I must confess to a certain amount of fascination, be this either, 'morbid' or simply 'justifiable', when I was first introduced to The Flange Collective's Human Menagerie. But I must say, as many others have before me, that inside they were just like *normal* people. Adding that, during the long years of my life, I have yet to have it accurately defined for me what exactly *normal* is supposed to mean. I have met many many folk, but none I regarded as *normal*.

First I was introduced to Peg, The Flange Collective's resident fat lady. Today, of course, fat ladies are two-a-penny (so to speak) but back in the sixties, they were a rarity. In England there was Peg and in America there was Mama Cass (who did *not* die choking on a pork sandwich!).

Whether there were any other fat women in the world, I couldn't say. But if there were, I never saw them.

Mind you, it's strange, that, isn't it? Because, again as far as I know, there were only two fat men in the sixties. In England we had Robert Morley and in America there was Alfred Hitchcock. How times change, eh?

The Flange then introduced me to Mr Shrugger, the World-Famous Shrugging Man. And he was a *real* shrugging man, not just some skilful actor mocking-up the shrugging. Mr Shrugger gave a free demon-stration of shrugging to me. And, even though I have since met men who walked upon the Moon, Hollywood actors and an entire pantheon of gods,* I do have to say that I would number Mr Shrugger right up there in the list of the Five Most Remarkable Men that I have ever met.

The Slouch I didn't think too much of. He was just a little too laid back for me. And as for Fumbling Fernando, the Bird-Brained Butter-Fingers, well, I could do *that* myself and I honestly think that the only reason he rose to prominence, and he *was* a *big star* at The Flange Collective, was because of his Spanish origins. Who back then could resist a Spaniard? Especially one who fumbled?

We might sneer at those times now, but remember, all the very best music came from then, and The Sumerian Kynges were the best of the best.

Let me tell you all about our first tour.

---

* This is not entirely true. In fact, it is not true at all.

I have mentioned how all grown-up myself and the other guys in the band had become. How responsible and professional. And so, when it came to our first rock 'n' roll tour, we realised our responsibilities. And we were determined to do the job properly and be remembered for so doing.

And so it became the original 'Bad Behaviour' tour. The tour that set the low standards of behaviour by which later rock tours, such as those of Led Zep, would be judged.

We did it first, I tell you, and the original is still the greatest. And when it came to sex and drugs and rock 'n' roll it was a case of been there, done *that*.

Especially when it came to the drugs.

Well, *one* drug in particular.

It changed my life for evermore.

Let me tell you all about it.

32

Apparently Mr Ishmael and The Flange had put their heads together and planned the tour of The Sumerian Kynges with The Flange Collective very carefully. It was designed to make an impact, the idea being that we would arrive in town, blow as many minds as we could possibly blow, then move on, leaving a legend behind.

At this time we didn't have a record to market. No forty-five single, nor indeed album. We were spreading the word, as it were. Putting ourselves before the public and so on and so forth and suchlike.

It was an interesting tour.

Ealing Common, London . . . . (Support Act to Mr Shrugger)
Acton Common, London . . . . (Support Act to Mr Shrugger)
Shepherd's Bush Common, London . . (Support Act to Mr Shrugger)
Hyde Park, London . . . . (Top of Bill)
Carnegie Hall, New York City . . . . (Top of Bill)
Fillmore East, New York City . . . . (Top of Bill)
Fillmore West, San Francisco . . . . (Top of Bill)
Woodstock Festival, NY . . . . (Top of Bill)
The Alhambra, New Begrem, Sumeria . . . . (Top of Bill)

Nine dates in all. Hardly taxing, one might have thought. Nothing to get too excited about.

Perhaps not on the face of it. But we did change the face of rock music for ever.

I will pass over our first three gigs. Much as I admired Mr Shrugger and what he did, I was somewhat egotistical, and I did think that The Sumerian Kynges were going to top the bill with The Flange Collective. I was, to say the very least, a bit disappointed to discover that we were only to be a support act. So we will pass over *those* gigs and take ourselves directly to Hyde Park, to the great free Festival in the Park of nineteen sixty-nine, known to this day as The Stones in the Park gig. Memorable to my mind for four main things. For the two hundred and fifty thousand beautiful people who turned out to watch *us*. For the appearance of Gilbert and George, who, in grey suits and metallic face paint, strolled about the park creating their very own legend. For the drug that changed my life for ever. And, fourthly, for the fact that nowadays no one at all actually believes that The Sumerian Kynges even played there, let alone topped the bill.

So, let me set the record straight.

There had been a bit of unpleasantness two days before when Brian Jones was found dead in his swimming pool. Mr Ishmael had informed us of this tragedy before it had become known to the public.

'A sad affair,' he said to us. 'But we must look on the bright side.'

I had no idea what this bright side might be, so I just shrugged. And Mr Shrugger, who was standing near at hand doing his shoulder exercises, smote me a blow to the skull.

'It is clear,' said Mr Ishmael, 'that as Mr Jones is dead, The Rolling Stones will, out of respect, cancel their free festival in Hyde Park. And so The Sumerian Kynges can step into their shoes, as it were.'

I rubbed my skull and shrugged no more, but I did glance at the other guys. Neil was polishing his shaven head with an early precursor of the J-Cloth, Andy was impersonating a chicken, Rob was eating cheese and Toby was grinning to himself in a manner that I can only describe as 'iffy'. And I *did* recall the threat he had made against Brian Jones so long before at Southcross Roads School, on the school dance night.

No, he wouldn't, I thought to myself. *He couldn't. He wouldn't. He didn't.*

'So we will be top of the bill?' said Rob. And Mr Ishmael nodded.

'But why?' asked Rob. 'Why *us*?'

'Because now is your time and you have to make an impression. And you have to succeed and become rich and famous.'

'Why?' Rob asked, once again.

'Does it really matter why, as long as it occurs?'

I shrugged once more, and dodged the swing of Mr Shrugger's fist. 'I'm good with it,' I said. 'Some fame and fortune would be nice. Any kind of wage at all would be nice, in fact.'

Mr Ishmael cast me a withering glance. And I felt an irresistible need to rush at once to the toilet. Which I did. When I returned, Mr Ishmael had gone and the guys of the band were looking a bit puzzled.

'Why these looks of puzzlement?' I asked them.

'He's got some purpose to this,' said Toby. 'Mr Ishmael. Everything is part of some great Machiavellian Masterplan. We are part of it. What this masterplan is, Heaven only knows, but he does put the wind up me.'

'Me, too,' I agreed. 'But we don't have any problem with being rich and famous, do we?'

This question occasioned a great deal of shrugging all round. And Mr Shrugger swore loudly, threw up his hands and stamped away in a right old huff.

'So we're good to go, guys, yes?' I asked.

And they supposed that they were.

And as history records, The Rolling Stones did *not* cancel their free festival in Hyde Park. They'd sacked Brian Jones from the band anyway and got in the replacement that few folk now remember. Brian Blessed, wasn't it? And they had no intention at all of cancelling such a big gig.

But we were hoping that they would and so when we arrived at the park in our Collective Wagons, we were somewhat disheartened to see Mick and Keith loafing about smoking cigarettes and chatting-up girls. Chatting-up girls! I ask you! Mick was going out with Marianne Faithfull at the time! Good grief!

Mick (you notice that he no longer called himself Michael) hardly even acknowledged our arrival. I later learned that he was under the impression that we were part of a circus act warming up for the bands. Outrageous!

Toby marched straight up to Michael. 'Wotchamate, Michael,' he said. 'So nice to see you again. Which way is the green room?'

'That Winnebago there,' said Mick. And he pointed in a rather drippy fashion.

And so we did *not* help to erect the candy-striped big top. We took ourselves instead to the Winnebago green room to avail ourselves of drugs and groupies, of which, we felt assured, there'd be plenty.

Our way was barred, however, by a very big man who asked us for our passes.

'Passes?' I enquired of him. 'What would passes be?'

'They would be special passes that license you to enter the green room,' the very big man told us.

'Licence?' I said. 'Again the requirement for a licence?'

'No licence pass, no entry,' said the fellow.

'This man deserves nothing less than death,' I heard Toby whisper.

'Would you respond to bribery?' I asked the very big fellow.

But he, in sadness, shook his head and told us that it was more than his job was worth.

'And what *exactly* is your job?' I asked him.

'I am a roadie for the Stones.'

'My dad was a roadie for The Stones,' I said, with a degree of wistfulness. As I hadn't seen my dad for a couple of years.

'Is your dad a big-bearded Scotsman?' asked the very big fellow who guarded the green room door.

I agreed that he was.

'Then your name would be Tyler. And that fellow with you, dressed as a postman – would be Andy.'

'Yes,' I said. 'But how do you know?'

'Because I *am* your daddy,' said my daddy. 'I thought I recognised you.'

And indeed it *was* my daddy. Although I would not have recognised him, he had changed so much. The rock 'n' roll lifestyle, I supposed. That, or he had shaved off his beard. (*That*, then, probably.)

And so we got into the Winnebago green room.

What a happy coincidence, eh?

We couldn't see much in there due to the dope smoke. The Beatles boasted that they'd smoked dope in the toilets of Buckingham Palace, when they went there to collect their CBEs. But they probably said that in an attempt to look cool. In the hope that it would take right-thinking people's minds off the fact that they had sold out and *actually accepted* CBEs. Outrageous!

But The Stones did have style and the green room heaved with dope smoke. And dope-smoking groupies.

'Hello, ladies,' said Andy, whose eyesight was perhaps the more acute. 'I'm John Lennon – does anyone fancy a shag?'

And how well did *that* used to work!

We availed ourselves of the dope-smoking groupies.

And indeed of the dope that they were smoking.

Well, at least the others seemed to, anyway. I just bumbled about somewhat trying not to step on writhing bodies whilst breathing in an awful lot of dope smoke. And this went on for a considerable time, until Toby chose to introduce something new into the proceedings. A drug that I had not even heard of before. A drug that Toby told me was called a Banbury Bloater.

'Banbury Bloater?' I enquired as I floundered about somewhat in the smoggy Winnebago, searching for a groupie I could call my own. 'What is a Banbury Bloater?'

'Who said that?' called Toby, his mouth somewhat muffled by bosoms.

'It's Tyler,' I said.

'Ah,' said Toby. 'Exactly who I'd hoped for.'

'What did you say?' I asked. Putting my hands upon something naked that didn't belong to me.

'Hands off my bum,' said Toby. 'I said, "Lets all do Banbury Bloaters." You can do one first.'

'Could I have some sex first?' I asked. 'I've been really hoping to get some sex, but so far—' And then I said no more, because I became aware of a lot of female sniggering.

'But I suppose that's how it goes,' I continued. *Loudly.* 'When you're Ringo Starr.' And the sniggering stopped. But no one offered me a shag.

'Down here,' said Toby. And I located him in the fug. But *did* have to turn my face away. Because he *was* having sex. With two women simultaneously. How *did* he do that?

'Stop ogling my bits,' said Toby, 'and score a Banbury Bloater.'

'You were going to tell me why it was so called,' I said. Accepting a large tartan something that strongly resembled a psychedelic gobstopper. 'And what am I supposed to do with this?'

'Firstly,' said Toby, who continued with his dual-lovemaking as he spoke, 'it is called a Banbury Bloater because it was developed in Banbury by a Druid named Pendragon Bloater. Pendragon was employed by the CIA to develop the drug. It was designed for soldiers in Vietnam, for them to take when they were dying.'

'To revive them?' I asked. Then I had to apologise to a groupie for stepping on her bottom.

'To revive them? No. To send them on their way in a correct fashion. I read all about in it *Conspiracy Theories Today* magazine. Those soldiers in Vietnam, they are nothing more than sacrificial victims offered up to placate the War Gods. I bet you didn't know that.'

'I'll bet you that I did,' I said. Because I did.

'Yeah, well, it *has* been in all the Underground Press,' said Toby. 'But the drug was designed to be taken at the moment of death to bestow a universal consciousness to those who took it. It's not so much a psychedelic gobstopper.' And Toby held this item towards me, between his forefinger and thumb, and I viewed it very closely amidst the swirling smoke. 'It's not so much a psychedelic gobstopper as a universe within itself. It isn't a chemical, it's a micro-universe. They're everywhere, apparently, but you have to know where to look and then how to encapsulate them into a form that can be taken orally.'

I was staring at the psychedelic gobstopper. And I could see that although it appeared at first glance to be a solid glass marble sort of a body, it was in fact something rather more than that. The closer I looked, the further away it seemed. There appeared, indeed, to be an eternity of nothingness within this spherical something. A fathomless, bottomless pit in which microscopic galaxies gently revolved, and all this was very, very cosmic indeed.

'How many of these do you have?' I asked of Toby.

'Just the one, so far.'

'And you are offering it to *me*?'

'Well, you don't think I'd be so dumb as to . . .' Toby paused for a moment, though not in his lovemaking. 'What I mean to say is that I'm not as cosmic as you, am I? You'd be the first to admit that you are *very* cosmic.'

I was aware of a lot of chuckling, but I did not consider that any of it could possibly be directed at me. Because, after all, Toby, with more awareness and wisdom than I would have given him credit for, had, in his way, struck the nail right upon its enlightened head. I *was* pretty cosmic. And if anyone would be the suitable someone to take such a cosmic drug, then that cosmic someone would be me.

Cosmically speaking.

So to cosmically speak.

'Orally?' I queried. Staring hard at the fair-sized cosmic something. 'It does look rather big.'

'What it *appears* to be and what it *is* are two different things,' said Toby. 'Just to the right a bit there, Marianne . . . yes, that's perfect.'

'What?' I queried.

'It has no absolute size. It inhabits no absolute time. It inhabits no absolute space.'

'How exactly did you come by it?' I enquired.

'Ask me no questions and I'll tell you no lies.'

'That isn't much of an answer.'

The groupies were growing restless. 'Bung it in your gob,' called Mama Cass.

'Well,' I said. And I wobbled a bit as I said it, because I *had* been breathing an awful lot of dope smoke. 'I *would* take it, because I *am* pretty cosmic, but I'm just wondering whether—'

But whatever it was I was wondering, and I cannot in truth

remember now just what that might have been, my wondering about whatever it was was abruptly curtailed by the opening of the green-room door.

And Mick Jagger entered, tripped upon bodies and fell forward, right on top of me. Knocking *me* forward and the out-held Banbury Bloater right into my mouth.

And right, in a Cosmicky kind of a gulp.

Right deep down my throat.

33

It didn't so much creep up on me as hit me straight in the brain. It felt as if I no longer had any flesh and blood and bone inside of me. These had ceased to be and I was instead literally filled with *the Spirit*.

Hugo Rune wrote about something that he referred to as *soul-space* – a kind of interior equivalent to the exterior space that surrounds the human body. An interior universe, inhabited by spiritual beings, where events occurred that had a separate reality from exterior events, but were nonetheless real for that. Rune believed that the imagination and what the imagination conjured up were real, but that their reality was only a reality within the soul-space. He developed the idea in many directions. Were, perhaps, the revelations of so-called visionaries the real and genuine revelations offered by entities that inhabited the soul-space?

The mind boggles, and the more you think about such stuff the more inwardly turning become your thoughts, until you begin to believe that what goes on *inside* is more real than what goes on *outside*. Or you begin to confuse the two.

And then you are, by definition, mad.

I suppose, then, that the first sensation I experienced was absolute terror. I had suddenly been thrust, as it were, into completely alien territory. I had nothing to cling on to.

Outside me I could see and sense the exterior universe: the Winnebago green room, with its dope-smoke and heaving bodies. I was aware of this and that it existed as a reality. But I had become aware of this so much more. So much more that I couldn't even have guessed existed. The internal universe. And although it was seemingly contained within the boundaries of my body, it was vast, endless, limitless. And it had been there all along, but I hadn't known it was there. A multiverse within me and I never even knew.

And *that* is a lot to take in.

And so I freaked. I foamed somewhat at the mouth and I ranted away like a loon. And I must have done quite a bit of leaping up and down also, because very, very soon, I was taken hold of by many hands and cast bodily from the Winnnebago. And how uncool was *that*?

You are supposed to care for people when they're freaking, not shout abuse at them and throw them out on their ear. Uncool. Uncool. Uncool.

I arose from the grass upon which I had landed. And became suddenly *completely* aware of *the grass*. And I mean *totally* so. I understood the grass. Knew its motivations. Sensed its sadness. I *knew* grass. I *was* grass.

For I had entered Phase II.

All the Phases of Banbury Bloater have now been thoroughly researched, studied and catalogued by many a Harvard scientist. Many a learned fellow has taken the old Christopher Mayhew journey into the other world of the hallucinogenic. Those who studied the Bloater were changed men for ever. And most dispensed at once with science and took to more spiritual occupations. They did, however, write *a lot* about their experiences.

And they all made a *big deal* of Phase II.

I looked down at that grass and grass looked up at me. And we both, in our way, came to terms with one another. And we were both, in our separate ways, *good* with one another. I stepped lightly over that grass. And then I beheld the sky.

And almost passed immediately into Phase IIa, which is defined as an 'overwhelming and all-encompassing mind-shock trauma, terminating in complete mental shutdown, followed by death'.

So not one of the better ones, that.

But I didn't die and I didn't go into shock. What I did was soar in the summer sky. I rose within myself and I soared. And I was at one with that sky.

And then I saw Woman. And *that* nearly had me over the edge. There was so much to Woman that I had never before been aware of. How could I not have seen Woman for what Woman truly was? How could I have been so totally blind, so wantonly ignorant, so completely lacking in perception?

Woman smiled at me and golden rivulets of cosmic ether bathed my cheeks. I could see the aura of Woman, her feelings and passions, loves and longings. I knew just what Woman was. And then once more I was filled with terror. Because I knew that if I could understand what Woman was, then I could also understand what Man was. And to do that might not be a pleasant thing. In fact, it might be a hideous thing. A thing too terrible to take in.

And so I looked down once more at the grass. The comforting grass that I was getting along with just fine. And I took off my shoes and my socks and I cast them away. And then I padded about on grass. Dear grass. My friend, the grass.

And I lay down upon that grass and rolled about on and in it. And I was a pretty good match, in my green baize jumpsuit. I was rather grass-like to behold.

And then I encountered Man.

And Man scared the baby Jesus out of me. He was big and rough and tough, was Man, and spiky at the edges. And a black fug of 'smelly' breathed out of Man and oozed from his pores like ichor. I liked not the sight nor the smell of Man. Nor did I like the feel of Man either. As Man hoisted me up to my feet and stared into my eyes.

And then I did not like the sound of Man either.

Man roared and raged. There was neither peace nor harmony in his voice.

'You're bloody stoned,' roared Man at me. And he roared in the voice of my brother.

'Andy?' I asked in a tiny whiney voice. 'Is that you, my brother?'

'It's me,' said Andy. 'That Toby has laid some very bad acid on you.'

'Not acid,' I said. And noticed, as I said it, that the words came floating out of my mouth as little colourful bubbles of stuff that burst all over his face.

'Sorry,' I said. Most sincerely.

'*He'll* be sorry,' said Andy. And his words were black like lumps of coal.

'No,' I said. 'It's all right, really. This is beyond acid. I am experiencing things that I had no idea even existed.'

Andy stared at me quizzically. 'Why are you reciting the alphabet?' he asked.

'I'm not,' I said. 'I think I have become at one with the universe.'

'Stop doing it now,' said Andy.

But—'

'Then end it with that zed.'

'But—'

'One zed is enough.'

I did noddings at Andy. It was clear, to me at least, that what I thought I was saying was *not* what I *was* saying. Which led me to believe that it was not possible to express what I was experiencing to someone who was not experiencing the same thing at the same time.

And that is another of those Universal Truths!

And then Andy said, 'There has been a bit of unpleasantness in the Winnebago. Mick told us all to get out. He wasn't too taken with Toby shagging his girlfriend. And someone had told him that we were intending to top the bill.'

I opened my mouth to speak, but thought better of it.

'So he wants us all to leave. And he's getting his security roadie boys to chuck us out of the park.'

I said nothing once again.

'But for some reason he has decided that he wants *you* to go onstage. He's got these boxes of butterflies, apparently, and he's going to read a bit of poetry "for Brian" and then release all these butterflies. And he wants *you* to bring them on stage.'

I opened my mouth. But Andy put his hand over it.

'I think Mr Ishmael put a bit of pressure on him,' he whispered into my ear. 'He's here in the park somewhere.'

And so I got to stand at the side of the stage minding the boxes of butterflies.

Now, I remember the Edgar Broughton Band and I'm sure some other band that had a black fella with a big afro playing the electric organ. And I do recall, with perfect clarity, the sight of Gilbert and George strolling through the crowd. And I also recall, with perfect clarity, how I became aware that they were *perfect Humans*, in the manner that they were Perfect Artists, in the manner that they *were* and, for all I know, still *are* their own art.

Which is why I recall seeing them *with* such perfect clarity.

And then a big roadie, who didn't have a beard, but who wasn't my dad, nudged me rather firmly in the rib-area and told me to, 'Get ready with those boxes, mate, the star-turn is going on next.'

And I have to confess that even in my cosmic and all but universally enlightened condition, I was a bit teed-off that The Sumerian Kynges were not going to be the star-turn, or indeed any turn at all. Because this *was* the Perfect Day that Lou Reed would later sing about and the sun was shining down and Hyde Park was filled with beautiful people. So The Sumerian Kynges really *should* be playing. Because we *were* here and this was supposed to be *our* time.

So yes. I was a little teed-off.

'And pull the Sellotape off the boxes before you carry them onstage,' said the roadie. 'Mick can't be having with de-Sellotaping. It wouldn't be cool.'

Which had me more than just a little bit more teed-off.

Not that I wasn't still cosmic. No, believe me, I *was*.

'And get your act together, you stoner.'

And *that* was an interesting one.

Because it seemed to me that that final remark triggered something. Or put something into motion. Or brought something into being. A physical/spiritual something. And somehow I *projected*.

And although I never touched him with my hands, I pushed that roadie. Very hard. And he flew backwards with a look of perplexity upon his face, the memory of which I still and will always treasure. And he hit the side of The Stones' limo *very* hard and collapsed in an untidy heap. And the driver of the limo issued from that limo and looked at me, some distance away, weighed up the possibility that *I* might have struck the roadie, mentally declared it a no-goer, looked down at the roadie, up at the big dent in the passenger door of the limo and then gave the roadie a very sound and thorough kicking.

Which caused me to turn my face away. As I was of a delicate disposition. And filled to the very brim with cosmic consciousness.

But I did smile and chuckle just a bit.

And I did regard myself and say, 'Oh yes,' and then, 'Oh joy,' and then, 'I'm Superman.'

Which, I agree, was a pretty dumb thing to say, because if I was going to be any kind of superhero, then that superhero would have to have been Doctor Strange. For he was the Master of the Mystic Arts. And probably a chum of Count Dante, the Master of Dimac, the Most Brutal and Disfiguring of the Martial Arts. Of whom I was a *great* fan. Although my Dimac manual had still failed to turn up. Even though I'd left a forwarding address for The Flange Collective.

And then suddenly The Rolling Stones issued from somewhere and made for the stage. The band with the black afro-hairstyled electric organ player (what *was* his name?)* were leaving the stage. But the two bands passed each other in complete harmony, which I felt very deeply (and was glad).

'Oi, boy,' called Mick Jagger. And I suddenly became aware that he was addressing *me*. 'Boy, bring on the butterflies when Charlie gives you the nod.'

And Charlie Watts, who was passing by, mimed this nod to me. The miming of the nod and the nod itself were indeed very similar. In fact it would have been, and indeed *was*, impossible to tell one from the other. Except for the fact that the miming of the nod occurred earlier.

I glared somewhat at Charlie. But I did *not* project. Because, in all

* The organist was Richie Havens. (Ed.)

truth, I had become something of a fan of The Stones, and of Charlie in particular. And was hoping to get his autograph later.

Charlie scuttled up the steps. And I bethought me of those other steps, the ones that led up to the school stage (from the left-hand side of the stage when viewed by the audience) on that night that seemed now so long ago.

'And don't muff it up,' said Mick.

And to some extent the rest is history. The Stones went on stage, Mick read a bit of poetry 'for Brian' – Shelley, I think it was, or perhaps Byron, or perhaps the Great McGonagall – and then Charlie gave me the nod and I lugged the boxes of butterflies onto the stage. Although hardly *lugged*, as they didn't weigh very much. And then Mick opened the boxes and shook out the butterflies, many of which were dead, as you're not really supposed to box up butterflies. And I looked up into the wonderful skies, and saw the wonderful butterflies and I knew, just knew. I just knew.

What?

Well, *that* would be hard to explain.

And then I looked out at the audience, the two hundred and fifty thousand beautiful people. And my, they *were* beautiful, in their beautiful clothes, with their beautiful hair and their beautiful beads and bells. Just beautiful.

But then I saw it.

It, as in something I hadn't expected to see. Could never have expected to see. And certainly wasn't supposed to see.

I saw *them*.

In my heightened condition I saw them. Was enabled to see them. Saw those who were real and those who were not. Saw indeed the living and the dead and could discern the difference between the one and the other.

Because out there, in that crowd, all that were out there were not living. *They* were there, too. And there were hundreds of them. The animated dead that I had encountered before (although even now, as it were, I do not have complete recollection). But the dead that Mr Ishmael had spoken of – and I *knew* that I remembered that, indeed *now* it seemed that I could remember everything – *they* were out there in the crowd.

And they were in their hundreds.

And they were dead.

And *I* could see them clearly.

34

And I got rather upset. Because there and then I had a revelation, within my soul-space, and I remembered everything. All the missing bits of what had happened in that cemetery in Hanwell. With our stolen equipment and the mausoleum of Count Otto Black. And the zombies rising in the glowing mist. And the helicopters and gunfire. And the Ministry of Serendipity beneath Mornington Crescent Underground Station. And Darren McMahon the mysterious doctor and Elvis lookalike. And all that was said and all that was done to me and how I suddenly woke up once more back at my luncheon table.

All as if it had happened only yesterday. And all in perfect clarity.

And I looked out across that vista in the park, at all those beautiful people. And I could see the others, lurking amongst them, looking on the outside to be as them, but on the inside, where I could see, not as the living. These were indeed the dead.

And I think, in all of my upsetness, that I must have projected once more, because suddenly now The Rolling Stones were finishing their set, to great applause, from both the living and the dead. And after their encores they were making their way off the stage. And the mighty crowd was stirring, making as to leave, for the show was all over.

But *I* projected.

And *we*, The Sumerian Kynges, came on stage.

They looked a bit rattled, the others. They were clearly stoned and Toby was still pulling up his trousers. And Andy was now wearing one of Mick Jagger's spare stage costumes, which he had apparently availed himself of from the boot of The Stones' limo. And he looked rather well in it, too, I thought.

And The Stones' instruments were still on stage. And we took them up. And we played. *How* we played.

You will note, with grateful thanks I am sure, how I have been sharing with you the original lyrics of The Sumerian Kynges' songs.

And so now I give you one more. The song that closed our

performance at The Stones in the Park gig. When *we* topped the bill. Although no one remembers it now.

The name of the composition is—

THE BLACK PROJECTIONS

He cursed the black projections as they grew
Though he knew it wasn't quite the thing to do
But the natives from the town
Turned their backs upon his gown
That he'd won from some old Hindustan gu-ru.

He cursed the black projections that he found.
He tore them off and flung them to the ground.
But the natives played at jacks
With their hands behind their backs
And sold little bags of white stuff by the pound.

He cursed the black projections on his arm.
When he saw them there he cried out in alarm.
But the natives turned away,
They were not inclined to stay
And they went and found new jobs about the farm.

And when the black projections took control
He found it rather difficult to bowl
But the natives in the slips
Stood with hands upon their hips
And dined on cottage tea and Dover sole.

And allow me to say once more that they really and truly do *not* write songs like *that* any more.

A standing ovation, I kid you not, from a quarter of a million beautiful people.

And then I felt suddenly exhausted. And I could project no longer. And I sank into a kind of sleep and that was that for me.

I awoke upon the road to Liverpool. Then slept, then awoke once more, on the dock.

'Where am I?' I asked. And Andy answered.

'Liverpool,' said he.

'Are we playing Liverpool?' I asked of Andy.

'No,' he said. 'We're not.'

'Then why?' But Andy shushed me.

And I awoke once more to find—

America.

America!

Blimey. Our ship had docked in New York. I had slept for more than a week. Which had caused Andy some concern. But clearly not too much, because he had, apparently, had an extremely good time on the voyage over. As had the other members of the band.

When I awoke I was anxious to talk about the Hyde Park gig and how we had shamed The Stones with our musical genius.

But none of the other guys wanted to talk about it at all.

In fact they made it quite clear that they had nothing at all to say on the matter. *And* suggested that I 'shut the f★★k up about *that*'. And so I said no more. And the subject of what happened that day was never brought up again.

I don't really understand why they didn't want to talk about it.

Modesty, perhaps.

But I wasn't going to argue with them. I had had a very special experience. A life-changing experience. And if there was one thing that I particularly wanted to do, then that one thing was to talk to Mr Ishmael about all that I had remembered.

And all that I had seen in Hyde Park.

The dead people, and everything.

But, I was told, Mr Ishmael was not with us on the ship. He might or might not be coming over to America to join us on our tour.

Mr Ishmael was rather busy at the moment.

So I held my tongue and beheld New York. And I really took to the place.

New York was seedy in a manner of exceeding seediness. London could be seedy, as could any other city in England, but never on the scale of New York. New York had really worked hard on perfecting its seediness and no other city could touch it.

I am told that Shanghai and Singapore tried. But failed.

And Penge put in a bid. Came close, but lost upon population numbers.

The New York club scene was just coming into its own. Club 27, the now infamous den of sin and iniquity, had just opened and it was where the famous went to indulge themselves on all levels. For such is the reward for being famous.

We breezed in on a Thursday night, having first checked in to the Pentecost Hotel. Which was *the* place to check in to. Thursday nights at Club 27 were Shadow Nights. And so we fell straight into that.

'What, *exactly*, are Shadow Nights?' Andy asked of Neil.

'Ah,' said Neil. 'I'm glad you asked me that question because I know all about Shadow Nights.'

I grinned a bit at Neil and nodded. He did know so much stuff. I wondered whether it would be a good idea to introduce Neil to a Banbury Bloater, so he could know some more.

But Toby had told me that he had no more such Bloaters and suspected that he might not be able to lay his hands on any more Bloaters ever. But then, of course, we were only in New York. We had yet to reach California.

'So,' I said to Neil, 'speak to us of Shadow Nights.'

'It's an extra thing,' said Neil. 'Like the shrinking buildings.'

'Not quite following you there,' I said, ordering, as I did so, a bowl of strawberries from the waitress and a quarter pound of cocaine to sprinkle over them.

'The woman from Croydon,' said Neil. 'You must have heard about the woman from Croydon.'

But strangely no.

And so Neil told us all about the woman from Croydon. And her connection with Shadow Nights at Club 27 in New York. And frankly, I have to admit that I was astounded.

Because I had never heard of her before. But her experiences fitted right in with my experience in Hyde Park and all that went before it.

And indeed was to come afterwards. Although, of course, I wasn't to know that then. But it put things into place. And exposed a bigger picture and all that kind of business.

And so, I give you another aside, but again a relevant one.

I give you, indeed, the revelations.

Of the woman from Croydon.

35

There was a young lady named Clara
Who crashed in her new Ford Sierra.
The results of collision
Caused hoots of derision
And stays in a home, with a carer.

When Hugo Rune wrote of the soul-space, he also wrote of what he called the mental-mesh. The mental-mesh was a physical thing, in Rune's opinion, and could be espied under a microscope within a dissected human brain. If you knew just where to look.

The purpose of the mental-mesh is to screen out the bad stuff that would otherwise interfere with the everyday running of human life. A filter, if you will, that prevents the admission of the stuff that would be too much to bear – the interference, cosmic and otherwise. The thickness of the mesh determines the range of the spectrum that our eyes have access to. Also the limitations of sound, both high-pitched and low. That which might be smelled and touched and sensed in all manner of ways. It is an evolutionary development without which humanity could never have raised itself above the animal kingdom. It is well known that birds can see better than Man, and dogs can smell much more and certain creatures sense much more than this. But Man, you will note, is the master of them all. Because by limiting the input, Man can concentrate upon other things, rather than being constantly under a massive sensory assault.

The question arose in Rune's mighty mind as to what might happen to a man if the mental-mesh was removed from his brain. Rune experimented upon several of his willing acolytes and although he could not claim a one hundred per cent success rate, he described the results as 'interesting'. And 'not without some humour'.

But as Rune was to discover, it was not necessary for him to slice away at his acolytes' heads in order to observe what happens when the mental-mesh is either partially or totally removed. There are some amongst us who lack for mental meshes, either wholly or in part. Or whose mental-meshes have become damaged or 'holed' due to some trauma or accident.

And these folk are to be found inhabiting the in-patients' wards of mental institutions. Here are those diagnosed as paranoid schizophrenic. Those who *hear the voices*. And as those who know of those who hear the voices know, those who hear the voices do *not* hear the voices inside their heads, they hear the voices coming from outside. And what they see is not internal, what they see is outside of themselves.

Because these unfortunates have holes in their mental-meshes that allow those things that it is better not to hear, to be heard. And those things that it is better not to see, to be seen.

It is not all bad, however, because there are those who hear and see the good stuff rather than the bad. And we call these people blessed, and holy, and prophets, and saints.

And thus it was that a change came unto the lady from Croydon called Clara, when she crashed her new Ford Sierra.

For those who have an interest in such matters – and let's face it, who amongst us does not? – it is to be noticed that the street plan of Croydon mirrors precisely that of the lost city of Begrem.

Coincidence? Perhaps. But then—

As those who have an interest in such things will also know, Croydon was originally founded as a fundamentalist Christian community by that famous son of a preacher-man Courage Croydon, Hellfire pulpit-thunderer. His South of England crusades in the eighteenth century were intended to instil the Word of God into the pagan peoples of Sussex. Especially Brighton, although even *he* was forced to give up on Brighton. Courage Croydon travelled with his entourage, the Ladies of the Lord, and was finally bequeathed 'the lands to all compass points to a distance of twelve leagues from the church founded upon common land by the Reverand Courage Croydon' by the reigning monarch.

History records that the reigning monarch did this in the hope of keeping Courage Croydon away from the gates of Hampton Court by giving him a goodly parcel of land on which to build what Courage described as 'the Earthly Kingdom of God'.*

* Should the reader yearn to know the full story of Courage Croydon, the best reference book would be Sir John Rimmer's *Croydon's Croydon: The Man, the Myth and the Sacred Geomancy of the Roundabout system*.

He chose to model this Earthly Kingdom upon the lost city of Begrem because he believed that the plans for Begrem had been drawn up by God and given to the first King in a vision. When a later King fell from favour with God by creating the Homunculus, the city, all turned to gold, sank beneath the Sumerian sands.

Where it remains to this day.

Courage Croydon saw all this in a vision of his own. And the voice of God spoke at his ear and so he took up vellum and quill and drew up plans for Croydon as they were dictated to him.

In his biography of Courage Croydon, Sir John Rimmer speaks of the city of Croydon's (now world-famous) roundabouts. Rimmer, something of a visionary himself, eschews the theory that crop circles are nothing more than the aftermaths of travelling fairy circuses and attributes them a more mystical significance. 'They are where the doo-dads dance,' claims Rimmer. The doo-dads being those creatures that are defined as 'halfway between Man and the angels', the communicators of Angelic Wisdom who speak into the ears of the soon-to-be enlightened when God and the angels are otherwise engaged.

'Thus,' claims Rimmer, 'the roundabouts of Croydon are based on the circular systems of Begrem. As the transportation of that early age was horse-drawn, such roundabouts were unnecessary, but were instead created to allow the unobstructed circular dances of the doo-dads, which in those days were invisible to most if not all of the population.' Rimmer refers to roundabouts as the tarmac equivalent of corn circles. Road circles are they. For doo-dad dances in the round.

Which brings us, rather neatly, back to the lady named Clara.

And the crash that she had on one of Croydon's roundabouts.

And the consequences of this crash. Which led to the creation of Shadow Nights at Club 27 in New York.

Matters came to pass in this fashion.

With swerve and with crash and with bang.

The morning was bright enough in its way, as Croydon mornings have the habit of being. Folk rose from their beds, stretched, flung wide their bedroom curtains and rejoiced. Beheld the glory that is Croydon, and rejoiced. Tea was brewed and toast was buttered, daily papers taken from the mat. Rosy-cheeked the children were as they were dressed for school. And the stockbrokers' clerks and the City professionals sang when they strolled to their trains. For Croydon, the good and the Godly, brought as ever joy to those who live there.

And Clara woke from dreams of whalers, hunting for a whale.

Whether this whale was white and Moby-Dickish, none can say, for Clara awoke before they'd found it. She awoke beside her husband Keith, a stockbroker's clerk in the City. Today was their third wedding anniversary.* And although Keith had planned a major dinner for two at the local Wimpy Bar, this was a well-kept secret and Clara knew nothing of it.

She had, of course, prepared a present for her spouse and this she gave to him before his breakfast. Which had his knees go somewhat numb and he fairly stumbled downstairs for his breakfast.

'Love is everywhere,' the singer sang. And who was to doubt him in Croydon?

The breakfast was the Full Welsh, with nothing spared. And, when brought to the perfect conclusion with a buttered bap and a handy shandy, Clara's husband Keith went off to work with a smile on his face and a twinkle in his eye. And love in his heart for Jesus.

For good and Godly are the folk of Croydon.

And Clara peeled off all of her rubber-wear and took herself off for a shower. And here, as she bathed, she sang a hymn to the Lord. For she sang soprano in Croydon Ladies' Choir and a fine soprano she had.

And once she had done with the singing and shower, she dried and dressed and left the house to go shopping.

Those who know Croydon will know of its internationally famed shopping center, a World Trades Fair of fancy goods and eco-kind comestibles. Where there is always ample parking and every shopper wears a sunny smile.

And Clara steered her Ford Sierra around Croydon's most southerly road circle and was, of a sudden, the victim of a freak accident involving a kitty hawk, a carrier pigeon called Dennis, a gunman on a grassy knoll, a garden gnome without a home and an off-side-rear-tyre puncture.

Such freak accidents are not unknown Up North, but in Croydon it was an incident distinctly beyond the norm.

And matters came to a terrible pass.

With a swerve and a crash and a bang.

And Clara awoke, some weeks later, in a room that she did not recognise, looking up at a doctor that she did.

Clara blinked her eyes and said, 'Surely you are Elvis?'

* Third wedding Anniversaries are 'cheese'. And are not easy to get anniversary cards for. As opposed to those silver, gold and diamond. But strange, at times, are the ways of Man.

The doctor smiled and stroked her brow. 'I'm Doctor McMahon,' he told her.

'Where?'

'Where are you, my dear? You are in the special recovery unit of the Ministry of Serendipity, beneath Mornington Crescent Underground Station.'

'W—'

'Why? Because you have been in an accident and your cranial X-rays show that there is extensive damage to your mental-mesh.'

'M—'

Mental-mesh? A technical term that at the present you need not concern yourself about. We are here to help with your rehabilitation. And to prepare you for what lies ahead.'

'W—'

'What lies ahead?'

'No,' said Clara. 'Where's the toilet? I am in need of a pee.'

There were no bones broken, and Clara, but for the occasional bit of stiffness, seemed otherwise to be in fine fettle. She was somewhat surprised and disturbed too that her husband Keith hadn't paid her a visit, and as one day passed into the next, she grew rather anxious withal.

She saw no one but Dr McMahon, who, although constantly assuring her that she was on the mend and would soon be returned to the bosom of her family, kept finding causes for more tests that resulted in an ever-prolonged stay in what was explained to her as being a subterranean Government facility.

And Clara did not take to Dr McMahon, who described his resemblance to Elvis as being 'passing and not noticed by many'.

And Clara began to fret and soon was fretting continually. And it is not good for someone in recovery to fret. It can have negative consequences and no doctor in the rightness of his mind would prescribe it as a pick-me-up.

Dr McMahon did, however, prescribe a good many drugs for Clara. Many that she had never heard of and some that she had heard of, but didn't really believe in the existence of. And time passed very slowly and Clara now plotted escape.

And although Dr McMahon stood over her and supervised the taking of her medication, she secretly regurgitated same upon his departure from the circular windowless room in which she now considered herself to be held a prisoner. And plotted her escape.

And the means of her escape presented itself in an unexpected manner. This being the arrival of a visitor, ushered into her room by the Elvis-like Dr McMahon.

'This,' said the doctor, 'is Vincent Trillby, Professor of Advanced Psychiatry at Harvard. He is most interested to study your case, in the hope that it will facilitate the early return of yourself to the bosom of your family. In particular to your husband Keith, who loves and misses you greatly.'

Clara from Croydon ground her teeth, but disguised this as a sniffly sneeze, said that she hoped she wasn't coming down with a cold, then put out a slender hand for a shake (for she was indeed a slender lady, as are most in Croydon) and smiled into the face of Vincent Trillby.

And then withdrew her hand at considerable speed and screamed very loudly indeed. And she screamed in that high soprano voice of hers that had brought great joy to numerous Croydon congregations, but which within the limited confines of her circular cell caused considerable distress to Dr McMahon and to Vincent Trillby, both of whom collapsed to their knees, a-covering of their ears.

And when they both appeared to be in a state of incapacitation, Clara screamed some more, and repeatedly doing so made for the door and from there, by diverse routes, to the surface. Where she stood, shivering somewhat even though it was another sunny day. There in the great booming heart of the metropolis, in her foolish do-up-at-the-back patient's smock. And had it not been for a passing stockbroker's clerk who took pity on her plight, escorted her, via taxi, to Selfridges and had her fitted out from head to toe in all the latest groovy gear, bought her a handbag and popped a five-pound note into it, there is no telling what might have happened.

And the stockbroker's clerk tipped his bowler to Clara, wished her all the bestest for the balance of the day and returned to his office with a story to tell. (But not of the shag he'd been hoping for.)

And so it came to pass that Clara, all spiffed-up and trendy-looking, found herself in Trafalgar Square.

And it was there that she looked all around and saw that things were *not* right. That something was in fact very wrong indeed, but that, it appeared, she was the only person who could see it.

Which is where those shadows come in.

So let us speak of them now.

36

Clara saw the shadows and she was afeared.

At first she thought it was some kind of optical illusion, or delusion, brought on by her sudden transition (via Selfridges) from subterranean prison to sunlit Trafalgar Square. But her head soon cleared itself of this thinking because a revelation was granted to her, through the medium of a voice, which whispered rather closely at her ear that she now had the gift to see *them*.

To see the extra shadows that were there.

The extra shadows of the men and women who passed by in that fine historic square, that was named for that great naval victory. Not *all* possessed them, but *some*. Few in fact were they, but Clara saw them. The folk who had an extra shadow. That is what she saw.

Certainly now many of us are aware of the phenomenon. It seems extraordinary today that anyone, particularly the cinema-goers to whom the phenomenon was ever on view in the movies of the day, failed to see it. Check out any Hollywood cowboy film of the late fifties and early sixties. Anything starring John Wayne, for instance. Check out the outside shots, those sunny-day gunfight scenes. Look at Mr Wayne, then look at his shadow. Or rather *shadows*! For he casts more than one. It's there in almost every movie, captured on the celluloid. And Clara saw it there in Trafalgar Square, that certain folk had more than one shadow. And that these folk were wrong from the inside to the out.

Her mental-mesh was damaged indeed, and she could see more than others.

But Clara kept her alarm to herself. She did not cause a fuss, because such a fuss might well have landed her in a police cell, then a psychiatric unit, then back at the Ministry of Serendipity.

No, Clara kept her alarm very much in check. She took herself off to a well-known American-style eatery and ordered a hamburger, French chips and a Brown Derby Ice-Cream Sundae, *and* a cup of tea, and pondered deeply on her situation.

And she viewed the waiters and waitresses coming and going in their elegant and distinctive red and white livery. And she noted well that one of them cast more shadows than she felt was strictly necessary and determined on a plan. Because she had now become a most determined woman.

At three in the afternoon there was a change of shifts and the waiter with the surplus shadow clocked off and, like Elvis, left the building. And Clara followed this fellow.

To the Underground Station she followed him. And there he purchased a ticket and she a Red Rover, as she hadn't seen which ticket he purchased. From there to a train and on this train, as fate would have it, back to Croydon.

Breathing God's good air, Clara emerged from Croydon Station and followed the caster of the double shadow, who, oblivious to the fact that he was being shadowed, strode on with that air of confidence and self-assurance that is the almost exclusive preserve of waiters the whole world over.

And eventually this waiter reached the ornate gates of the Croydon Municipal Burial Ground, paused for but a moment and then entered there. And though Clara followed him closely, very soon he was gone. To where? And how? Clara did not know. But she was rattled.

And in that state of rattledness she returned home. And at the corner of the street that was her own she paused, because there ahead of her was a long black car with blackly mirrored windows. And it was parked right outside her house. And there were men dressed in black standing around in her front garden.

And one of these was talking to her husband Keith (who should surely have been at work) and Keith was wringing his hands and looked a little weepy overall.

And Clara flattened herself into a hedge of a privetty nature and realised that she was indeed in *very* big trouble. And was somewhat stuck as to just what to do about this.

And so she hid and she waited. And eventually the men in black returned to their black limousine and this drove away at some speed. And Clara crept down a side alleyway and along to the rear of her house, and from there into her back garden where she sneaked to the living-room window and peeped in.

And there was her husband, wringing his hands and pacing up and down. And Clara was overcome by his obvious emotions and she tapped upon the window. And her husband Keith saw her and broke into a smile and they were reunited there and then.

And Neil concluded the story there, as we sat in Club 27.

'Hold on,' I said to Neil. 'That can't be the end of the story. What else happened?'

But Neil was now dipping strawberries into a bowl of cocaine.

'Come on,' I said, reaching for a strawberry and giving it a dip. 'That can't be the end of the story. What has it got to do with Shadow Night at Club Twenty-Seven?'

Neil chucked a strawberry down his throat. 'Oh, all right,' said he. And carried on.

Clara's husband Keith made a pot of tea for his wife, and at length he joined her in the lounge room. Clara was a bit sobby and sniffy now, what with the emotional reunion and all that had gone before it, and her husband poured her tea and asked her to tell him *everything*. Because, as he told her, the men in black who had visited had told him she had died.

And so Clara told him *everything*.

And Keith listened to this everything with a perplexed expression on his normally cheery chops. And when Clara had done with the telling of everything, he reclined back in the Parker Knoll Recliner* and said, 'By golly, by gosh.'

'By what?'

'By golly?'

'Golly, where?'

'Not here.' And husband Keith patted the wrist of his wife and told her that this was a right old pickle, as well as being a fine kettle of fish and a rum one, to be sure. And then he took to thinking. And then he said, 'Wait here.'

And he went upstairs and rummaged about. And then he returned, bearing in his hands his old service revolver, which he had been allowed to keep at the end of the Second World War, as a gift from a grateful officer-in-command for the many valorous deeds that the then Private Keith had performed that were above and beyond the call of duty. And he showed this service revolver to his wife.

And his wife was further alarmed by this display of hand armament. Although also strangely comforted. And she asked her husband Keith what his intentions were concerning the deployment of this weapon.

And husband Keith twirled it upon his finger, as John Wayne was

* Still reckoned to be the most comfortable recliner of all time.

wont to do in the movies. And he told his wife that it would put an end to their particular problems.

And then he aimed it at Clara's head and pulled the trigger.

And the last thing that she noticed, before all-encompassing blackness closed in about her, was that the raised arm of her husband cast two shadows.

And Neil dipped once more into the strawberry bowl.

'No, no, no,' I said to Neil. 'Although very good in an *Outer Limits* kind of a way, that still doesn't explain Club Twenty-Seven's Shadow Night. Or much else when it comes right down to it.'

'Well, there is *another version*,' said Neil, who now seemed to be growing rather animated.

Clara noticed that double shadow as her husband raised that gun. And she screamed once more in that high soprano, which had her husband flinching. And Clara wrestled away that gun and ran in fear of her life, far away from Croydon, and was never seen again.

And Neil had one more strawberry and great big dippings did.

'I will punch you, Neil,' I told him. 'And if not me, then Andy will.'

'I'll punch him anyway, if you want,' said Andy. Who, I noticed, was dressed in the police uniform of one of New York's Finest.

'I'll have him killed,' said Toby.

And Neil continued with haste.

She left England (Neil continued, with haste). Jumped a liner to New York. Submerged herself into the New York scene and wrote about her experiences in the Underground Press. You'll find a lot of her stuff if you flick through back issues of *Flaky Fruitcake Today* magazine. She played the part of the mad old bag lady.

'Hold on there,' I said to Neil. 'Mad *old* bag lady?'

'Oh yes,' said Neil. 'This all happened back in the nineteen-thirties.'

'They didn't have Ford Sierras in the nineteen-thirties,' said Toby, who already had several cars of his own.

'They did in Croydon,' said Neil.

'And what about the doctor who looked like Elvis?' said Andy.

'I think she added that into the story later,' said Neil. 'She met the real Elvis, you see, and realised that he was the dead spit of the doctor that she had met twenty years before. Which is kind of weird, isn't it?'

Andy grunted that it was and had another strawberry.

And Neil continued, 'So Clara became an outsider, an eccentric, a bogus bag lady, to avoid the attentions of the Men from the Ministry. But she could see who was who. And she published her findings in all kinds of off-the-wall publications. And some folk took her seriously, these folk being those whose own mental-meshes were either damaged, or missing.'

'And Shadow Night at Club Twenty-Seven?' I asked.

'She founded Club Twenty-Seven,' said Neil, 'as a means of Purging the Taint.'

And I knew *that* expression. I had heard it used to describe what went on when the helicopter gunships strafed that Hanwell cemetery.

'How does this work?' I asked Neil.

'They are lured into the club,' said Neil, 'the *others*, those casters of the double shadow. They are reanimated corpses, you see. Clara eventually figured it all out. They have their own shadow, but also another – the shadow of the ungodly thing that has been inflicted into them. Shadow Night sorts them out.'

'How?' I enquired. Although, in truth, I wasn't particularly caring too much by then, because I had by that point eaten my way through about half a pound of snowily dusted strawberries.

'Well, *you* didn't know what Shadow Night meant until I explained it to you,' said Neil. 'So neither do *they*, and no one explains it to *them*. *They* come into the club, looking for a good time, but *they* never leave. There's a hotel over on the West Coast, also founded by Clara, where the same thing goes on.'

'The Hotel California?' I said.

'You know of it?'

'Only a lucky guess.'

'So they get exterminated. And it's really entertaining to watch, apparently.'

I registered the looks upon the faces of the other guys in the band. Apart from Toby, who appeared altogether keen, the other guys, even though now buoyed-up considerably by copious quantities of coke, didn't look altogether enthusiastic.

'It's one of those *rich* people things,' Neil explained. 'Those exclusive things that only the rich are privy to. We can watch because we are rock musicians. I'm up for it – what about the rest of you?'

'How do they do the actual butchering?' Andy asked.

'I think you can have your choice of weapons.'

'*What?*' I said to Neil. 'What did you say?'

'Oh, I forgot to mention *that*. If you bung a contribution into the

Extermination of the Undead Fund, you can butcher one of the blighters yourself. With your choice of weapons.'

I did shakings of my head. This was all a bit sudden. And a bit unexpected.

'Well, I'm up for it,' said Toby. 'Can I choose one of those General Electric miniguns? They look like a lot of fun.'

'Well, I'm *not* up for it,' said Rob. 'It all sounds most dubious to me. What if they're not undead? And frankly I don't think I believe in the concept of the undead. It sounds rather cheesy to me. You might kill some innocent party instead.'

And so we did *not* attend Shadow Night. It was a group decision. A band decision. And I for one am glad that we took it. It wouldn't have been right if we'd got involved in something like that and butchered an innocent party.

So we all went back to the hotel and to our original plan for the evening: to live the rock 'n' roll lifestyle and set the standard by which other rock bands would be judged in years to come.

Yes, follow our original plan.

And eat one of the groupies.

37

We didn't eat *all* of the groupie.

We left the trotters and the snout.

I really took to New York, which, I learned, was so good they had named it twice. It was midsummer, but as this *was* New York, it was snowing heavily and folk were skating about on various outdoor ice rinks. All the women looked like Barbra Streisand and the blokes like Elliott Gould. Which meant very little to me, because I was English.

I had no idea just how much kudos being English held in America. Folk just 'love that English accent', and we were asked repeatedly whether we owned bowler hats and regularly had the Queen round to tea. Which was handy for Toby because, apparently, he *did*!

This was nineteen sixty-nine and New York was in the throes of a big Jewish craze. Being Jewish was *the* in thing and people who did not look even the remotest bit Jewish were adopting yarmulkes and Jewish accents, greeting each other with *oy veys* and catching gefilte fish. The year before it had been fashionable to be Irish. And in the early seventies you weren't anyone in New York if you weren't black and didn't sport an afro. I don't know what the present fashion is in New York, but I have heard talk of cross-dressing.

But as Jewish was the look, we trooped into a downtown boutique and got ourselves kitted out. Black. All black. Black suit, black coat, black shoes, black homburg. It was a really cool look, and we took it with us back to England and unwittingly started the Goth movement.

And there's something about black, isn't there? There's really nothing cooler to wear than black. You can go anywhere in a black suit and folk will always show you respect. Because you will always look sophisticated. We didn't wear black onstage in America, though, because after all, we *had* invented Glam Rock and we wanted the American public to appreciate our glamour. Before they got too deeply into our sophistication. We did have an ingrained natural sophistication, though, which is why we didn't eat the snout, or the trotters.

Andy just loved New York. He acquired an all-black police uniform, augmented with silver trimmings and badge, and took to performing random stop-and-searches on young women and issuing on-the-spot fines for breaches of style. Andy adored New York, and in its turn New York, it appeared, loved Andy.

Neil loved New York also and hung around the recording studios, mixing with the big stars of the day. Rob checked out Madison Avenue, home of advertising, and found favour in all that he met with there.

Toby engaged in all manner of wheelings and dealings, some of which, I felt certain, *had* to be legal.

Which left only me.

And I suppose that I loved New York also, even though it was so cold. But I had so many things on my mind that I could not concentrate on looking cool and having a really good time.

This whole undead business was really getting me down. I just didn't know what to make of it. I'd seen it with my own eyes – the zombies in the cemetery and the undead at the Hyde Park gig. And the knowledge that Shadow Night *really* existed at Club 27 meant that it was not just me, Mr Ishmael and the mysterious crew at the Ministry of Serendipity who knew about it. This thing was big and growing ever bigger.

What I didn't know, but really wanted to know, was *who* or *what* was behind it. Was it some evil necromancer? Or a black magician, or perhaps the Homunculus himself? It was definitely a baddy of some big-time description. A super-baddy. And whether Mr Ishmael had been telling me all of the truth, or indeed *any* of it, I had no way of knowing.

So I *really truly* did want to talk to Mr Ishmael.

But Mr Ishmael was nowhere to be found.

I still had his telephone number – I'd found it in the lining of my mother's trench coat – and I called several times, using the special trans-Atlantic prefix and everything. But there was no answer. And thinking about that scrap of paper and the trench coat had me feeling all nostalgic and gave me a crinkly mouth. I quite missed my mum and dad, and even though I was now a rock 'n' roll star, on the way up with a glorious future ahead of me, I actually missed being a private detective.

And this line of thinking set me to thinking of something else. So to speak. And had this been an animated cartoon rather than real life, you would have seen, at this point, a little light bulb materialise above my head and frantically start flashing.

And the word 'IDEA' might even have appeared within it.

And there might also have been heard the sound of a bell ringing.

Flash and Ding and IDEA. Just like that.

Because I was in New York. And New York was the home of the private detective. Los Angeles was too, of course. But not really. Los Angeles was the home of the private detective in the Hollywood movies, because the studios were all in Los Angeles and if they shot the movie in LA they didn't have to travel, or pay the cast and crew's hotel costs. Cheapskates!

But this *was* New York. And New York *was* the home of the private eye. In fact, the real Lazlo Woodbine lived and worked in New York. Or at least *had*, in the nineteen-fifties. P. P. Penrose based his Lazlo Woodbine thrillers on a real-life New York private eye and I wondered, just wondered, whether this fellow was still practising his craft. And if so, whether he might care to take on an English sidekick for a couple of weeks, at no charge to himself. It would be a dream come true for me, to work with the legend that was Woodbine. But hold on! Even better than *that*! Although the great Lazlo Woodbine might not take to some complete stranger (no matter whether or not he had experience in the field of Private Eyedom) trying to muscle in on his field of activity, he would never refuse a commission. Especially from a stylishly clad Englishman. If I were to offer him a job, then *he* would work for *me*. And how cool would *that* be?

Very cool, that's how.

That little light bulb over my head grew burning, burning bright.

And popped.

I awoke early on what I recall was a Monday morning, dressed in modish black, stepped carefully between the bits of groupie that were scattered about my room and left the Pentecost Hotel.

I knew that Laz had his office somewhere in Manhattan and that he drank in a pub called Fangio's Bar, where he regularly sat and chewed the fat with Fangio, the fat-boy barman. And talked the toot also. Because talking the toot was something that Laz and Fangio did in a manner that surpassed any other toot-talking, past, present or future. And if he *was* still in business, then he was bound to be in the telephone book.

Now, I'm sure you've noticed it in Hollywood movies, so I will not dwell upon it here, but isn't it odd how all American telephone numbers begin with 555? What is *that* all about?

In a public phone booth, which didn't have a door and looked very much like the record booths they had in the Squires Music shop in Ealing Broadway, I beheld a telephone book.

It had pages missing and smelled somewhat of wee wee – but the vandals who had been abusing it had not got as far as the classified section. And so I ran my finger down the list of private eyes.

And I saw him! Large as life!

Lazlo Woodbine
Private Detective
2727 27th Street
555 272727

Result!

And just two blocks away. I could walk it.

And so I did. For those who don't know New York, allow me to explain to you about it. New York divides itself into quarters. You have your Irish Quarter, your Latin Quarter, your Trinidadian Quarter and your Tierra del Fuego Quarter. And many many other quarters, all to do with commerce. These quarters are also called districts. So you have your Slaughterhouse District, Fashion District, Tiger's Eye Pottery District, et cetera and et cetera. So, once you have a map of New York with all these quarters/districts marked upon it, you can't go wrong. And at least you know where everything is. And there *is* a quarter for *everything* in New York.

Twenty-Seventh Street is the Detective Quarter. It's just past the Gay Plumbers' Quarter, but before you reach the Elvis Impersonators' Quarter. Depending upon which way you approach it, of course.

I *really, really* liked 27th Street. It may have changed now, of course, but back then, in the heyday of private detectivedom, it was *the* place (for private detectives) and it was *very* seedy indeed. It was all run-down 'brownstones' and crumbling nineteen-thirties Art Deco office blocks. There were alleyways a-plenty and each owned its fair share of cast-iron fire escapes with those retractable bottom sections. And trashcans and the rear doors of down-at-heel nightclubs. And each and every one of these alleyways echoed softly to the music of a solitary saxophone. Sweet.

I did most approving noddings as I strolled along 27th Street.

And then I saw it, and, I kid you not, my heart skipped a beat. It was Fangio's Bar and it was open.

The neon sign flashed out its message and the shatter-glass door opened before me at my touch. And then I was there, in that very bar immortalised by the poignant pen of P. P. Penrose.

Long and low and loathsome was Fangio's Bar. With photographs of boxers all framed up on the walls. And a lengthy bright chromium bar counter that ran the lengthiness of the room (on the left, looking from the front door). There were bar stools, there were booths, and there, behind that bar counter, he stood. It had to be him: Fangio, the fat-boy barman of legend.

I straightened up my shoulders, disguising my scholar's stoop, dusted non-existent dandruff from said shoulders and nonchalantly made my way to the bar.

Fangio was stuffing olives. Into an old army sock.

He looked up from his doings and I caught his eye.

'Out of this bar,' quoth he.

'Excuse me?' I said, with politeness, as I viewed Fangio.

He was somewhat broader than he was long, having about him a respectable girth. Yet although his belly was running to fat, his feet weren't running anywhere. He stood four-square upon the floor of his bar, a man amongst men and a titan. Bald of head and bulbous of nose and, 'Out of this bar,' quoth he.

'Excuse me, sir?' I said, this time eager to show my respect.

'This is a non-denominational bar,' said Fangio, 'and I don't want any trouble.'

'I think there must be some misunderstanding,' I said.

'Some?' said Fangio. 'I think you will find that in this bar there is a very great deal of misunderstanding.'

'Will I?' I asked.

'There's just no telling,' said Fangio. 'But tell me this, while you are still here, do you think that if I were a woman, it would be a viable proposition for me to give birth to myself? When cloning is finally perfected, I could then self-reproduce. It would be the next best thing to immortality, don't you think?'

'You have me on that one,' I said, 'because I do not have the faintest idea what you are talking about.'

'A likely story,' said Fangio.

And I just shook my head.

'Perhaps we have got off on the wrong foot,' said Fangio.

'Perhaps we have,' I agreed.

'So let me put it in a more straightforward way. Get out of my bar, Mr Doctor of Death, or I shall be forced to shoot you.'

'It's definitely a misunderstanding,' I said. 'I am not a doctor of any sort.'

'Oh, I hate it when that happens,' said Fangio, and he tied up the neck of his army sock with a Gordian knot that he formed from a sinister shoelace. 'There are always so many official forms to fill in after the shooting.'

'I'm *not* a doctor,' said I.

'But you are dressed as a Swiss doctor of the Anabaptist persuasion. And that fails to satisfy upon so many levels.'

'I thought this was a Jewish coat,' I said.

'A *Jewish* coat?' And Fangio took to laughter. And with considerable gusto he took to it. He placed the now-knotted sock onto the bar counter, placed his ample hands upon his ample belly and laughed himself fit-to-go busting.

And I shook my head one more time. And then twice.

'A *Jewish* coat,' said Fangio, between great gales of gusto. 'That's a good'n, that is. Wait until I tell my wife. You don't know a dame who might want to marry me, do you?' And he laughed again.

'I really don't see what's so funny,' I said.

'You Swiss,' said Fangio, wiping big tears from his eyes. 'You will be the death of me. And indeed of all of us,' he added, 'with your cuckoo clocks and chocolate and all that neutrality. How many borders do you have? No, don't get me going on that.' And he laughed a little more. Then stopped.

'So what would you care to drink?' he asked. The model of sobriety.

'Well,' I said, well flummoxed. 'What would you recommend?'

'Well,' said the Fange. 'Now you're asking.'

'Yes I am,' I said. 'I am.'

'Which calls to mind a most illuminating and entertaining anecdote that was passed on to me the other day by one of those Jimbos who seem to be so popular in England nowadays. It concerns this fallen angel who is trying to get his car started and he—'

But Fangio didn't get any further with the telling of his tale because the shatter-glass door now opened and in *he* walked. The one, the only, the man, the myth.

The Private Eye, Lazlo Woodbine.

It was he.

Applause.

38

He looked a little past his sell-by date.

But given the life he had led and the adventures he'd had, this was hardly surprising. But it *was* him, it definitely was.

There could be no mistaking those gimlet eyes, those chiselled cheekbones, the hammered hooter and that joineried jawline. And he wore the fedora and he wore the trench coat. And he looked like Lazlo Woodbine.

It was he.

'Fange,' said Lazlo Woodbine.

'Laz,' said Fangio.

'A bottle of Bud and a hot pastrami on rye.'

'A ploughman's umbrella and a parsnip in a poetry.'

Lazlo looked at Fangio.

And Fange looked back at Laz.

And oh how they laughed.

Well, they *did*. Don't ask me why, but they did. It was a *talking the toot* thing, I suppose. I had unconsciously engaged in it with Fangio a little earlier, but I did not as yet understand how it worked. The strict rules of the vernacular and the inflective. The subtleties of variant pronunciation. The coordinating and subordinating conjunctions.

Not to mention the connotive labels or the cross-referenced etymologies.

Which neither of them ever did.

'So, would you care for a drink, sir?' said Fangio to Laz.

'A bottle of Bud?' said Lazlo Woodbine, seating himself on a bar stool.

'A bottle of Bud?' And Fangio now took to the stroking of one of his many chins. 'A bottle of Bud? I'll get it in a minute, I'm sure. It rings a bell somewhere.'

'You're thinking of Quasimodo,' said Lazlo Woodbine. 'He rings a bell somewhere – Paris, I think.'

'Paris?' said Fangio, selecting another chin for a stroking. 'Now don't get me going on Paris.'

'Still that trouble with bicycles?'

'Bicycles?' said Fangio. 'It's Amsterdam for bicycles and Paris for the Orient Express.'

'You can catch the Orient Express in London,' said Laz. 'But then you can catch almost anything in London.'

'I once caught a tiger by the tail,' said Fangio, 'but that was in India. And let's face it, I've never even been to India.'

'Don't get *me* going on India,' said Lazlo Woodbine. 'Cambay, Chandrapur, Chikmagulur, Coonoor, Cuddalore, Cuttack—'

'You sure know your Indian cities that begin with the letter C, buddy.'

'Friend,' said Lazlo Woodbine to Fangio, 'in my business, knowing your Indian cities that begin with the letter C can mean the difference between a clean-cut curr in curlers at Crufts and dirty dogging in Dagenham.* If you know what I mean, and I'm sure that you do.'

And Fangio knew what he meant.

'Excuse me,' I said, and two eye-pairings turned as one to view me.

'Who's the Swiss Anabaptist abortionist?' asked Lazlo Woodbine.

'*Abortionist?*' I said.

'Doctor of Death,' said Fangio. 'By any other name. I speak as I find and you won't find me speaking of raffia.'

'He abhors raffia,' Lazlo Woodbine explained. 'And also Koya matting.'

'Any form of matting,' said Fangio. 'Raffia, coir, logo, anti-slip, fitted, Milliken Obex – a revolutionary matting system unequalled in performance – rustic, rush or rag-rug.'

'Buddy, you sure know your matting,' said Lazlo.

'Friend,' said Fangio the barman, 'in this business, knowing your matting can mean the difference between an uncovered linoleum floor and one that has a mat on it.'

There was a moment's pause. Outside the sun went behind a cloud and a dog howled in the distance.

'It's not quite as funny when you do it as when I do it, is it?' asked Lazlo.

'Abortionist?' I said once more.

'We did that one,' said Fangio.

'Yes, I'm sure you did. But I'm sorry – you're talking the toot, aren't

---

* Which rather impressed me at the time because dogging had yet to become an English national pastime.

you? The now legendary toot that Lazlo Woodbine and Fangio the barman always talk. Especially when Laz is on a case.'

'The Swiss,' said Lazlo Woodbine. 'They'll be the death of me. And indeed of us all, with their cuckoo clocks and chocolate bars and garden gnomes called Zurich.'

'I did that bit,' said Fange. 'I mentioned Swiss neutrality, though.'

'Don't get me going on *that*.' And Lazlo Woodbine doffed his fedora and wafted it round and about.

'I'm really *not* Swiss,' I told the both of them. '*Really*. *Not*.'

'Ah,' said Fange. And he tapped at his nose with a thumb like an unsliced pastrami. 'You're here undercover. I understand.'

'And I'm *not* undercover. And I am certainly *not* an abortionist. And I'm not even sure what an Anabaptist is.'

'Don't get me going on *that*,' said one or other of them, but I couldn't tell which one.

'It was me,' said Fangio. 'I have the deeper and more resonant voice. A natural baritone, I am.'

'But not a natural blonde,' said Lazlo Woodbine.

'But I do have all my own teeth.'

'I'll bet you can't open a beer bottle with them.'

'Oh yes I can.'

'Then a bottle of Bud, please, barman.'

And I applauded this.

And Fangio bowed and Lazlo Woodbine bowed. And Fangio brought Laz a bottle of Bud. 'I was lying about the teeth,' he said as he opened it with an opener.

'So, young lady,' said Lazlo Woodbine to me, 'what is it that I can do for you? You are a long way from Switzerland, and your vast bank vaults of Nazi gold.'

'And I'm *not* a young lady,' I said. 'You're supposed to be a detective, aren't you? Swiss? Anabaptist? Abortionist? Young lady?'

'One at a time,' said Fangio. 'I only have one pair of hands. Form an orderly queue, if you will, Swiss boys to the rear.'

'Do they?' said Laz to Fange. 'I thought *that* was an English thing. All those Jimbos and everything.'

I took to massaging my temples. I had never encountered the talking of the toot before, and frankly it was giving me a headache.

'Freemason also,' said Fangio to Lazlo as he passed him over his Bud. 'They always do that thing with their temples. It's called a Masonic temple, you know. But I can't tell you more than that or they'll cut my nipples off and post them through a vicar's letterbox.'

'They're only being cruel to be kind,' said Lazlo Woodbine, and he drew on his bottle of Bud.

'And I am *not* a Freemason,' said I.

And Lazlo Woodbine placed his bottle on the counter. 'And now,' said he, 'we have established all the things that you are not. You are *not* a woman, neither are you Swiss, an Anabaptist, a Doctor of Death, a Freemason, nor, I believe, a dogger.'

'Certainly *not* a dogger,' I said. Although I did harbour some secret yearnings to dog. But then whom amongst us does not?

'And so,' Lazlo Woodbine continued, 'I conclude therefore that you must be English, a private detective who is presently serving his time as a rock 'n' roll musician, a stranger to New York and a young man with a problem that he believes only Lazlo Woodbine can solve.'

'Well,' I said. And then no more, for I was somewhat speechless.

'Never underestimate the power of the toot,' said Fangio, the fat-boy barman. 'Many before you have and all have paid the price.'

'Right,' I said. 'Right, well, I don't quite know what to say.'

'Then you must accompany me to my office,' said Lazlo Woodbine. 'And there you will outline to me the nature of the case in point. And I, Lazlo Woodbine, will then endeavour to solve it for you.'

'Really?' I said.

'Honest engine,' said he.

And so we left Fangio's Bar and crossed the street to the building that housed Lazlo's office. Fangio left his bar and followed us halfway across the street, complaining that Lazlo Woodbine had *not* paid for his beer and that the Swiss maid hadn't even bought a bar of chocolate.

And concluding that it would be a cold day in Cairo before he let autumn leaves start to fall, he returned to the comfort of his bar.

'Have you and the Fange been friends for a very long time?' I asked Lazlo Woodbine as I followed him up the stairs that led to his office.

'We were Marines together in the last war,' said the great detective. 'Both won Purple Hearts in the Pacific. I won mine for outstanding bravery and Fange won his in a pie-eating contest.'

'I won't get you going on *that*,' I said.

But Lazlo Woodbine ignored me.

And soon I found myself in the famous office. And it was just as I would have imagined it to be. Indeed, as anyone who is a fan of the nineteen-fifties American genre detective's office would have imagined it to be. There was the carpet that dared not speak its name. The water cooler that cooled no water and the hatstand that stood alone without a hat. There was the filing cabinet, the detective's desk with its telephone on top, and, I felt confident, its bottle of Kentucky bourbon in a drawer.

There were the two chairs and the ceiling fan that revolved slowly above. And *there* was the venetian blind. And I could definitely hear a solo saxophonist playing outside in the alleyway. I breathed in the ambience and then had a very good cough.

'You hawk it up,' said Lazlo Woodbine, patting at my back. 'You never know, it *might* be a gold watch.'

'It never is,' I said. And I concluded my coughing.

Lazlo Woodbine removed his hat and his coat and flung them in the general direction of the hatstand. He seated himself behind his desk and gestured for me to take the chair before it (which I did). Then he leaned back in his chair and placed his feet upon his desk. And then he took from his top drawer a bottle of Kentucky bourbon and two glasses, uncorked the bottle and poured out two golden shots.

'Down your shirt,' said Lazlo Woodbine. 'As you Brits will have it.'

'Up your Liberty Bell,' I replied, a-raising of my glass. 'As you Yanks will have it.'

And oh how we laughed.

But not much.

'And so,' said Lazlo Woodbine, 'you will now tell me all about the case, but first you must understand certain things. They are very important things and you must understand them now if we are going to work together.'

'Work *together*?' I queried.

'Lazlo Woodbine works *with* his client, never *for* his client. There is a subtle distinction, but an important one. Are you sitting quietly?'

I nodded. Noisily.

'Then put a sock in it.'

'A sock?'

'A sock all filled with olives. Such as this one that I recently liberated from Fangio's Bar. But hear me now and take heed of what I say, because I will only be saying it once. My name is Lazlo Woodbine, private eye, and some call me Laz. In the tradition of all great nineteen-fifties American genre detectives, I work only the four locations. An office where clients come to call. A bar where I talk the toot with the barman and meet the dame who does me wrong. An alleyway where I get into sticky situations. And a rooftop, where I have a final confrontation with the villain. Who then takes the obligatory long from-the-rooftop-fall-to-oblivion. These are the only locations that I work. No private eye worthy of his trench coat and fedora ever needs more. Do I make myself understood?'

I nodded my head and said that he did.

'And one more thing,' said Laz. '*I* am always the hero, and as such I work strictly in the first person.'

'Ah,' I said. 'Now that might be tricky.'

'Tricky, kid?' said I.

And the kid looked kind of cock-eyed at me. But ain't that the way with those Brits?

39

The snow dropped down like dandruff from the Holy Head of God.

In my business, which is one of private detection, you see these cosmic similes all the time. You have to keep in touch with your spiritual side, never forgetting that every next step could be your last and a watched boil never pops. It's keeping this balance that helps you succeed; that and the pistol you pack.

I always pack a trusty Smith & Wesson. In this town, packing a trusty Smith & Wesson can mean the difference between pursuing a course in elegant maths and perusing the corpse of the Elephant Man, if you know what I mean and I'm sure that you do. You got to keep a balance, see, and that is what I do.

I do what I do from my office at 2727 27th Street. The office has my name on the door. And also my profession.

'Lazlo Woodbine', it says. And 'Private Detective', too.

Sometimes it also says 'GONE TO LUNCH'. But that's when I've gone to lunch.

I hadn't gone for lunch on the day that the young guy walked into my office. But then it wasn't lunchtime. If I'd had a clock, then it might have struck ten. But I didn't, and so it struck nine. The young guy had come all the way from England just to seek my help on a case. He didn't tell me that this was the way of it, but then he didn't have to. In my occupation you either *know* things, or you don't. It's an *instinct*, a *gift*, if you like, and some of us have this gift, though most of us do not.

The young guy wore black, but he wasn't Swiss, nor was he Jewish, it seemed. He was a musician, travelling with a band called The Sumerian Kynges, in the company of something called The Flange Collective, a kind of five-and-dime carny that was presently encamped in Central Park. Although he and his fellow musicians had taken rooms at the Pentecost Hotel because, unlike carny folk, all musicians are cissies and don't like the cold weather. And the guy's name was Tyler and he had worries on his mind. And in this town, if you have worries on your mind, you either hit a bar or call your shrink. And if neither of those hit the spot and there is the possibility that the quelling of these worries might only be facilitated by a lot of gratuitous sex and violence, a great deal of trench-coat action and a denouement that involves a final rooftop confrontation during which a villain takes the last dive to oblivion, then you call on me.

If, however, you have Georgia on your mind, then I'd recommend the jazz club down the street.

So the young guy sat down in the chair that I reserve for clients and I poured him a glass of Kentucky bourbon to ease his passage whilst he spilt his beans. His beans, it seemed, were curious beans, beans of an outré nature. In my business I encounter many a curious bean. A curious bean, a wayward sprout and a parsnip in a pale tweed. It's all meat and fish to a guy like me. And I wouldn't have it any other way.

'So, kid,' said I as I tipped him the wink, 'what is it worries your mind?'

The guy sipped his bourbon and looked ill at ease, but ain't that the way with the Brits? It was obvious to me from the start that getting the full story out of him was going to take some time. But I was prepared to take this time as I had to know all the facts. It is of the utmost importance to know all the facts. Facts are the lifeblood of a private eye. As would be a very small whip to a trainer of cheese. So I sat back and let him speak. I let him spill his beans.

'I'm in no hurry,' I told the guy. And anyhow I charge by the hour.

'It is this way, Mr Woodbine, sir,' said the kid, with respect in his voice. 'I have become involved in something so strange, and indeed horrifying, that I hardly know where to begin. Corpses are being reanimated, imbued with souls that are not their own. A plan is afoot to destroy all life upon this world and reduce the planet to a Necrosphere. I have seen these undead with my own eyes and I am not the only one who has. In England an organisation that calls itself the Ministry of Serendipity is involved in the extermination of these undead creatures whenever it locates them. A gentleman called Mr Ishmael told me all about this. And there is something very wrong about this gentleman, but *that* is not why I am here.

'Mr Woodbine, I am here to call upon your expertise. I wish to employ your services to investigate this matter, with a view to identifying the evil mastermind behind it.'

And I made the guy pause there. 'Kid,' I said to him. 'Kid, did I just hear you use the words "evil mastermind"?'

'That you did, Mr Woodbine, sir,' said he.

I paused for a moment, in case he wished to add the words, 'Gawd strike me dead, guv'nor, if I'm telling you a porkie pie', in that manner so favoured by the Brits. But as he did not, I spoke certain words of my own.

'Kid,' I said, 'to use the downtown vernacular, you may well be blowing Dixie out of your ass, but if there is an evil mastermind involved, then you came a-knocking on the right detective's door this brisk morning.' And I topped up my glass and that of my client and let him go rambling on.

He was no literary eruditioner, like some of those famous Brits are. Your Walter Shakespeare, or your Guy Fawkes-Nights. But he could put his sentences together in the right order, and he kept his feet off my desk, so I kinda took a liking to the guy. Clearly he was suffering from a mental condition, chronic schizophrenia allied with an acute persecution complex resulting in audio/visual hallucinations, or was simply a fruitcake, as we in this town would say. But I liked the cut of his shoulders and as business was slack for the time of the year, what with most of the New York criminals being down in Miami at Crim-Con 69, I agreed to take the case and see which way it led.

'Kid,' I told the guy, 'you may have bumblebees in your watering can, but who can say what your uncle keeps in his shed?'

The kid said, 'Eh?' But he knew what I meant. And I knew that he knew I knew.

'So,' said the guy, 'what do we do next?'

'We?' I said. '*We*? Well, I'll tell you what *you* do. You hoik your bankroll out and peel me off two hundred bucks.'

I noted a certain hesitation here, but I put this down to that British reticence and sexual repression that I'd heard so much about. From Fangio, who had once been to Brighton. At a barmans' convention, Toot-Con 55. Fangio had sung the praises of the English women, whom, he claimed, rarely wore anything other than three trained ducks. And wellington boots for the rain.

The guy paid up front with two fifties, three twenties, two tens, four fives, nine ones and a three that I handed back to him. Those crazy Brits, eh, what do you make of them? And they say that *they* won the war.

'Where to?' asked the guy of me.

And I said, 'Fangio's Bar.'

Like I told the guy earlier, I work only the four locations. No genre detective worthy of his ACME sock-suspenders and patent-pending ball-and-socket truss needs more. And once I'd interviewed a client in my office, the next stop was always the bar. It can be *any* bar, let me be clear on that, but it must be a bar. It is the way things must be done, if they are to be done with style. And according to format.

I put the 'GONE TO LUNCH' sign on my door, although you wouldn't have seen that because I do not work corridors, and moments later, as if through the means of a lap-dissolve, found myself in Fangio's Bar.

As it was nearing lunchtime now, the joint was beginning to jump. The uptown chic in natty black and downtown noncer in beige. A cheese-trainer from Illinois, here searching for a venue for Cheese-Con 70.* A couple of Dacks, a McMurdo and a chim-chim-cheree-chim-cheroo. The McMurdo was sitting on my favourite bar stool, so he got the short shrift that was coming to him.

'A bottle of Bud,' I said to Fangio, the fat-boy barman. 'And whatever my client here is having. And put it on my client's tab, as soon as you've written one up.'

'That all sounds rather complicated,' said Fangio. 'Would you care to run it by me again? Or perhaps not so much run as jog purposefully?'

'Not as such,' I said to Fange. 'Especially not on a day like this.'

'This day is a new one on me,' said the fat-boy, with wisdom. 'And I'd just come to terms with yesterday when this one turns up and oh dear me.' And he began to sob.

'Do you need a hankie to dry those tears?' I asked him.

'No,' said Fange. 'I have a hankie of my own.'

'Then stick it in your mouth and bring us over two Buds.'

'I'd quite like to try a cocktail,' said the young guy called Tyler as he leaned upon the bar counter and ogled the ashtrays in the way that strangers so often do.

'Don't get me going on cocktails,' said Fangio, weeping away like a woebegone woman bewailing a badly drawn boy.

'Two Buds,' I said, using the natural authority that God in His infinite wisdom had seen fit to grant me.

'Coming right up, sir,' said the barman.

'Might I ask you something, Mr Woodbine?' said the guy.

I nodded in the affirmative. 'Not now, kid,' I said.

'But it's important. Please.'

'Well, all right. Go on. And don't feel that you have to rush yourself.'

* That's probably enough Cons, now, thank you. (Ed.)†
† Hey, buddy, don't footnote Woodbine – I ain't a footnoted kind of guy.

'All this talking of the toot – it really does help you to solve your cases?'

That was some question and I was the fella to answer it.

'Kid,' I said. 'Kid, over the years Fange and I have talked a great deal of toot in this bar. We talk the toot and we chew the fat.' And as it *was* nearing lunchtime, I dipped into the complimentary bowl upon the bartop and helped myself to a prize gobbet of said chewing-fat. 'It's the way things are done, kid,' I continued, munching as I did. 'You might argue that it is a tradition, or an old charter, or something. But I would argue that it ain't nothing of the sort. It's more of a dynamic symbiosis. Or, more rightly, a symbiotic dynamic. You can't squeeze salt from a billiard ball, no matter how long you soak it.'

The guy looked thoughtful and nodded his head. 'Right,' said he, 'So all this talking of the toot – it really does help you to solve your cases?'

'Ah,' I said. 'Here's our beers. And Fangio's brought your tab.'

'I'm not sure that it really is a tab,' said the fat-boy, presenting us with two glasses of cherry brandy. 'It looks more to me to be something connected with golf. A tee, possibly, or a five-iron-gone-apeshit-crazy.'

I gave the item he'd brought out a stern looking-over. 'Nope,' I said, in the negative. 'That's a bar tab all right. See the words "BAR TAB" printed at the top? That's your guide to its correct identification, right up there in lights, as it were.'

And Fangio smiled, which brought joy to the world. 'God bless you, Lazlo,' said he.

The guy sipped at his cherry brandy and asked me whether it was a cocktail. I didn't want to complicate things and so I nodded that it was, discreetly, without any fuss.

'Tastes just like a cherry brandy,' said the guy. 'But I was asking you about the toot.'

'Kid,' I said, 'we've been through that. And repetition does nothing more than labour a point. It's the way things are done and that's that. I'm on *your* case now, so everything that happens from now on will be pertinent to *your* case. These folk in this bar – pertinent. Those Dacks and that McMurdo lying on the floor—'

'The one who was sitting on your bar stool?' said the guy.

'Same one. All pertinent. What we have to do is to wait here, talking the toot, until *she* arrives.'

'*She?*' asked the guy.

'The dame that does me wrong. You've read the novels, right? *Everyone's* read the Lazlo Woodbine Thrillers, right?'

'From the poignant pen of Penrose? Yes.'

'Well, you must then understand that you must *never* mess with a winning formula. All the big guys know this, which is why they *are* big guys. Right?'

'Right,' said the guy. 'So we sit here talking the toot until the dame that does you wrong turns up. Right?'

'Right.'

'Right. And is this the same dame every time, or a different dame?'

'Different dame.'

'Right,' said the guy. 'Because if it was always the same dame, you'd probably be forewarned that she was going to do you wrong. Right?'

'Right,' I said once more. 'So it would lack for the element of surprise. Which would mess with the format. The dame that does me wrong always furnishes me with some vital clue that is necessary to the solving of the case. But she *will* do me wrong, in that at the end of the chapter she always strikes me hard on the back of the head and sends me down into that whirling pit of black oblivion that all genre private eyes get sent to in that chapter.'

'This chapter, right?'

'Next chapter.'

'Quite so.'

'Don't you mean "right"?' I asked.

'Right,' said the guy.

And then I saw her. And she was beautiful. She breezed into that bar like a bat out of Hell that would be gone when the morning came. But without a hint of the bat about her. By the way she walked I could tell that here was a dame who knew what the sound of one hand clapping was like. And if she wasn't built for the pleasures of the flesh, then Rome was built in a day with a bucket and spade. She was long and blonde and when God designed her, She wasn't kidding around.

The guy nudged the elbow of my trench coat and asked me, 'Is that the dame?'

'I wish, kid,' and I shook my head. 'It's that great fat munter behind her.'

40

Now, I retract that word 'munter'. It's a cruel word, that, and although it rarely fails to raise a titter, that's no need to go using it willy-nilly. Especially in a derogatory fashion.

And especially when referring to Mama Cass.

'Hi there, Laz,' said the legend from the Mamas and the Papas.

I tipped the lady the brim of my fine fedora, told her to pull up a bar stool and park her big butt and join me in taking a drink.

'I can't stay,' said the rather broad broad. 'I need to use the phone. Our limo broke down and we have to get to Woodstock for the festival.'

'I'm playing at Woodstock,' said the guy, 'with my band The Sumerian Kynges. Perhaps you've heard of us – we closed the Hyde Park gig for The Rolling Stones.'

'Don't go getting all bent out of shape,' I told the guy. 'The Rolling Stones closed the Hyde Park gig for The Rolling Stones, and I should know, I was over there on a case. And Mick Jagger let me into the green room. He's a big fan of my work, you see.'

'But—' said the guy.

'It's a true story,' said Fangio. 'Tell him about the kid, Laz, the one who got really stoned on a Banbury Bloater and had to be chucked out of the green room. How uncool was *he*?'

'What?' said the guy.

'What indeed,' said I.

'Woodstock?' said Mama Cass. 'You and your band are playing Woodstock?' But she didn't address this question to me, rather to my client, the kid.

'Yes,' said the kid. 'I think we're on just after you. This is a real pleasure.' And he stuck out his hand for a shake.

But I edged this hand aside. 'Kid,' I told him, 'you're muddying the waters here. Sending the plot off on a tangent. Lazlo Woodbine doesn't do tangents. He's a real straight arrow. He talks the toot, yes, but he gets right on with the job in hand. So kindly step aside and watch how the dame that does me wrong does me wrong. Pay attention, now – it will be an educational experience.'

The guy made a noise that sounded like 'Hmmph' but which might have been 'Yes, sir' in Swiss.

'So,' said Fangio to Mama Cass, 'Woodstock, eh? I've heard tell of this. An outdoor Hippy Life-Affirming Cosmic Celebration. Or as we right-minded Republicans would say, a bunch of them no-good peace-queers and drug fiends smoking reefers and supporting the cockney work ethic.'

'What?' said the guy. And I for one joined him in this.

'Are you for real?' asked Mama Cass of Fangio.

The fat-boy felt at his person.

'That is disgusting,' said Mama Cass.

'It's *my* person,' said Fangio, 'and I'll feel at it if I wish.' Adding, 'And as it's also *my* bar, I can propound right-wing bigotry also, if I so wish. It's the prerogative of the barlord. That and fiddling the change.'

'And skimping on the toilet rolls in the gentlemens' John,' I added.

'That goes without saying,' said Fangio.

'So, where *is* the phone?' asked Mama Cass.

'Now *that*,' said Fangio, '*is* a question.'

'But you *do* have a phone?'

'It depends on what you mean by "have",' said Fange. 'I had measles once, but I'm damned if I know whatever became of them.'

'I had a lost weekend once,' I said to Fange. 'But I'm damned if *I* know whatever happened to *that*.'

'I was with you on that weekend,' said Fangio. 'And I *do* know, but I'm not telling. Being enigmatic is also the prerogative of the barlord.'

'So, no telephone,' said Mama Cass.

Fangio the barman shook his head. 'Don't you just long for the invention of the mobile phone?' he asked. 'Or *cell* phone as we'll call it over here. Because people will use them in prisons, I suppose.'

There was a small but perfect silence.

'My mum predicted that,' said the guy. 'And do you know what? I miss my mum.' And he got a rather sad face on.

'You're going off on a tangent again, kid,' I told him. 'Never take your eye off the ball. Except if you're in a gay pub quiz.'

'But where *is* this leading?' he pleaded.

'Just stick around and you'll see.'

'Oh dear,' said Mama Cass. 'Well, if you don't have a phone here, I suppose I'll have to go elsewhere and look for one. I must get in touch with Mr Ishmael.'

'*Mr Ishmael?*' went the guy. But I silenced him with a raised fist and single look so intense that it could have swallowed a pigeon, beak and trotters and all.

'Mr Ishmael?' I asked Mama Cass. 'Who is this Mr Ishmael of whom you speak?'

'You have a lovely way with words,' said the talented, if slightly overweight, chanteuse. 'Would you care for some free love in the back of the limo?'

'Lady,' I told her, 'in my line of work, I don't have time for love. I have time for danger and time for trouble. And time to talk the toot. But to Lazlo Woodbine, love is a stranger who wears a tweed jacket with ink on its right lapel. And leather patches on its elbows. Which can say so much, whilst still remaining mute, if you know what I mean and I'm sure that you do.'

'Don't get me going on tweed-jacket elbow patches,' said Fangio.

'I won't, my friend,' I told him.

'But this is *free* love,' said Mama Cass. 'It's not like *real* love. In fact, it doesn't really have anything to do with love at all, really. It's more about meaningless sex. It just sounds nicer to call it free love. It's one of those new buzz words, like Flower Power, that the Big Apple Corporation create.'

'The Big Apple Corporation?' I questioned.

'The BAC, that's right.'

'Pray tell me, madam,' I asked of her, 'what do you know of this uptown organisation?'

'Not very much,' said Mama Cass. And she took the cherry brandy from my client's hand and quaffed it away at a gulp. 'They're behind the Woodstock Festival. Although they're very secretive about it and not many people know. I just happened to overhear a conversation that Mr Ishmael was having.'

'That name again,' said I. 'Who is this Mr Ishmael?'

'The backer of Woodstock. The chairman of the Big Apple Corporation.'

'This is news to *me*,' said the guy.

'Be still,' I said. And I meant it. And I showed him that I did.

'Mr Ishmael is the driving force behind the BAC,' continued the ample diva. 'And it was the BAC that came up with not only Free Love and Flower Power, but Peace and Love, Man also. And a good thing, too, because if the BAC hadn't got the Flower Power thing going, me and my band could never have found a record label to take our stuff.'

'You're on Dunhill, aren't you?' I said.

'It's Mr Ishmael's label really. But I must be going. I need to find a phone.'

'It's very cold out,' I said to the girl with the golden voice. 'What say you and I sit here and sink a few Buds, chew the fat and talk about the good old days.'

'You mean memories? Misty watercolour memories?'

'The very same. Can I buy you a beer? My client there is paying.'

'The young guy lying on the floor next to the McMurdo?'

'The very same.' And I hailed Fangio. 'We need some service over here,' I said. 'And none of your service-with-a-smile-without-the-smile.'

'I missed his earlier smile,' said Mama Cass, 'because it was before I came in. But I just bet it brought joy to the world, for it certainly did to me.'

'Sister,' I said to her, 'you know how to talk the toot. Let's crack a bottle of bubbly.'

I ordered that bottle and by three of the clock that ticks out the afternoon it was delivered to us, along with a bar tab that I signed on my client's behalf and a kitten that I petted gently and returned to Fange. Who placed it in a cardboard box to be mailed to our boys in 'Nam.

I filled glasses and toasts were exchanged.

'I have a black eye,' said my client, rising unsteadily from the floor and viewing this in the mirror behind the bar.

'I'll drink to that,' I said.

Fangio excused himself from a crowd of Jimbos who had recently entered the bar and returned himself to my company.

'What very big women,' he said. 'And such deep voices. And they smell a bit iffy, too.'

I noticed my client glance over his shoulder.

'Are you okay, buddy?' I asked him.

'Jimbos,' said my client. 'I told you about them. At The Green Carnation Club. I think they might be undead.'

'But you can't tell for sure because you're not on the drug, right?'

'Right,' said the guy. 'And that wasn't funny, what you said earlier. You weren't in the green room at The Stones in the Park gig. I would have seen you.'

'But you did,' I told him. 'I was in disguise.'

'As what?'

'As *whom*. As Marianne Faithfull.'

'I think I'm drunk,' said the guy. 'I don't believe you actually said that.'

'I didn't,' I said. 'Just keep telling yourself *I didn't.*'

'And add *I must pay Fangio's bar tab,*' said Fangio. 'And, a little while later, when we're all very drunk, you can sing us a song, also.'

'I don't want to,' he said. 'I've been sitting around here for hours now, drinking and lying on the floor unconscious also, although I don't remember how *that* happened. And I'm beginning to believe that Mr Woodbine here is just treading water, as it were, because he is being paid by the hour.'

Things went suddenly quiet in the bar. And outside the sun went behind a cloud and a dog howled in the distance. Same sun. Different dog.

Fangio broke the sudden quiet. 'Out of my bar,' cried he.

'Out?' said the guy.

'Out indeed. Coming in here with your beguiling gypsy ways, disguised as a Swiss abortionist. I can stand just so much and then no more. Like Popeye. And *he's* a sailor!'

'But I'm the client,' said the guy. 'If you chuck me out then Mr Woodbine won't have a case to work on. And I won't come back and pay my bar tab.'

'You fiend in human form,' quoth Fangio. 'Are there any Cosa Nostra in the bar? I must have this man killed.'

'Let's all stop there,' I said, as ever the voice of reason. 'We have all had something to drink and Mr Tyler, being a Brit, cannot be expected to either hold his drink or enjoy the benefits of the American dental system.'

'What?' asked the guy.

'And I,' I said, 'feel that I am perched upon the threshold of a major breakthrough in the case. I am only moments away from this breakthrough and I for one would not wish to be denied this breakthrough, as the repercussions for the case – and in fact for humanity as a whole – are too horrendous even to contemplate.'

'You don't say?' said Fangio.

'Oh yes I do.'

Fangio grinned and said, 'Oh no you don't.'

'Oh yes I do.'

'Oh no you don't.' And Fangio laughed.

'Have to stop you there,' I said.

'But—' said the guy. But I had to stop him, too.

'A major breakthrough is coming,' I said, 'so let us not mess with the method. Mama Cass, is there anything else that you would like to tell me regarding Mr Ishmael and the Big Apple Corporation?'

'I can't think of anything,' said Mama Cass.

'Think *very, very* hard.'

And Mama Cass thought hard. 'There is *one* thing,' she said. 'It seemed a trivial thing at the time, but the more I think about it, and I often do, I think that it might mean something.'

'Would you care to whisper it into my ear?' I asked Mama Cass.

'I certainly would,' said she.

And Mama Cass whispered. And I listened hard to her whispering. And my client tried to listen too, but he couldn't hear because Mama Cass was whispering.

And when her whispering was done, she stopped whispering.

'Your words are sweet soul music to my ears, Mama Cass,' I told her.

'You think it means something?' she asked.

'It has the case all but solved.'

'Case?' said Mama Cass. 'What case?'

'Oh, nothing,' I said. 'A trivial matter. But let us talk about us. You are a fine-looking woman, and I a virile man. What say we jump into the back of your limo and get our rocks off?'

And Mama Cass cried, 'Look, Zulus, thousands of them,' and pointed, and I peered in the direction of this pointing. And then she hit me hard on the back of the head. And I felt myself falling, down, down into a whirling black pit of oblivion.

And right on cue, at the end of the chapter, which worked out perfectly.

41

Frankly, I could do without the blow to the back of my head and the long and horrid fall into that whirling black pit of oblivion, which I always have to take at the end of chapter two in every adventure I have. Frankly, and I use that word again and advisedly, I wish that there was some other way to expedite matters with the *dame that does me wrong*. Because, *frankly*, it gives me a headache. But for we genre detectives, the tried and trusty methods are the ones that get the job done. So I guess that you just gotta take the knocks along with the good times and never say die. And never *ever* change format.

I really cannot impress upon you too strongly the importance of format. A *correct* format, that is. A prize-winning, bestselling format. Correct format has seen me through thick and thin and no matter what kind of inexplicable conundrums I might find myself faced with, I will always stick to format and I *will always* succeed in the end.

And for any of you out there who might have forgotten the format, or possibly speed-read through that paragraph because you were anxious to get to the end of that particular chapter, probably in the hope of some really hot trench-coat action coming up in the next, I will run through the format just the once more and ask that you commit it to memory because it will prove so very important when the time comes.

So, just the once more and no more.

As a nineteen-fifties genre detective I work only the four locations:

1. An office where a client comes to call.
2. A bar where I talk the all-important toot with the barman and meet the *dame who will do me wrong*, who will impart important information, but *will* do me wrong. And strike me on the head to send me down into that black whirling pit of oblivion.
3. An alleyway where I will get into sticky situations (this is where there will be a lot of trench-coat action).

4. And a rooftop, preferably during a thunderstorm, where I will encounter the villain for that final rooftop confrontation. And from which the villain will take that final big tumble to ultimate oblivion.

And that is it. That is how it works. How it has always worked and how it *will* always work. You can call it a tradition, or an old charter, or something, if you wish. But I just call it a perfect winning format.

But why, you might ask, am I telling you this now? Where does me telling you this fit into the format? When would I have time to tell you this? Take my steel-trap mind off the case in hand at the present and tell you all this? When, Laz, when? I hear you ask, and the answer is oh so simple.

Right *now* is that oh-so-simple answer. Now, when I am unconscious, spinning around and around and around in that whirling black pit of oblivion. And I will have to part company with you now, because I think I'm coming round.

Wap! went a mug-load of beer to my mug and someone shook my trench-coat lapels all around.

'Oh, whoa, hold hard there,' cried I, striking away this douser of my person, unhanding their hands from my spotless lapels and making a very fierce face.

'Sorry, Mr Woodbine,' said the kid who was my client, 'but Mama Cass lamped you one on the noggin.'

'That's no excuse to besmirch me with beer.' I was on my feet now and wiping beer froth from my chops. And also from the shoulders of my trench coat. And that was *not* a good thing to be happening. Beer besmirchment of the trench coat. That was a big no-no.

In my profession, which can be likened to life in general, appearance, smartness and suavity, elegance, too, and panache – and style, of course, let's not forget style, and cleanliness, but then cleanliness is a given – all these things make us *us*. Raise Man above the brute beast. Make us what we are.

Why, in my line of malarkey, having a clean trench coat can mean the difference between cutting a dash at a dandy's conservatoire and cutting the cheese in the shed. If you know what I mean and I'm sure that you do. By golly, yes siree.

The kid who was my client was dispatched, at my behest, back to the bar to fetch napkins in order to facilitate trench-coat refurbishment. I did dustings down of myself and perused my situation.

I was in an alleyway. The one to the rear of Fangio's Bar. But it could have been any alleyway. That Brit playwright Wayne Shakespeare once wrote that 'all the world is an alleyway and every man and every woman, a private eye'. And he wasn't talking slash-sleeved turkey for once. And so I perused my situation, fingering the bulge of my trusty Smith & Wesson as I did so, because in my game an alleyway can spell trouble. And one must always remain alert.

But enough of this gay badinage.

I dipped my hand into my trench coat, drew out the trusty Smith & Wesson, turned upon my toes, adopted the position and let off two rounds straight and true. Two bullets spent and two men hit the dust.

One had been crouching upon one of those cast-iron fire escapes with the retractable bottom sections; the other, half-hidden behind a trashcan. Both had sniper rifles and both of these had been trained on me.

Moving with more stealth than a Vatican pimp and more élan than a Lotus, I made my way to the guy who now adorned a trashcan, turned him over with the polished toe of my classic Oxford brogue, taking great care to avoid any trouser cuff/blood contamination, and viewed my erstwhile assassin.

'God dammit,' I said, in a manner that would soon find favour with the villains of dubbed kung fu movies. 'I've plugged me a dame.' And although dames *do* do me wrong, I always feel a little pang of something whenever I have to torture vital information from one, or gun one down in an alleyway.

'Ah! But hey.' And I perused a wig piece. Not a dame at all, but a guy done up as one. A Jimbo. I went through the cross-dressing SOB's pockets to check for any ID.

And at that moment the kid who was my client came out of the rear door of Fangio's and all but hurled when he saw the blood and the body.

'Oh my God,' he wailed. 'You've shot a woman. Oh my God.'

'Be grateful, kid,' I told him. 'I spied them out as soon as I came to consciousness again. I sent you to get tissues to keep you out of the crossfire.'

'Really?'

'Certainly did. And to get these beer stains off my trench coat. And this ain't no woman – it's a Jimbo.'

The kid was looking paler than Typhoid Mary's Triumph Herald, which was a whiter shade of green.

'A Jimbo?' he said. 'One of *them*?'

'Could be, kid.' I emptied the last of the cadaver's pockets. 'No ID. And the body's as cold as an Eskimo's love bite on the Feast of Saint Stephen. Ah now, what is this?' And I drew into the alleyway's light what looked to be a cardboard skull. 'What do you make of that?' I asked the kid.

The kid shrugged and said he didn't know.

'Top-class shrugging,' I said, because praise never costs and kindness comes even cheaper. 'This is a membership card to a very exclusive club. And if there isn't another of these membership cards in the pocket of the other dead boy up there—' and I gestured with aplomb towards the cast-iron fire escape '—then I'll be a Crowleyian cowboy at a Rosicrucian rodeo. Which I ain't.'

'Another body?' went the kid.

'Do try to keep up,' I told him. 'This is a turning point in the case.'

'How so?'

I displayed the card. 'The membership card of a most exclusive club. Perhaps *the* most exclusive club in New York City – Papa Crossbar's Voodoo Pushbike Scullery.'

'Voodoo?' said my client, the kid. With justifiable awe.

'Voodoo,' I affirmed. 'And the way this case is shaping up, it could involve almost any god in the voodoo pantheon – Loco, the god of the forests; Papa Legba, benevolent guardian of the gates; Damballa Oueddo, the wisest and most powerful, whose spirit is the serpent; Maitresse Ezilee, the blessed Virgin, or Ogoun Badagris, the bloody dreadful.'

'Mr Woodbine,' said the kid (my client) with just a smidgen more awe, 'you certainly know your voodoo pantheon.'

'Kid,' I told him, 'in my job, knowing your voodoo pantheon can mean the difference between breaking the ice in the governor's black carriage and breaking wind in a gargler's back passage. And the distinction ain't too subtle. If you know what I mean and I'm pretty damn sure that you do.'

'I am coming to recognise certain patterns,' said the kid. 'I suppose you'd like me to swarm up the wall and fetch down the club membership card from the pocket of the other stiff.'

'You're catching on fast, kid,' I told him. Because charm never dates and time and tide wait for Norse men. 'And give me those tissues before you do, so I can save what I can of this trench coat.'

Now, a bar is a bar is a bar, as an alley's an alley's an alley.

And Papa Crossbar's Voodoo Pushbike Scullery was, though a club, a bar by any other name. And as I do bars as part of my four-location format, the kid and I presumably flashed the membership cards that we had availed ourselves of and now found ourselves inside.

I remembered this place when it had been The Pink Camel's Foot, an all-night topiary joint where landscape gardeners who were down on their uppers would congregate, hoping to hook up with new clients, or just to shoot the breeze with fellow artistes and swap some land-scaping yarns. Those were the days, I told myself. But thankfully they were over.

The décor was of that subtle persuasion that says so much while presenting so little. There had clearly been some degree of graveyard looting involved. You just can't get hold of that many human skulls simply by asking around. And although most morgue attendants will pretty much let you have the run of the place for a couple of Bacardi and Cokes, they don't like to part with the heads of their stiffs because too many questions get asked.

There was a lot of red velvet all around and about and young dames in high heels and sou'westers mingled with the clientele, giving weather-forecast updates and offering love for sale.

I spied the look of bafflement on the kid's face. 'Something troubling you, kid?' I asked of him.

'The weather girls,' said my client. 'What is their relevance here?'

'Aha,' I said in reply. 'You've touched upon a salient detail. You will of course be aware that God takes no direct action in the affairs of Man. He is like Switzerland, neutral. Even when the most hideous atrocities are being committed, God will not intervene.'

The kid did noddings of an agreeable nature.

'But He does intervene in the ways of Man in a subtle and sometimes not so subtle way. God has control of the weather. You will note that you cannot insure your property against earthquake or flood, because these things are referred to on the insurance forms as *Acts of God*. I got involved in a case involving a Mr Godalming once and I learned all about this stuff. God is in charge of the weather, and through the weather He controls the future of Mankind.'

'And *you* know *this*?'

And I nodded. 'And this is a voodoo bar, where practitioners of voodoo congregate. And if they wish to invoke a particular voodoo god to achieve a particular end, they are going to need regular me-teorological updates so that they don't mess around with God's overall purpose. It is never good to contradict God, especially if you know what He has in mind. God doesn't take kindly to that sort of behaviour. And although He remains out of human affairs, do you really think that the folk who get struck by lightning do so through sheer coincidence?'

The kid made a face of some surprise. 'Are you telling me that it might be possible to divine the overall purpose of God by studying weather forecasts?'

'It is a reasonable proposition.'

The kid did further shruggings. And then, it appeared, the barman caught his eye. The barman was a beery guy in typical barman's duds. And but for his black-dyed head with the white skull painted upon it, you might have had him down as any other barman, in all of the bars, in all of the world, and so forth. And suchlike. And so on.

'I recognise that barman,' said the kid.

And I perused the barman and did, likewise, recognise him.

'Fangio,' I hailed the barman. And took myself up to the bar.

The kid followed, but he didn't look keen.

'What is your problem?' I asked him.

'Well,' said the kid, 'if Fangio's here too, then you're going to talk the toot again. And I was really hoping that you'd be getting on with the case, because I have to leave New York tomorrow to head off to Woodstock. Our New York gigs got cancelled and Woodstock is now the next on the list, and it would be really brilliant if you could solve the case today.'

'Solve this case in a single day?'

'You *always* solve the case in a single day.'

'Kid, it might seem like I do, because that's the way that Penrose writes it up. But cases do *not* get solved in a day. These things take time, but things *are* happening. Already we've had the dame that did me wrong do me wrong and me gun down two assassins in an alleyway. Although I admit that you missed that bit. So although I might appear to have been mostly talking the toot, things *are* moving along.'

'So you *won't* be talking the toot with Fangio.'

I tipped my fedora to the kid. 'Only if it's strictly necessary.'

'And do you feel that there might be the vaguest chance that you might solve the case today?'

'Kid,' I told him. 'Kid, I *will* solve the case today. Okay? Just because you are a Brit, and you're in a hurry, I will solve this case today.'

And I felt certain that I would. Because I was Lazlo Woodbine, Private Eye, and I had never failed to solve any case that I had taken on. And although this one had certain outré qualities about it, I felt absolutely sure that ultimately I would triumph. And I would ultimately triumph *today*. And that would be that would be that.

But I was wrong. So terribly wrong.

So terribly, fatally wrong.

42

There were a great many bicycles. But then of course there would have been, because this *was* a Voodoo Pushbike Scullery. There were bikes aplenty, hanging from the ceiling and mounted on the walls and modified to act as tables and chairs and lampstands and whatnots and suchlike.

And these were not all just standard sit-up-and-begs, not a bit of it. Here you had your drop-handlebarred aluminium-framed Claude Butler racers, your Louis Orblanc mountain bikes, your Mulberry drop-head traditionals—

Oh yes, in my career path, knowing your bicycles can mean the difference between knowing your bicycles and not knowing your bicycles. And there I paused and took stock. That wasn't right, surely? There should be a little bit of witty double entendre stylish wordplay jobbie going on there. But oddly there didn't seem to be, and this made me feel most uneasy. I looked all around and about at the weather girls and the clientele.

The weather girls looked sound enough. One of them was singing a song, and I caught the line 'It's raining men, Hallelujah', so all was well with them. But as to the clientele, I viewed them with care.

They were not right at all. They had about them the look of uptown swells, bankers and traders and big city muck-a-mucks. But there was something out of kilter about these chaps.

And I paused once more. Did I just say *chaps*?

And I began to feel most uncomfortable. There was something altogether wrong. I knew who I was – I was Lazlo Woodbine, *the* Private Eye and very likely the last in my line. There wouldn't be any more like me. The fedora and trench coat were, unbelievably, going out of style and a new breed of private dick appeared to be on the cards. No one had really noticed when the world of Sherlock Holmes was no longer the world of Sherlock Holmes. And perhaps no one would notice the passing of the world of Lazlo Woodbine.

In fact, perhaps that world had already passed and I was now nothing more than a cliché and an anachronism. Something that had become a parody of itself. Something, God forbid, to be sniggered at.

I felt a shudder pass right through me, from the snap-brim of my fedora to the leather soles of my classic Oxfords.

I looked at the kid who was my client. 'Kid,' I said to this kid, 'how do I look to you?'

'Uneasy,' said the kid. 'And strangely, now that I look at you, not altogether in focus. You seem a little fuzzy around the edges.'

I took a great deep breath and leaned my elbows on the bar.

'A bottle of Bud and a hot pastrami on rye,' I said to the barman.

'Coming right up, sir,' he replied.

'What?'

'Pardon me, sir?' said the barman.

'Fange,' I said. 'It's me.'

'Well, of course it's you, sir. Who else would it be?'

'But you are serving me my order.'

'That's what barmen do, sir.'

'It's not what *you* do.'

'Ah, have to correct you there, sir. It's not what I *did*, when I was the barkeeper at my old bar.'

'That was only about ten minutes ago!'

'It feels like that, doesn't it, sir? But time passes so quickly. Tick and tock and tick again and the clock doth slice away our lives. But I cannot waste your time with idle conversation, sir. I must attend to your order.'

'Fange,' I said, 'What is happening here?'

'I've no idea what you mean, sir. A hot pastrami upon rye and a bottle of Bud. Anything else, sir? Anything for this young gentleman here?'

'I'll have a bottle of Bud, too,' said the kid. 'But you are certain that you just want to serve Mr Woodbine? You don't want, perhaps, to talk some toot with him?'

'Talk some toot?' And the barman laughed. It wasn't a good look, or a good laugh. And Lazlo Woodbine took his bottle of Bud and poured much of its contents down his throat.

'Are you all right?' I asked the man in the trench coat. 'You really *do* look more than a little fuzzy round the edges.'

'What did you say?' asked Lazlo Woodbine, replacing his bottle on the bar. 'And *how* are you saying it?'

'I'm just opening and shutting my mouth, like I always do.'

'No you're not.' And Lazlo Woodbine took off his fedora. 'You can't do *that*!' he cried.

'Do what?' I asked him. 'What is the matter?'

'You're in the *first person*. You suddenly moved into the first person. You can't do that. *I* work in the first person when I'm working on a case. I made that perfectly clear to you when I agreed to take your case.'

'Oh yes,' I said. 'I believe you did.'

'You're doing it again. Stop it at once.'

'I'm sorry,' I said. 'Oh dear, I've done it again.'

The face of Lazlo Woodbine took on a curious expression.

No! No! No! My face took on a curious expression. *I* am Lazlo Woodbine. And something forceful moved inside my brain. And it said, 'Hold on, hold on, something is happening to you, right here in this bar. Something altogether beyond the world of the outré. Something altogether anomalous.'

And I gritted my teeth and I thought myself back to the centre of things and back into the first person. 'Kid,' I said. 'Kid, who is the greatest private eye of all time?'

'You are, Mr Woodbine, sir,' said he.

'And why are we in this bar?'

'Because *you* are pursuing a case – to find out who is the criminal mastermind behind the plan to zombify this entire world.'

'And only *I* could solve such a case, yes?'

'Only *you*, Mr Woodbine. Because *you* are the greatest of them all.'

'Yes, kid. You're right. You're right.' And I patted the kid on the shoulder. 'Perhaps it was that blow to the skull that the dame who did me wrong dealt me. Or perhaps—' And I looked once more all around and about.

'Perhaps it is something more, Mr Woodbine.'

And I turned and I beheld. A figure of considerable strangeness and one that I did not take to in the slightest. He was short and plump and baldy-headed and if I had to pick out some historical character that he put me in mind of, I would have had to say Dickens' Mr Pickwick. With the hint of a shaven-headed Shirley Temple and a little too much of a bucktoothed Caligula.

And there was an intensity and a density to this being that I found alarming and I took one pace backaways.

I might add that he wore a dapper black suit and carried a silver-topped cane.

'Buddy,' said I, 'I don't think we've been introduced.'

'Mayhap not,' he replied, 'although you have already felt my power,

Mr Woodbine. An uncomfortable sensation, is it not? Trying to define just what you are. Who you are. Whether your existence actually serves any purpose whatsoever.'

'How do you know my name?' I enquired. 'Are you a fan? If so, whip out your pen and I'll give you an autograph.'

'Such bravado, Mr Woodbine. You are putting a brave face on it, anyway.'

'What is going on?' asked the kid who was my client. 'Is this the villain, Mr Woodbine? Should you shoot him now?'

'Priceless,' said the stumpy fellow with the cane. 'Absolutely price-less. One of Mr Ishmael's little puppets. And so far from home. And oh, such thoughts of triumph.'

'What?' went the kid and he clutched at his head. 'You are reading my thoughts. And it hurts. Stop doing it. Please stop doing it.'

And all around and about the kid and myself and the stumpy guy with the seemingly supernatural powers, the clientele of the club just kept on talking with their companions and downing their beers. And the weather girls came and went and Fangio the barman, in his skull make-up, served customers to the right and the left of him, with never a hint of the toot being talked.

And I squared up to the stumpy guy and stared at him eye to eye. 'Who are you, fella?' I asked of him.

And the fella laughed. And it was a terrible, terrible laugh and it rolled all about me and all through me and it made me feel sick at heart. 'I do hate to use such a dreadful cliché,' said the fella. 'And as I have already made you aware that you are now a cliché yourself, it does seem such a shame. But as I have no feelings for you, or indeed your race, let it be known to you that I am Papa Crossbar. And I am your worst nightmare.'

'*The* Papa Crossbar, High Priest of voodoo?'

'And so very much more besides. And one by one I take from this world, take life and replace it with death.'

'It *is* him,' cried the kid. 'Shoot him, Laz. Shoot him now.'

And I reached for my trusty Smith & Wesson. But my trusty Smith & Wesson wasn't there. The stumpy guy that was Papa Crossbar had it. He had somehow lifted it from my shoulder holster. And he twirled it about him on a stumpy little finger.

'I can hear you thinking,' he said, 'all of you, and the din is deafen-ing. You make so much noise, don't you? And so much mess, too, and you stink out this part of the universe. But soon I will be done with all of you. With *all* life on this planet, down to the tiniest noisy little microbe. All will be gone and all that will remain will be a Necro-sphere. A planet of the dead – the totally dead. No bacteria rowdily feasting on corpses, no loudly chomping maggots. *All* will be dead. Each and all. But *you* will not be here to witness that, I am thinking.'

'But why?' I asked. And I took a step back. 'Why would you want to do such an awful thing?'

'Awful?' asked the stumpy Papa Crossbar. 'Awful in what respect?'

'To annihilate an entire race. Eradicate life from an entire planet. Why would you want to do such a thing?'

'Pest control, if you will. Life is *not* universal. Death is universal. This little pocket of life is an anomaly. It ruins the perfection that the universe would otherwise attain. Nasty, noisy, smelly little planet. All must be expunged. All must die.'

'You too?' I asked.

'Oh yes, but in my way, not yours. While I am here, upon this world, I am as you are. As mortal as you but so much more than you. I am Papa Crossbar. And when my work here is done, I will ascend into the darkness to enjoy eternal peace.'

'Might I ask a question?' asked the kid.

'You might, but I doubt whether I will feel inclined to answer it.'

'Well,' said the kid, 'I will ask it anyway, if you don't mind. Because I got involved in all this weird stuff a while back. It was your zombies at the cemetery in Hanwell, I suppose.'

'There have been many and there will be many more.'

'And—'

'And so what does Mr Ishmael have to do with this?'

'Oh,' said the kid. 'You really *can* read my mind. And it really *does* hurt.'

'Indeed. And so I know what you are now thinking. You are thinking that you will try to distract me with some toot so that Mr Woodbine here can strike me down and hopefully kill me by so doing.'

'Hmph,' went the kid.

'No go, I'm afraid. Not that you couldn't possibly pull off such a scheme, but you would have to guard your thinking so well that I could not penetrate your thoughts. And *you* do not have *that* skill. And so goodbye.'

'Are you off?' said the kid, with some bravado. 'Please don't think that you must hurry back.'

'It is goodbye to Mr Woodbine,' said Papa Crossbar. 'This man could pose a genuine threat to me, and so he must depart now from this plane of existence.'

'Not quite yet,' I implored. 'Lazlo Woodbine's time has not yet come. I have years left in me. And my adventures might well enjoy a renaissance. There might even be a TV series made of them. With, perhaps, Robert Culp playing me.'

'Yes,' the kid agreed. 'You can't kill Lazlo Woodbine.'

The being that was Papa Crossbar shrugged. And he did this with a wicked smile upon his face. 'It is goodbye, Lazlo Woodbine,' he said. And he raised his hands. And then he projected. As I had projected, me, Tyler, on the Banbury Bloater drug at The Stones in the Park gig. I knew what it was to project. And just how much power it had. And one moment there was Lazlo Woodbine. And the next moment, there wasn't.

'Gone into the ether,' said Papa Crossbar. 'Will you be next, or will you choose to run?'

And I chose to run and so I ran.

And I ran and I ran and I ran.

43

And I ran back through the streets of New York, to the Pentecost Hotel.

And I felt sick to my very soul and took myself off to the bar therein.

Now, a hotel bar is a hotel bar and they all have points *for* them and points *against*. This one had mostly *points for*. It was *not* Papa Crossbar's Voodoo Pushbike Scullery and it did *not* have Fangio for a barman.

I ordered a Kentucky bourbon, double, on the rocks. And I sat at the bar and I hung my head, feeling very bad indeed.

It occurred to me that it would probably be for the best if I didn't mention to Andy that I had met Lazlo Woodbine, what with Andy being such a big fan of the great detective and everything. He might just be a bit jealous and perhaps ask me why I hadn't taken him with me when I went to visit Laz. And then the conversation might turn to what exactly went on when I did meet Laz. And then I might have to explain, just in passing, that Lazlo Woodbine *had passed*, so to speak. And that, *perhaps*, I was partially to blame for this passing. And it might all get rather messy and embarrassing and there might be some unpleasantness. And Andy might point accusing fingers at me and maybe knot these into fists and throw them likewise in my direction.

So it would probably be better just to say nothing.

But I still felt sick at heart.

It *was* my fault. *I* had got Laz into that fatal situation. I *was* to blame.

And as to Papa Crossbar! Well! So *he* was the super-villain. A black-magic voodoo evildoer. And it was *he*, Papa Crossbar, whose intention it was to destroy every vestige of life on this planet and reduce the Earth to a Necrosphere.

Scary stuff indeed it all was and I knew it all to be true.

And Papa Crossbar *knew* that I knew and so it was odds-on favourite that he would be sending some of his awful minions to butcher me horribly before I passed my information on.

I did nervous lookings around to the right and the left of me. Were any of his awful minions already here? He could read my mind, which was probably why he had let me run – for a bit of sport, because he knew where I was staying. The clientele looked normal enough. But, as I have already mentioned, I have never been able to define exactly what *normal* might be. And so the apparent normality of these folk, these chaps in their business suits and ladies in sweatsuits and pearls, might well belie the awfulness of what they really were.

I became now not only sick to my soul but *frightened*.

I would have to tell someone. Mr Ishmael, that was who I must tell. And he must help me. It was *his* duty to help me. After all, it was he who had got me into this mess in the first place. In fact, it was *all* his fault that I was involved in it. And so it followed that it was really *his* fault that Lazlo Woodbine had come to such a terrible end. But this was really absolutely no consolation whatsoever, so I sat and sulked and fretted and feared and gulped away at my bourbon.

And then the barman sauntered along to me and pushed the bar bill that I had signed for my double Kentucky bourbon on ice (although the ice was complimentary) under my drooping nose. 'This is no good,' he told me. 'You'll have to pay with cash.'

'Of course it's good,' I told him in reply. 'That's my room number. Stick it on my bill.'

'Sir does not have a bill to stick it on, *sir*. Because *sir* is not a resident at this hotel.'

'Don't be foolish,' I said. 'I'm booked in with the rest of The Sumerian Kynges. We're a really famous rock 'n' roll band. You must have heard of us.'

'Indeed I have, sir,' said the barman, adopting that obsequious tone that oh-so-easily becomes sarcasm. 'In fact, I have two of The Sumerian Kynges' albums, one of them signed by Andy, the lead singer.'

'You *what*?' I asked. 'What are you talking about?'

'I am talking about The Sumerian Kynges, *sir*. I am a big fan. But they are *not* staying at this hotel and neither it seems are you. Now, do you wish to pay for your drink, or should I call for the services of the doorman? He is a master of Dimac, I understand, and although he only uses his vicious martial skills in self-defence, it is remarkable how much damage he does to folk whom he clearly believes, although perhaps misguidedly, are trying to attack him.'

'Hold on, hold on,' I said. 'I don't want any trouble. I *am* booked into this hotel. And I *am* one of The Sumerian Kynges. And all of us are booked in here. *But* we haven't any albums out *yet*.'

'Sir would appear to be wrong on all counts there,' said the barman. And he reached down beneath the counter top.

Fearing the arrival of a knobkerrie, I took a cautionary step back. But no such cudgel was brought to light, rather a long-playing record in a glossy twelve-inch sleeve. 'Wallah,' went the barman. 'Doubt *this* if you will.' He held out this album to me and I stepped up and took it from his hands.

The Sumerian Kynges
~ CHEESEMANIA ~

That's what it said on the album cover, all in psychedelic writing in the style of Rick Griffin. And there was a picture of The Sumerian Kynges, wearing kaftans and looking suitably trippy. There was Andy and there was Rob and there was Neil and there was Toby.

I flipped the album over. It was a Greatest Hits album.

'The Smell in the Gents'. 'The Land of the Western God'. 'The 'Two By One Song', not to mention 'Your Soul Will Burn'.

Which I did not.

But I gawped at that album cover. Gawped at it and felt a tad more sick. Well, more than a tad, an avalanche of pukiness. It had to be a hoax of some kind, surely. We hadn't even had a single single out. How could there be a Greatest Hits album? It was a trick, wasn't it?

I pulled out the vinyl record inside. It certainly looked real enough, though.

'Careful with your fingers on that,' said the barman. 'I know there's millions of them about, but that one is mine.'

'Millions?' I said, in a breathless, whispery voice. And I peered closely at that record. And I read the date upon it: 1973.

'It's a fake,' I cried. 'Nineteen seventy-three! It's a fake.'

'No, it's *not*,' said the barman. 'It came out in nineteen seventy-three. I know it's four years old, but it's *mine* and it's signed, so hand it back here.'

'Four years old?' I said. 'Nineteen seventy-seven?' I said.

'Do you know what?' said the barman. 'The Sumerian Kynges *did* stay in this hotel. Way back in nineteen sixty-nine, it was, before my time. That must have been about the time New York was going for the Jewish look and folk were dressing the way you're dressed now.'

I sank down onto my bar stool. But missed my bar stool and fell down onto the floor.

'You're drunk,' cried the barman. 'I'm calling the doorman. He'll make it look like self-defence.'

'No,' I blubbered and I got to my knees. 'Something is very wrong.

It can't be nineteen seventy-seven. It was only nineteen sixty-nine this very morning. The Sumerian Kynges were leaving tomorrow to play Woodstock.'

'I understand they were brilliant at Woodstock,' said the barman, leaning over the bar counter to further enjoy, it appeared, the spectacle of me on my knees on the floor. 'I wasn't there myself. Too young. And The Kynges don't appear in the movie of the festival. Contractual differences, apparently. Which is why The Beatles and Bob Dylan, who also played there, aren't in the movie.'

'What?' I went. 'What? What? What?' It couldn't be true, could it? Nearly nine years had passed. The Sumerian Kynges had become world famous *without me* and had a Greatest Hits album out. Was I dreaming this? And if not, how could it have happened?

I climbed giddily to my feet. 'I need another drink,' I told the barman. 'And I will pay in cash.'

'Happy to serve you, *sir*.'

I paid in cash and happily I had enough. I quite expected the barman to tell me that my money was out of date and thus no good, but he didn't. Apparently American dollars have remained the same for the last one hundred years. Apparently so that if you do commit a bank robbery and get caught and sent to jail, but manage to avoid giving back any of the money, it will be waiting for you wherever you buried it, ready for use when you get out of prison. And not be out of date. It is something to do with the American Dream, Democracy and Freemasons running the world. Or something.

So the barman accepted my money.

And I tucked into my bourbon.

'Has the mobile phone been invented yet?' I asked the barman. 'Or the jet-pack?'

The barman shook his head sadly. 'Shall I call for the doorman?' he asked.

And I shook my head. Sadly. 'No,' I said. 'I will be all right. I won't cause any trouble. Something very weird has happened to me. I must have lost my memory or something. Perhaps I had an accident.'

The barman eyed me, queerly. 'Are you telling me,' he asked, 'that the last memory you have is of nineteen sixty-nine?'

'Yes,' I said. 'It seems so. One minute it's nineteen sixty-nine and I am over on Twenty-Seventh Street. Then I run back here and it's nineteen seventy-seven. How weird is *that*?'

'Most weird,' and the barman nodded. 'Twenty-Seventh Street. That used to be the Detective Quarter, didn't it?'

'Used to be?' I shrugged.

'Nice shrugging,' the barman observed. 'Did you know that *the* Shrugger once got drunk in this bar?'

'I just bet he did,' I said. 'I *was* with The Sumerian Kynges, you know, *really* I was. And we were in New York with The Flange Collective.'

'I've read about that – a sort of freak show, wasn't it?'

'Something like that, yes. I wonder whatever became of it.'

'It closed this very year. The Flange, that was the guy who ran it, retired to Brentford in England to pursue a sacred quest of his – to create The Lounge Room of Christ, to bring about the Second Coming of Jesus.'

'That is, perhaps, a little bit more than I can take in at the moment. Although I do think he might have talked about that. Although it's getting a bit hazy now. But then, I suppose it *was* over eight years ago.'

The barman went off to serve some normal people. I picked up a copy of *American Hero Today* magazine from the bar top and gave its cover a good looking over. It was the March edition for nineteen seventy-seven. I gulped down some more Kentucky bourbon and made a mournful face. What was I going to do now? Where was I going to go? I supposed I could assume that Papa Crossbar wasn't going to have me killed. But, I supposed also, that it was he who had done this to me somehow. Through voodoo? I didn't know, but *somehow*. But perhaps I *was* free of him. Because what was I going to do, expose him? Tell everyone what I knew about him?

What, a mad boy with a defective memory? The more I thought about this, the more it all fell into place. In a weird and twisted fashion.

And I wondered, and I feared, too, just *what* had been happening during these missing years. Was most of the world now dead? How far had the bad things gone? I rubbed my hands at my temples. If I wasn't careful, I might soon become a truly mad boy.

And mad *boy*? Had I aged? That was an interesting one. I took myself off to the toilet, which hadn't really changed much. But for the bowl of flowers and the nail brushes. I examined myself in the mirror. I *hadn't* changed at all. Which meant that although nearly nine years had passed for the rest of the world, they had not done so for me.

So what did *that* make me? Something special? Some*one* special? I liked the idea of *that*. Although I suppose I had always considered myself to be someone special. So this was confirmation, really, wasn't it?

In fact, perhaps God had done this, and *not* Papa Crossbar. I liked the idea of *that*.

And I gazed at my reflection in the mirror. 'I am really, truly messed up here,' I told it. 'My thinking is all out of kilter. I'm lost and alone and falling to pieces.' And I gazed some more at my reflection. But my reflection did not have anything to say on the matter, so I returned to the bar.

The barman was awaiting my return.

'That's him,' he said to the fellow standing beside him. A burly, useful-looking fellow dressed in a doorman's livery.

'I don't want any trouble,' I said. 'If you want me to go, I'll go.'

'I don't want you to go,' said the useful-looking one. 'I have a message for you.'

'You do?' I said, reseating myself. 'Do you think you might pass it to me, along with the double bourbon on the rocks that you have most generously purchased for me?'

'That, I think, can be done.' The useful one nodded to the barman, who returned to his place behind the bar and did the necessary business.

'I'll have the same,' said the useful one. And the same was also dispensed.

My drink was pushed in my direction and I gratefully accepted it.

'Drink up,' said the fellow, and I did so. 'Now then,' said the fellow. 'The message.'

And I said, 'Yes, go on please, the message?'

'Your name is?' asked the fellow.

'Tyler,' I told him, and he nodded.

'Tyler, yes, it is you. He said that one day you would return here and that you would probably be rather confused. And that I was to give you this.' And he withdrew from an inner jacket pocket a very dog-eared envelope. 'I've carried it with me since nineteen sixty-nine. He said you'd come back sooner or later and now you have.'

'Who said I'd come back?' I asked.

'Mr Ishmael,' said the fellow. 'Oh, and he said that the future of humanity rested upon you receiving this letter. And that I wasn't ever to open it, just wait until you turned up and give it to you.'

I looked this fellow up and down. 'And he told you *that*, and you have had the letter in your possession for all these years and never opened it to see what was inside?'

The fellow nodded. 'That is so.'

'And you *really* never opened it?'

222

'No,' said the fellow. 'Never, ever, I swear.'

'But why?'

The fellow made the face of fear. 'Have you ever *met* Mr Ishmael?' he asked.

44

I took the envelope from him and he sighed. Deeply. *Very* deeply, he sighed. And then he made a joyful face and shouted, 'I am free! I am free!' And he ran from the hotel bar. Somewhat madly.

Leaving his drink. To which I helped myself.

'I shouldn't let you steal his drink,' said the barman, 'but I will turn a blind eye to it if you let me see the contents of that letter. That doorman has sat on that letter for so long, like a lady hawk on a nest. It's nearly driven him insane. But he wouldn't open it. He'd been told not to and he did what he was told. Have *you* ever met this Mr Ishmael character?'

'Yes,' I said. 'I have.'

'So open up the letter, let's have a look.'

I glanced up at the barman. 'If you will stand me drinks in this bar until I want no more, I will.'

'It's a done deal.' The barman stuck out his hand for a shake and I shook it.

'Then let's have a look inside,' I said. And I opened the envelope. There was a sheet of paper inside, good quality vellum. And a message, handwritten, upon it.

Dear Tyler (it read)

If you are reading this, then it means that you survived your encounter with Papa Crossbar. And if this is the case, then it means that I chose wisely when I chose you. I have orchestrated your life since you were a child, and for one purpose only: that together we may thwart the plans of the Evil One. You and I, together. Do not return to England. Feel free to call your family and tell them that you are alive, but do not return to England. Your future lies here. There is much that I will explain to you, but not yet. You will not know at this moment what you should do next. So have a drink and give it a moment and it will come to you. As if delivered. As if it was meant to be. I enclose a one-hundred-dollar bill. Use it unwisely.

> *Yours sincerely*
> *Mr Ishmael*

And there was a one-hundred-dollar bill enclosed in the envelope.

The barman examined it. 'It's real,' he said. 'Real as real.'

'And why wouldn't it be?' I asked him.

'Well.' The barman took up the letter *again*. Because he *had* been reading it with me. 'This is pretty far-out stuff. *You* coming in here, thinking it's nineteen sixty-nine. And this letter. I mean, "thwart the plans of the Evil One". That's not the kind of line you hear every day. Except, perhaps, down on East 2001 Street, the Science Fiction Quarter.'

'There isn't *really* a Science Fiction Quarter in New York, is there?' I asked the barman.

'No, not really,' he said.

'I thought not.'

'It's in San Francisco.'

'And that's not true either, is it?'

The barman shook his head. 'Give me a break,' he said. 'I was just trying to big-up my part a bit. If you are some kind of Saviour of All Mankind, then just being in the same room as you and talking to you is probably going to be one of the most significant things in my life.'

'You think?'

'Of course. So when I get to tell my grandchildren that I met you and they say, "So what did you talk about, Grandpop?" I don't want to have to reply, "Nothing. I just poured him drinks." '

'Fair enough,' I said. 'But as I, although I might at times have a high opinion of myself, do *not* believe that I will be a Saviour of All Mankind, I doubt very much whether it matters what you tell your grandchildren.'

'Well, thank the Lord for *that*!' said the barman.

'*What?*'

'Well, I'm gay, aren't I? And the thought that I was going to have to go straight and get married and have children, so that *they* could have children, so I could tell *them* that I met *you*, frankly had little appeal.'

'So it's all worked out okay for you,' I said. 'Would you care for a drink?'

'I would.'

'Then help yourself to the optics as all barmen do.'*

The barman went off in a bit of a huff and I gulped on with my drinking. And I reread the letter and I did a lot of deep, deep thinking.

I really didn't like that bit in the letter about Mr Ishmael having

---

* Allegedly. But hey, come on!

orchestrated my life since I was a child. But the more I thought about it, the clearer it became that he *had* been orchestrating my life from the moment I met him at the Southcross Roads School dance, and from then until now. Which I didn't like one bit.

I drank my drinks, ordered more and paid with the hundred-dollar bill. And I counted my change when I recovered it, because I wasn't *that* drunk yet. Although I was obviously sufficiently drunk as to have forgotten that the barman was supposed to be paying for all my drinks that evening, because I'd showed him the letter. And then I had a bit of an idea. I would phone home. Speak to my mum and dad and to Andy.

That was a good idea.

That was *not* a good idea.

I phoned and I did get through. And I spoke to my mum, who was up even though it was three a.m. English time, hoovering the carpets. But with the Hoover turned off, so as not to wake my daddy, who was no longer working as a roadie for The Stones but now as a roadie for T. Rex.

My mum got all tearful when she heard my voice. And then she told me that I was a very bad boy for not calling for so long and how had it been in prison?

'Prison?' I asked her.

'Your brother Andy said that you had been taken off to prison for being naughty with children.'

'What?' I said. Considerably appalled.

'Well, I was so worried that you were dead or something. And I kept on and on at Andy to find out the truth. And finally he said that you were okay, in perfect health and being well looked after in the psychiatric ward of Sing Sing.'

'Oh splendid,' I said. 'Good old Andy.'

'But I don't see much of him now,' said my mum. 'He mostly lives on his island.'

'*His island?*'

'In the Caribbean. Near Haiti. Andy Isle it's called, I think. He flies there on his private jet.'

And I groaned very loudly.

'You should have stayed in the band,' said my mum, 'rather than getting yourself involved in illegal playground activities.'

'Thank you, Mother,' I said to her. 'And goodbye.' And I replaced the receiver and never spoke to my mother ever again.

And I returned to the bar.

'Are you going to buy me a drink *now*?' asked the barman.

'Yes,' I said and I sighed when I said it. 'Why not? Go on. What will you have?'

The barman helped himself to the drink of his choice, took my money, cashed it up in the register and obligingly short-changed me.

I just sort of smiled at this and said, 'Life.'

'It's a funny old world, ain't it?' said the barman.

'Oh yes,' I agreed. 'I have no idea at all exactly what the purpose of my life has been up until now. Or even if it had a purpose. I am inclined to think that life is totally without purpose.'

'And you would be correct in this thinking,' the barman agreed.

'You think?'

'Of course. Life is a finite entity. Men live, men die, and whatever they leave behind – literature, music, art – will eventually die also. Nothing lasts for ever. All creations have a finite existence, therefore all creations are ultimately without purpose. Because once they have ceased to be, and the memory of them has also ceased to be, it is as if they have never existed. It is *all* without purpose. Well done for noticing it.'

'Thanks a lot!' I said.

'My pleasure. So how do you intend to go about your mission of saving Mankind? You apparently being the Chosen One and everything.'

'I have no idea at all,' I said, downing further bourbon. 'In fact, I have no idea what to do. It feels as if my whole life really *has* been orchestrated and I have absolutely no free will at all. I am just a pawn in some terrible game. Or, more precisely, a puppet, with someone pulling my strings.'

'Nasty,' said the barman. 'That must be horrid. Perhaps you need something to take your mind off all this. A distraction. A hobby or something.'

I shrugged. 'I suppose.'

'You're out of work at the moment, right?'

'Absolutely. I was a musician. And also a private detective. But I'm out of work now and totally lost.'

'A private detective, did you say?'

'I did say that, yes.'

'Well, that's a coincidence. Perhaps *this* is what you need.'

The barman pulled that copy of *American Heroes Today* magazine towards him and leafed through its pages to the small ads. 'This might be what you are looking for,' he said.

He had circled the ad in question.

With a thick-nibbed pen.

> The American Heritage Society is proud to announce that due to Government funding, the 27th Street Private Detective District is to be saved from redevelopment. A number of office placements have been made available to suitable candidates. One remains.
>
> Lot 27. The office of Lazlo Woodbine, Private Eye, missing, presumed dead. Comprising hatstand, carpet, ceiling fan, filing cabinet, desk, two chairs, venetian blind.
>
> To be sold as a single lot. Including also the remaining wardrobe of Lazlo Woodbine, comprising trench coat, fedora, Oxfords, trusty Smith & Wesson, etc.
>
> Eighty-five dollars.

'How much change do you have from your one-hundred-dollar bill?' asked the barman.

And I took out my change and counted it.

'Eighty-five dollars,' I said.

45

Exactly eighty-five dollars! How handy was *that*?

It was indeed a happy coincidence and with its coming I recalled once more that the barman was supposed to be paying for my drinks, and so I let him buy me a few more doubles before I made my way back to 27th Street.

Now, I suppose you might say that I was a wee bit tiddly by the time I got to the famous office where the famous detective had met with his clients before heading off to his other three locations in order to solve his cases. Well, perhaps a tad tiddly, rather than just a wee bit. But I was able to tap on the door without putting my hand through the glass and string sufficient words into sufficient sentences to make myself understood.

The man from *American Heritage* was very nice. He was just going home when I arrived, but he looked quite pleased to see me. He said that if I *hadn't* arrived, then he was preparing to give the whole thing up as a lost cause, auction off the contents of Mr Woodbine's office and let the building be demolished to make way for a proposed detective-themed shopping mall.

'I'm sure the developer will be very pleased when I tell them that someone has agreed to take over Mr Woodbine's business,' he said, 'because it will save them all the trouble of building that brand-new mall.'

I agreed that it was a possibility and asked where I had to sign.

There wasn't much in the way of paperwork involved. And I was certainly never asked any probing or personal questions. It was just 'sign your name on this here dotted line and hand over your eighty-five dollars'. And that was that. And he shook my hand, gave me an official deed to the office and a licence (another *licence*! But this time one that would work in my favour). Handed me a set of keys, told me that the water cooler needed refilling and that if I wished to make a complaint to City Hall regarding the solo saxophonist, whose dreamy rhythms drifted even now through the window, then I would have to do so in writing.

Then shook my hand once more and took his leave.

Chuckling.

Yes, that *is* what I said, *chuckling*. Why chuckling? Well, I have absolutely no idea at all. But that's what he did. Perhaps it was just relief at finally getting the perfect tenant to take over from Laz. Who can say? Not me.

He shut the door behind him and I was left alone. And as it was now getting dark, I switched on the light. And then recalled that the man from American Heritage had also mentioned something about the electricity having been switched off. Although I hadn't really been listening carefully to that bit. So I upped the venetian blind and let what light there was enter the office. It was rather a cool light, really, being composed of a street lamp on the alleyway corner and the flashing neon of a night club called The Engine Room. I sat down in Lazlo's chair – Lazlo's chair that was now *my* chair – and put my feet up on the desk that had also been Lazlo's but was now *my* desk.

And I smiled considerably.

The office wasn't quite how I remembered it. It had been tidied up a bit. And repainted in a colour that I did not know the name of. And the carpet that dared not speak its name had been replaced by one whose name I wouldn't have listened to even if it *had* dared to speak it. So it wasn't *quite* Lazlo Woodbine's office. But it *was* his office. If you know what I mean, and I'm sure that you do. And I thought to myself, as one might think—

HOW COOL IS **THIS**?

I was now, to all intents and purposes and things of that nature generally, Lazlo Woodbine, Private Eye.

HOW COOL WAS **THAT**?
Well cool.

Although, all right, there were certain things that weren't all *that* cool.

The years that were missing out of my life.

The entire horrible Papa Crossbar business.

The fact that I had missed out on fame and fortune with The

Sumerian Kynges and hadn't even got a songwriting credit on the Greatest Hits album.

And that it was *I* who was, let us say, *indirectly* responsible for Lazlo Woodbine vanishing into the ether.

I have not, perhaps, printed this list in order of priority. But these things were *not* cool.

But having this office *was*.

And so I smiled, somewhat contentedly, which is not to say also *smugly*, and thought that what I should do now would be to go somewhere and celebrate my good fortune. Back to the Pentecost Hotel, might it be, to take advantage of the barman? No, it was a long walk back. Across the street to Fangio's Bar, then?

That was a better idea.

The light was now uncertain in the office and I stumbled about a bit, bumping into some things and knocking other things over. But during this stumbling I did come across three things that very much took my interest: a fedora and a trench coat and a trusty Smith & Wesson. Lazlo Woodbine's spares, I supposed. So I took off my coat and togged up, and tucked the trusty Smith & Wesson into an inside trench-coat pocket. The fedora fitted and I knew I looked cool.

And then I left *my* office. Locking *my* door behind me.

And I crossed the street to Fangio's Bar and pushed open that famous shatter-glass door. And Fangio's Bar had *not* changed at all. It was the same woe-begotten dump of a dive, and this I found a comfort. I mooched in with a grin on my chops and hailed the fat-boy barman.

Because there he stood, as large as *Life*, but slightly less glossy than *Vogue*. He wore the look of a man who knew just where he was. And also an eyepatch and cutlass.

'Hello there,' I said to the fat-boy. 'And so we meet again.'

'Arrr, aharr harr,' went Fangio and he rolled his visible eye.

As I was already somewhat in my cups, I felt I was up to the challenge.

'Old war wound, is it?' I asked, approaching the bar counter and hoisting myself onto the bar stool that had formally been Lazlo Woodbine's favourite and would now be *mine*. 'Or is it medieval mouth-music from the mountains of Mongolia?'

'Well, swab me decks,' said Fangio. ' 'Tis you, so 'tis, so 'tis.'

'Give me just one clue,' I asked, 'and then I can join you in this.'

Fangio sighed and did thumbings. To a sign above the bar:

FANGIO'S BAR WELCOMES PIRATES
(It read)

'Oh,' I said. 'I see. Pirates.'

'You see pirates?' asked Fangio, lifting his eyepatch. '*Where?*'

'No,' I said, shaking my head. 'What I said was, I see, *full stop*, pirates.'

'Right,' said Fangio. 'So what will it be, Laz – a tot of rum, a parrot or a flog-around-the-fleet? The last one is a cocktail, before you ask.'

'I wasn't going to. But why are you calling me Laz?'

'The guy from American Heritage drinks in here every day and just popped in for a quick bottle of champagne to celebrate the fact that some sucker, I mean, some *plucky* son of a gun, had purchased the franchise. And you're wearing Laz's spare clothes, so it must be you.'

I was impressed by Fangio's reasoning. But had he just said *sucker*? I glared pointy daggers at him.

'Of course, I *was* thinking of buying it myself,' Fangio continued, 'But I couldn't afford the inflated price. Oh damn.'

'Hold on,' I said. 'Inflated price?' I said. 'Franchise,' I said, also.

'I read in this month's copy of *Detective Franchises Today* magazine that P. P. Penrose was selling franchises worldwide now,' said Fangio. 'He started out with one in Brentford, England, and due to its success he started selling them all over the world.'

'But I bought the office of the *real* Lazlo Woodbine,' I said.

'Which makes *you* the real Lazlo Woodbine now. Doesn't it, Laz?'

'No, it *doesn't*,' I said. 'I can pretend to be. And to be honest I did pretend to be, for a while, in England. But neither I, nor anyone else, can ever be the *real* Lazlo Woodbine. There can only ever be *one* Lazlo Woodbine.'

'And so what do you think ever became of the *one* Lazlo Woodbine?' asked Fangio.

'Ah,' I said. 'Ah.'

'No,' said Fangio, 'it's "arrr, harr-harr". The way that Robert Newton did it in the television series of *Treasure Island*. Newton is *the* Long John Silver against which all future Long John Silvers must be measured. Measured and found to fall short, in my opinion. Arr-harr. Harr.'

'Quite so,' I said. 'But there will never be another Lazlo Woodbine.'

'So what *did* become of him?' asked Fangio.

'A bottle of Bud,' I said, 'and a hot pastrami on rye.'

'Do you want a couple of pieces of eight with that?'

'No,' said I. 'Nor a sunken galleon.'

'Don't go refusing my cocktails before you've tried them,' said Fangio. And he actually went off to fetch my bottle of Bud. So things *had* changed just a little hereabouts.

Fangio returned with a Bosun's Whistle. A cocktail of his very own formulation, he assured me. So perhaps things *hadn't* changed after all.

He did not discuss the matter of immediate payment, so, out of politeness, nor did I. I sipped at my Bosun's Whistle and picked a bit of seaweed from between my teeth.

'I'll bet you can't identify all the different ingredients in that cocktail,' said Fangio.

'I'll bet you'd be correct on that,' I said.

'How much do you bet?' Fangio asked.

'That you are correct and that I cannot identify the ingredients?'

'Precisely. How much?'

'Ten dollars?' I said.

'You pussy. Arr-harr-harr-harr.'

'One *hundred* dollars?' I suggested.

'That's more like it. Shake.' And Fangio extended a hand across the bar counter. 'Sucker,' said Fangio. And chuckling away, as had the man from American Heritage, he stumped off along behind the bar counter upon his newly fitted wooden leg.

Leaving me to ponder one of life's eternal questions.

Why had I not pressed him further to explain about the pirates?

I viewed the clientele of Fangio's Bar. None of them were dressed as pirates. Although I did notice two fellows and a lady sporting wooden legs. But that was not necessarily an indication of piratical leanings. Most who know anything about New York in the nineteen-seventies will know that there was a brief fashion for *bums*. Bums being the American word for tramps. Fanny, apparently, being the American word for bum. The famous bums' bible, *The Autobiography of a Supertramp*, which was written in the nineteen-twenties, had been reprinted, and along with Jack Kerouac's *On the Road* had become *the* thing to read. And in the final chapter of *Supertramp*, the author, who is riding-the-rods on an American train, falls off and loses a leg and *this* caught the reading public's imagination. And many folk went out and had a single leg amputated. Weird, eh? Of course, that kind of thing would not happen today, because the readers of autobiographies are far too sophisticated. And intelligent. And beautiful. And sexy. And—

'Life, eh?' said Fangio who, having served others, had now returned unto me. 'You can't live with it, but you can't live without it. Or is that *women* I'm thinking about?'

'Probably women,' I said. 'I think a lot about women. But I never seem to have sex with any of them.'

'Perhaps you're gay,' said Fangio.

'How dare you,' I said.

'Oh, I'm so sorry,' said Fangio.

'Quite so.'

'I should have said perhaps you're gay. *Ah-harr-harr-harr.*'

'I should think so *too*.' And I sipped at my Bosun's Whistle.

'Getting anywhere near a solution regarding its ingredients? Ah-harr? Ah-harr-harr?' asked Fangio.

'Sadly not,' I said. 'If I can't come up with something soon, I will just have to accept defeat and take the hundred dollars for failing.'

'And that will serve you right.' And Fangio chuckled again. 'Harr-harr-harr-ah-harr,' he went.

And then he said, 'Ah-harr slice-me-membrane and walk-me-plank (also cocktails), there was a guy in here earlier, asking for you.'

'Asking for *me*?' I said.

'That's right. Aar-harr-harr—' and then Fangio coughed. 'I don't know how pirates keep it up,' he said. 'It makes my throat sore. But yes, asking for you. Well, asking for Lazlo Woodbine, Private Eye.'

'A client?' I said. 'Well, if you see him again, you send him over to *my* office.'

'No,' said Fangio, shaking his head. 'I can't do *that*. Oh no.'

'And why not?' I asked, and I downed the last of my Bosun's Whistle and then picked a pair of lady's underpants out of my teeth. 'Why can't you send them to *my* office?'

Fangio beckoned me close and whispered into my ear. 'Between you and me only,' he whispered, '*that* was the *real* Lazlo's format. The four locations. You'll have to come up with your own special format. I'm not going to help you to copy his.'

And I thanked Fangio for his whispered words. And I concluded, in my rather drunken state, that he did have a good point there. I mustn't copy the way Laz had conducted his business, even if I was going to work under his name. And I *was*. I would have to come up with my own special way of doing things. Perhaps, learning by Laz's fatal mistake, not such a *hands-on*, *in-your-face*, *get-up-and-go*, *jumping-directly-into-danger* kind of way of doing things. I would definitely have to come up with my own. Some way to get the job done with no direct danger to myself. Some technique, in fact, that mostly involved sitting down, preferably in the office, or in this bar, and thinking things out. A technique of my own. A technique for Tyler.

The Tyler Technique, that's what.

And I would have ended this chapter right there. At that momentous moment, when I made my momentous decision. But for the fact that Fangio suddenly tapped me briskly upon the left trench-coat sleeve and said, 'Hey, Laz – that's the guy. The one that wants to speak to you. About a case. I think.'

And he pointed and I turned to look. And there he was in the doorway. And I raised up my fedora to the guy.

Because he was Elvis Presley.

46

Well, it certainly looked like Elvis Presley.

But then, how was I to be sure?

Because I remembered Dr Darren McMahon, the Scouse one at the Ministry of Serendipity. So was *this* the *real* Elvis Presley, or just *another* Elvis Presley? Whatever that might mean. But think about *this*. If this really *was* Elvis Presley. And he had a case he wanted Lazlo Woodbine to solve. And I was, for all the world, Lazlo Woodbine now. It would mean that *I* would be solving a case for *Elvis*. How cool would *that* be? *How cool?* I tried to hold on to myself and my composure. I would have to act professionally here. *Keep calm*, I told myself. And so I kept calm. *Very* calm. Very very very calm, I kept. Though really rather drunk.

The chap that might be Elvis Presley caught sight of me and he grinned, with that most-distinctively-Elvis-lip-curl grin, and swaggered in my direction.

And I use the word 'swaggered' without fear of correction. Elvis *was* a swaggerer. He sidled also, did Elvis. In fact he combined swaggering and sidling into a walk that was quite his own. Unique, one might say. So perhaps I shouldn't say that he *swaggered*. No, he swaggered and sidled simultaneously.

He swiddled.

'Mr Lazlo Woodbine, sir?' he said to me, swiddling up and sticking out his hand. He smelled very strongly of 'product', this fellow did, and I found myself almost immediately engulfed by an overall cloud of it. I know folk like to write that in his last years Elvis rarely washed, taking the occasional 'whore's bath' – a wipe under the armpits and around the willy and bum/fanny regions – but *I* can vouch for his cleanliness. It was scrupulous. And so he smelled of 'product'. Of product*s*.

A musky aftershave. A cedarwood-based body lotion over vanilla soap. An olive-essence hairspray that kept those roguish darkly dyed strands* in place and a lily-of-the-valley-flavoured foot powder, which

---

* Elvis was in fact a natural blond, although not a lot of people know that.

ensured forever freshness of the feet. I did not know at the time, and in fact never did find out, that these personal products had all been promoted through a Fifth Avenue advertising agency in which my old chum Rob of The Sumerian Kynges now owned a controlling interest. I'm glad I never knew, really, because I'm sure it would probably have upset me.

'You *are* Mr Woodbine, ain't you, sir?' asked the sweetly smelling swiddler.

I nodded in the manner that suggested that yes, I might be, but who was it who was asking.

'The name's Presley, sir,' said the fellow. 'Elvis Presley – you might have heard of me.'

'I *might*,' I said. Enjoying the moment. A *drunken* moment, it was.

'Help me, Mr Woodbine. You are my only hope.'

I bade the fellow seat himself beside me. And I glanced around at the clientele, who had now all ceased to speak, but not to whisper, and were staring slack-jawed at my would-be client. 'Back about your business,' I cried at them. Firmly, with authority.

'A drink?' I asked Elvis. Because it appeared to be him. The accent was certainly right. And the manner. And the swiddling.

'Well, thank you, sir.'

I called out to Fangio. But not too far, as he was leaning right across the bar counter behind me.

'It is *him*,' whispered Fangio, his big face once more close against my ear. 'It *is* him, isn't it? Say it is him.'

'It *is* him,' I whispered in reply.

And Fangio whistled. Tunelessly. 'Richard Nixon,' he said. 'Right here in my bar. Just wait until I tell the guys at the tennis club.'

'Tennis club?' I said. 'You?'

'I'll have you know that I *do* own a tennis club,' said Fangio.

'*Own* a tennis club?'

'Certainly. It's a thing about yay-long.' Fangio mimed the yayness. 'Made of wood, with criss-crossed strings at the fat end.'

'That's a tennis *racquet*,' I said.

'Not the way *I* use it,' said Fangio.

'Two Bosun's Whistles,' I said to Fange. 'And don't feel that you need to skimp on the speed when serving them up. As fast as possible will do just fine.'

Fangio made the sound that a sparrow will make when pushed through the strings of a tennis club. And went to mix our drinks.

'An honour to meet you, sir,' said Elvis. 'Might I say that you're younger than I figured you'd be.'

'I keep myself fit,' I told him, 'because in my business, keeping yourself fit can mean the difference between serving up a winning storm at Wimbledon and serving time in Sing Sing with a swarm of bees up your jumper.'

Elvis looked at me blankly.

'Yes,' I said. 'You're right, it *was* rubbish. I promise I'll never do it again.'

Elvis looked at me some more. Even more blankly this time.

'Right,' I said. And then our drinks arrived.

'Shall I put these on your bar tab, Laz?' asked Fangio.

'No,' I said. 'Take the cost out of the one hundred dollars you owe me. I give up on these cocktails. I have no idea what's in them.'

'And you never will,' said Fangio. And chuckling once more he took himself off to the cash register.

'Were you just talking the toot, sir?' asked Elvis. 'Only I read about that, in the Lazlo Woodbine Thrillers.'

'You've read those, have you?'

'Well, no, sir, not really. I have them read *to* me.'

'Right,' I said. 'But you need my help. You have a worried mind. And a problem that only Lazlo Woodbine can solve for you. Am I correct?'

'You are, sir, yes.'

I was really rather taken with the way Elvis spoke. He didn't just smell nice, but he was so polite, too. So well mannered. All right, he was rather fat. And I didn't mention this at the beginning of the chapter, although perhaps I should have, because he *had* put on weight. He was now a bit of a bloater. But I didn't mention it, and what with him being so sweetly smelling and so polite, I am not going to mention it. Not even in passing. No.

'So,' I said to Elvis Presley, 'what can I do for you?'

'Well, sir, I gotta problem. I been playing Végas, six nights a week, two shows a day, practising for my big tour. This tour is going to take me all over the world. I never left America before, except to go to Germany for my call-up, and now I'm going to England. And through Europe. And Africa. To Sumeria.'

'Sumeria?' I said. 'Why Sumeria?'

'I don't know, sir. It's on the tour list – New Begrem, Sumeria.'

'Begrem?'

'Yes, sir. But that ain't the problem.'

'You might need me to accompany you on that leg of the tour,' I said. 'In fact, we should probably write out a contract to that effect right now.' And you do have to understand that me saying this was *not* going against the Tyler Technique even before I'd had a chance to put it into operation. Because, come on, I really did have to get to the Lost Golden City of Begrem if there was any chance at all. Didn't I! 'Fangio, fetch paper and pen,' I said.

'Coming right up, sir,' said Fangio. But he didn't move an inch.

'So what, *exactly*, is the problem?' I asked Elvis.

'It's my brother,' said Elvis.

To which I said, '*Your brother?*'

'Not so loud, sir, if you please.'

'I'm sorry,' I said. 'I'm sorry. But your brother – I didn't know that you had a brother.'

'I was born one of twins,' said Elvis.

'Yes, well, I know that. But your twin died in childbirth. I know that, too. Very sad.'

'He didn't die,' said Elvis. 'They took him away. He was a special boy. He *is* a special boy.'

'Have you ever heard of the Ministry of Serendipity?' I asked Elvis.

'Yes, sir, I have. And that Doctor McMahon ain't no brother of mine.'

'But you do know of him?'

'Certainly, sir. He was part of the experiment.'

And yes, I confess, I was warming to *this*. Elvis Presley's twin brother. The Ministry of Serendipity. Part of *the experiment*. Oh yes, I was certainly warming to *this*.

'I will have to ask you to tell me everything as clearly and precisely as possible,' I told Elvis. 'The facts are the most important thing to a detective. Oh, and one more thing—'

'Yes, sir?' said Elvis.

'Not you,' I told him. 'Fange.'

'Yes?' said Fange the barman.

'Clear off,' I said to Fange. 'This is private.'

And Fangio stumped away in a right old grump and a battered tricorn and I spoke on with Elvis.

'Tell me everything,' I said. And he told me everything.

'You must understand, sir,' said he, 'that I only know what I am going to tell you because my daddy told it all to me. After my mummy died—' and Elvis crossed himself, though I never thought he was Catholic '—my daddy took me aside and said, "Son, I have things to say to you, and you'd better listen when I say them." And I listened and so I'm telling them to you now.'

'And very well, too,' I said. And Elvis continued.

'You see, sir, there's a war going on. And I don't mean a war like Vietnam. This war has been going on for ever. Between Good and Evil, God and the Devil.' And I thought back to Captain Lynch and all he had told me when I was young. And I thought that I knew what was coming. And I did. To some degree.

'Good and Evil, God and the Devil,' said Elvis. 'But God, He doesn't war too much Himself. Though the Devil keeps right on. And the bad guys who work for the Devil – black magicians, I tell you, sir, real black magicians.' And Elvis looked at me. Deeply, right into my eyes.

And, if I *had* been gay, well . . .

'Please carry on,' I told him.

'Powerful bad magic, sir,' said Elvis. 'And every century the most powerful black magician performs the most powerful spell there is and causes the Homunculus to be born – a human being with the soul of an unholy one. He's kinda the Devil in human form, but not quite.'

'And how do you and your brother, and indeed Doctor McMahon, fit into this?' I asked.

'It was meant to be me,' said Elvis. 'I was supposed to be the Homunculus.'

'Golly!' I said.

'Where?' said Elvis.

'Never mind. Please continue. Please.'

'I don't know what you know about the Second World War,' said Elvis, 'but it wasn't all fought with tanks and bombs. It was fought with magic, too. And Adolf Hitler got raised into power by black magicians and the SS was a black-magic cult.'

'I have read of such things,' I said. 'And you believe this to be true?'

'I know it to be true, sir. The Nazi magicians were trying to create the twentieth-century Homunculus, Hitler being the nineteenth-century Homunculus. The new one was to be his unholy son. But there were other magicians, all around the world, all waging war in their own ways. And the most powerful of all was in England. Have you ever heard of a guy named Aleister Crowley?'

'Yes,' I said, and I nodded also. 'My father met him once.'

'Your daddy met the Great Beast of the Apocalypse?' And Elvis had awe in his voice and he crossed once more at himself.

And I felt rather good that I had impressed him.

'The British Government,' Elvis continued, 'a secret department of war in the British Government – the Ministry of Serendipity – recruited Crowley to beat the German occult war machine by raising the Homunculus before they could.'

I looked on as Elvis spoke all these words. And I admit that I was pretty slack-jawed. Because you really wouldn't have expected such stuff to come out of the mouth of Elvis Presley.

Would you?

'Mr Crowley was an old man,' Elvis continued, 'but still strong with spells. They brought to him a woman who would be mother to the Homunculus. My mummy. Their idea was simply to beat the Germans to it. And once they had brought the Homunculus into being, they would then kill it straight away, and so void the chance of another being created for another one hundred years.'

'Rather clever,' I said. 'If a little horrid.'

'So, Mr Crowley – he—'

'Had sex with your mum?' I asked.

'Please keep your voice down, sir.'

'So *you* are the son of Aleister Crowley?'

Elvis looked to the right and the left, then nodded. 'Through magical invocation.'

'Well, damn me!' I said.

'That's not really *my* line, sir,' said Elvis.

'Go on, please.'

'I was one of twins, sir, like I told you. The English magicians beat the German magicians in the race to create the Homunculus. And eventually they managed to kill Hitler also and end the war. The Americans did that, sir, not the Brits.'

'Why did it come as no surprise to me that you were going to say *that*?' I said.

'Because you are Lazlo Woodbine and always one step ahead of the game, sir?' Elvis suggested. And I agreed with him. And so he went on—

'It wasn't twins, sir,' said Elvis. 'I have to be honest, sir. On January eighth nineteen forty-five, six boys were born. Because Mr Crowley *was* the Beast Six-Six-Six. Three boys died. I survived, and my brother. And my *other* brother – Doctor McMahon, as he calls himself now.'

'And the actual Homunculus?' I said. 'It's not *you*, is it? And it's not Doctor McMahon?'

'No, sir. It's my other brother, Keith.'

'Keith?' I said, both slowly and surely.

'Keith,' said Elvis.

'Keith,' I said once more. 'Your sextuplet, Keith, the evil Homunculus.'

'That's about the size of it, sir. And I want you to find him.'

'Ah,' I said. 'I see. He's gone missing, this Keith?'

'He escaped, sir, yes.'

'Escaped?' I asked.

'The Ministry of Serendipity intended to kill him at birth, sir, but then someone got to thinking that maybe they should study him instead. Keep him under control and under constant surveillance, but keep him, as their own. For their purposes.'

'And the British Government thought this?'

'The Ministry of Serendipity, yes, sir. So they moved Mummy and Daddy over to America. They were originally from Brentford in London, England, but the Ministry resettled them in Tupelo, Mississippi. My brother Keith was kept a secret – he never left the house. He has ways about him, sir. Horrible ways. Wherever he goes, things die. All things. So my mummy and daddy kept him indoors. And time passed and now I'm kinda famous. Which I hear don't please my other brother Darren too much. And he's kinda angry too that Mummy and Daddy left him behind at the Ministry. You see, sir, they couldn't care for three children – they didn't get much of a Government grant.'

'And so *why exactly* do you want to employ *me*?' I asked Elvis.

'I want you to find my brother Keith, Mr Woodbine. If anyone can find him, you can.'

'This is true,' I said to Elvis. 'So when did he escape?'

'About twenty years ago.'

'*Twenty years?* Haven't you waited rather a long time to report him missing?'

'I guess so, sir. But I guess I thought, like my daddy and my mummy thought, too, that he was dead. We thought that the Ministry of Serendipity men had changed their minds, taken him away and killed him. But he ain't, sir. He ain't dead.'

'How do you know?' I asked Elvis. 'How do you know he isn't dead?'

'Because I saw a picture of him in the newspaper. He's still alive.'

'Let me get this clear,' I said. 'You recently saw his picture in the newspaper? Did it tell you where he was?'

'Yes, sir, I have the address.'

'Then he's not really all that lost, is he? Why do you want me to find him if you already know where he is?'

'Mr Woodbine, sir, this is my brother, Keith. He is at large in the world. He is the most evil man who ever lived, capable of channelling all the powers of Evil through him. He is the Homunculus.'

'Yes, I see,' I said.

'I don't think you do, sir,' said Elvis. 'I don't want you just to find him.'

'You don't?' I asked.

'I don't,' said Elvis. 'I want you to kill him.'

47

Now, to be honest, I *was* having some problems with this.

And I now felt suddenly sober.

It might well have been that I had drunk myself sober. I had heard of such a thing happening, but never actually experienced it myself. I always fell asleep. But I was definitely feeling rather sober now and it was probably down to all that the King of rock 'n' roll had just told me.

And how I was having some problems with it.

With quite a *lot* of it, actually.

Such as, well, that was an awful lot of deeply personal secret stuff that Elvis had just spilled out to a complete stranger. Even if he *did* believe that the complete stranger was Lazlo Woodbine, Private Eye.

And there was a rather big gaping hole in the timeline going on here.

If Elvis was born in nineteen forty-five rather than nineteen thirty-five, as I had otherwise been led to believe, then he would only have been nine years old when he went into Sam Phillips' Sun Studios to record 'That's All Right (Mama)'. And that didn't seem all that likely.

And then there was the matter of him seeing a picture of his brother, Keith, in a newspaper. Surely this would be his *twin* brother. So whatever Keith was pictured doing, folk would have thought it was Elvis doing it. Which might well have had Colonel Tom Parker asking questions. These and other problems I was finding with this.

Ah, yes, and *one* in particular.

And this being that I was Lazlo Woodbine, Private Eye.

And not Lazlo Woodbine, *Assassin.*

'Are you okay, sir?' asked Elvis. 'You look kinda strange. Do you want that I should sing a song or something? I always do that in my movies when folk get that strange look on their faces.'

I stared hard at Elvis and said, 'Do you know any Sumerian Kynges songs?'

And he might very well have said to me, 'Why yes, sir, they're my favourite band.' But happily he didn't. Instead he just shook his head, showering me with a fine film of olive essence. 'There's only one King,' said Elvis. 'And that one and only King is me.'

'God bless you, Elvis Presley,' said I.

'Well, thank you very much, sir,' said he.

'And so then,' I now said, 'I do have many questions that I need to ask you, because things do not tie up as neatly as they might. But I do have to say to you that I am *not* an assassin.'

'But the villain always dies, sir,' said Elvis. 'At the end of every one of your cases. In the final rooftop confrontation. They take the big, long fall to ultimate oblivion. They always do. And that's why I came to you. Most other detectives bring the criminal to justice by taking him to stand trial. But the criminal *always* dies when *you* take on the case.'

'Ah,' I said. And, 'I see.'

'You do, sir, yes.'

'Right,' I said. 'Right.'

'I have the newspaper cutting here, sir,' said Elvis, 'so you can recognise my brother, Keith.'

'I think I'd know him if I saw him,' I told Elvis.

'How, sir?' he asked me. ' 'Cos you ain't ever met him.'

'Right,' I said once more. But nevertheless Elvis pulled from the pocket of his jumpsuit (because he *was* wearing a jumpsuit – white, rhinestoned, big-golden-belted, bell-bottomed-trousered) a rather crumpled-up newspaper cutting. And he flattened out the creases in this with his hands and patted it down on the bar top.

And I viewed the photograph before me.

And then I fell back in surprise.

Although, fair doos, it should not really have been a surprise, should it? Because I am sure, fair reader, that *you* knew who that picture was of.

A rather stumpy-looking fellow, who resembled an amalgamation of Dickens' Mr Pickwick, a shaven-headed Shirley Temple and bad old buck-toothed Caligula of Rome.

Papa Crossbar. That's right.

' "Keith Crossbar",' I read aloud from the text beneath the photograph. ' "New York entrepreneur night-club owner to open brand-new venue – Papa Crossbar's Voodoo Pushbike Scullery Two. 'It is a dream come true for me,' said the colourful man about town, 'combining my favourite hobbies – clubbing, cycling, cooking and the Black Arts—' " ' And there was more, but I didn't bother to read it.

And I weighed up the pros and the cons of the matter. It *was* Papa Crossbar who had dispatched Lazlo Woodbine into the great beyond.

And it *was* Papa Crossbar who was threatening to dispatch everyone on Earth into the great beyond. So killing Papa Crossbar would be at the top of the list of anyone's priorities really. It was right there at the top of mine.

But, and this was a big but, *I* didn't really want to kill anyone. And *I* was determined to stick with the Tyler Technique. Because the Tyler Technique would keep me out of danger.

But – and the ideas were now spinning around inside my sober head – but perhaps I could call upon the services of my brother Andy to do the actual assassination. He had dispatched the Zeitgeist without so much as a second thought, so he might well go for it. And he wouldn't need to take a share of the very large fee I intended to extract from Elvis. He'd probably do it just for the buzz and for a chance to wear the real Lazlo Woodbine's trench coat. Yes, the ideas were certainly spinning around, so I ordered further drinks and Fangio, who had remained throughout my conversation with Elvis, stumped off to prepare them.

'All right,' I said to Elvis. 'I will take on your case. But as you are well aware, your brother Keith is a very powerful being. I have already met him and it will be no easy matter to catch him unawares and assassinate him—' (I couldn't really believe I was actually saying such things and saying such things to Elvis. But as I *was*, I continued) '—so it will be a very expensive case and I will need some money·up front.'

And Elvis now produced an envelope from another jumpsuit pocket.

And he handed me this envelope, and I, in turn, tore it open.

And lo, there was a cheque for ten thousand dollars.

And lo, this cheque found favour in my eyes and brought joy unto my heart. And I was thankful, withal. Blessings unto thee, oh Elvis Presley.

'Many thanks,' I said. 'That's the first couple of days covered, then.'

Elvis rubbed his hands together. 'Thank you, sir,' said he. 'Shall we head for the alleyway now? Or do you want to wait around for the dame-that-does-you-wrong to come in here and bop you on the head?'

'Ah,' I said to Elvis. 'We're not doing it like that any more. That was the old format. That's old-fashioned. Now we have a brand-new nineteen-seventies-style format. It's a more Zen kind of thing. It's not quite as hands-on as the old format, it's—'

And I looked up at Elvis and the blankness on his face.

'Never mind,' I told him. 'I will be doing it *my* way. You have nothing to worry about. You can go back to your rehearsals. You want to be your best for Begrem.'

'But, sir,' said Elvis, 'I took a week's vacation so I could help you out. And I brought this.'

And wouldn't you know it, he had another pocket in his jumpsuit, an inner pocket this time, and from this pocket he produced a pistol. And it was a very big pistol.

'This is a World War Two Colt Forty-Five, just like the one I gave to President Nixon in the Oval Office.'

'Put it away!' I told him. And Elvis tucked it away.

'You still carry the trusty Smith & Wesson?' he asked.

'Yes,' I said. 'But neither of us will be involving ourselves with guns at the present.'

And Elvis gave me another blank look.

And Fangio arrived with our drinks.

'Two Jamaican Longboats,' said Fangio.

'Jamaican Longboats are Wimpy Bar ice-cream desserts,' I told him. 'One scoop each of vanilla, chocolate and strawberry ice cream, topped with glacé cherries.'

'Arr harr-harr! Correct,' cried the fat boy. 'Then that makes us even. Do you want to go for a double-or-quits on the next ones?'

'Of course I do,' I said. 'And bring us some alcohol. We don't want these ice-cream desserts.'

'I do,' said Elvis. Although it was difficult to make out his words as he was already tucking into both Jamaican Longboats.

Fangio left our company and later returned to it in a company of his own. A company of two Avast-Behinds. 'You are *never* going to figure out what I've put in these,' said Fangio.

'I'll just bet that I won't,' I said.

'You're on.'

And we raised the stakes and Fangio went off, chuckling.

I fished a napkin from the chromium-plated napkin dispenser that stood upon the bar top and handed it to Elvis. 'You might need this,' I told him. 'You have a bit of ice cream . . . on your . . . well, everywhere, really.'

Elvis looked somewhat baffled.

'You don't actually do wiping yourself, do you?' I asked him.

'Would you?' asked Elvis. 'If you were me?'

And I supposed I would not.

And so Elvis and I drank on into the night. And I ordered further drinks and failed to identify their ingredients. And at the end of the night's drinking, Fangio handed over the deeds to his bar and told me that I had the luck of a Latvian.

And so I didn't have to stagger back to my unelectrified office. I was able instead to pass out on the floor of *my* new bar.

Which I did, with a smile on my face. Because I had only been Lazlo Woodbine for about twelve hours. And already I was chumming it up with Elvis. Had become ten thousand dollars richer than the nothing I was previously worth. And was the very proud owner of Fangio's Bar.

It was clear that Fate had finally decided to smile upon me, and that my fortunes were already changing.

And so I kipped down with a grin on my chops.

And ne'er a care for the future.

48

And do you know, I sometimes think back to that night in Fangio's Bar as being one of the happiest moments of my life. Really. Truly. And for a man such as myself, who has done so many things, that might sound strange. I had played Hyde Park in front of a quarter of a million people. And made love to some of the most beautiful women in the world. Well, the former, anyway. But that night, in Fangio's Bar, I was happy. Which, I suppose, is why I remember it so well. Because I was never happy again.

I think it may be that prior to that night in Fangio's Bar, my life never had a focus. I might have thought it did and that I had a purpose, but it wasn't true. And I *was* manipulated. And my life *was* orchestrated. But now, for the first time, I acquired that focus, that purpose, that sense of direction. I knew what I was and what I had to do. And I will write more of such things, but not now.

Because something else happened that night. Something that shocked me and set my focus, my purpose, my sense of direction all to the same grim goal.

To destroy the being that called itself Keith Crossbar.

It happened to me while I slept, but it wasn't a dream. I had a vision. The detail was so precise. And I watched every bit of it as if I was watching a television show.

I had a vision of Death that night as I lay upon the floor of Fangio's Bar. Or Tyler's Bar, as it might soon be renamed.

And in this vision I learned the identity of Death.

And Death was Keith Crossbar, brother of Elvis and evil Homunculus.

And I awoke in a sweat.

Which is why I remember the night before with such fondness. Because in the days that followed, things got very grim indeed.

Elvis was asleep on the counter, with his sweetly smelling head resting upon the chromium-plated napkin dispenser. I rose from the floor, clicked my limbs, did stretchings, clutchings at my skull, searchings and findings of my fedora and, at length, quiet stumblings towards the bar counter.

Where I beheld the other King of Kings.

The King of rock 'n' roll.

True, it was a fair old time since Elvis had actually done any real rock 'n' roll and he had long ago sacked Scotty Moore and the other members of his original backing band. But he *was* the King. Elvis was a one-off.

Except, of course, I had now learned that he was anything but. He was one of a three-off. But a *good* one. And he lay there, sleeping like the King he was. And yes, I confess it, I had a little sniff.

And Elvis smelled sweetly even there.

Captain Lynch had once told me about the *odour of sanctity*, which issues from the incorruptible bodies of the saints. He had personally sniffed Saint Bernadette of Lourdes, he told me, and could confirm the smell. She smelled of lilacs.

I had a good old sniff at Elvis. And yes, he smelled of lilacs, too.

And my sniffing awoke the King of rock 'n' roll and I had to back off in a hurry.

Elvis roused himself and yawned and saw me and said, 'Hey, Laz, sir. Have you been awake all night, guarding me?'

'Ah,' I said. 'Yes, I have. I will add that to the bill, if you don't mind.'

'Nope,' went Elvis, and he straightened his hair. 'I was having me a weird old dream there. And my brother was there, and he was Death, and—'

I said, 'Really?' and yawned a bit myself.

'Do you think it might mean something?' Elvis asked.

'No,' I said. 'Don't worry about it. You leave the thinking to me.'

And Elvis made the face of relief. 'I love it when folks say that to me,' he said. 'Colonel Tom, or the movie director, or some Jimbo that the manager of Caesar's Palace has had sent up to my room.'

I opened my mouth, but then closed it again. We wouldn't go into *that*.

'I could do breakfast,' said Elvis. 'Peanut butter and banana-stuffed French toast with cinnamon butter and maple-beer syrup, washed down with strawberry shasta.'

'Sounds delightful,' I said. 'Do you think you could get it delivered?'

'Am I Elvis?' said Elvis.

And I agreed that he was.

And so Elvis made a phone call from the phone that Fangio had denied all knowledge of to Mama Cass. Or perhaps he'd had it installed later, in case any other rock icons needed to use it. Elvis, for instance.*

And soon as you like, Elvis and I were chowing down upon peanut butter and banana-stuffed French toast with all the trimmings and the strawberry shastas.

And I rather enjoyed mine. And Elvis clearly enjoyed his. Because he telephoned for further helpings. And then Fangio came down in his dressing gown and Elvis made another call for even more breakfast.

'I don't normally do my own phone calls, you understand, sir,' he said to me, 'but as this *is* a special occasion.'

'And it is for me, too,' I said. And it *was* – breakfast with Elvis. But I *wasn't* happy any more. I just had too many things all gnawing away at my mind.

'So,' said Elvis, when finally done with breakfast, 'are we going to my brother's night club now? So you can lure him onto the roof and send him on the long and final journey down?'

'Ar-harr,' went Fangio. 'Can I come too and watch that?'

'Ah, no,' I said.

'Do you mean "Ah-harr, no"?' asked Fangio.

But I just shook my head.

'So what is your plan, Mr Woodbine?' asked Elvis.

'Well,' I said. And I made a face suggestive of deep thinking. 'This is not something that can be rushed into. It will be necessary to set up a surveillance network. Plot your brother's every move. Work out graphs and pie charts. Get sample opinions from the general public. Do market research into key areas, which may need re-examination to determine prime targets. Define—'

'Why are you reading from the copy of *Advertising Executive Today* magazine on the bar counter?' asked Fangio.

'Shut up,' I said to him.

'Oooh,' went Fangio. And he mimed the holding up of a handbag.

'We can't just go in all guns blasting,' I said to Elvis.

'Why not?' asked the King of rock 'n' roll.

'Because, for one thing, I am not certain whether it can be *proved* that your brother has actually broken any laws. I know I've seen him do—' And I cut myself short. I didn't want to mention what had happened to Laz to Fangio. But regardless, I couldn't *prove* anything. Not, I agree,

---

* Everything makes sense when you give it sufficient thought. Doesn't it?

that it mattered, as he was going to have to be killed. I just didn't really want to be around when the actual killing was done.

'That's no reason not to shoot him,' said Fangio. 'It sounds like he's a wrong'n. That's good enough for me.'

'So do *you* want to do the actual shooting?'

Fangio stuffed peanut buttery stuff into his face. 'Not as such,' he said. 'But if you want him throwing out of this bar, then I'm your man.'

'I will bear that in mind.'

'Why doesn't Elvis shoot him?' asked Fangio. 'It's a family affair, after all. As Sly Stone used to say when he drank in here. Before I threw *him* out.'

'Uh uh,' said Elvis. 'I can't kill one of my own, no matter how evil nor intent on the extermination of all human life they may be.'

'I'll just make a note of that,' said Fangio. 'Not that anyone I tell will ever believe you said it.'

'Mr Woodbine must do it,' said Elvis, 'because this will be Mr Woodbine's greatest ever case. The one everyone will remember him for. And be forever in his debt—'

'Hold it there while I get a pencil,' said Fangio.

But Elvis continued, 'This case will be *the* case for Lazlo Woodbine. And who but Lazlo Woodbine *could* solve this case? My evil brother must be tracked to his secret lair and destroyed. And the world will be saved and all the world will honour Lazlo Woodbine for saving it.'

'Got it,' said Fangio, raising a pencil. 'One more time, if you will.'

But Elvis shook his head. 'Mr Woodbine will deal with this,' he said. 'And he was right – I must return to Vegas and prepare for my tour. I will leave this case in the safe hands of Lazlo Woodbine.'

And he reached out a hand to me and I shook it.

And Fangio stuck his out for a shake, but Elvis did not shake his.

And then Elvis said, 'I have your address, Mr Woodbine. I'll have further money sent on. And you know my address – keep me informed, if you will. And thank you, sir. The whole world will thank you when this is done. But I can thank you now.'

And then he sort of bowed. And did that thing where he whirls his arm about and goes down on one knee. And he produced from *another* pocket a silk scarf, and this he hung about my neck. And then he swiddled from the bar. *My* bar. Like that.

Just like that.

Elvis had left the building.

And I looked at Fange.

And Fangio looked at me.

And we shared a moment. An *Elvis* moment. And it was a special one, too.

'Who was that masked man?' asked Fangio.

'Why, don't you know?' I said. '*That* was the Lone Ranger.'

And then we both laughed and shared another moment. And I came almost close to being happy, but not quite.

'So what would your plan be now, Laz?' asked Fangio. 'If you are no longer going for the four-location format, how do you intend to deal with this Case of Cases, this Case to End All Cases, this Ultimate Case, this Case Beyond—'

'Shut up!' I said to Fangio. 'I'm thinking.'

'Do you wish to indulge in further pirate repartee? Or do some more guessing-the-ingredients-of-cocktails humour? Or should we simply talk the toot and see what comes to pass?'

'It's a Woodbine format thing, talking the toot,' I said.

'I'll miss that, then,' said Fangio, sadly.

'Oh, don't worry, you'll have plenty to think about, training for your new career.'

'My what?' asked Fangio. 'I mean ah-harr-harr-harr. My *what*?'

'New career,' I said. 'Don't forget, I own this bar now, so you can consider yourself sacked. And I'll take over behind the bar. Where I can think about this case in peace. Dawn of a new era and dawn of a new format, eh? Lazlo Woodbine, Private Eye/Barman. Hold on, it's coming to me – Lazlo Woodbine, Private Barlord. A pint, a quip and another case solved.'

'Please tell me you're joking,' said Fangio.

'I am,' said I. 'But not entirely. I wish to employ my newly developed Tyler Technique to this case. Which, I agree, will be the Biggest Case That Ever There Was. It would appear to be my fate to deal with this evil being that is the brother of Elvis. So, Fange, today will be the dawning of a new era in crime detection. And it will all begin here. What is today's date, by the way?'

'The sixteenth of August, nineteen seventy-seven,' said Fangio.

'All right,' I said. 'And so this is the date that people will always remember. As the day *I* took on the Ultimate Case.'

And yes, folk *would* remember that date.

And I'm sure *you* know why.

49

'What do you have in the way of cocktails?' I asked of Fangio.

The fat-boy did blinkings of his patchless peeper. 'Won't you be heading off to have a showdown with the bad guy?' he asked me.

I made major tutting sounds. 'Mustn't go rushing into things half-cocked,' I said. 'These matters take time.'

'Well, some things never change, then,' said the barlord-for-now. 'The original Lazlo Woodbine used to make his cases last and last.'

'What are you implying?' And I raised an eyebrow, but lowered the brim of my hat.

'Oh, nothing.' Fangio did innocent whistlings. 'I'm *not* suggesting that as you are being paid by the day, it might be in your interests to keep the case going for as long as possible.'

'Such a thought has never crossed my mind,' I said. And I made the face of one appalled. Which, added to my raised eyebrow and lowered brim, presented Fangio with a formidable impression of outraged innocence.

'Hm,' went Fangio. 'But hey, I *am* interested – exactly how does this Tyler Technique of yours work? You just sit about doing nothing and hope that something will happen – is that it?'

'It's much more complicated than *that*.' And I waved the barlord on his way with an order for cocktails and quickly.

I sat on my favourite bar stool and gave this matter some penetrating thought. The Tyler Technique had not as yet been tried and tested, so it might take a while to perfect. And if I *was* getting paid by the day, and I *was*, then these days would not be wasted. They would be spent bringing the Tyler Technique to perfection. And with it the case to a satisfactory conclusion. And, pleased with the logic of this, I awaited my cocktails. And yes, I did mean cocktails in the plural.

And eventually Fangio returned with cocktails in the plural.

'A Round-of-Chainshot, a Dead-Man's Chest and a Bloke-on-the-Blower,' said Fangio.

'There's only two drinks here,' I told him.

'Correct,' said the barlord. 'The Bloke-on-the-Blower *is* a bloke on the blower – a guy on the telephone, for *you*.'

'You see, the Tyler Technique is already kicking in,' I told the Doubting Thomas of a barlord-for-now. And I went off to answer the phone.

And then I returned to Fangio.

'Where *is* the phone?' I asked him.

'Right here,' said the barlord-for-now. And he presented me with a big black box about the size of a house brick. 'It is the portable, or *mobile*, phone. It was just invented this morning.'

'This morning?' I said. 'And you already have one?'

'Not just me,' said Fangio. 'Folk all over the city. So I suppose that August the sixteenth nineteen seventy-seven will indeed be a date to be long remembered, just as you predicted.'

I made certain grumbling sounds but answered the phone anyway. I had to rest it on the bar counter because it was so heavy and then shout into it.

'Who is this? I shouted.

'It's Elvis,' Elvis shouted back.

'What can I do for you?' I shouted.

'Nothing,' shouted Elvis. 'I just wanted to try out this new mobile phone that I got today.'

I made certain other grumbling sounds. 'Where are you now?' I shouted into the portable telephone.

'Home in Graceland.'

'That was quick.'

'I travelled through one of the new teleportation booths. They just went "online", as they say, today. So I suppose this date will be forever remembered for that.'

'Teleportation booth?'

'On the corner outside Fangio's Bar. It looks a bit like a telephone booth, but more futuristic.'

'Right,' I said. And rolled my eyes. This was clearly a wind-up.

'Well, have to say goodbye now, Elvis,' I said. And with some sarcasm, 'Have to test out my new jet pack.'

'Did yours arrive today, too?'

I switched off the portable phone.

And pushed it across the bartop to Fangio.

'Teleportation?' said Fangio. 'Ah-harr-harr. And jet packs? What a historic day this is turning out to be.'

'Yes indeed,' I said and I tucked into my Dead-Man's Chest. And presently pulled a digital watch from between my teeth.

'Perhaps this is the dawn of the New Tomorrow that we have been promised since back in the nineteen-thirties, when Hugo Gernsback edited *Amazing Science*. Not to mention *Future Scientist Today* magazine.'

So I didn't mention it.

'Well,' I said, 'it's been a long time coming. Let's be grateful, eh?' And giving my eyes another roll, just for the Hell of it, I downed the rest of my Dead-Man's Chest. And at least I did *not* pull an iPod from between my teeth. Which was something.

'Well,' said Fangio, 'I can't keep chatting here all day. Have to open up the bar for business. I do hope that delivery comes soon.'

'And what delivery might this be?' I asked. As this was now *my* bar.

'The microwave oven,' said Fangio and he stumped away.

I downed my other cocktail, gave up on identifying its ingredients, took myself away to behind the bar counter, cashed up 'No Sale' on the publican's piano and helped myself to some fifty-dollar bills.

And then I thought I'd go for a walk. And that is what I did.

The folk on 27th Street were looking pretty spivvy. Today they mostly favoured silver jumpsuits with Dan Dare-style flared shoulders and platform-soled boots. Hairstyles were combed up very high and slim little sunglasses worn. I watched as a solar-powered dirigible crossed the sky and marvelled just a little as a hover-car moved by.

'New York,' I said to myself. 'When New York takes to a fashion, it *really* takes to a fashion.' And then I spied the teleportation booth.

There was a bit of a queue formed beside it. And I joined the end of this queue. Just to have a look-see, you understand. *Not* to do anything purposeful. And not to do *anything* involved with the case I was on. I was sticking with the Tyler Technique for now. What would happen would happen, and as long as I was in the right state of mind when it did happen, then I would benefit from it happening. So to speak.

A guy at the head of the queue now entered the booth. He spoke into a sort of grille, received instructions, inserted money, pressed certain buttons. Then there was a buzz and a flash and a puff of smoke and the guy had vanished away.

'Now *that*,' I said to a lady in a straw hat, who was before me in the queue, 'is *very* clever, don't you agree?'

'We've had them on my planet for years,' said the lady.

'On *your* planet?' And I viewed the lady. Her skin was quite grey and her eyes rather black. 'You are not from *this* planet?'

'I am from Planet Begrem in the Sumerian Constellation. Haven't you been watching the news? Our ambassador landed his craft upon the White House lawn this morning and made first contact with your President.'

'It's true as true,' said a fellow before her in the queue. 'A fellow in a weather dome, with a zero-gravity briefcase. August sixteenth, nineteen seventy-seven. This date will go down in history, eh?'

And I agreed that it probably would and got in a right old grump.

And presently all the folk in the queue before me had vanished away in little puffs of smoke, and I found myself standing before the teleportation booth.

'I wonder how this works,' I wondered, into the little grille.

'Please place a fifty-dollar bill into the slot provided,' said a strangely mechanical voice. And I shrugged, and having nothing better to do, fished out a fifty-dollar bill and slipped it into the slot provided.

'Where to, sir?' asked the artificial voice.

'I don't know,' I said. And I didn't.

'Have to hurry you, sir,' said the voice. 'There are other people waiting behind you.'

'Yes, get a move on,' said a different lady in a different straw hat. 'I need to go to the toilet.'

'This isn't the queue for the toilet,' I told her.

'The toilet in Graceland.'

'*Graceland?*' I said.

'Graceland it is,' said the voice.

'No, hold on—' I said. 'I—'

But there was a buzz and a bang and a flash.

And I vanished off in a puff of smoke.

And I appeared in a kitchen.

It was a rather attractive kitchen, really. All mod cons. All well beyond mod, really. There *was* a microwave oven, although I did not recognise it as such then. And what I did not recognise as a plasmascreen TV a-hanging on the wall. And a computerised food-synthesiser and a device for peeling potatoes that involved the transperambulation of pseudo-cosmic anti-matter. And a Teasmaid.

And a large black lady, who looked like the cook in the Tom and Jerry cartoons. And she was frying up peanut butter and banana on French toast in a frying pan about the size of a dustbin lid.

And I gave this lady a bit of a shock through my unexpected and sudden arrival.

'Oh Lordy, Lordy, Lordy,' said this lady, as it was still permissible to say such things back in nineteen seventy-seven. 'By the laser-lav of Lady Raygun, Queen of the Pan-Galactic Ukulele All-Stars! Where did you spring from all of a sudden?'

'New York, New York,' I told her. 'It's a wonderful town.'

'And what you doin' of here?'

'No purpose whatsoever,' I assured her *and* myself. 'I am *not* here on a case.'

'A zero-gravity briefcase?' she asked, and she flipped the frying pan by means of remote control.

'A detective case. I am a private detective. The name's Woodbine, Lazlo Woodbine,' and I added, 'some call me Laz.'

'Well, pleased to meet you, Mr Woodburn.'

'Wood*bine*,' I said.

'Wood*bine*,' she said. 'But you'd better hightail it outta here. This is Masser Elvis's kitchen. And Masser Elvis don't take too kindly to strangers in his kitchen.'

'Elvis is a friend of mine,' I said.

'Elvis is a friend to all Mankind,' said the black lady. And she crossed herself above her ample bosoms. 'The Pope says Masser Elvis is the Blessed Second Come.'

'The Pope says *what*?' I asked, in some surprise.

'That Masser Elvis is Messiah Elvis. Praise the Lord and pass the phase-plasma rifles in a forty-watt range. Lordy Lordy.'

'Right,' I said. As I was wont to do on such occasions. 'And when *exactly* did the Pope say this?'

'About half an hour ago. He teleported in from the Vatican to take lunch with Masser Elvis. That's what I'm cookin' up here.'

'Hm,' I went. 'This is all most unexpected.'

'Maybe for you, Mr Widebum, but not for the rest of the world.'

'I think the rest of the world may take my side on this issue,' I said.

'You think?' And the black lady diddled with some futuristic-looking contrivance that was strapped about her wrist. And the wafer-thin (mint-coloured) plasma TV lit up like the Fourth of July. Or the fifth of November, back home.

'I am standing here, outside the gates of Graceland,' said a TV news reporter. And there he was, doing that very thing. 'Where myself and news teams from all around the world and thousands of followers of Elvis are gathered.' And the TV camera panned around and there were indeed thousands gathered around Graceland. And there were news crews and police cars and ambulances, too. 'For this momentous day,'

258

the TV news reporter went on. 'Within Graceland, his Holy Fatherness Pope Keith the First is at this very moment issuing the private blessing and sorting out all the complicated paperwork that will confirm Elvis as the Second Come. And usher in the End Times. For which all we Christian folk rejoice. Praise Jesus, praise Elvis. Amen. Lordy Lordy.'

And I looked at the black lady.

And the black lady looked at me.

And I said, 'No, this isn't right.'

And then she hit me with the frying pan.

And I found myself falling down and down into the whirling black pit of oblivion that nineteen-fifties American genre detectives always fall into at this time.

Which was definitely *not* supposed to happen.

50

And then I awoke to find Elvis looking down at me.

And he was dabbing at my brow and singing.

And he was singing 'The Smell in the Gents''. And *I* wrote that. But he sang it very nicely. And Elvis smiled and said, 'Are you all right, buddy? You took a bit of a tumble.'

And I lifted up my head a tad and felt the lump on the back of it.

'Your cook welted me with a frying pan,' I said. 'And although that looks very funny on TV, it doesn't half hurt in real life.'

And Elvis said, 'Lo, you are healed.'

And I said, 'What?'

And the Pope who was standing nearby said, 'It is a miracle.' And added, 'Lordy Lordy.'

'It is a *what*?' I said. 'No, it's *not*!'

'Elvis has raised him from the dead,' said the Pope, 'as he formerly did Lazarus.'

'He never did,' I protested. 'I was just unconscious.'

'You were dead,' said the Pope. 'I saw you at it. You weren't breathing.'

'I was *too* breathing. I was.'

'Delirious and no surprise,' said the Pope. 'This is the final proof I needed to confirm your divinity, O Holy One.' And he fell to one knee and touched the hem of Elvis's jumpsuit bell-bottom garment ending.

'Hold on there,' I complained. 'This is all some mistake. *All* of it. And a very big mistake, too.'

'How did you get here, sir?' asked Elvis.

'I teleported,' I said, 'from the same booth-thingie that you did. From the corner near Fangio's Bar.'

'Never heard of such a place,' said Elvis. 'It sounds like some den of vice, where shameless women and wanton men meet to engage in acts of filthy congregation.'

'It's not quite as much fun as that,' I said. 'But it's my bar now, so I might think about giving that a go.'

'Antichrist!' cried the Pope, and he whipped out a cross from his papal robes and waggled it at me with menace. And I stared into the face of that Pope and *then* I saw who he was.

For it was indeed Keith, though Pope Keith he called himself.

Keith, the brother of Elvis.

'Oh my God!' I shouted at Elvis. 'It's *him*!'

'The Pope,' said Elvis. 'Show some respect, sir, please.'

'It's *him*,' I said. 'And I'm *me*. Elvis, don't you know me?'

'I don't think we've made acquaintance, sir. My name is Elvis Presley and—'

'It's *me*, Elvis – Lazlo Woodbine.'

'Lazlo Wormwood more like,' said the Pope. 'The Evil One himself.'

'*I'm* not the Evil One,' I shouted, rising as I did so to shake a fist or two. '*You* are the Evil One. The Homunculus. The Evil Twin of Elvis.'

'Twin?' said the Pope.

'Well, brother then. I know who you are.'

'An auto-da-fé,' said the Pope. 'The public burning of a heretic. That would begin your Earthly reign with a big media event, O Holy One.'

Elvis nodded. 'It would,' he agreed.

And as he nodded I smelled him.

I didn't mean to smell him. I wasn't doing furtive sniffings, not like I had done earlier that morning. I just sort of smelled him because his smell came wafting all over me. It positively engulfed and took to drowning me. And Elvis no longer smelled of all those nice things.

Elvis smelled of sulphur.

Elvis smelled of brimstone.

'It's *you*,' I said. 'You lied to me. You tricked me somehow, I don't know how. But it's *you*. You are the Homunculus.'

'I think you've been drinking, fella,' said Elvis, and he took me by the trench-coat lapels. And I tried to struggle, as well I might, but Elvis *did* know karate and he flung me rather hard, right across the room, and I bounced off a rather hard wall at the end.

'Handcuff him,' I heard Elvis say to someone, 'and we'll get him ready for that burning automobile thing.'

'Auto-da-fé,' said Pope Keith.

'That,' said Elvis. 'Yeah.'

And big hands were laid upon me fiercely. And someone else welted me hard.

And I awoke once more from that whirling black pit of oblivion.

To find to my surprise and, I cannot emphasise this enough, my *absolute horror*, that I was now in the garden of Graceland. Lashed to a post and surrounded by sundry combustibles. And cameras were trained upon me. And Pope Keith was intoning something in Latin and waving a burning torch (of the kind so beloved of villagers when they storm the castle of Frankenstein). And I was very upset by this turn of events and took to voicing my protests.

And Pope Keith ceased his intonations and called for someone to tape up my mouth. And this that someone did.

Which considerably increased my panic and caused me to come near to all but peeing myself. Which I might well have done had not a sudden and quite ludicrous thought entered my head: that I should save my pee until the Pope lit the combustibles, in the hope that I could pee out the flames. It's funny what you think in times of crisis, isn't it? Although I didn't think it funny at the time.

'The dawn of a New Age,' I could hear the TV news reporter saying, over the Pope's resumed Latin stuff. 'The Final Age. The Glorious End Times. When the Second Come will defeat the powers of Evil and lead us all – well, we Christians at least – to Paradise.'

'Mmph mm mmm,' I went. Which meant something along the lines that a big mistake was being made here. And please would someone kindly untie me as I dearly needed the toilet.

And then Pope Keith chimed in with, 'Burn the heretic. Burn the Antichrist.' And wouldn't you just know it, this cry was taken up by the assembled multitude and chanted again and again and again.

Which rather drowned out my mumbling of, 'Mmph mm mmm.'

And the chanting sort of turned down a bit in volume, as it might do in a movie when someone has something to say over it, and I heard the TV news reporter say, 'And the winner of our Light Up the Antichrist for the Lord competition is – oh and this is something of a surprise – the actual brother of the heretic–Antichrist himself. And he's here with us right now – let us give a big Second Come Graceland welcome to Andy.'

And the chanting ceased and cheering began.

And I looked on at Andy.

Well, sort of *down* at Andy. Because I *was* atop a goodly heap of combustibles. And Andy appeared, making his way through the cheering crowd. And he looked pretty good, did Andy, older now, of course, but still slim and with all of his hair. And very fashionably dressed in the chicest of silver jumpsuits, all sequinned, and just like the look that we had in those early days of The Sumerian Kynges. My brother! And I breathed a sigh of relief. Through my nose. He had come here to save me. Good old Andy. And I copped Andy a wink. And Andy winked at me.

'Andy,' said the TV news reporter, shaking Andy by the hand, 'and tell us all the truth now. This is *not* a happy coincidence, is it?'

'Well, no, Keith,' said Andy. *Another Keith!* 'Actually, I did not *win* the competition. I *bought* the competition. I have put twenty million dollars into the Elvis Messiah Fund to promote the Second Come. Indeed, finance His own situation comedy show on TV.'

And the crowd took once more to cheering. And I looked on all forlorn.

'Let's hear it even more for Andy,' crowed the TV news reporter. 'A true American hero.'

I might have managed, 'A *what?*' had I been able to speak. But as I could not, I fought even harder to free myself and made a mental note that if by some miracle (and that *was* what I was going to need) I did get out of this mess, then I was going to beat seven bells of Bejabbers out of Andy at the very first opportunity.

'Let's hand over that flaming torch to Andy,' said the TV news reporter man. And Pope Keith did the jolly handing over.

And Andy took that flaming torch and raised it high above his head and cried, 'For Elvis,' and then plunged it down into the combustibles that were all piled up most high about my feet.

And the combustibles did what was natural to them. And smoke and flames rose up all around me. And if I'd ever had any doubts about commending my soul to the Lord, I lost all of those doubts right then and I prayed for forgiveness to the *real* Lord Jesus. And put in just a *little* word with God that if He would like to break His rule of non-involvement in human affairs just this once, then I for one would not hold it against Him. Perhaps, I suggested, a mighty thunderstorm to staunch the flames. That was in His remit, thunderstorms. I'd be fine with a thunderstorm about now. And then the flames reached my feet and ankles and I couldn't think any more.

All I could do was scream.

And I *could* do *that*. Because the excruciating pain brought sufficient power to my jaws to burst the tape that bound my mouth. And I screamed most loudly.

And I glimpsed the TV news reporter through the smoke and flames, beckoning to someone to tape me up again. Because my screaming was drowning out his commentary.

And suddenly amongst the smoke and flame and agony that was my existence came fellows clawing their way towards me, trying to fan the flames away from themselves and stuff things into my mouth. And I wasn't having *that*. And I wrenched my head from side to side and tried to avoid them. And the flames were rising higher. And I was suddenly aware that one of these fellows was now well ablaze too and he sort of flung himself towards me in a rather futile bid for escape. And the bottom of the pole I was lashed to was burning away. And he fell against me and I reared backwards and the pole snapped and we both toppled back and down and out of the roaring flames.

And I suppose it must have looked to those who viewed the conflagration from the front as if we had simply vanished into the flames. Which must have been why no one came rushing round to roll me back into the fire.

And I was fast, believe you me. I rolled over and over and I managed to free myself from the pole and get my hands under my feet and use my teeth to gnaw away the knots. And all that kind of stuff. And the guy who had tried to stuff things into my mouth was howling on the ground, somewhat on fire. And I went over to him and didn't half put the boot in!

And then I kicked off my boots, because they were still on fire. And then I looked all around and about. And having assured myself that I was unobserved, I took to my blistering heels and I fled.

I knew that I couldn't escape from Graceland. Yet. There were too many people. I would have to wait until the crowds had melted away. As crowds will do, when all the excitement is over. And so I crept back into Graceland mansion, snuck upstairs and hid myself in the bathroom. There was a TV in there, too, of course, so I switched that on, with the sound turned ever so low.

And I watched that terrible bonfire. And my own brother dancing around in front of it. And Elvis and the Pope having a knees-up, too. And the crowd all cheering. It was all most unpleasant, I can tell you, and it upset me no end.

And I lowered the lid on the toilet and sat down upon it, broken-hearted. What had happened today? I asked myself. This was all insane. And Elvis was the Antichrist, for surely that was what he was. Was I hallucinating? Was this all some awful drunken dream, brought on by too many of Fangio's nautical cocktails? That was a possibility. But it was all too real. Too detailed. And I couldn't wake up. Nor could I do any of those impossible things that you can do in dreams. Especially in those rare dreams when you know you're dreaming. Those lucid dreams.

So, *not* a hallucination.

And *not* a dream.

Then what?

I didn't know. But I knew that I was angry. And I knew that I was sore. *Very* sore. My feet were badly blistered and my wrists were red raw. This was real enough. But how could it be? I just had no idea.

And then I heard voices. So I switched off the TV and hid myself behind the shower curtain in the bath. And I saw the bathroom door open, and Elvis come in. And shut the door behind him, lock it and drop his trousers, for he now wore a T-shirt and a pair of tracksuit bottoms. And he raised the toilet lid and settled himself down upon the toilet.

And I drew from my inner trench-coat pocket the trusty Smith & Wesson and I emerged from hiding.

And Elvis looked up from his ablutions. And the startled look on his *big fat face* was almost comical. Almost.

'Well, well, well,' I said to Elvis. 'Matters adjust themselves. To my advantage this time.'

And Elvis now had a look of horror on. And he blubbered, 'How?' And he blubbered, 'Please don't shoot me.'

And then what with the sound and the accompanying pong, it was clear that he *had* pooed himself.

And I relate that here because I was *really, really* angry.

'Second Come?' I said. 'The Messiah?' I said.

'It's not what you think,' said Elvis.

'*Not what I think?* You claim to be Jesus. You had me burned at the stake.'

'But you live. Is this not a miracle? Bow down now and give thanks and I will say no more about it.'

'*What?*' And I waggled my pistol at Elvis.

'Please don't shoot.' And he waggled his hands and he pooed a whole lot more.

And I fanned at my hooter and said, 'You thoroughgoing rotter. I should shoot you dead right here and now.'

And Elvis grinned a sly little grin. 'But you cannot, can you?' he said.

'Oh, I can,' I said. 'And I should.'

'I don't think you can.' And Elvis was now arising to his feet.

Which exposed certain parts of himself that I really had no wish at all to see. Although, if I had been gay . . .

'Sit back down,' I told him. 'Sit back down and shut your mouth.' And I cocked the trusty Smith & Wesson and pressed it to his forehead. Just to show him that I meant business. And that I might well shoot him if I had a mind to.

Well, I might.

And I would have been justified in doing so.

Because he really *did* have it coming.

And I hesitated for just a moment and considered that yes, perhaps in this world now turned all upside down, I had a duty to shoot him. For the good of all Mankind.

And Elvis looked up at me. Directly into my eyes.

And then a dire look flashed over his face. And he clutched at his heart. And he groaned. And he floundered. And he fell.

Before me, right on the mat.

Stone dead.

51

'Well, pardon me for saying so,' said Fangio, 'but you have only yourself to blame. Women and cheese don't mix. They are an unhealthy combination.'

'What did you say?' I asked him. Coming to, as it were, in Fangio's Bar.

'Your wife,' said the barlord. 'That's what.'

'My *wife*?' And I did many double takes. I felt as if I had awoken suddenly from a dream. Or been brought to the surface of some murky-watered lake with a great big rush and a good gulp of air. And I said, 'What is this?'

'What is *what*?' asked Fangio. 'There's a whole lot of whating going on.'

'This,' I said. And I pointed to the back of my left hand. 'I've got a tattoo. When did I get a tattoo?'

'Oh, you're not going to start all that again, are you?' said Fangio. 'Because you'll only go getting yourself banged up in the booby hatch again. And although I know that "being in therapy" is oh-so-very-nineties, it does keep you away from this bar. And I do remain quietly confident that one day I will win it back from you.'

'Slow down. Slow down. Slow down,' I said. 'I am in some confusion here. But *not* mad, understand me? I haven't gone mad. *Say it*, if you please.'

'You haven't gone mad,' said Fangio. And I'm sure he *tried* to put some conviction into his voice.

'I'm sorry,' I said, 'but I'm having a bit of a moment here. I'm a little confused. And you did say *wife* to me a moment ago, didn't you?'

'Hatchet-faced harridan,' said Fangio.

'Excuse me?'

'Heaven-faced honey-bunch?' Fangio suggested. And then he looked me squarely in the eyes. And I could see that he'd aged. He'd aged again. By at least another ten years. Perhaps nearer twenty.

And I said, 'Oh no, not again.'

'You've lost your memory again, haven't you?' asked Fangio. 'I bet you don't even know what day of the week it is, do you?'

And I shook my head, rather sadly.

'Or what year?' asked the barlord.

And I shook my head once more.

And Fangio now shook *his* head. 'So go on,' he said, 'what is your last memory? What is the last date you remember?'

I must have got a fearful look on then, because Fangio told me not to worry and that he wouldn't turn me in to the men in white coats again. And I told him that the last date I could remember was 16th August 1977.

'Ah, that terrible day,' said Fangio. 'And today is the twentieth anniversary.'

'Terrible day.' And I said those words very slowly. '*Twentieth* anniversary.'

'The death of the King,' said Fangio. 'The death of Elvis Presley.'

'Ah,' I said. And, 'Yes, but that *was* all for the best, you know.'

'For the best? But I'd hoped to get free tickets, for when he was going to play Carnegie Hall.'

'As the new Messiah?' I said.

'As the King of rock 'n' roll. What a tragedy that was. And he was in this *very* bar, that *very* day. Did you know that?'

'Yes,' I said, 'because I was here, too.'

'You?' said Fangio. 'You were never here that day. You left here the day before that, said you had some pressing business down South. But twenty years, though. You suddenly can't remember the last twenty years of your life?'

And I clutched at my aching head. Because my head, which *hadn't* been aching, was certainly aching now.

'I remember *that* day well enough,' I told Fangio. 'That terrible day. With the teleportation booths and the flying saucer landing on the White House lawn and everything. And the Pope confirming that Elvis was the Second Come and—'

And I looked at Fangio. And he had a certain look upon his face. A look that said so much without there being a need for words. So to speak.

'No teleportation booths?' I said. 'No flying saucers? No Elvis being made the Second Come?'

'Only Elvis dying on his toilet,' said Fangio. 'A tragic way to go. A heart attack, they say it was.'

'It *was* a heart attack,' I said. 'And I should know because—' But then I said no more. And hunched somewhat over my drink.

'What is this I'm drinking?' I asked the not-quite-so-much-of-a-fat-boy-as-he-used-to-be-but-twenty-years-older barlord.

'*Spritzer*,' said Fangio. 'Welcome to the nineteen-nineties.'

I did burying of head in hands and lots of groaning, too.

And Fangio brought me another spritzer and patted me on the shoulder. 'So you really can't remember anything about the last twenty years?' he asked. 'Nothing at all? You're kidding me, right?'

'No jet-packs?' I asked.

'No jet-packs.'

'I think things might be coming back just a little,' I said. Because odd things were beginning to stir in my head. Memories, perhaps? Returning, perhaps? I took a peep into the mirror behind the bar. And this time I *had* aged. But not in a way that I found too terrible to behold. I looked pretty trim, somewhat greying at the temples, but it was a dignified look. But if twenty years of my life were missing— 'You did say *wife* to me, didn't you, Fangio?' I said.

'If you can't remember her, then perhaps it's all for the best,' said the barman. 'She cost you plenty in the divorce.'

'*Divorce?*' I said. 'Oh no. I actually get a wife. Which *must* mean that I finally got some sex. But I can't remember her or the sex and I've got a divorce. That is *so* unfair.'

'Be grateful,' said Fangio. 'I remember her and she was a stinker.'

'Not nice?'

'Dog rough.'

'Oh,' I said. 'And when did I marry her?'

'You really can't remember, can you?'

'I'm not doing this for effect. When did I marry her, Fange?'

'Thirtieth of August, nineteen seventy-seven. You met her here in the bar. The two of you were drunk, both being so upset about the death of Elvis. And you both had the tattoos done.'

I examined the tattoo on the back of my left hand. 'It's Phil Silvers as Sergeant Bilko,' I said.

'You asked for Elvis.'

'But it doesn't look anything like Elvis. It's Phil Silvers as Sergeant Bilko.'

'You were drunk. She was drunk. The tattooist was drunk.'

'And so I got Sergeant Bilko?'

'I'd never tried tattooing before . . .' Fangio's voice trailed off. 'You should see what your wife got. Or perhaps you shouldn't. I think it is what started her hating you, really.'

'Hating me? I see. Do you think I had any sex at all during my marriage?'

'You never mentioned to me about having any. And I think you probably would have mentioned it if you had.'

'And I think I probably would have, too.' And I gulped down my spritzer. 'This tastes disgusting,' I said. 'What is it?'

'Would you care to guess? We could have a bet on it. I think I've figured out where I've been going wrong with my betting, all these years.'

'All good things must pass,' I said. Philosophically.

'So anyway. You split up with her after she stabbed you.'

'*What?*'

'Repeatedly. In the gut area. Lift up your designer T-shirt and have a look.'

And I beheld that I *was* wearing a designer T-shirt. Not that I had previously known what a designer T-shirt was. Although I suppose I must have, because I probably bought it. Unless I had a lovely girlfriend who had— But probably not. So I upped this designer T-shirt and now beheld the multiple scarring and stitching-up marks on my gut area.

'Oh my God!' I cried out loud. 'I'll bet *that* hurt. I am *so* glad I do *not* remember that.'

'Your memory will probably return.'

'I do hope *not*.' But it *was* returning. And fast. And I grabbed at my skull and squeezed it hard between my hands and howled.

And twenty years' worth of memories returned to me. Twenty dismal years of me trying to scrape a living as a private eye. As if sleep-walking. And I realised that during those twenty years I had not been able to remember what had gone on before. All the horrible stuff involving Elvis's Homunculus brother, Keith. It was as if I had just returned from a hypnotic trance at the hand-clap of an evil hypnotist.

'You remember *now*?' asked Fange.

'It's all coming back,' I said. 'But how, I don't understand.'

'You'll figure it out, I'm sure. By the by, now that you're returning to normal, did you get me those tickets you promised me?'

'Tickets?' I said. 'That I promised?'

'For The Sumerian Kynges Thirtieth Anniversary Tour. It's thirty years since they played their first professional gig on Ealing Common with The Flange Collective.'

The Flange Collective? That felt like a lifetime ago. 'That feels like a lifetime ago,' I said. 'They're all still alive, I suppose.'

'Depends on what you mean by "alive",' said Fangio. And there was a certain something in his voice as he said it. A certain gravitas, perhaps.

'I know *exactly* what I mean by "alive",' I said. 'I mean, as opposed to dead.'

'Ah,' said Fangio. 'You certainly haven't recalled everything yet, then. I know a lot of people think it's just a lot of talk and conspiracy theory nonsense. And I know that for the last twenty years you have been telling me that it's all nonsense and that you don't believe in it and nor should I. But I *do* believe in it.'

'Believe in *what*?' I asked.

'The Undead thing,' said Fangio. 'The Dead-Walk-Amongst-Us thing.'

'*That*,' I said, in the tone known as leaden. 'I believe in *that*.'

'Sudden change of mind,' said Fangio. 'You've been making public statements for the last twenty years that the whole thing is a communist hoax.'

'I have *what*?' And more terrible memories returned. I *had* done that. I really had. I had literally become the spokesman for the There-Are-No-Undead-Amongst-Us lobby.

'Oh my God,' I said, and I hung my head once more. 'Oh my God. I was manipulated. Hypnotised. Drugged. I don't know what. But somehow I have been controlled for twenty long years. And before that, on the day that Elvis died, I was in some kind of trance. That has to be it – some mind-controlled drug-induced brainwashed trance. Or something.'

'Or something,' the barlord agreed. And I am reasonably sure that at this point he would probably have gone off to serve another customer. If there had been another customer. But there were no other customers in Fangio's Bar. There was just him and me in that bar.

So he stayed.

'Business not too good?' I asked.

And Fangio sighed. 'Not since you closed the bar to everyone except yourself,' he said.

'Oh dear,' said I. 'And when did I do that?'

'At the time of your divorce. Which came after just the three weeks of marriage. But let's not return to that topic of conversation, eh?'

'Let's not,' I said. 'But I am now awake from that terrible twenty-year walking nightmare of a life. That's half of my life nearly, all wasted away. I can't believe it, it's too terrible. But I *do* believe in the undead.

And I want you to tell me all about what *you* know of them. And I want you to take the "CLOSED" sign off this door and reopen this bar for business.'

'Praise the Lord!' cried Fangio, throwing up his not-quite-so-podgy fingers. 'Praise the Lord, Lordy Lordy.'

'And never say "Lordy Lordy" again,' I told him.

And Fange promised that he never would.

And Fange left the shelter of his bar counter, crossed the floor (rather smart trousers he wore, and the wooden leg was only memory), reached the door, turned the 'CLOSED' sign to the 'OPEN' side and returned to from whence he had come.

'A job well done,' said Fangio. 'And welcome back, Laz. It has been a very long time.'

'It *has*,' I agreed. 'And I am very angry about this state of affairs. Someone has been playing awful games with my life, and I'm damn sure I know who. And I will do something about it and about *them*. You see if I don't. Okay?'

'Okay,' said Fangio. 'But you did of course say that the reason for your last twenty years of mostly inactivity was because you were perfecting the Tyler Technique. Does this new-found positivity mean that you have now perfected it? Or is it a by-product of the nineties Zeitgeist? The post-yuppie work ethic?'

'Tell me about the undead,' I said to Fangio. 'And get me a proper drink. And get one for yourself. And we'll both have doubles. Okay?'

And Fangio did as I bade him to do.

And then he settled himself down upon his side of the bar and he told me things. And these things were terrible things.

But I had to be told them and so I listened.

Quietly, like this.

I listened.

52

'There's a lot of different versions of this story regarding the undead,' said Fangio. 'Some say the whole thing started here and others say it started there. No one is exactly sure where and when it all began, but there are a growing number of informed and intelligent folk who *do* believe it. And folk have been piecing things together. And folk talk in bars. And I listened to these folk. And I have been listening to folk during the last ten years, in this bar, having meetings, while you have been out at *your* meetings propagandising to the contrary on this matter.'

I made certain groaning sounds. 'Please continue,' I told him.

And so Fangio continued.

'Legends say that it started in Vietnam, but researchers have found anomalies that date back as far as the First World War. There was the case of a man named Billy Balloon, a Punch and Judy man in Edinburgh. He went off to fight for his King and his country, and returned to join the family business and perform as a Punch and Judy man. And he is remembered in the annals of Punch and Judy men as being one of the greatest that ever there was. But the mystery of it is this: he had his arms and his tongue blown off during that dreadful war, so how could he work the puppets and do all the voices as well?'

'My father told me this story,' I said to Fangio. 'He told me that as a child he'd been taken to see Billy Balloon's Punch and Judy show. And later, when Billy died, my granddaddy told him the story. But he didn't know the truth. Do you?'

'He was dead,' said Fangio. 'He died at the Somme. But his comrades didn't know that he had died. They thought he had been terribly wounded, but had survived his injuries.'

'But he was dead? Was it a dead man that my father saw perform the Punch and Judy show?'

'A dead man,' said Fangio. 'By force of will, by utter determination, he refused to let go of his physical body. He clung on to it. He urged it back into animation. But he had no arms. And he could not speak.'

'So how did he work the puppets? And do the voices?'

'He didn't. Not physically, anyway. He didn't touch the puppets. Those puppets climbed up onto the little stage of the Punch and Judy show tent booth and performed and spoke by themselves.'

'He brought the puppets to life?'

'He was undead. His soul had left his body back in the Somme. What remained was the force of his will. Witches have their familiars, animals with the souls of demons that do the witches' bidding. In the same way, he had his puppets. He conjured into those puppets the souls of departed comrades. How many millions died in the First World War? How many lost souls wandered those battlefields?'

I felt little shivers run through me. This was sinister stuff.

'Oh,' said Fangio. 'A customer. And my first, other than yourself, in twenty years. Please pardon me while I serve him.'

And off he went to do that very thing.

And I did some thinking on what he had said. It was that thing about souls again. That thing upon which the creation of the Homunculus was based. The Punch and Judy man had somehow cheated Death, in that although he had died and his soul had left his body, the being that was *him* had somehow remained there, by sheer force of will. And this will-being had reanimated his own body. A dead body. But what about those Punch and Judy puppets? The souls of fellow soldiers animating the bodies of puppets? That sounded rather horrid. But then perhaps it was better than being in your own rotting corpse lying unrecovered on some foreign battlefield, awaiting your call to salvation or otherwise. As an option, perhaps it wasn't too bad a one. Although how had Billy Balloon managed to achieve it?

'He was outside this world,' said Fangio, as if reading my thoughts. 'Sorry if I startled you there, but you were probably going to ask me how Billy Balloon managed to instill the souls of his war buddies into puppets. Yes?'

'Yes,' I said. 'So how did he do it?'

'He was outside this world. The world that we understand. The world of the living. That is the only world that we, the living, understand, insofar as we *do* understand it. But it's all that we know anything about. Beyond that? The Great Mystery. Our rules no longer apply. What the dead are capable of, we the living do not know. What really goes on in Heaven or Hell we only can speculate on.'

'This is rather deep stuff for you,' I said to Fangio.

'Sir,' said Fangio, 'I am a barlord. We can do deep and we can do shallow. We do what we are called upon to do. That is our skill. That is our gift. That is why we became barmen.'

'Good grief,' I said. 'Then it is a vocation? Like joining the priest-hood?'

'Precisely. Though somewhat deeper and more mystical than being in the priesthood.'

'I will never look at you in the same light again,' I said.

'It would be oh-so-simple to stick in a little bit of *shallow* here,' said Fangio, 'but I will resist the temptation and carry on with the deep stuff.'

And that was what he did.

'So,' he continued, 'a dead man walking and orchestrating the movements of puppets imbued with the souls of his dead companions. He achieved his goal. He wanted to make his family proud of him, maintain the family traditions. And he did. And when he had done so, he gave up the ghost, if you like. He let his long-dead body finally find peace in the ground.'

'It's a sad story,' I said. 'But uplifting, in a curious manner.'

'Quite so. But what comes later is not quite so uplifting. We have the Second World War. Which, I am assured, was not just fought with conventional weapons, but also with magic. A great battle of Good against Evil. And this led to the creation of the Homunculus. Do you know what that is?'

'Actually I do,' I said. 'I know all about the Homunculus.'

'There is much rumour,' said Fangio. 'Some even claim that he is the brother of Elvis, who was one of six children, the magical sons of the English magician Aleister Crowley.'

'And how do you feel about this idea?' I asked Fangio. As it now appeared certain that Fangio had no recollection of the conversation that he had overhead two decades before, in this very bar, between myself and Elvis Presley.

'I poo-poo this idea,' said the barlord. 'How about you?'

'If you poo-poo it, that is good enough for me,' I said. Because I did want to learn more. 'Please continue with your most interesting narrative.'

'The Homunculus,' said Fangio. 'As with the reanimated corpse of Billy Balloon, the Homunculus is outside of our world. He exists in a manner that we do not understand. *Cannot* understand. His motives are inexplicable to us, as inexplicable as our motives must be to him.'

I gave this some thought. Some very hard thought. And Fangio continued.

'Where he goes, Death follows. Death. For he is an aspect of Death. He would destroy all life. All of us. We cannot understand why because we cannot understand him. But death is what he wills upon us.'

'Death,' I said. And slowly.

'Death,' said Fangio. 'And so, this much *I* understand, and others all over the world understand – a secret department here in the States, a secret ministry over in England. *We* understand that the Homunculus is raising an army of the dead. Here. All over the world. A growing army. This has been going on since the nineteen-fifties, when he escaped from the custody of those who controlled his actions.'

I did some more hard thinking.

Fangio clearly had part of the story. And *I* had part of the story. And all over the world other concerned parties had other parts of the story. It was a very big story. And it came in many parts.

'An army of the dead,' I said to Fangio. 'Why?'

'To do what armies do, of course. This is all about war, isn't it? Everything is ultimately about war. The war between Good and Evil. This war becomes the war between the dead and the living. When the reanimated dead are of sufficient number, when they outnumber the living, then they will rise. The war will be swift, the outcome inevitable.'

'That is horrible,' I said to Fange. 'That is absolutely horrible.'

'It is no laughing matter,' said the barlord.

'And when the dead have won and there are no more living, what then?'

'What indeed?' said Fangio. 'I have told you. We, the living, cannot understand the motives of the Homunculus. He is beyond our worldliness, beyond our comprehension.'

'That is a cop-out,' I said to Fange. 'You must have *some* theory.'

'I have many,' said the barlord, 'but they are only theories, nothing more. I do not understand the motives of the Homunculus. But I and other concerned parties have no wish to understand them. All we want is for him to be destroyed, before all of the Earth and every living thing on it are destroyed.'

And off went Fange to serve another customer. Leaving me all alone.

'Well,' I said. To nobody but myself. 'All this makes a lot of sense. I wonder if, perhaps, I should pass on to Fangio and to his concerned parties the fact that I know the identity of the Homunculus.'

'Probably not the best idea in the world.'

And I looked all around and about. And, 'Who said *that*?' I asked.

'Oh, surely you remember *me*.'

And there he was, as large as life, although not perhaps *of* it. The short, stumpy man with the odd Pickwickian looks. And that hint of a hairless Shirley Temple. And all that buck-toothed Caligula business also.

'Mr Woodbine,' said Papa Keith Crossbar, seating himself upon the next bar stool. And extending a hand.

I did not accept that lumpy paw. In fact I drew back in some alarm and kept my hands out of reach.

'You,' was all I managed to say. In a rather breathless voice.

'And no other,' said Papa Keith Crossbar. 'And long time no see. Why, when was the last time I saw you? Oh, I know – at that bonfire party in Graceland's garden. What a laugh that was, eh?'

'It was real,' I said. And I began to shake as I said it. 'All that *was* real, wasn't it? The futuristic stuff. The teleportation. The auto-da-fé?'

'Real,' said Papa Crossbar, the Homunculus. 'But not *this* reality. Your barman friend is correct. The world I inhabit is not the world you inhabit. Not altogether. Although there are tangents and cross-overs here and there. I allowed you to enter into my world. Into one of my worlds. A parallel world. An alternative reality where Mankind had achieved all the things that it would have achieved if it had not devoted so much of its time to fighting each other. The parallel world that exists in parallel space where the fighting did *not* occur and Mankind *did* go forward. I granted you a view of that. A little visit to it.'

'A world where Elvis was being hailed as the New Messiah?'

'Yes, wasn't that hilarious? All that futuristic technology, and Mankind was still ultimately as stupid and gullible as it ever had been. What hope for humanity, eh?'

'And *I* killed Elvis,' I said. 'Or if not actually killed him, I was responsible for his death.'

'Where the worlds connect, mine and yours, you killed Elvis. And he died in both worlds, yours, mine. You did what I intended you to do. You killed the man who was employing you to kill me. Job done, eh? Exactly as I planned it. Done.'

And I looked on in horror. 'You thoroughgoing swine.'

'And you were sufficiently traumatised by what you had done that you literally sleepwalked though the next twenty years of your life,' this thoroughgoing swine continued, 'as my puppet, campaigning against those ludicrous conspiracy theories about a rising army of the dead.'

'You thoroughgoing—'

'You said that, yes.'

'Wife,' I said. In a hopeless little voice.

'Yes, wasn't that a laugh? The memories will all return. You won't enjoy them. And you didn't get any sex. Your life has really been a bit of a waste of time, hasn't it? If you were to go outside now and throw yourself under the first car that came rushing by – an old Ford Sierra, that would be, imported from Croydon – then who would blame you? You would be doing the right thing. And you really *should* do the right thing, shouldn't you? After doing so many wrong things for so long, the right thing would make a pleasant change. What do you think?'

And the Homunculus looked at me. Deeply at me. Intensely at me. *Completely* at me.

'It would be the right thing to do,' he said. 'Wouldn't it?'

And I nodded bleakly. It *would* be the right thing to do. It really would. I had been a total failure in life. Everything I had ever done had come to nothing. Life had failed me and I had failed life. I would be better off out of it. Death would be better than this life.

Anything would be better than this life. Death especially.

And so I got up from my bar stool. And I walked across the bar, opened the shatter-glass door and walked out onto the sidewalk of 27th Street.

And stood there.

And a Ford Sierra came streaking towards me. It ran straight through the lights. An old woman was driving it and I saw her face clearly. And she saw mine also. And we looked into each other's eyes.

And I flung myself into the path of her on-rushing motor car, which struck me with deadly force.

53

Tick tock tick tock tick tock tick.

My life all ticked away.

And had it been worth it? Something to remember? Something to be proud of? Would I have made my mother proud? Or my father? Had I achieved anything? Anything?

I looked deeply into that woman's eyes and felt a sense of ultimate betrayal. The Homunculus had governed my life for the last twenty years. I had been his puppet. My life had ticked and tocked away and I had walked through it as a somnambulist. And I looked into her eyes.

And in slow motion, as it always is, that car ploughed into me, breaking first my ankles, then one hip bone as I struck the bonnet, then several ribs and a right arm bone or several. And then my nose as my head passed through that windscreen. And much glass dug in well and deep, into my forehead and cheeks.

And then, as the car swerved and slammed to a halt, momentum shot my body forward, into that lamp post, shattering further ribs and doing all manner of horrible damagings deep internally.

This was not one of those accidents where someone was going to walk away with a bit of minor chafing and a good-luck tale to tell. No, this was one of those statistic jobbies, another one chalked up dead.

And then I watched it all happening. The crowd that formed, the eager helpers who knew nothing of first aid and caused more damage through their helpfulness. The arrival of the emergency services. Those flashing beacon lights and banshee-wailing sirens. And the policemen, stringing up that 'DO NOT CROSS' tape. Asking questions, taking notes.

The woman in the car did not walk away with a bit of minor chafing and a good-luck tale to tell. She was decapitated. Her head rolled across 27th Street and came to rest in the doorway of Fangio's Bar.

Fangio had watched the whole thing happen. He stood gnawing a bar cloth.

'That is very sad,' he told another eyewitness. 'But on the bright side,

279

the bar will no doubt revert to me.' And then he went back into *his* bar, carefully stepping over the fallen head.

They had to use the jaws of life to free the rest of the driver's body. Jaws of life? That was a bit of a joke. And no one really troubled much to rush over and gather up my Earthly remains. What with me being twisted up into such a dire-looking Gordian knot and everything.

And if it hadn't been for a lady in a straw hat who drew the attention of one of New York's Finest to the fact that I *was* still breathing, they would probably have just tossed a tarpaulin over me and carted me off to the morgue.

The fact that I *was* still breathing caused much excitement amongst the paramedics, who had been standing around, sniffing the oxygen and smoking cigarettes, and they fell upon my helpless body with great enthusiasm. They were clearly delighted at having an opportunity to use *all* of the equipment. *All* the different Band-Aids and braces. All the splints and pads and drips and dual monitors, LIH vascular packages, en-mode image intensifiers and portable nebulisers. Not to mention the hydro-colloid dressings, wound-closure strips, tubular bandages, Hemcom haemostatic bandages and chest-seal tapes.

Which I, in my present state, was quite unable to do.

And once they had transformed me into a passable facsimile of King Tut's mummy, they loaded me onto a gurney, pushed this into the back of an ambulance, hooked me up to all manner of tubes, wires, chest-drains and whatnots, and then got the driver to drive away fast with flashings and hootings and wailings. And I watched all this happening. All of it. Even though my eyes were bandaged over. I watched it from outside my body, kind of hovering above it, free of gravity, as if in a dream and unable to feel the pain that the mash-up me below was clearly suffering.

And then we hit the ER. And my gurney was rushed along corridors and bumped through double doors and then surrounded by shouting surgeons, all of them shouting at once.

And they shouted all those things that they shout in movies.

'Give me one hundred ccs of sodium bi-pli-nick-nack, hook up the defibrillator, bring a line in on the pulse oximetrical poliscope.'

'Hand me a phase-nine sphygmomanometer and chips.'

'We're losing him. We're losing him.'

'Charge up the defibrillator. Full power. Stand back. Stand back.'

And then *wallop* went that electrical shock right on through my body.

And *wallop* I was no longer out of my body. I was back. But then I was out again.

'No response. Stand back, I am going to shock him again.'

I was now hovering well above my body. I was drifting, in free fall, but falling nowhere. And I could see what was going on outside the Emergency Room. I could see folk in the corridor. I could see Fangio. He had come along. Which was decent of him. Although he did keep going on to passing medics that he had something really important that he needed me to sign before I snuffed it.

And there was someone else I knew. Although now this someone was truly a face from the past. It was Mr Ishmael. And he was remonstrating with medics, demanding that they save my life. That was nice of him.

Then *wallop* again.

And again I was back in my body.

'We're getting something,' I heard someone say, not too far from my ear. 'I've got a heartbeat, or something.'

And I was back in my body and I stayed.

And they said it was a miracle. But also that I'd never walk again. Nor speak, nor do anything much, really, other than impersonate a vegetable. And I lay there, saying nothing, doing nothing, but *hearing* everything.

And feeling it, too.

All those operations they did with the minimum or *no* anaesthetic, because, after all, I *was* in a coma, so what was I likely to feel?

Well, *everything*, really!

The cuttings, the probings, the sewings-up. The knittings together of bones. But I lay there saying nothing, doing nothing, unable to move, or to speak, just being.

As tick tock tick tock, my life went ticking by. And then all feeling left me.

One day the members of The Sumerian Kynges came to pay me a visit and sing me a song. The only member from the days when I'd had some involvement was Andy. And I *could* see him, even though my eyes were closed, as I seemed to be developing some very strange abilities within my vegetative state. Andy looked well; he looked older, of course, but he still had his hair and he still wore that hair in the everstylish mullet.

I tried like damn to communicate with Andy, to force my thoughts into his head, to persuade him to take me home with him, but it didn't work. And presently he, and the three Chinese girls who now composed the other members of The Sumerian Royalty as they were now apparently renamed (a gender-neutral thing apparently), cleared off and left me all alone.

They came back once or twice, but as the media showed no particular interest after the second time, there were few other visits and I was left truly alone.

Apart from Fangio visiting me. He came every week. He brought me fresh flowers to put in my vase. And a box of chocolates, which he proceeded to eat, assuring me that 'the nurses would only eat them otherwise'. And he never mentioned that piece of paper that he wanted signing. Which *did* make me wonder whether, perhaps, he had simply forged my signature onto it. But he *did* come. And it's odd when you are really ill, isn't it? Who does come and visit you and who does not. Who your real friends turn out to be. And all that kind of caper.

And what was really, really strange was that I found, as time passed, as time all ticked and tocked away, that I was able to do all sorts of things that years and years ago I had read about in comic books.

In Doctor Strange comics.

I could see with my eyes closed.

Leave my body in my astral form and travel around and about.

Smell people coming from quite a considerable distance.

And, though it was faltering and not altogether reliable, read people's minds. Hear their thoughts.

I was becoming a regular Master of the Mystic Arts. Which was all very well and quite wonderful really. But lying on my back in a coma was really doing my brain in.

The big change came one Tuesday morning, early in May in the year 2007. Because yes, I had lain in that bed being poked and bed-bathed and massaged and messed with for ten more years of my wasted, useless ticked-and-tocked-away life.

But a big change came one Tuesday morning, beginning with the arrival of a very old man. He looked to be a veritable ancient and he wore an old-fashioned uniform that perhaps once fitted him, but was now several sizes too big. And he took off the cap that was also too big and placed it upon my bedside table. And he took my left hand between his crinkly paws and stroked at my foolish tattoo.

'Hello there, young Tyler,' he said, in a wheezy, creaky old voice.

'I'll bet you won't remember me. But I knew you when you were very young.'

And I looked hard at this venerable elder, hard through my closed eyelids.

And I said, 'Captain Lynch,' to myself. For none but me could hear it.

'I'm Captain Lynch,' said Captain Lynch. 'Well, Major Lynch now, but long retired. Your mother told me you were here. It's taken me a few years to save up the money to fly over from England, but I have and now I'm with you.'

And I looked on at Major Lynch, Captain Lynch as was.

'I had to speak to you before it is too late for me to do so. I have to give you something. It's an important something that we spoke of many years ago. More important than ever now, what with the way things are. I've talked with others and I know that you know all about *them*. And you know who it is – the Homunculus that I spoke to you of, all those years ago. It wasn't Elvis, was it? Elvis is gone, but the Evil goes on and grows daily. You must stop it, Tyler. You will need this.'

And he produced from the pocket of his superannuated uniform a crumpled, dog-eared piece of paper.

'I have carried this with me for sixty years,' he continued. 'It is the map. The location of Begrem, the Lost City of Gold. I never got to Africa. The Church Army said that I was *not* missionary material. There had been some trouble, you see. Certain Indiscretions. Certain scandals. But I kept your mother's name out of it. But I never went. And I never married or had children. Well, only *you*. Well, oh never mind, forget I said *that*. But I was supposed to train you from when you were young, so that you would know what to do when the time came. So that you would have sufficient power to kill *him*.'

'*What?*' I went. But only to myself.

'The map,' said Major Lynch. 'It's there on the map. The location of the lost city. You must lead an expedition, Tyler. Find the city. There are secrets to be found in that lost city, secrets that could help you to destroy the Homunculus, before he destroys us all.'

And then the major patted my head, stroked my brow and, rising, kissed me on the forehead. Which was somewhat unlovely, as he lacked for several teeth and was a bit drippy in the mouth regions.

But I didn't mind. Because his heart was in the right place. Although this business about him training me when I was young – what was *that* all about? And I tried to read his thoughts, but could not, because they were old and confused and chaotic.

And then he upped and put on his cap. And he saluted me, as the old soldier of the Lord that he was, and he said, 'You *will* rise again, Tyler, as our Good Lord rose again. And you *will* slay the Evil One, as our Good Lord should, but can't, because it is not in His remit. Good luck, my boy.' And he saluted again. And about-turned and marched as best he could from my room.

And I lay there, saying nothing at all.

But thinking an awful lot.

And then, about an hour after the good major had departed, two fellows entered my room and stood at the foot of my bed, a-chatting.

'Ten years?' said one.

'All but,' said the other.

'And who is paying for this?'

'His brother made a donation, but that ran out some time ago and he is not on any Medicare programme.'

'So why is he still alive?'

'I don't quite understand the question, sir. He lives because his body is healthy enough and one day he might awaken from his coma.'

'But that is not altogether likely, is it? After three months in a coma, the chances fall and fall away. After two years the chances are almost zero.'

Nobody had told me *that*!

'New advances are being made in the fields of neurosurgery all the time, sir. This man may be revived and go on to live a useful life.'

'We do have a very thick CIA file on this individual. He did not have a useful life before his accident.'

'No, sir, he didn't.'

'He's too expensive. We need his room. We are going to extend the children's ward. Children's wards get funding. Vegetables taking up valuable bed space do not.'

'I can't just pull the plug on him, sir. That would be unethical.'

'There will be a power cut at three p.m. Essential maintenance work outside. All staff have been notified of this, yes?'

'Yes, sir, because the equipment that maintains the life-functions of patients such as this must be reset immediately after the power cut or they will not restart.'

'And you are responsible for restarting this patient's equipment?'

'Yes, sir.'

'Then I am ordering you to take the afternoon off. Go home, watch the Lakers game on TV. Here, take these.'

'And these are, sir?'

'Tickets to Carnegie Hall. The Fortieth Anniversary tour of The Sumerian Royalty. Have a good time. Take your wife.'

'Well, thank you, sir. But the patient—'

'I don't think you need to worry yourself over this patient. *I* will take responsibility for him.'

And the fellow who said this smiled a cruel smile and drew a finger across his throat. And then the two of them left my room.

Giving me plenty more things to ponder upon.

54

Tick tock tick tock, time all passing by.

And me on my bed, all alone in my room, with plenty of things to ponder. And a certain rage growing within me that it would be very hard to describe to anyone who has never been in a similar situation.

They call it an *impotent* rage. And there is no rage worse than that.

And this rage roared through my body, boiling and foaming.

And the time on the clock ticked by.

So this was to be it, was it, then? Had some mighty cosmic force that *wasn't* God (because God didn't intervene) finally decided that enough was enough? That I had suffered enough? That now would be the time to put me out of my misery? That now I was just a waste of space?

I wasn't having *that*.

I was not going to be switched off. Have my plug pulled good and proper. Be dispatched upon my way. No. And so I raged and boiled and foamed. And then I felt it twitch. It was a finger. The little finger on my left hand twitched and I could feel it doing so. And then I got the thumb going and another finger. And then I could feel my wrist. And my toes tingled and my nose ran. And I rose up from my bed.

Rose, as a titan from the depths.

As one born again. Although not *that* one, obviously.

Rose and tore out the tubes and the wires and set my feet on the floor.

And collapsed in a most untidy heap. A groaning, moaning heap.

Because feeling had now returned to my body and I hurt *everywhere*. My eyeballs hurt, and how can your eyeballs hurt? Even my hair hurt. And my toenails. But I climbed up to my feet, swayed gently, clutched the bed for support. And I savoured that pain, every red-hot-firey needle of it. Because I *could* feel again and even pain felt good. And I breathed great drafts of air unaided and I opened my eyes and I stared at the world. And the world didn't look too good.

My room was shabby. In fact it was more than just shabby, it was filthy. It hadn't looked like that through my astral eyes. It had just looked like a room. But with my normal eyesight, shabby grim. And with my nasal passages working once more, it smelled dreadful. As if some blighter had pooed in the corner and no one had cleared it up.

I steadied myself against the bed, sat myself down on it and pulled out the last of the bits and bobs that connected me to this and that.

'Well, you can have your room back,' I said. 'I hope the dear children like the smell.'

My clothes hung in a cupboard in the corner of the room. I patted at the trench coat. They had taken my trusty Smith & Wesson, but the rest of my stuff was there, though smelly. All musty and fusty and greatly in need of dry-cleaning.

I tore off the horrid surgical gown that unflatteringly adorned me and it came away in pieces, it was so rotten. 'No expense spent,' I concluded as I togged up in my Lazlo Woodbine gear. And I took up that map that the major had left and stuffed it into a pocket.

The Woodbine gear didn't fit me too well. It was, I confess, a bit big. I had clearly lost weight. The belt did up by another three holes. I was virtually skeletal.

There was a mirror over the sink by the window and I limped over to it and peered therein. And I didn't like what I saw.

I looked awful. Sunken, drawn, my skin like yellow parchment, stretched across my cheekbones. Killer cheekbones, though. Like Elvis used to have, when he was young and *really* the King of rock 'n' roll.

But I was a mess. My eyes were bloodshot and sunk deep in dark sockets. I opened my mouth. Had nobody cleaned my teeth? They were as yellow as my skin, with nasty black lines between.

'Look at me,' I howled. And I *did*. 'I'm a wreck. I look like a plague victim. How did they let me get in this condition?'

And I felt that rage all boiling once again.

And very energising that rage was. And I splashed some water on my face, used my finger as a toothbrush, was disgusted by the blackness of my tongue. Pulled my fedora way down low and stormed from my hospital room.

And nobody stopped me. Nobody spoke to me. Nobody even seemed to notice me. The medics just went about their business. Gurneys were pushed, some folk shouted, other folk wept. Nurses came and went.

And presently I was outside in the street.

And I took great breaths of New York air and those great breaths were not rewarding or beneficial to the good health of my person. New York stank. It reeked. It was horrible.

It was a nice day, though. Bright sunlight.

Although—

There *was* bright sunlight, but there was a certain dark quality to this bright sunlight. It was difficult to quantify, really, but things *weren't* right. Things were, shall we say, out of kilter.

Somehow.

And then I saw the policeman. He was just a policeman. He stood on the corner, twirling his nightstick as old-fashioned policemen used to do. And the sun, the dark sun, shone down upon this policeman and cast his shadows before him.

And yes, I did say shadow*s*. He cast two shadows, that New York cop. And I could see them clearly.

Two shadows! And I thought about that woman in Croydon who had had the crash on the roundabout and woken up in the Ministry of Serendipity. She'd seen the double shadows. And was it her who had ran me down and died in the crash?

Probably yes, I supposed.

And I glanced here and I glanced there. And saw them here and there. *Them*. The dead, the animated dead. The ones that cast two shadows.

'And I can see the shadows now,' I said, in a whispery kind of a voice, 'because I have been in a coma for so long and developed these weird abilities.'

'What a wreck!' A woman walked by me. A good-looking woman. She'd said that I was a wreck. I opened my mouth to answer her back. But then I realised that she *hadn't* said it. She'd only thought it. And I had heard her thoughts. I watched her as she walked away. The woman had only one shadow.

I shrank back against a wall and tried to look inconspicuous. It's a detective thing. And I viewed the people of New York. And I counted them as I viewed them. And wouldn't you know it, one in three was casting a pair of shadows.

One in three? Did this mean that one in three New Yorkers was dead? The conclusion had to be *yes*.

I turned up the collar of my trench coat. The dark sun seemed to cast no heat and I felt chilly withal. He was winning. The Homunculus. One in three. All over the world? The army of the dead growing in numbers, awaiting the moment to arise against the living.

I felt chilled to the bone.

And I was starting to shake.

Going into shock? I couldn't have that. I couldn't end up back in the hospital again. What I needed now was a big fat drink.

A big fat drink in Fangio's Bar.

I had no money for cabs, so I walked. And as I walked, I fretted. He was going to win, that Homunculus horror, and I was powerless to stop him. What could I do, a single living man against an army of the dead? And how had all these people come to die anyhow? I didn't believe that they had died, been buried, then risen from their graves and gone home to their friends and family, saying that it had all been a big mistake and that they were all fit and well again. That didn't make any sense. They must have been murdered secretly and then zombified, as the voodoo priests did to their victims in Haiti.

So what did that mean? That there were zombie hit-squads roaming around at night, picking folk off at the order of their evil master, the Homunculus?

That, in all its horror, seemed most probable.

I trudged on, in an ill-smelling trench coat and a right old fug.

And Fangio's Bar hadn't changed. But had Fangio? The not-so-fat-boy barman hadn't attended my bedside in a while. Had he succumbed? Did he now cast double shadows and call the Homunculus 'sir'?

It was with some foreboding, and no small degree of thirst, that I pushed open the now-legendary shatter-glass door and once more entered the bar.

And there was the now elegantly wasted boy behind the bar counter and he looked up from a magazine and copped a glance at me.

'A bottle of Bud, please, Fange,' I said. 'And a hot pastrami on rye.'

And he fainted. Dead away.

And I roused him with the contents of the ice bucket. And he rued the day that he had not worn a wetsuit to work (this day) and arose all dripping to his feet.

'It *is* you,' he said. 'And you are awake and here.'

'And looking like dog poo,' I said. 'How come nobody gave my teeth a wash?' And I displayed my teeth to Fangio. Who fell back before the onrushing of my severe halitosis.

'You're going to need some alcohol to mask that breath of yours,' said the barlord. 'And then we are going to have to talk some very intense toot. If you know what I mean and I'm sure that you do.'

And he popped the top from a bottle of Bud and served up a pastrami on rye.

And I tucked in to all that he served and did so gratefully.

'I cannot tell you how wonderful it is to see you up and about,' said Fangio. 'Even if you do look somewhat dog-pooish. So do you wish to pay in cash, or should I start a tab for you?'

'I'll have these on the house,' I said. 'As this is *my* bar.'

'Ah,' said Fangio. '*Was* your bar. The court order came through just last week. When you were declared officially braindead.'

'Which quite clearly I am *not*!' I said. In the voice of outrage.

'Opinions vary,' said Fangio. 'You're entitled to your own, of course. Personally I incline towards the opinion of the magistrate who signed the court order. But that's me all over, isn't it? Upholder of the law and friend to one and all.'

And I did grindings of the teeth. And bits of teeth fell off.

'I need a wash,' I said to Fangio. 'I stink and everything I'm wearing stinks and I need to clean my teeth. A lot.'

And Fangio let me use *his* bathroom. And he said that he would not charge me for the towels. On this occasion. The man was clearly a saint in the making. And, as he cast but a single shadow, still in the land of the living.

I returned to the bar smelling as sweetly as Elvis once had and rea-sonably shining-white in the railing regions. And I smiled my almost pearly-whites at Fangio and this time he did not fall back clutching at his nose.

'It really *is* good to have you back,' he said. 'What are your present opinions regarding the undead? Believer, or non-believer?'

'Believer,' I said. 'Firm and fervent believer. And instrument of vengeance upon the Homunculus. If I get half a chance.'

'Top man,' said Fangio. 'Bonnie Tyler was in here the other day and she was holding out for a hero. I don't suppose you're related?'

'I didn't know that you knew my real name,' I said.

'It was on your hospital records. Which came from extensive CIA files on you. Apparently.'

'So I heard. Perhaps I should go and speak to the CIA, tell them everything I know. And I know *a lot*.'

'Best not,' said Fangio.

'You think?'

'I *know*. Best not.' And Fangio pushed the magazine he had been reading when I entered across the bar counter to me.

It was a copy of *American Alpha Males Today* magazine, which incorporated *American Jocks Today* magazine. And *American Teenage Dirtbags Today* magazine. And *Hard-Core She-Males Monthly*, but this last was in very small lettering.

And there he was on the cover.

In big glossy all full colour.

Keith Presley, brother of Elvis.

Otherwise known as Papa Keith Crossbar.

The Homunculus.

And there was a big blurb on that cover. And that blurb said—

LOOK OUT

VILLAINS BEWARE AND TERRORISTS FLEE

Keith Crossbar Crowned New
Head of the CIA

'Head of the CIA?' I said. 'That's him, you know. That's the Homunculus.'

'Of course I know,' said Fangio. 'All of us in the Underground know now. But what can we do? Assassinate him?'

I glugged down another bottle of Bud.

And Fangio served me up another. 'I'll put it on your tab,' he said.

'Head of the CIA,' I said. 'How did that happen?'

'Folk died,' said Fangio. 'Anyone who stood in his career path met with an unfortunate accident. Not always fatal, though, because when they had "recuperated", they no longer stood in his way – they endorsed his rise to power.'

'And I bet they all cast two shadows?' I said.

'I've heard that story, too,' said Fangio. 'And I'll just bet that they do.'

'How much would you be prepared to bet?' I asked on the off-chance.

Fangio scratched at what he had left of hairs on his head.

'Surely I would win that bet,' he said.

'You might,' I replied.

'I think I'll pass anyway.'

I raised my bottle of Bud to Fange. 'It is very good to be sitting here in this bar talking to you,' I said. 'Even if we are *not* talking the toot. It's good. Cheers to you, my friend.'

'And cheers to you, too,' said Fangio.

And we shared a moment. A special moment.

And then the shatter-glass door opened and a newsboy entered and hurled the evening paper onto the bar.

Fangio almost caught it, but didn't. And the newsboy departed, chuckling.

'The news,' I said to Fangio. 'Now, I have not exactly been too privy to the news lately. Let's have a look at what's going on in the world.' And Fangio smiled and pushed the evening paper across the counter-top to me.

And I perused the front page.

And guess what. And wouldn't you just know it.

There was a great big photograph of me on the front page. And below this were printed the words—

PSYCHOTIC TERRORIST SERIAL-KILLER ESCAPES
FROM STATE MENTAL INSTITUTION
CIA Head Orders Cops to Shoot on Sight

'Oh sweet,' I said. 'Just perfect.'

55

So I was Public Enemy Number One.

Which rather spoiled my afternoon.

Not that I'd been having the best afternoon of my life, you understand, what with discovering that one in every three New Yorkers was a walking corpse. But, looking on the bright side, I *was* up out of my hospital bed and I *was* in a bar, having the first beers I'd had in ten years.

And my, those beers tasted good.

But Public Enemy Number One? On the front page of the newspaper? That wasn't funny. That wasn't fair. That was downright spiteful.

Fangio cast eyes across the newspaper and whistled the whistle of surprise. 'Psycho-terrorist?' said he. 'I wonder if there's a reward.'

'Don't even think about it,' I told him. 'And bring me another beer.'

'You won't go blowing the place up when my back is turned?'

I gave Fange that certain look and he fetched further beer.

'This is a fine kettle of fish,' I said, upon his return. 'A right how-do-you-do and a rare turn-up-for-the-books.'

'Are we talking the toot now?' asked Fangio. 'Because you are getting me confused.'

'I'm upset,' I said. 'And I'm angry. A wanted man? That is going to make things rather difficult for me, isn't it?'

'These things happen,' said the barlord. 'The secret is not to let them get you down. I've recently joined a travel club. That takes my mind off my problems.'

'A travel club. But you never travel anywhere, except to the toilet.'

'Ah,' said Fangio. 'But that is one of the beauties of the present age. I don't have to travel. I can employ other people to do it for me.'

'That doesn't make any sense at all,' I told him, in no uncertain tones.

'Ah, but it does.' And Fangio rested his elegantly wasted elbows upon the bar counter. 'I pay for someone to travel to exotic lands and in return they send me postcards telling me all about it and thanking me for being so wonderful as to finance their journeys for them. So it satisfies on so many levels, really.'

'It's nonsense,' I said. 'And anyway, where would you get the money to finance them from?'

'Out of your insurance pay-off . . .' said Fangio. And then his voice trailed off.

'My *what*?' I said.

'Curious thing,' said Fange. 'And I would have told you about it. I just forgot, with all the excitement of you being up and about and everything.'

'Really?' I said.

'Well, there's a chance that I *might* have mentioned it,' said Fange. 'There's *always* a chance.'

'I'll just bet there is. But not *now*. Tell me all about this insurance pay-off.'

'Well,' said Fange, and he did that grin that roadkill does to perfection. The rictus grin, it is called. 'Well, when you were struck down by that car. Curious thing. A fellow standing in the doorway of this bar, beside me – because I followed you out, you see, when you went a bit weird and just walked out – this fellow saw the crash and said, "What a coincidence, I happen to represent the insurance company that covers that old woman in the Ford Sierra. And we're having a special offer this week and there's a half a million pay-out to whoever she runs down."'

'What?' I said. 'That is rather unlikely.'

'Well, be that as it may. He asked whether I knew you. And I said, for the sake of convenience, that I was your only brother. And your only living relative.'

'For the sake of convenience?'

'I like to call it that, yes.'

'Go on,' I said. And I sighed.

'He made out the cheque on the spot. What a happy happenstance, eh?'

'What a far-fetched load of old cobblers.'

'Would you like to see my bank statement?'

'Very much indeed.'

And so Fangio showed me his bank statement. And wouldn't you just know it—

'Golly!' I said.

'*Where?*' said Fangio.

'But there's only a quarter of a million dollars in this account.'

'I've had expenses.'

'Such as paying people to go on holiday for you.'

'Well, actually, no,' and Fangio shook his head. 'I was just about to finish organising that this very afternoon but I got all distracted by you walking in.'

'So many distractions,' I said. 'I don't know how you cope.'

'Oh, I think it's being so cheerful that keeps me going.'

'Right,' I said. In the way that I always said, 'Right.'

'So I'm glad that's all sorted out.' And Fangio turned his attention once more to the newspaper. 'There *is* mention here of a reward,' he observed.

'Travel club,' I said, thoughtfully. 'Tell me, Fangio, would you still care to invest in someone going on holiday for you?'

'Oh yes, I certainly would. I was getting rather excited about the whole thing. The travel. The digging up. The discovery. The glory.'

'The what?' I asked.

'I was thinking of financing an expedition,' said Fangio. 'I thought it would be more exciting than just a plain old holiday.'

'An expedition?' I said.

'An archaeological expedition. To seek the Lost City of Begrem.'

The dark sun went behind a cloud and a dog howled in the distance.

'Don't you just hate it when that happens?' Fangio asked.

'Right,' I said once more. 'And so, and I have to ask you this, have you had anyone volunteer to go on this expedition for you?'

'No, like I said, I was hoping it would get organised this afternoon – I put an ad in *Freeloader Today* magazine (incorporating *Australian Backpacker Today* magazine and *Off-to-Kathmandu-to-Get-My-Head-Together Today* magazine) and applicants were supposed to turn up here by—' And Fangio checked his watch.

'Isn't that *my* watch?' I asked him.

'Hard to be sure, what with all the excitement and everything. But—' and he checked this watch once more '—they should have been here by now. So no takers, I suppose.'

I sighed deeply and drew some more on the neck of my bottle of beer. Fate can play strange tricks, can't it? And if I didn't know better, and know, as I *did* know, that God did *not* intervene in the ways of men *except* by tampering with the weather, I might well have come to the conclusion that this opportune coincidence was the work of Divine Providence.

'Oh well,' said Fange. 'You can't win them all. I'll go back to my original plan and advertise for someone to take their family to Butlins in Bognor, England.'

'Not so fast,' I said to Fangio.

'Oh, it wouldn't be *that* fast. I'd want to spend some time composing the words of the ad very carefully. I don't want to blow it a second time, do I?'

And I shook my head and sighed a bit more.

'That's very plaintive sighing, Laz,' said Fangio. And I rather liked it that he called me Laz. 'You want to cheer yourself up. Get away from things. Escape from your troubles. My God!' And Fangio brought his right fist down into his left palm. 'I've just had an idea. You will never believe what has just occurred to me.'

'No,' I said. 'I'll just bet that I won't.'

'How much?'

'Don't start. I'm not in the mood right now.'

'But it's the solution to your present worries. It was there staring me in the face all the time and I never even saw it.'

'Go on,' I said, in as tolerant a tone as I could muster up. 'Surprise me.'

'This holiday business,' said Fangio.

'Yes? Go on.'

'Oh come on,' said Fange. 'It's obvious, isn't it?'

'Is it?' I asked. For I was, at least, enjoying this old toot.

'Well, *you* need to get away from it all. And *I* have the where-withal—'

'Yes?'

'So why don't *I* go on holiday and *you* can stay here and mind the bar for me?'

And I never hit him. Not at all. Because I wasn't up to hitting. And because he was a friend. But I did explain things slowly and clearly.

'Oh,' said Fangio. 'I see. So I finance *you* to seek the Lost City of Begrem. That's a bit of a left-fielder. I would never have thought of anything as radical as that.'

'Given time you might,' I said, kindly.

'I think you're only being kind,' said Fangio.

And I agreed that this was probably the case.

'You haven't, perhaps, purchased any tickets?' I asked.

'To The Sumerian Royalty reunion? No.'

'To Begrem?' I suggested.

'Ah, no,' said Fangio, 'because no one knows where it is. It is a *lost* city. And you have to *find* a *lost* city.'

'I know where it is,' I said.

'I would like to express considerable surprise at that statement,' said Fangio, 'but I regret that I can't, as I have to go and serve another customer. I should have done it earlier, really, to punctuate our conversation in a better place. Sorry.' And Fangio wandered off to serve a customer.

Which gave me a moment to do some thinking.

And I pulled out that scrunched-up piece of paper.

The piece of paper that Major Lynch had left upon my bedside table.

And I unfolded it carefully and spread it out upon the bar counter.

It was really a bit of a mess, all tea-stained and beer-stained and otherwise stained in a manner that it was not perhaps decent to speak of openly. But stained it *was*, nonetheless.

I viewed this stained and crumpled piece of paper. It *was* a map, this was clear. But that it *was* a map was all that was clear.

It was all just lines, interlocking, with little dots spread here and there along them. And one big dot surmounted with a cross and the words *Begrem, it is here*. But as to spot-heights, benchmarks, Cartesian co-ordinates, coincident line features, demographic data, grid references or link-node topology, or indeed any number of other wonderful things that you find when you check the Ordinance Survey Database, there was nothing that could even place the map as being part of any particular country. No go.

And then the shatter-glass door opened. And wouldn't you just know it, although I hate like *damn* to have to use that phrase again, but wouldn't you just know it, in walked two of New York's Finest. Big guns and nightsticks and all. And I sank low over my little map and kept my eyes averted.

And Fangio smiled towards his newly arrived clientele, bid them the big hello and served them the beverages of their choice without of course asking for payment, because these *were* policemen after all. And he directed them to a cosy corner booth where they could drink undisturbed and then he returned to me.

'Fancy *that*,' he said. 'Two policemen coming in *here*.'

'I don't fancy it at all,' I said. 'Thanks for tucking them out of the way. I think I might have to take my leave quite soon.'

'So do you want to settle up before you go?'

'Fangio,' I said to Fangio, 'you have tricked me out of the bar that I tricked you out of *and* half a million dollars. And you still think I should pay for these beers?'

'You'd think I'd know better, wouldn't you?' said Fange. 'But I don't.'

And I sighed once again. But took unto myself a solemn vow that it would be the very last time I sighed today. I mean, it's all so depressing, sighing, isn't it? And although I did have good, sound reasons for being very depressed, there were also now reasons to be optimistic. If Fangio financed my expedition to find Begrem. And I *did* find Begrem. And in Begrem there was some secret something that would enable me to defeat and destroy the Homunculus. Then *that* would be a result, wouldn't it?

Yes, it would, I told myself. It would. It would. It would.

'What I am going to do,' I said to Fangio, 'is let you finance me to form a one-man expedition to find the Lost City of Begrem. That is what is going to happen. What do you think of that?'

Fangio did shakings of his head.

'You are shaking your head,' I informed him.

'Because I'm bored with Begrem,' said Fangio. 'I don't think anyone's ever going to find it, so I'm not financing that expedition any more. Would you care for two two-weeker tickets to Butlins?'

And, well, yes, I *did* hit him this time. But not *that* hard. It would have been harder, it would have been *much* harder, had I been able to muster up the strength. So he got off quite lightly, did Fangio.

'Most unsporting,' said he.

'Begrem,' I said. 'You will finance my expedition to Begrem. Right now and right out of the cash register.'

'Well, I suppose I do have the money in the cash register that I put aside to finance the expedition. There's fifty big ones in that register.'

'Fifty thousand dollars?'

'It's been a slow week.'

And I almost sighed again, but didn't.

Instead I said, 'Give me the money.'

'Are you sure you wouldn't prefer Butlins?'

'*Begrem!*' I said. '*Now!*' I said also.

'And you *will* send me postcards?'

'Every single day, I promise.'

'Splendid,' said Fangio. 'And you'll probably need this. I have been keeping it for you.' And he brought up, from beneath the counter, my trusty Smith & Wesson. 'Had it serviced for you and everything,' he said. 'Just in case you did make it back from the hospital.'

'You are a saint,' I told Fange. And I smiled. And I pointed the trusty S & W at him and said, 'Give me the contents of your cash register.'

And Fangio humorously raised his hands. And said, 'Don't shoot, Mr Burglar.'

Which is where, perhaps, things went so seriously wrong. When it looked as if they were just about to go so right.

I think it was the New York cop getting up to get another drink. And seeing me with the gun, demanding money, and Fangio with his hands raised and everything.

And the fact that the cop then shouted, 'It's that psycho-terrorist guy. Shoot to kill!' As he and his chum drew their guns.

56

You have to be sprightly when bullets start to fly.

You have to know how to take cover.

You notice that I say you have to *know*, rather than you have to *learn*. The thing is, if you don't instinctively *know*, then you will get shot and you won't have an opportunity to learn.

I leaped over the bar post-haste, over that bar counter and straight down to the other side, taking my treasure map with me. To join Fangio, I might add, who was evidently skilled in knowing how to take cover, for he was already on his hands and knees in the foetal position.

The cops opened fire and shot up all the liquor bottles on the glass shelves behind Fangio's bar counter. Why? Well, they had their guns drawn and they were clearly prepared to use them. On anything.

A friend of mine from my teenage years, who was once in the TA, told me that the only soldiers who are really any good to the army are the psychopathic ones. They've joined the army *to shoot guns at people*. Most people who join the army never really think about the shooting people side of it, and when they find themselves in a combat situation they will spend a lot of time instinctively taking cover. Whereas that one solider in every hundred who is psychotic will be blasting away at the enemy and chalking up kills. My friend who was once in the TA also told me that war consists of two things: boredom and fear. Waiting and waiting for something to happen and then being terrified when it does.

This friend, who was neither psychotic nor a fan of being afraid, left the TA as quickly as he was able and took work with the council in Cardiff. And I was caused to think of him when I took the dive for cover because I didn't really want to shoot a policeman, but neither did I want to have one shoot me.

'There is a back door,' shouted Fangio, close by my ear. 'Perhaps if you left by it, those cops might stop shooting my bar to pieces.'

And further shots crackled overhead. And bottles of Bud now went to ruination. 'Please take all the money with you,' said Fangio.

'I was intending to, yes.'

'Oh good. Because *then* I can claim it back from my robbery-cover insurance.'

'Financially speaking, you have acquired certain wisdom over the years,' I told him as I crawled in the direction of the cash register.

The clientele had taken to fleeing and above and between the bursts of gunfire I could hear one of the cops calling for backup. The words 'bring everything you have' stick in my memory. And also 'the SWAT Team psychos'.

I made a leap for the cash register and I brought it down to the floor and I emptied it. And I filled my pockets with these emptyings. Especially the inside pockets of my trench coat, as they were big 'poacher's pockets' with plenty of room for loot. Not that this *was* loot. It wasn't. It was *my* money, for God's sake!

And I was *not* leaving this bar *without* my money.

'How would you feel about me using you as a human shield while I back out of the rear door?' I asked Fangio.

And there was a moment of silence. And the dark sun went once more behind a cloud. And another dog howled in the distance.

'I'm glad those howling dogs never come any closer,' shouted Fangio to me as the police gunfire resumed, 'because I'm sure they must be very big and fierce. But in answer to your question, I'm not particularly keen.'

'I could force you,' I shouted into his earhole. 'I do have a gun.' And I flourished this at Fange.

'It doesn't have any bullets in it, though.'

'What?'

'I forgot to put them in.'

'Ah,' I said. 'But if I hold it to your head, how are *you* going to know *that*?'

'Good point.'

But I decided against it. I didn't want Fangio to get hurt. When it came right down to it, he was probably the only friend I had, and I didn't want to be responsible for something horrible happening to him.

Because, let's face it, there was a rare, outside chance that I might best the Homunculus and return one day to this bar to claim my share of all the money Fangio had managed to snaffle away.

All right, it *was* a rare and outside chance, but I had to stay positive. Even if, as now, I was being shot at.

'Farewell, Fangio,' I said. 'I hope we will meet again in more favourable circumstances. You have been a good friend to me. Give us a shake of the hand.'

Fangio stuck out his hand for a shake. 'I'm just thinking,' said he, 'that if I were to disarm you and make a citizen's arrest, I would be considered a bit of a hero. And I'd get the reward. I don't suppose you'd let me bop you on the head?'

'Goodbye, Fangio,' I said to him.

'Goodbye, Laz,' said Fange.

I think the police backup must have arrived because there was suddenly a whole lot more gunfire and from lots of different directions. And I make no bones about it, it frightened six bells of Shadoogie out of me. I was really scared. And I crawled along behind the bar counter and edged through the rear door, passed into the unspeakable kitchen, of which there has been no former description and of which there will be none now, and slipped out of the rear doorway and into the alleyway beyond.

The alleyway where Lazlo Woodbine used to get into sticky situations.

That alleyway made me feel almost nostalgic. Almost. I crept along that alleyway, moving from the cover of one trashcan to another, and mostly beneath those cast-iron fire escapes with the retractable bottom sections. I paused, briefly, to check whether I was being followed. And savoured the atmospheric ambient sounds of a solitary saxophone.

And then, when I was almost at the end of the alleyway, a police car swerved to a halt right before me and cops piled out, all carrying guns, and I was forced to run.

And my, can't you run fast when cops are shooting at you!

And me, not being particularly physically fit and, in truth, a wee bit tiddly from the bottles of Bud – *although* this *was* all rather sobering – even so, I *did* run fast, I can tell you. And I did dodgings, too. And police bullets ricocheted off trashcans and cast-iron fire escapes. And a bum who camped in that alleyway, and whom fate had not perhaps treated as fairly as it might, copped a round or two to the head, which was tough, but such is life.

And I ran. Right down that alleyway and out of the other end. And yes, there were more police cars. And I really had to get a burst of extra speed on to try to lose myself amidst the New York traffic and all the comings and goings.

And presently I found myself in Times Square, breathing very heavily, but at least breathing. And I took deep breaths to steady myself and steadied myself. And then I looked up at that big television jobbie that Times Square is so famous for. As opposed to the Pepsi Cola sign that Piccadilly Circus is so famous for.

And *yes. Wouldn't you just know it—*

There was my face right up there on that screen.

Interspersed with shots of Fangio's Bar.

And I sighed. Once more, I confess it. And I turned up the collar of my trench coat and pulled down the brim of my snap-brimmed fedora, which all but fell off because it was so mouldy. And I trudged along amidst the crowd, keeping my head hung low and feeling not altogether the jolliest fellow around.

And I found a Donut Diner and I slipped into it. And with my head bowed, I ordered a donut and coffee. And after some considerable time negotiating exactly which type of donut, and which variety of coffee would 'truly fit my personality', which caused me to wish that there *were* bullets inside my gun, I paid an outrageous sum for something-or-other to eat and something-or-other to drink and retired with these to a quiet corner table.

And of course there *was* a television set in that Donut Diner.

And yes, of course it *was* tuned to a news station that was broadcasting pictures of my face. But I kept my head down and feigned interest in my donut and coffee. Whilst trying to formulate a plan.

I would have to get out of New York as quickly as possible. This was a given. And seek Begrem? Yes, I had the financial means and the aching need. But *not* the knowledge of where to seek it. Sumeria would probably be a good starting point. But I did not have a passport. And even if I'd had a passport, it was odds-on that this passport would lead to my arrest at the airport. Difficult times.

And I sat with my head way down low and glowered at my donut.

I was all messed up here, I knew it, the whole thing was hopeless, I was done for. I had no intention of giving myself up, so all I could do was run. Far away from here. Get to Begrem. How? All I could do for now was try to escape to somewhere safe. But where? And how? I knew not.

And sighing and glowering, I diddled with my donut.

'Difficult times for you, Tyler.'

'Difficult times indeed,' I agreed.

'Difficult, difficult times.'

'Yes, I know they're difficult.' And then I looked up. Because I wasn't having this conversation with myself. Someone else was speaking to me. Although not *speaking*. I could hear them thinking.

'That will prove a most valuable asset.'

And I looked all round and about.

And there he was, sitting beside the counter, eating some kind of something that was probably a donut. And he was grinning at me. And I rose to greet him, but he beckoned me to stay. And so I sat still and he joined me at my table.

Mr Ishmael.

'You don't look quite as well as you might,' he said. And I saw that he said it because I saw his mouth open up. And I saw too that he hadn't changed much. He looked very well. 'It is good that we meet again,' he said. 'Very good.'

I gazed at Mr Ishmael and I hated him.

'Harsh thoughts,' said Mr Ishmael. 'I have always had your interests at heart.'

'You are a liar,' I said. 'You have always had your own motives at your own heart. I have been nothing more than a pawn in your game.'

'You are a great deal more than that, young Tyler.'

'Young?' I said. And I laughed a hollow laugh. 'You have stolen away my life. Look at me – I am old and wrecked. What life have I had?'

'You have yet to have your finest hour.'

'I hate you, Mr Ishmael,' I said. 'And if I had bullets in my gun, I would surely shoot you.'

'Oh dear, very harsh words.'

'It is because of you that I am a wanted man. The Homunculus will surely have me killed. I hold you responsible for this. And if there is any kind of an afterlife, be assured that I will return to haunt you.'

'Oh dear,' said Mr Ishmael. 'This is not the merry reunion I was hoping it might be.'

'Leave me alone,' I said. 'Go away and leave me alone.'

'But I can help you, Tyler. That's why I'm here, to help you. I have kept a careful eye on you all these years. You have been under my protection.'

'Yeah, right,' I said.

'I watched you leave the hospital, I followed you to Fangio's Bar, I followed you here.'

'Only so you could get me into even more trouble.'

'I don't think it would be possible for you to get into even more trouble than you are in now.'

'Then take satisfaction in what you have achieved.'

'It is not me who will achieve our goal, but you. Everything that has happened to you so far has all been a part of what is to come. A preparation for what you must do. And you are prepared now. You are ready. You have all the skills. All the abilities. You are the weapon of our deliverance. You are the Bedrock of our Salvation.'

'Oh, yeah, *right*. I spent twenty years of my life as a puppet for Papa Crossbar, then another ten in a hospital bed. I have been robbed of my life and it is all your fault. And I would so love to kill you. And as I have no bullets, I think I'll just bludgeon you to death with the gun.'

'So much anger,' said Mr Ishmael. Without moving his mouth. 'And justified, too. But you are directing your anger in the wrong direction. You know you are special, Tyler. You don't know why, because no one has told you. Major Lynch didn't tell you, did he? But he almost did, he almost let it slip. I disciplined him for that.'

'*Who* are you?' I asked. '*What* are you?'

'You *do* know who I am. You just haven't given it sufficient thought. But *I* am not the issue, Tyler, *you* are the issue. *You* are the future. *You* must succeed.'

'Bend your head down,' I said, 'and I'll welt it with my gun.'

And Mr Ishmael sighed.

'I hold the present franchise on sighing,' I told him. 'You are infringing my copyright.'

'I'll leave you to it, then. You clearly do not want my help.'

'No, I *don't*,' I said. 'I don't want anything more to do with you at all.'

'I'm sure I could help you with something.'

'And I am sure you cannot. Please leave me alone now. And never again come into my life.'

'I ought to give you something. If we are never to meet again.'

'You have nothing I want,' I told Mr Ishmael. 'I hope that you live an unhappy life from now on and die painfully.'

'Sadly, that *is* what will happen. But I *will* give you something, Tyler. Something you need.'

I said nothing more. For I had tired of this.

'The map,' said Mr Ishmael. 'The treasure map showing the location of the Lost City of Begrem.'

'You want it?' I said. 'Because you can't have it. Tell you what, I think I'm up to it now, up to taking you on. You scared me before. You had power that scared me. But I'm not scared any more. Tell you what – I'll put the map on the table and the one who remains alive can walk out of the door with it. Come on, what do you say?'

And I even surprised myself with that little speech. But I was oh so very angry.

'I don't want it,' said Mr Ishmael. And he raised his hands. 'That map is for you. It has always been for you. I don't want to take it. I want to tell you what it represents. Where the lost city is. Exactly where.'

'And *you* know *that*?'

'Of course.'

'So where is it?'

And Mr Ishmael looked at me and I looked at Mr Ishmael. And it was really *hard* looking that we did. One upon another. And Mr Ishmael smiled. But I did not. And Mr Ishmael said, 'We will never meet again, Tyler. This is my final gift to you. Use it well.'

And I said, '*gift?*' and got even angrier.

And Mr Ishmael said, 'That map is of the New York underground railway system, Tyler. The City of Begrem is here. Right here. Beneath your feet.' And he pointed downwards and smiled. 'Where "X" marks the spot, that is the entrance.'

And then he got up and just walked away.

Out of my life for ever.

I never saw him again.

57

The New York underground railway system.

Now why hadn't *I* thought of *that*?

It was all so obvious, really, when you thought about it. Really.

Well, perhaps if you screwed up your mind just a little and thought about it. Because, as is well known to all Londoners, there is a lost race of troglodytes inhabiting the London Transport Underground railway system. Descendants, it is believed, of a Victorian train disaster down there, when a train all-filled-up with Victorian ladies and gents got all-walled-up in a tunnel collapse. The London Underground Railway Company covered up this terrible tragedy and denied all knowledge of it, because it was bad for public confidence in the Underground system. It appears that there were survivors, living on rats and mushrooms, who eventually burrowed into the present-day system, where, when the hunger is upon them, they will snatch some lone commuter from a late-night platform and descend with him or her into their secret subterranean lairs, to feed. And surely it can be no coincidence that that most secret of all secret Government departments, the mysterious Ministry of Serendipity, is housed beneath Mornington Crescent Underground Station in London.

No.

And so, *what*, a lost city beneath the present-day streets of New York? An unlikely proposition? No, I don't think so.

I took the treasure map from my pocket and gave it a good peering at. It did look like a railway system, yes, it really did.

I hailed a waitress who was passing by, whistling that old Sumerian Kynges classic 'The Land of the Western God', and I enquired of this beauteous personage as to whether she might have a map of the New York underground railway system anywhere about her beauteous person.

And she replied in that feisty manner for which New York women are renowned and told me exactly what I could do with myself and precisely *how* I could do it.

'That would be a no, then,' I concluded. But I was not going to be thwarted quite so easily in my bid to enter the Lost City of Begrem and avail myself of whatever there was to be had once I was there. And so I asked a young black gentleman of the burly persuasion, whose attire sported a comprehensive selection of gang-affiliated patches. And he gave me his map and said that I could keep it.

And I thanked him very much for his generosity.

And he in turn said that it was a pleasure to be of assistance and that if I wouldn't object to giving him one hundred dollars as a 'handling fee', he would kindly refrain from disembowelling me with his shiv.

And so I handed over one hundred dollars, on the understanding that 'fair exchange is no robbery' and 'a trouble shared was indeed a trouble halved'.

And then it occurred to me that I had indeed been talking the toot with *myself*. Which was novel enough, and cheered me up slightly, though not very much.

And then I unfolded the map the young black gentleman had 'given' to me. And discovered it to be a flyer for some rap band appearing that night in a nearby club.

And I was about to hail the young gentleman, who was leaving the Donut Diner, and inform him of his regrettable error when the feisty waitress took me by the arm, advised me against it and then pulled out a map from her apron and handed it to me.

'You're not from around these parts, are you, stranger?' she asked me.

'Well, curiously,' I said, 'I've been living in New York for the last thirty years. But I haven't been out and about much lately.'

'Are you someone famous?' she asked me. 'Only I think I recognise your face from somewhere.'

'I'm the public face of a very private grief,' I told her. As some women find enigmatic men fascinating, and take them back to their homes for extended periods of sexual activity.

'Yeah, right,' she said and went straight back to her work.

And then I unfolded the map she had given me. And lo, it *was* a map of the New York underground railway system. And lo, when I held my map up against it and got it round the right way and everything, the two were an all but perfect match. And I carefully traced the railway lines with my finger, noting that my fingernails dearly needed cutting, and I concluded that the location of the entrance to the Lost City of Begrem had to be right there, beneath *that* particular station.

And I peered at the name of that particular station. And the words on the map read Mornington Crescent East (discontinued usage).

Mornington Crescent! I was amazed. Discontinued usage? That would mean *closed*, I supposed.

And I folded up my map and stuck it back into my pocket. And I folded up the waitress's map and kept that, too. And I got a bit of a smile going then (even though I wasn't *that* happy) because I *did* now have the location of the entrance to a lost city of gold. So I had pretty much cracked everything that needed to be cracked and so must be on the home straight and about to storm across the finishing line as an outright winner. So to speak and things of that nature generally.

I'd just have another cup of coffee, and another donut, because I couldn't be sure when I'd be eating later. Then I'd saunter on over to Mornington Crescent East, gain access to its murky depths and hit the lost city of gold. Job done.

And you really would have thought that it would have been as simple as that, wouldn't you?

So I ordered more coffee and a further donut. And then I ducked very low to avoid the coffee pot that was swung at the back of my head.

Which I did because I heard the thoughts of the waitress. And these went, 'It's that psycho-terrorist, and if I smash his brains in now, I can claim the reward and put the money towards a Butlins holiday at Bognor in England.'

Which made me feel rather glad that I had developed those extraordinary sensitivities whilst I'd lain in my God-awful coma. And I didn't hit the waitress, because hitting women is wrong, but I did make my getaway from that Donut Diner, leaving my latest coffee undrunk and half a donut uneaten. Which was a waste, really, but what was I to do?

And I ran once more through the streets of New York, ducking and diving and dodging. And the late-afternoon sun shone down darkly, casting long shadows of the New Yorkers, some singles, some doubles, and I ducked, dived and dodged.

And presently after much asking and, I confess, some degree of misdirection and requests for alms upon the part of native New Yorkers, I found myself standing outside Mornington Crescent East (discontinued usage) Underground Station. It was ancient, run-down, fly-blown, plastered over with posters. And above it, soaring up into the sky, was a mighty office block of a building. And upon this a mighty sign of a sign that read 'THE BIG APPLE CORPORATION'. Which rang a distant bell with me, as this was the corporation that Mr Ishmael was supposedly the managing director of.

'It figures,' I said to myself. 'Right here, over this station.'

And a New York bum approached me and enquired whether I might be of a mind to transfer some of my own funds into his possession. He was a rather splendid bum, as it happened, smelling strongly of Thunderbird wine and bodily odours and sporting the wildest hair and beard and the shabbiest clothes I've ever seen. What a wretch. It made me feel most superior to encounter such a degraded specimen of humanity.

'Come on, buddy,' he said to me. 'We bums have to look after each other, right?'

'What?'

'Knights of the Road, *buddy*,' he said. 'Hobo Chang Ba and all that kind of a carry on.'

'Hit the road, *buddy*,' I told him, 'or fear the wrath that comes in the shape of a trusty Smith & Wesson.'

'God damn company man,' he said. And he spat, as they do, those bums.

'Company man?' I said. 'What of this?'

'I saw you looking up there at the BAC. I used to work there. I was big in advertising, would have made CEO but for the takeover.'

'Go on,' I said. 'I'm listening.'

'The company was bought up. A hostile takeover. And not by another advertising company, oh no. Do you know who took over the BAC?'

'No,' I said and I shook my head. To indicate that I didn't.

'The CIA,' said the bum. 'That Keith Crossbar had me sacked. Threw me personally out of my office on the very top floor. Said, "This will do me nicely," and out I went. He had me thrown down the lift shaft. But luckily the lift was coming up from the floor below so I only broke my back and spent ten years in a coma.'

'Right,' I said. And who could say 'right' much better than me?

'Fifty dollars will do me,' said the bum.

'Take a hundred,' I said. And peeled one out of my pocket.

'God bless you, buddy,' said the bum. 'And if there's anything I can do in return, don't hesitate to mention it and we can negotiate a price.'

'There is one thing,' I said. 'This here station.'

'The Subway?' he said.

'Oh, that's what they're called. The Subway, yes. As a Knight of the Road, I'll just bet you'd know a way of getting in here. Right?'

And I watched as the colour drained from his dirt-besmirched face. And he threw up his hands and he waved them at me and he grew most animated.

'You don't want to go in there, mister,' he said, dropping the less formal 'buddy'. 'Terrible things go on in there. Terrible things. They say a train got walled-up in there in Victorian times and that the descendants of the trapped victims of the walling-up have become cannibals and—'

'Have to stop you there,' I told him, 'but thanks all the same. Farewell.'

And on the understanding that no further largesse was to be granted him, he shuffled away, mumbling words to the effect that he *would* kill again and that it was God who told him to do it.

And I realised exactly how much I had missed New York while I had been all banged-up in my hospital bed. And I realised that perhaps it wasn't really *that much* at all.

And I viewed once more the abandoned Subway station and wondered exactly how I was to gain entry to it. And then what exactly I would do when I had. I really needed some kind of a plan. Or some kind of a something. And I stroked my chin and shuffled my feet and wondered just what it would be. And glancing, as if by chance, across the street, I noticed a shop with a great big sign above it. And this sign read *ACME Subterranean Expedition Outfitters and Forcible-Entry Specialists.*

'I wonder if they have a phone?' I wondered to myself. 'Then I could phone someone for advice.'

Right.

It was a wonderful shop. Never in my life have I seen a more comprehensive selection of subterranean expedition outfittings. I was particularly impressed by the chrome carabiners, the belay devices, the braided cords, cap lamps, caving helmets, chest harnesses, dry sacs, elbow-patches, dynamic ropes, Maillon Rapide screw links and polyester webbing.

Not to mention the shock-absorbing lanyards and the semi-static ropes and the micro-slim emergency cord.

Which on this occasion I did, because I wanted to buy all of it.

I pointed to this and that and indeed the other and told the proprietor, Mr Ashbury Molesworth, that I would have them. And I purchased a really over-the-top-of-the-range sleeping bag, and some special chocolate that gives you energy. And I also purchased some *other stuff*!

'Are you going in *deep*?' he asked. In a suitably dark voice.

'Very possibly so,' I said. 'Could you recommend a decent torch?'

And he did. The Astra Multi-Beam one-million-candlepower mega-torch. And also an ACME Ever-Lite Varie-Flame cigarette lighter, to light candles once the battery of the Astra Multi-Beam had given up the ghost.

And I took everything he recommended, including a ukulele, which he said was good for relieving boredom when trapped several hundred feet below the surface of the Earth, with little or no hope of rescue. And Mr Molesworth encouraged me to take a telescope and a 26.5 mm Very flare pistol with a telescopic sight. And although I said that I really couldn't see the point of taking them on a subterranean journey, he assured me that they might prove to be invaluable. So I took them.

'I'll take a spare set of strings for the ukulele, too,' I said, 'in case once I've fired my flares it takes a really long time for me to starve to death.'

'Well prepared is best prepared,' said he. 'Why, I'm really getting quite excited myself.'

'Why?' I asked him. Because I wanted to know.

'Because,' he said, 'you're English, aren't you? I can tell by your voice.'

'I am,' I said. 'And *that* makes you excited?'

'Not as such. It's just that you Brits never get the hang of American dollars, so you won't notice just how much I grossly overcharge you for all this specialist equipment.'

'Ah,' I said. 'Well, you have probably made a fundamental error there, because I have no intention of paying for any of these items. I have a gun in my pocket and shortly will be pointing it at you.'

And oh how we laughed.

Until I produced the gun.

But eventually we came to an arrangement, which involved him selling me the items I required for a fair price, in exchange for me not holding him up at gunpoint and taking everything for nothing.

I remain to this day uncertain as to which of us came out best upon the deal.

But finally I was all togged-up. And all paid-up. And as night was falling, the proprietor all closed-up. And I found myself back in the street.

Although this time perfectly attired and equipped for the task that lay ahead.

To enter Mornington Crescent East (discontinued usage).

Descend from it to the entrance of the lost city beneath.

Enter the lost city and avail myself of whatever there was to avail myself of.

Return to the surface, bearing same.

Defeat and destroy the Homunculus.

Beer at Fangio's.

Bed.

Done and dusted.

Piece of cake.

And all that kind of caper.

58

Orpheus descended into the Underworld. He went there to rescue Eurydice, I think, although I never paid as much attention to that particular Greek myth. I liked Odysseus shooting that big arrow into the eye of Polyphemus the Cyclops. And the Gorgon, with all those snakes on her head. And Hercules mucking out the stables. Anything, really, that involved Ray Harryhausen doing the animation. And I wondered, to myself, privately, as I prised open an entry into that long-deserted station, whether, just perhaps, if everything did go well and I did win and everything, I might attain the status of mythic hero and Ray Harryhausen might do the animation for any of the monsters I might encounter. When they made the movie.

Monsters? Now why had I thought *that* word? I squeezed between boards that I had parted and found myself within. Little light was there to greet me and so I switched on the brand new Astra Multi-Beam and revelled in its million candlepower.

There is something rather special about old deserted stations. Well, old deserted anythings, really. They are redolent with all kinds of things. They are the stuff of memory. There are faded posters and ephemera and ceased-to-be cigarette packets. And the dust has that certain smell and things have made nests. And what was once commonplace is now mysterious and intriguing.

I viewed a crumbling poster that advertised a wartime ersatz cheese, that was manufactured from hand-laundered pine cones. And the word 'cheese' made me nostalgic. I thought of Rob and those early days with The Sumerian Kynges. He'd always had this thing about cheese. And I wondered what had happened to him and whether he was even still alive. And I thought of Neil and of Toby and of Andy. And what *they* would think if they knew that I was *here*, right *now*, doing *this*.

And I shrugged off the sadness that had suddenly descended upon me and shone my torch about a bit more. I was in the concourse of what must once have been quite a substantial station, with marble flooring and etched-glassed ticket booths. And stairs leading down. And I took them.

The torchlight tunnelled ahead of me as I descended those stairs. And my footfalls echoed and I felt very alone. Perhaps, I thought, I should establish a base camp here, get a fire going and bed down for the night. I was very much looking forward to getting into my over-the-top-of-the-range sleeping bag. And that special chocolate that gave you energy sounded particularly tempting.

'Perhaps a bit further down,' I told myself. 'At least as far as the platform.'

And I continued down and down with the light going on before me.

And it didn't smell so bad down here. Not nearly as bad as it smelled topside. But then there were no people down here.

No people!

That was it, wasn't it? That smell. That rancid smell that cloaked New York above. It was the smell of death.

The smell of the dead. The walking dead. How horrid. And the living must have let it creep up on them, more so and more so, without even noticing it.

Very horrid.

The platform formed an elegant arc, tiled in glazed terracotta. There were lamps in the Tiffany style, hanging at intervals. There were more wartime posters, this time for violet wands, which had evidently been in great demand, along with electric enemas and patented pneumatic trusses. Thinking about it, there appeared to have been a very great deal of illness back in the war days, all of which required specific patented equipment of the electrical persuasion to effect all-but-miraculous cures. Most of which plugged in and vibrated. So no change there, then. Boom-boom.

And the sun may well have gone behind a cloud somewhere and a dog may well have howled somewhere else, in the distance, but I was deep down down below, so I was unaware. I also spied upon the wall something that I might not have expected to have seen. To whit, a number of posters advertising the movies of George Formby. It appeared that there had been showings of his movies right here on the platform during the war years. Perhaps to engender some kind of Blitz spirit amongst New Yorkers. To prepare them in case *they got theirs*, as it were. Which they didn't, of course, but they might have.

What to do now, though? Wander down a tunnel?

I wasn't keen on that idea. The friend I mentioned earlier, who had once been in the TA, had also once worked for London Transport, on lifts and escalators. And he told me that it was forbidden for any London Transport sub-ground operative to walk down a tunnel unaccompanied.

'Because,' he told me, 'if you fell over or got knocked down or something, the rats would eat you up.'

So not, perhaps, down the tunnel.

'So,' I said to myself, 'if I was a lost city of gold hereabouts, where would I have my hidden entrance?'

And an answer returned to me in an instant. And *hidden* this answer was. Because it would be hidden, wouldn't it? Because if it hadn't been hidden, then wartime travellers would have stumbled upon it. Wouldn't they? And I agreed, with myself, that they would.

'I think that maybe I should establish base camp right here, right now, get a fire going, get into my sleeping bag and eat the special chocolate, was my considered opinion. Finding this city might just take a bit longer than I might have hoped. And it would be best to go about searching for it all bright and fresh.

But do you know what? I didn't do that. Because many-togged as that sleeping bag might have been and inviting to equally many, I had just spent ten years on my back and had probably had all the sleep I needed for the foreseeable future.

So, press on. But to where?

And now I considered the *other stuff*. I previously mentioned the *other stuff*, but only briefly and in passing and was in no way specific or indeed even hinted as to what the *other stuff* might be. And this I did because I didn't know whether I would need to use the *other stuff* or not. And if I wasn't going to use it, then I didn't want to get the reader's hopes up that I *might* use it, only to dash them down when I didn't.

But *now* I considered the *other stuff*. Because the *other stuff* might just be the solution to finding the hidden entrance.

And so now I will name the *other stuff* specifically.

It was manufactured by ACME.

And it was dynamite.

A dozen sticks of it, with fuses.

Well, I couldn't let dynamite slip by, could I? I mean, how many times in your life have you ever had the chance to let off a stick of dynamite? Probably never, that's how many.

Dynamite! I divested myself of my multi-denominational rucksack, un-Velcroed the windproof, rainproof coverall top flap and dug down deep into the contents therein and came up with a stick of dynamite. And examined it by torchlight.

Dynamite! A red sealed tube, like in the movies, with a fuse sticking out of one end.

Dynamite! I gave it a little loving stroke.

In all truth, I had been looking for the slightest opportunity to use it. I had even thought of letting off a stick upstairs by the ticket booths, just to see how much damage it would do. But I wisely considered that at ground level it might draw some unwanted attention from passers-by.

But down here . . .

Dynamite!

'Calm yourself, Tyler,' I told myself. 'It's only dynamite.'

Only!

But I did calm myself down. And I had a good think. Where should I place this dynamite? Lowest point in the station seemed favourite. But surely I was there now. On the track, then? Sounded good. Where-abouts?

So many questions!

'Right in the middle,' I said to myself, and my words echoed up and then down the ancient platform.

I took myself, my rucksack and my torch and my dynamite along that platform until I had reached roughly the middle. And satisfying myself that this *was* roughly the middle and that I *was* now having a very exciting time, I laid down my rucksack and shone my super-torch onto the track. A rat scuttled by and I didn't like that. But I did have the dynamite. So how much to use? How powerful *was* dynamite? How many seconds would I have to make away to a place of safety once I'd lit the fuse? How far *was* a place of safety?

Too many questions.

'In answer to the first question, how much to use,' I said in a whispery tone, 'I have twelve sticks, so let's say, well . . .' And I counted on my fingers and made that thinking-face. 'Six?' I said. Yes, six sounded like a nice round figure. If there was a lost city below, then six sticks of dynamite should be able to blast a way through to it.

Six it was, then.

I fished out another five. And by the megawatt light of my most excellent torch, bound them together with a length of ACME Patented Climbing Cord. Cut to length with my multi-blade Swiss Army knife.

I got my rucksack back onto my shoulders, then took from my pocket my brand-new ACME Ever-Lite Varie-Flame lighter and thumbed it into flame. I figured that to light just the one fuse would probably be enough. And this I now did. Noting the wonderful fizz as it lit and all the pretty sparks.

And then I tossed the bundle of dynamite sticks down onto the railway track and took to my heels at the hurry-up. And if it was interesting, from a detached point of view, just how fast you can run when pursued by policemen firing guns at you, it was equally, if not more so, interesting to note that you can run *even faster* when faced with the possibility of being blown to pieces by dynamite.

So to speak.

I legged it up that platform and up those steps and all the way back to the ticket booths above. And I flung myself down into one of those booths and assumed that foetal position Fangio had favoured earlier in the day and I switched off my torch and covered my ears and held my breath and waited.

And I won't draw things out. I reckon it couldn't have been more than thirty seconds later when that dynamite went off. And it wasn't deafening where I was, all huddled. But there was a terrific *woomph!* and a terrible shudder, as of an earthquake starting up. And then there was the dust. And I hadn't really allowed for the dust. Or given the dust a moment's thought. Even imagined that there would be any dust.

But that dust came rushing up the stairs and suddenly the darkness was a stifling darkness. A choking darkness. A fatally asphyxiating darkness.

And I coughed and croaked and spluttered in this lung-filling darkness and it was pretty horrible, I can tell you.

And I don't know whether I passed out or not. But I do recall switching on my torch and finding myself looking like a grey snowman. And having to empty my nostrils and cough up clouds of dust. And then do a lot of manic pattings to restore myself to a measure of sartorial elegance.

'I must remember in future about the dust,' I said. In a hoarse and baritone voice. 'But let's go and look at the damage.'

And I descended once more to the platform of Mornington Crescent East (discontinued usage). And, shining my torch all around and about, declared that it was a mess.

It was now a most untidy platform, all smothered in great boulders and rocks and everything velvet with dust, and I steered my way between the boulders and rocks to view the epicentre of the concussion.

And shone my torch down into a very large hole indeed.

It was a real humdinger of a hole.

A veritable pit-shaft.

And as I flashed my flashlight down, I thought I discerned amongst gentle twirling risings of dusts a certain degree of twinkling.

And as I looked and as I saw, certain words came to me.

From my memory. Words I had once read in a book about the discovery of the tomb of Tutankhamun. And of how Howard Carter had knocked a small hole through the wall of the tomb and shone *his* torch inside.

'What do you see?' Howard had been asked.

And he said, 'Wonderful things.'

59

And thus did I descend into the abyss.

Upon braided cord, secured by a chrome carabiner and employing certain belay devices, shock-absorbing lanyards and polyester webbing.

A veritable sight to behold.

But no one beheld me as I lowered myself carefully down. Down, down to where I beheld the beauty of sparkling gold. For sparkling gold there was a-plenty. My big mega-candlepower torch, affixed to my person with the appropriate chest harness, cast its brilliant light across burnished walls and dazzling, glittering spires. I was above the city of Begrem, which, it appeared, was enclosed within a monstrous cavern. One that now had a dirty great hole in its ceiling. Happily, I had not skimped upon the braided cord. And I had gone for the best-quality ACME nail-clamp-pseudo-sprockets, so the pulley-wheels whirred upon frictionless bearings as I went abseiling down.

To land in some central plaza, surrounded, it appeared, by buildings of the Byzantine persuasion. There was much in the way of helmed and hipped roofs, Palladian-style minarets, fluted in the Isabelline fashion. Lancet windows were in evidence, but also Diocletian, in the clerestory regions. And there were cusps and cupolas and flying buttresses a-plenty.

And so on and so forth and suchlike. So, a somewhat eclectic collection of archaeological styles. To say that I was entranced would be to severely underplay the emotions that were whirling all around and about within me.

I had found it. I had actually found it. It actually existed.

I had dreamed of this moment. When I had lain there in that hospital bed, I had dreamed of finding Begrem. I had pictured myself strolling amongst its ruins, picking up this golden gewgaw and that. Tossing them into my rucksack. Returning to the surface in glory.

And now I was here. And I felt desperately lonely. All of a sudden, I did. It just swept over me. I was all alone here in this lost city, and no one knew of it. Mr Ishmael, he knew of it. But he wouldn't know that

I was here now. Nor my family, nor any one of the few friends that I had. I was totally alone. And I really hated it.

But I did love it, too. Being *here*. Incredible.

I disconnected myself from the braided cord, unclipped my torch and flashed it all around. And the gold of the buildings twinkled and glittered, and then I saw something more.

And I switched off my torch. Because there was light here, here in this sunken realm, a soft effulgence that seemed to swell from the very golden buildings themselves. It was so unspeakably beautiful that I sank down to my knees and, lacking any words that could be said, I had a little cry.

And then I pulled myself together. And took myself off to explore.

There was quite a lot of rubble on the central plaza, all blown down by the force of my explosion above, and I have to admit that it did somewhat sully the golden cityscape. And that made me feel rather guilty, because this place had lain here hidden from the eyes of man for centuries and now I had arrived and littered it up and made mess.

And that made me sigh somewhat. But then I thought, well, what the hey, I can always get it cleaned up before I open it to the tourists (*live* tourists) and get a few food concessions going down here.

So I went off to explore. And all about me the buildings twinkled and glimmered, magically, magically, weaving wonderful spells.

'I wonder where the King's palace is?' I wondered. Because if I was going to set up camp here, and I *was*, well, where better to set it up than in the palace of the King? In fact, where better to spend the night than in the King's bedchamber itself? And then another thought struck me, for many thoughts were now coming my way. I could live here. In this magical city. In the King's palace. After all, *I'd* found it. This was all my discovery. This was *all mine*! And I could have electrics run down here and set myself up in the palace.

I sniffed at the air. And the air smelled good. None of that taint from above. There was a golden purity down here. Living here would be as near to living in Heaven on Earth as surely was possible.

This and many other such thoughts, some supportive and others contradictory, blustered about in my head, bumping into each other, big ones elbowing smaller ones aside, mad ones rising to prominence, then getting all dashed away. And I had to sit myself down upon a golden pavement and take a few breaths to steady myself. Because a man could well go mad with all this thinking and I didn't want *that* to happen, not now I'd come this far.

And I had travelled far and no mistake from my upbringing in Ealing and Southcross Roads School. Being a detective with my brother Andy. Being with The Sumerian Kynges. Meeting Lazlo Woodbine. And meeting Elvis also. Although I didn't want to dwell too long on *that*.

It had been a very strange trip and I knew now that it was nearing its end. That my journey through life, a life that had ticked and tocked and ticked itself away, was coming to an end. I knew that I would find what I wanted here and with it I *would* defeat and destroy the Homunculus. I just *knew* that I would do this, though don't ask me how I knew.

And so I set out for the palace. And the palace was not too difficult to find. I reasoned that it would probably hold the best, most prominent position in the city and be the biggest, grandest building there was. So I returned to my dangling braided rope, shinned up it a bit and took a good look all around.

And it didn't take too long to spy out a vast building of enormous and imposing grandeur. Which just *had* to be the palace, really. And so, shinning down, I set out in its direction.

As I strode along through the ancient streets, I did wonder one thing, amongst all the others. And that one thing was, I wonder what happened to all the people?

Would I come across skeletons in regal robes seated about a grand table in the royal dining room? I wondered. And might there be a skeleton waiting to greet me around the next corner?

And might there be ghosts?

Now *that* was a thought, *ghosts*. If God smote this city, and it was a pretty dead cert that he had, then did He smite all the people in it straight to Hell? Or did He doom a few to wander for ever throughout the sunken city, bewailing their foolishness in falling out with the Almighty?

And that sent a bit of a chill up me. Because this wasn't then just a sunken lost city of gold. This was a *cursed* sunken lost city of gold.

And I might now be one of the cursed for entering it.

And I had to have another sit down and take a few more deep breaths. And I helped myself to a bit of special chocolate, because I reasoned that my energy levels might well have fallen somewhat, which might account for all this gloominess of thought.

And after I'd had the special chocolate, *all of* the special chocolate, and washed it down with a bottle of special glucose drink, I felt a lot more chipper. Quite bouncy, really. In fact, more than just a little hyper.

And I pressed on with a goodly spring in my step.

And soon reached the gates of the palace. And these gates were golden, which came as no surprise to me. And also open, which came as a bit of a surprise. Although I'm not entirely certain why I'd thought they would be closed. Probably so that I could dramatically fling them open, I suppose. And so in order to have just one more thing to remember, I edged the gates closed and then I flung them dramatically open. Nearly taking both my arms out of their shoulder sockets. Because they *were* most heavy gates.

And then I entered the courtyard and then I entered the palace of the King, of King Georgius, who had struck the deal with Satan and created the first Homunculus. How many centuries back? Well, many more indeed than I could clearly recall being told of.

And within, all was gold.

I spied out tables and couches and settles and settees. Vases and knick-knacks and whatnots stacked in threes. Plates and pans and flowerpot stands and fixtures and fittings and a great big throne.

And all of these were of gold.

And there were tapestries and tabards and tablecloths and toiletries and tambourines and tricycles and tubas and trumpets, too.

And these too all of gold.

And I sat down upon the King's throne. And I felt suddenly sick. Because it was too much. It was all too much. It was too much gold. More gold than the human mind was ever intended to see. Gold is precious because it is pure and because it is *not* commonplace. But a golden city, where everything is gold, was simply too much. And frankly it made me feel rather poorly. And so I sat in a slump on the King's golden throne and buried my face in my hands.

And then I heard the voices.

And that did make me worried. Because, let's face it, when you start to hear the voices, you know you're in really big trouble, mentally.

But hear the voices I did. And I heard the voices chanting. It sounded to me like a Latin chant, which would probably be about right for a place like this. But as I listened more carefully to these chanting voices, I came to realise almost immediately that they were not the product of madness. They were the product of real people chanting. Real people? Or the ghosts of real people?

I huddled on that throne and I listened. It really did sound like Latin.

> *Wennem clennum wendos.*
> *Wennem clennum wendos.*
> *Ukenem siewott iken sennun.*
> *Wennem clennum wendos.*

Well, that's what it sounded like to me. It was definitely Latin, and once more I fretted that I'd never been taught Latin. At a time like this, a working knowledge of Latin would have come in very handy.

And the chanting voices drew closer.

And everywhere I could hear the sounds of marching, charging feet (boy!).

And something told me that these sounds were not the sounds of ghosts, but indeed the sounds of men. But men? And here? Here in this sunken world? *My* sunken world?

'Oh dear me,' I said to myself. 'It's *their* sunken world *I'm* in.'

And *that really* upset me.

And it worried me also, because the chanting was becoming ever louder and the marching, charging feet were growing closer and closer. And it seemed very likely that they were marching and charging to this very throne room. And that if they were and if they found me here, trespassing, as it were, they might not take to me altogether kindly.

Of course, there was always the chance that they might. That they might welcome me eagerly and ask me to marry the present King's daughter, if there was one. But this thought did *not* cross my mind. Because sometimes, when I'm really up against it, I can be just plain pessimistic.

But whatever the case might turn out to be, I shinnied right out of that big throne and scuttled around behind it and hid myself from view.

But peeped out a little from the side, to see what was going on.

And presently people entered the throne room, marching, charging and chanting.

> *Wennem clennum wendos* (they went).
> *Wennem clennum wendos.*

And I beheld these underground folk and they were, frankly, gorgeous.

Their complexions, their clothing and their hair colour shouldn't have surprised me. It was all-over gold. And I could see that their eyes were golden, too. As were their tongues. And although they presented by this colouring a most alien appearance, it was one of such striking beauty that I found my eyes popping wide and my lower jaw dangling down.

And they marched and charged and chanted. And then they stopped. And I beheld, in the midst of them, that they carried aloft a saintly statue of a grinning man of benign appearance. And although the golden folk who carried this statue wore the robes of olden days, this statue appeared to be attired in twentieth-century clothing. Or indeed an impression of it, as a child might draw a house from memory. But the face of the statue was well crafted. The grin was a big one, which exposed a goodly array of teeth, and the eyes were crinkled and friendly.

And there was something familiar about that face. It was as if I had seen it before somewhere. Knew the owner of that face.

But then a fellow gold all over and slightly taller than the rest approached the golden throne, bowed before it and then turned to face the congregation before him.

'*Ettas ternowt nysee gen. Ettas ternowt nysee gen,*' he intoned, most solemnly. And the golden folk did bowings of the heads and mumbled the same in reply.

And I looked very hard at that statue. Stared very hard indeed.

And as the congregation took up their former chant once more, I heard it. Heard it for what it really was. Saw *him* for who *he* truly was.

> *Wennem clennum wendos.*
> *Wennum clennum wendos.*
> You can see what I can see
> When I'm cleaning windows.

And yes, it was him. It *was him*.
That statue, carried aloft, was *him*.
George Formby.

> *Ettas ternowt nysee gen.*
> It has turned out nice again.

And I began to laugh.

And that, it turned out, was a bad thing. And it did not turn out nice again at all.

Because I was overheard in this laughter and I was set upon and I was battered a good many times until I fell once more, and almost willingly, considering all the pain, down and down into that whirling black pit of oblivion.

60

You know that dream you have, where you're on your holidays and you're on a coach going off for a day trip to see some well-known tourist thing, like the Grand Canyon or the Taj Mahal, but the driver takes a wrong turn (and you never know whether he did this on purpose) and you end up in the square of an ancient Aztec city, one of the ones with the big stepped pyramids with the sacrificial altar on the top. And the next thing you know, you are being hustled out of the bus by all these natives with exotic jewellery and up to the top of that pyramid and onto that altar. And a high priest sort of chappie has you all held down and then bares your chest and brings out this razor-sharp dagger and raises it high—

And then the alarm goes off, so you miss the exciting bit.

Well, I was having one of those dreams and it was just getting to that exciting bit when, wouldn't you know it, I was woken up, and so I missed the exciting bit once more.

Woken up by a splash of cold water right across the gob. To find that I was strapped, all spreadeagled and half-naked, across what, from my limited field of vision, appeared to be a sacrificial altar.

Is that ironic, or what?

And I was about to remark upon its irony, or what, when a certain cold, hard hit of reality informed me that I might well be in a bit of a fix here. Because the high priest chappie, who had been intoning the 'it's turned out nice again' line, was looming over me, holding in his golden mit a whopping great golden dagger.

And I spoke out regarding my disinclination towards him bringing that item of weaponry into close proximity with my person, or indeed to a proximity that was well within it. But found that I could not. As someone had stuffed up my mouth. Which caused a real speech impediment.

And I recalled the fear I'd felt when I'd been made the target of an auto-da-fé in the garden at Graceland. And I felt a similar fear right now. At least this death would probably be a quick one. Although I did recall that Captain Lynch had once told me how the priests were so skilled with their knives that they could plunge in, slice away arteries and withdraw the heart, still beating, to display before the victim's still-living eyes.

And I didn't fancy that one bit.

And so I tried, with renewed vigour, to give voice to my misgivings. But again without success.

And the priest began a new chant, which again sounded like Latin but was more like pidgin English when I listened carefully. And he chanted the first verse of . . . 'Mr Woo's a Window Cleaner Now'.

And then he ceased his chanting and he spoke unto me.

In a broad Lancastrian accent.

Which I will not attempt to imitate here. But he did use the phrase 'well, I'll go t't foot of our stairs' more than once.

'Oh monster,' he spake unto me. 'Oh horrid pink beasty from the overworld. We have now beheld the terrible ruination of Hindoo Howdoo Hoodoo Yoodoo Man Plaza. How you cast down your thunderbolts from above and descended upon a coloured rope of doom to destroy us all. We who have remained true to the True Faith, who worship at the shrine of the cheeky chappie.'

I thought that Max Miller was the cheeky chappie, but no matter. George was, after all, a generic, or indeed archetypal, cheeky chappie.

'As the words of the George came down to us in the ancient days, it was prophesied that an evil one would descend upon us. And that he would be all pinky pink. But that if we captured and ate him, it would all turn out nice again.'

And I said, 'Mmmph mm mm.' Which, I agree, had never proved to be much of a winner as a means of communication.

'So die, pinky overworlder!' And the blade, held high as ever, rose a tad higher.

And I went, '*Mmmph!*' which meant, '*Please.*' But no doubt sounded like mmph! And then the terrible blade came down and I closed my eyes and I prayed.

'Please, please, God,' I prayed. 'I know You're not going to help me. But I also know that in Your infinite wisdom You are infinitely wise and so me dying now in this horrible fashion is all part of Your divine plan. Although, and pardon me for putting in my three-pennyworth here, but it is my considered opinion that it would have been a better deal for Mankind, for *Your* Mankind, if I lived to fight another day and destroyed the evil Homunculus.'

And obviously, you have to understand, I prayed this *really, really* fast, because that blade was heading on down towards my heart and I didn't want to get cut off in mid-sentence.

And I heard the swish of that blade. And then nothing. And then whispering. And I opened my eyes and looked up. And there was someone rabbiting away into the priest's ear. And this rabbiter had one hand over the priest's knife-hand and had stayed its progress towards my heart. And I heard the priest say, 'Are you certain?' in a Lancastrian kind of a fashion. And the other fellow nodded hugely and replied, 'They are bringing it here even now.'

And I heard the priest say, 'Well, this puts an entirely different complexion on things. I will need to cogitate upon this intelligence.'

And with that he sheathed his dagger and marched and charged away.

Which left me to say thank you very much indeed to the Almighty and promise that I would not let Him down when it came to the slaying of the Homunculus and the saving of Mankind.

'Amen,' I said.

Though it sounded like, '*Mmph*.'

And then I was left alone for a bit. And then the priest returned, but this time *not* in the company of his dagger. *This time* he appeared in the company of several young and most nubile golden girlies, scantily clad and looking well up for it.

And he ordered one of these lovelies to unstrap me from the sacrificial altar and he began to speak to me words of apology.

'I, I mean *we*, are most humbly, humbly sorry, your mightiness,' said he. Which I liked the sound of. 'There has been a terrible, terrible mistake. A clerical error, I suppose. And fear not, I will find the individual responsible and have him hung up by his wedding tackle, whilst many blows are dealt to his snout with a stout stick.

'That it should happen today of all days. Upon this sacred day, which is to say *your* sacred day. Which, of course, would be why you chose this day to bestow upon us the wondrousness of your presence.'

And the lovelies were now dusting me down in a most intimate fashion and readjusting my clothing. And that did get a bit of a smile playing about my lips. But I really had no idea what this priest fellow was going on about.

And so I asked him.

'Hmmph mm mmph?' I went.

And then I removed the stuffing from my mouth. 'What *are* you on about?' I asked him.

'And he speaks the sacred Lancashireland.' And the priest fell down on his knees. And the lovelies fell down on their knees too all around me. And *that* was a really good look, I'm telling you.

'Up,' I said. To the priest. Eventually. 'Speak to me clearly.'

'Yes sir, yes.' And he called out now to some underling, 'Bring the sacred pouch. Display the sacred tools of Godhead.'

Which made me a trifle edgy. Because there was always the chance that a sacred pouch might contain the celestial castrating shears, or some other such sacred tool.

And an underling scuttled in and this underling had my rucksack.

'Oi!' I said. 'That's mine. Give it back.'

'Oh yes, your sirness, yes,' said the priest. 'But please, might I display the sacred tools? Might I touch the sacred tools?'

'If you must,' I said. And I shrugged. Which reminded me of the Shrugger. And I wondered whatever had become of him.

But not for long, as the priest had now taken my rucksack from the underling and had reverently opened it and was now spreading its contents out upon the sacrificial altar.

'You have them,' he said, in a hushed and awestruck tone. 'As it was prophesied. In a different prophecy altogether. The one about the coming of the Special One. You have the sacred tools.' And he pulled out a stick of dynamite. Which made me flinch somewhat. But there weren't any naked flames about, so I relaxed *slightly*.

'You have them!' he cried, in an exalted fashion.

'I do,' I said. 'And they're mine, so be careful.'

'Oh yes, sir, yes.' And he stroked the stick of dynamite. 'The Little Stick of Blackpool Rock,' he said.

And I remembered that song well enough – I'd rehearsed that particular George Formby number a goodly number of times in the music room of Southcross Roads School.

And the priest laid out the six sticks of dynamite. 'One for each of the ministers of the church,' he said.

'Absolutely,' I said. *What is this all about?* I thought.

And then his hands were once more inside my rucksack. In a rather intimate manner, I thought. Although I suppose it had never occurred to me that one could get all precious about the contents of a rucksack. But then I'd never owned one before.

'And *yes!*' cried the priest. 'You *do* have it. The sacred strumm-upon. The Instrument of God.' And he drew out the ukulele that Mr Ashbury Molesworth had sold to me as a useful means of passing the time when trapped hopelessly far beneath ground level.

'That's *also* mine,' I said. And I took it from his hands.

'And so,' he said, in a breathless fashion, 'can you strum the holy hymns upon the sacred strum–upon?'

'Can I!' said I.

'Well, can you?' said he.

'Yes, I can,' said I. 'Would you care for me to sing you a song?'

And the priest was speechless. But he nodded. And then he said, 'Sing one of the holy hymns of the George. Oh yes.'

And I took to checking whether the uke was in tune.

'It's G, C, E and A,' I explained. 'Or as we musicians say, *my dog has fleas.*'

And his head bobbed up and down.

And I said, 'Okay, it's in tune. So what would you like to hear?'

And the priest just turned up the palms of his hands and said, 'Anything, Lord sir.'

'Okey-dokey,' I said. 'In that case I will play one of my own compositions. I wrote this number in my head, when I lay in a coma in a hospital bed. But you don't need to concern yourself with that. I wrote it for one of my favourite authors. He is known as the Father of Far-Fetched Fiction and his name is Robert Rankin.'

The priest viewed me, blankly.

'Well, he *is* something of an acquired taste. But I wrote this song for him to sing. And it is sung to the tune of George Formby's "When I'm Cleaning Windows".'

'It's called—'

WRITING FAR-FETCHED FICTION

'And it goes something like this.' And I played and I sang. And it sounded something like this. To the tune of 'When I'm Cleaning Windows'.

> *Now I write Far-Fetched Fiction*
> *To earn a couple of bob.*
> *For a lazy blighter*
> *It's really the ideal job.*
> *I sit in pubs for hours and hours*
> *I drink Harveys, I drink Flowers,*
> *Then I go home for golden showers.*
> *Writing Far-Fetched Fiction.*
>
> *I sit about and sit about*
> *I sometimes get my ballpoint out.*

That really makes the barmaid shout.
Writing Far-Fetched Fiction.

In my profession I work hard
But no one gives a *uck.
It's blinking J.K. Rowling
Who rakes in every buck.

I drink until my guts explode
I stumble drunken down the road
I wish I'd written The Da Vinci Code
Instead of Far-Fetched Fiction.
   (Ukulele solo, with much finger-picking,
   cross-strums and scale-runs, not to mention
   an effective use of grace notes and chromatics.)

In my profession I work hard,
Well no, perhaps I don't.
I bet I'll win a Nobel Prize,
Well no, perhaps I won't.

But like the Murphy's, I'm not bitter
As long as I can raise a titter.
I think I'll pop out to the *hitter
And write some Far-Fetched Fiction.

                Thank you very much.

  And the priest just stood there. Speechless.
And then he cried, 'Off with this head.'
Which I didn't like too much.

61

And then, oh how we laughed.

Because, can you believe this, he was winding me up, that priest. Having a laugh. And he clapped his hands together and told me that it was a beautiful song, so beautiful, in fact, that the George himself might have written it. And he commented upon the quality of the lyrics and enquired what the phrase *golden showers* meant.

And I told him.

And he nodded and said that he was rather keen on that kind of thing himself. But then as everything was golden hereabouts, what was I to expect? And then he begged me to play some more. And so I did.

I did straight, classic George this time. 'Leaning on a Lamp Post', 'Grandad's Flannelette Nightshirt', 'Riding in the T. T. Races', and of course 'Little Stick of Blackpool Rock'. To which the priest waved one of my sticks of dynamite about and I had to stop playing and ask him to put it down.

But my performance drew much applause, especially from the golden girlies, who were still kneeling down all around me. And I figured that I was definitely going to get some hot group-groupie action later on.

Or as soon as possible, if the chance arose.

And the priest wanted more, but I told him that enough was enough for now and that I was actually a bit hungry, because it had been a trying day and I wouldn't say no to a good sit down and some tucker. And the priest said that yes, there should be a celebrational banquet to greet the arrival of the Special One, and he clapped his hands together and got some of his underlings straight onto the job.

And I gazed upon these golden people and considered that perhaps now my luck was in and that if things worked out, they could very well soon be *my* golden people.

And I recalled, well enough, that the name George Formby became, by anagram, *Orgy of Begrem*, so things *were* looking up. And they might work out.

But *what*, I *did* have to ask myself, was all this Formby nonsense all about? They literally seemed to worship the Duke of the Uke.

And then thoughts came to me of a conversation I had engaged in as a child with Captain Lynch. Who it seemed had taught me oh so much. It had been about the Melanesian cargo cult of Jon Frum. During the Second World War, the Americans set up an airstrip at Tanna, an island in Vanuatu, Melanesia. Planes flew in delivering all manner of cargo and the natives, who had never seen anything like this before, sat down and gave the matter a jolly good thinking about. And then drew some logical conclusions.

It was clear to them that these Americans were in touch with Flying Gods who brought them cargo, and that they had built the airstrip to lure down the aeroplanes of the Gods.

And so the natives built their own airstrip next door to the real one. And they dressed up in pretend American uniforms and imitated all the things the Americans did. And waited for their planes with their cargo to land. And they got it into their heads that the pilot, the Godly sky pilot who brought the cargo, was called Jon Frum. And they set up shrines to him and lit candles.

Of course, no aeroplane ever did land on their pretend airstrips and after the war the Americans went home and no more planes at all landed. But the natives never gave up hope. They maintained their airstrip and went through the magical motions.

I recall seeing a TV documentary about Tanna and the Jon Frum cargo cult, and this smart-arsed Christian reporter was interviewing an old cargo-cult priest. And he said to this priest—

'How long have you been waiting for Jon Frum's return?'

And the priest said, 'Twenty years now.'

And the Christian reporter said, 'Then don't you think that perhaps you should give up? Because he's clearly not coming back.'

And the old priest said, 'But you have been awaiting the return of your Jon Frum for nearly two thousand years.'

And the interview went no further.

And I remember that it really tickled me at the time.

And so I assumed that this George Formby business must be something like that. But exactly *how* had it come to pass?

Now *that* was a question.

And it was one that I put to the priest – the *high* priest, he was – over dinner.

And dinner was served in the big royal dining room, on the big royal dining table, from all the very best royal plates. The gold ones. And there were thirty or so of Begrem's top bods seated about that table and I was issued with three scantily-clad golden girlies to attend to my every need. But, not wishing to take any risks regarding protocol, I didn't get any of them to administer to certain manly needs in an oral fashion from underneath the table.

The food was, happily, not of gold. It wasn't too heavy on meat, but it was pretty big on mushrooms. And there were things in bowls that looked startlingly like cockroaches with their legs pulled off, which failed to tickle my taste buds. The wine was good, though, as was the bread. And there's always bread, isn't there? No matter where you go in the world, there's always bread in one form or another.

And I've always wondered about this. How did Man discover how to make bread, eh? It's quite a complicated process and you could never just stumble upon it by accident. But every culture appears to have invented bread. It's one of life's mysteries.

'What do you think of the bread?' asked the high priest, who sat on my right hand (well, not actually *on* my hand), for I had the big best seat in the house, right at the top of the table. On a big throne chair.

'It's splendid bread,' I told him. And I told him also how I'd always wondered about how Man came to invent bread. And he told me that in his opinion there was very little mystery.

'Just grind up your cockroach legs, mix with water and bake,' he said. And I moved on to the soup.

But I did broach the subject of George Formby. In as subtle a manner as I could. Because he was under the impression that I was a follower of the cult, a missionary or something, I supposed. So I had to tread with care.

'Speak to me of the George,' said I, 'and of how the word of the George came unto your kingdom. Ee-oop, Mother.' And I did a Formby giggle.

'Ah,' said the high priest, speaking with his mouth half-filled with bread, which frankly I could have done without. 'In ancient of times, there was a former priest of Begrem, one who held to the old wicked ways of necromancy and the breeding of the Homunculus. He claimed that he had received a divine revelation that there was a world above this one. That we inhabit an underworld, this dull, monochrome, worthless world, but high above there is a beautiful world where there are more colours. And you are here, from this world, which proves it. Although we did get it wrong initially when we thought that you were an evil demon sent down to destroy us all. But I *have* apologised for that.'

And I nodded and I smiled and said, 'Go on.'

'The priest had a mighty tower constructed that reached up to the rocky sky. And he set his underlings to cut into the rocky sky and tunnel upwards. And this they did for a considerable length of time, but as we have no concept of night and day, it is difficult to say quite how long.'

And I made a certain face to this, but bid him continue anyway.

'They tunnelled up and finally broke through into a tiled tunnel above. And it was not all mono-coloured. It was of many colours. And then they saw the folk above, gathered in congregation before the George.'

And I did noddings of the head to this, recalling the George Formby movie posters I'd seen in the station above. The tunnellers had clearly broken through during one of the nightly showings.

'And the priest passed down word of what he had seen, many words, the holy hymns – "The Lancashire Torreador", "Limehouse Laundry Blues" and all the rest. Because he saw the George as a great vision upon the wall, far bigger than any man.'

The movies for sure, I thought.

'And he passed on all of these wonders to our people, who turned then from their old evil ways to embrace the hymns and sayings of the George, that all might be happy and go to the foot of their stairs in a state of grace and abiding joy.'

'That's a lovely story,' I said.

'Story?' said the high priest.

'Well, I know it's all true, obviously.'

'And so our people prepared to go above, to join the worshippers in the Tunnel of the George. But as the priest climbed up there, the terrible Wheelie Monster mashed him all to pieces.'

'He was run over by a train,' I said, with some degree of sadness. And some degree of a smirk, which I hid. But I could see the funny side.

'A train?'

'It's a Wheelie Monster, like you said.'

'And so we knew that we were not yet worthy, that we had not yet earned the right to go above. And so the tunnel was filled in and the great tower demolished. But our prophets claimed that some time in the future, someone would descend to deliver us from this terrible place and take us above into the Tunnel of the George.'

'Yep,' I said, raising my glass. 'That's me. But why did you think I was some horrid monster and want to stab me up with your big knife?'

'It would appear that an underling turned over two pages at once of

The Great Book of All Knowledge (and Selected Lyrics). For it is written that two shall come down from above, The *first* being the Deliverer, the *second* being the pinky-pink monster that must be all cut to pieces at the hurry-up.'

'Well, *that* explains everything,' I said. And I smiled. 'Things are always so simple once they're explained, aren't they?' And then I whispered an enquiry as to whether I could do *anything* I wanted to do with the golden girlies.

And the high priest said that yes, I could, but *not* at the dining table as it would upset his mum, who was sitting down at the end. And I waved to his mum, a lady in a golden straw hat, and she waved back to me.

'Well, isn't this all very nice,' I said to the high priest. 'But I seem to be all filled up now, so I think that perhaps I will skip pudding and take myself off to my sleeping accommodation with a couple of golden girlies.'

But the high priest said that although he was happy enough with that, his mum, who was now very old, and who had always been a devoted follower of the George and had only clung on to life this far in the hope that she would live to see the Deliverer, would be sorely miserable if she was not able to bathe in my glorious presence for just a bit longer.

So I said, 'Okay, just a *bit*.' And the high priest offered me more wine, and I most gratefully drank it.

And although there were one or two things right in the forefront of my mind, these being scantily clad and golden, other thoughts came crowding in upon me. And these thoughts were all concerned with the Homunculus.

And I did think a great deal about the nature of coincidence. Because there seemed to be a lot of it about. Because if these people *hadn't* converted to Formbyanity, they would still be evil Homunculus fans, and I would surely have been sacrificed simply for the fun of it. But they were now goodies, all told, and they were anxious that the Deliverer deliver them from this place and lead them above.

Although I did wonder whether they were going to be very disappointed when they finally arrived topside. They'd probably be impressed with the sky and the sun and the moon and all that kind of cosmic caper, but all the walking dead and the horrible pongs? They probably were not going to be altogether taken with that.

But we'd just have to see.

And then a thought struck me. And it was a wondrous thought. I had come here hoping for gold, and I had found plenty of *that*. I had also come here in the hope that there would be something that could aid me in destroying the Homunculus. And I *had* found that also.

Because it wasn't a some*thing* that I needed.

And here, I suppose, I had a bit of a revelation.

It was a some*body*. And not just *one* somebody. I needed a lot of somebodys. An army of somebodys, to be precise.

Because if I was to go against an Army of the Dead, then I would need an army of my own. And what better army to take on an Army of the Dead than an Army of the Underworld?

And, satisfied that this was the solution, the answer to all my problems, I had another glass of wine.

And then another.

And then another one, too.

62

And then I awoke.

Of a sudden, and quite painfully and *not* upon a golden bed, flanked by golden girlies. But still in my seat at the banqueting table, face down in a bowl of cockroach.

And I went, 'Whoa!' And then I went, 'Sorry, all, too much wine there, must have dozed off for a moment.'

But I found, to my surprise, that I was addressing these words to no one in particular. In fact to no one at all. For all around me were empty chairs and dirty pudding dishes.

'Oh dear,' I said. 'They've all gone off to bed without me. What a bummer. I wonder where the golden girlies went?'

'*Up the cord*,' I heard someone think. And then I heard them say it. And it was the high priest's mum, the lady in the golden straw hat. And she sat where she had been sitting, spooning spoons of pudding into her gob.

'Up the cord?' I asked her. 'Whatever do you mean?'

'Up *your* cord, to the Tunnel of the George, as it is foretold in *The Great Book of All Knowledge (and Selected Lyrics)*.'

'*What?*' I shouted. Loudly.

'There's no need to shout,' said the lady. 'Although it says that you do, in the Book. When you have awoken after drinking the wine with the sleeping draft in it.'

'*What?*' I went, even louder.

'You have to hand it to those ancients, don't you?' said the lady. 'When it comes to prophecy they were pretty hot stuff. You wouldn't get that kind of accuracy nowadays. If we had days to now, as it were. But as we don't understand the concept, we don't, so to speak.'

'They've gone up the cord?' And I rose from the table. And staggered a bit and my head really hurt. 'I was drugged and the whole population of Begrem has absconded up my braided cord?'

'That sounds mildly obscene,' said the lady, 'but in essence you are correct. Only I remain behind, to attend to your every desire for ever and ever. Well, at least for as long as I last, which won't be too long with my health, I shouldn't wonder.'

'I appreciate the sentiment,' I said. Because politeness never costs. 'But I will have to pass on your kind offer. I have to get up the cord myself. It's not safe for them to go wandering around up there, all by themselves. And *drugged wine*! I'll have stern words to say about *that*!'

'Oh no you won't,' said the lady.

'Oh yes I will.'

'Oh no you won't.'

'And why will I not?'

'Because they pulled the cord up after them. Would you care for a bit of hanky-panky to take your mind off things?'

'*What?*'

And she told me what she had in mind.

'Oh *no*,' I said. 'Not *that*. I have to get out of here. Is there another way out?'

And that was a very silly question, wasn't it? Because of course there was *not* another way out. And so I sat in my big throne chair and had a good sulk and *almost* drank some more wine by mistake. And I glowered occasionally at the lady in the golden straw hat and knotted my fists and was grumpy. And the lady fluttered her eyelashes and carried on with her pudding.

'I'm trapped,' I said. And I threw up my hands. 'I could end up spending the rest of my life down here.'

'So you'd better get that hanky-panky while you can.'

'I have to escape. My whole life, so it seems, has been moving – or has been moved *for* me – towards a single goal. I have a purpose. I cannot deny my purpose. I *have* to escape.'

'*Amazing accuracy*,' thought the lady.

'What did you say?' I asked her.

'I didn't say anything, dear.'

'But you thought it.'

Can he be reading my thoughts?

'Yes, I can,' I told her. 'And you thought "amazing accuracy". And I know why you thought it.'

The Book. He'll want to see the Book.

'Thank you,' I said. 'I do. I want to take a look at this book of prophecy.'

It's hidden under your chair. 'My son took it with him,' said the lady.

But I delved under my chair. 'Aha,' I said. 'What is this?'

But the lady just spooned up pudding.

And I swept bowls and plates and drugged wine from the table and laid out the book (a golden book) before me. And leafed it open.

And there were illustrations and everything. And the illustrations of the Deliverer looked just like me.

'Uncanny,' I said and did some further leafing. And then I went, 'Well,' because I had come across an interesting page. I read from this, aloud.

' "And so did the Deliverer rail against his forced confinement and seek a way of escape. And it came to him, as if by the influence of the George Himself, that there was a simple solution that—" ' And I gazed across at the other page.

' "Knew he had been thwarted," ' I read. 'What?' And then I examined the Book with care. 'Someone has torn out the page,' I observed with bitterness in my voice.

'My son,' said the lady, looking up from her pudding bowl. 'For such was it written in the Book that he would.'

I made growling sounds, above and below my breath. 'And did it say also that the Deliverer would be prepared to torture the necessary information out of the high priest's mother, should she fail to divulge it willingly?'

'I believe it must have,' said the high priest's mum. 'Which is why I was never allowed to read the page in question.'

I slammed shut the Book. 'All very clever,' I said. 'But I *will* succeed. The question is, just how.' And I asked the lady whether she would be kind enough to direct me to an undrugged golden carafe of wine and she kindly did so. And I let her try some first, just to make sure.

And I drank wine and had a good think. And I do have to say that my thinking was *very* focused thinking. I feel that my situation and future prospects down there truly focused my thinking. Which was all geared towards the matter of escape.

And presently, and although I didn't see it myself, a certain look appeared upon my face. And it was the look of one beatified, enlightened. And I said, 'Eureka,' and brought my right fist down into the palm of my left hand. Which sadly had a cake in it. But I had had my Eureka moment.

'Where is my sacred pouch?' I asked the lady.

Under my chair. 'My son took it with him,' she said.

And I fetched my rucksack from under her chair.

And I sorted through its contents until I found those two things I really couldn't see the point of when I purchased all the other stuff: the telescope and the 26.5 mm Very flare pistol with the telescopic sight.

'Yes!' I went. And I punched the air. As one will do, when enlightened.

And I said my farewells to the lady in the golden straw hat. And she said that she was sad to see me go, but had rather been expecting it. And that I was to give her love to her son when I saw him and say that the pudding was nice.

And I returned to the central plaza, the Hindoo Howdoo Hoodoo Yoodoo Man Plaza, and I squinted up towards the hole I had blown oh so far up above. And it was a goodly hopeless distance above. But I did not despair. I took up my telescope and I focused upon the hole. It was still a hole. They hadn't blocked it up, by the look of it. So it was possible that—

And I took up the 26.5 mm Very flare pistol with the telescopic sight and I peered through the telescopic sight and did focusings with that also. And I went, 'Hmm. This might just work. Well, it had better.' And I took from my rucksack my coil of micro-slim emergency cord and also one of the three flares I had.

And I secured the cord to the end of the flare and I aimed at the hole through the telescopic sight and I fired.

And the flare shot up towards the hole, bringing a most wonderful illumination to the golden city. But fell short by several yards and nearly hit me on the head when it came down.

'Fair enough,' I said. 'A higher elevation would be favourite.'

And I entered the nearest tall building and went right up to its roof. Which made a great deal more sense.

And then I took another shot at the hole.

And I missed again. And the flare set fire to my cord and tore all away from it.

At which point some seeds of desperation began to take root in my mind. I only had one more go at this.

I damped down the end of the micro-slim emergency cord with a great deal of spit. Tied it to the remaining flare. Slotted the flare into the pistol. Took very, very careful aim and fired—

And the flare shot up into the air, glorifying the city with its light, and passed into the hole and upwards. And I watched the light above in that hole, that flare lying somewhere in the Subway station above now. And I watched the light dim away and die. And then I gave a little tug upon the rope. Because this *was* going to be tricky. And also it was going to be extremely dangerous and potentially life-threatening. Because it was only going to be luck if that flare caught on something up there that could support my weight as I climbed that goodly way aloft, upon that very slim line, which was going to be pretty tricky in itself. Really.

And I sighed and I took a deep breath. And I considered having another little pray to God. But I decided that I had surely worn out my requests of the Creator. One more would, perhaps, be looked upon unfavourably. So I did testings of the line. And it did feel sound and I considered how best to lighten myself.

Take everything off? Climb naked? Perhaps not. But take off the heavy stuff and don't bring the rucksack. Although perhaps do bring—

I tucked the item I had decided to bring into a trouser pocket. Tested the line once more, let it bear my weight, then took to climbing. And I do have to tell you, it was no easy matter. But I kept at it. Tenaciously. With dedication. With resolution. And steadfastness. And more dedication. And things of that nature.

Specifically.

And there I was, this tiny figure dangling above this sunken city of gold. A rather strange and anomalous sight, I supposed, to anyone who might have been looking. And, peering down, I noticed that the lady in the golden straw hat *was* looking.

And waving.

But I really couldn't wave back. But I smiled.

And I inched upwards, the slim cord cutting into my fingers and me growing all hot and bothered and very short of breath. But I pressed on. Onwards and upwards. And after what felt like a very long time indeed, but probably didn't seem like anything much at all to the lady in the golden straw hat, who had no concept of time, I was inside the rocky ceiling above the Golden City of Begrem. And here I was able to get a purchase with my feet upon rocks and this made the going easier. Although it did involve some rocks getting kicked away and hurtling below.

And I did register a distant scream, followed almost immediately by a sickening thud. But I did not give that too much thought, as I had other things on my mind. The lady had probably been able to dodge the falling rock in time.

And I climbed onward and upward.

And eventually emerged into Mornington Crescent East (discontinued usage) Subway station.

And I had a really good puff and a really good cough and I rolled over and lay there, between the ruination of the tracks, and I breathed a great big sigh of relief.

And then I all but pooed myself.

Because someone cried, 'It is he. The prophecy is fulfilled.' And I looked up, blinking and cowering, to find the high priest looking down upon me, and others of Begrem, and they were all holding burning torches to light up the platform, and cheering.

And the high priest had my flare in his hands and had evidently been holding it steady while I climbed.

'You,' I said. 'You held the rope for me.'

'I caught the flamy thing,' said the High Priest. 'It was very hot. It burned my hands.'

'You *waited* for me? You *helped* me? Why?'

And he flourished the page that had been torn from the Book. 'Because that is what it said I would do.'

'Oh,' I said. 'Well, splendid.'

'And we are all here, awaiting your orders. As we awaited your ascent of the cord.'

'Awaiting my orders?' I said.

'To engage in battle against the Evil One,' said the high priest, 'As is written. We all have our weapons and we await your orders.'

'Right,' I said.

'Your Army of the Underworld, to defeat the Army of the Dead.'

'Yes,' I said, with a great big grin. 'And how *cool* is *that*!'

63

And thusly did the golden Army of the Underworld smite the evil Army of the Dead. And verily did they smite them and did trounce them, too. And Tyler was made King of the City of Begrem and many were his golden concubines and muchly did he take his joy in them when he was not a-strumming upon his ukulele.

Or, so I thought, it could oh so easily be.

And I wished I'd read a few more pages of *The Great Book of All Knowledge (and Selected Lyrics)*. Just to make sure.

But I hadn't and I'd have to wing it.

But the golden warriors crowded all about me upon the rubbly platform of Mornington Crescent East (discontinued usage), all a-cheering mightily and rattling their sabers, and waving the flaming torches that they held.

And I gave hearty cheers to them and called them mighty men.

And I gave a little speech then of the 'once more into the breach, dear friends' persuasion. And I counted up those who crowded round me, some thirty in number, lit, rather nobly I thought, by the flaming torches, and bade them call to their comrades in arms, who were surely lolling about on the stairways checking out the ancient posters, that all should gather round to listen to, what I felt, would be later considered a historic speech.

As soon as I had managed to compose it in my head.

And the high priest did the calling out.

And he called out to me, saying—

'What other warriors, sire?'

And I liked the 'sire' part of that, but said, 'What do you mean by that?'

And he said, 'By which part of which?'

And I said, 'The bit where you asked me *what other warriors?*'

And he said, 'Oh, that bit, well, because there are no other warriors, sire. We are all the men of Begrem.'

'And the women also,' added a golden girlie.

'Except for my mum downstairs,' said the high priest.

And I said, 'Hold on there, what are you telling me? That you, noble fellows that you undoubtedly are, are *all that remain* of the people of Begrem?'

And the high priest shrugged and said, 'Well, how many folk could *you* sustain in a closed environment on a limited diet of cockroaches and mushrooms?'

And I did not like the tone of the high priest and did tell him so. And the high priest shrugged and said he was sorry, but surely thirty men *was* a pretty big army. And how many warriors did *I* think they were liable to run up against? Because they were all well hard and up for it. And the other army could come and have a go, if they thought they were 'ard enough.

Well, you had to admire his courage, anyway.

'So,' I said, suddenly downcast, 'just the thirty of you.'

'Thirty-one, including my mum.'

'Forget your mum,' I said. 'Although she did ask me to pass on her love and say that she really enjoyed the pudding.'

'Aie,' said the high priest. 'She's a bonny lass and no mistake.'

To which I raised my eyebrows, but had no reply to make.

'So, sire,' said the high priest, 'would you care to make your rousing battle speech now?'

And I took to shrugging and said that I was no longer in the mood and perhaps I'd make it later. But the high priest said that *now* really would be the best time. And that he had memorised the bit in the Book that said that I did. So it would probably be better for me if I didn't try to mess with prophesied Fate. And there was something about the way he said it that suggested he really, really meant it.

'Oh, all right then,' I said. All sulky. 'Gather round, oh mighty warriors, and hearken unto me.'

The high priest gave me the thumbs-up to this and winked an eye in my direction.

'Now is the winter of our discontent,' I began, 'when we must fight them in the fields and on the beaches and keep a welcome in the hillside and gird up our loins and ride 'em, cowboy. Cometh the hour, cometh the man. Cry God for Harry and the George. And the show's not over until the fat lady takes tea with the parson.'

And I paused and did noddings of the head. But nobody cheered.

So I continued in a likewise manner, 'The time is right for fighting in the street,' I said. 'War, what is it good for? Absolutely nothing. But you can't make an omelette without breaking eggs. Oh, and kill everyone and let God sort it out. Geronimo!'

And I stopped there and did some shakings of the head. And one of the golden girlies clapped a little.

'Oh, listen, fellas,' I said. 'I don't have any great battle speech to give you. Directly above us there is what you will consider to be a mighty tower. And at the very top of this tower sits the Evil One. Except at weekends, when he probably plays golf with the President, or something. But I'm pretty sure we can catch him in on weekdays. And although you don't understand the concept of days, I will explain it to you. But he's up there and we're down here. So the idea is that we get ourselves up there somehow and slay him, pretty much as bloodily as you fancy, really.'

And the golden warriors looked at one another and then they looked at me. And then one of them whispered some words into the ear of the high priest.

And the high priest said to me, 'He wants to know what an omelette is.'

'Right,' I said. And rightly so.

And then I had an idea.

'Anyone hungry?' I asked. And all of them nodded.

'Would you like to try a little top-side tucker?' And all of them looked rather blank.

'Food,' I said. 'Good food. No cockroaches. Well, possibly *some*, but they're not supposed to be included in the dishes. I'll treat us all to dinner – I've still got loads of money.' And I dug into my trouser pockets and I did still have loads of money.

'You lot stay here,' I said, 'in the Tunnel of the George, because he might appear at any moment to greet you.'

'You think so, sire?' said the high priest.

'I wouldn't be at all surprised. But I will go upstairs, and I'll bring us back food. Pizzas and Coca-Colas. I'll get lots. An army marches on its stomach, doncha know?'

And they all looked blank again.

'Just stay here,' I said, 'and I'll get food.'

'Do you wish to take a couple of underlings to fetch and carry for you, sire?'

'No,' I told the high priest. 'I'll be fine. Now, I'm going to leave you in charge down here.'

'I'm always in charge,' said the high priest. And he folded his arms rather huffily.

'Well, of course you are. So exert your authority and make sure that everybody stays put and no one goes upstairs.'

'Why?' asked the high priest.

'Because I say so?' I ventured.

'That's good enough for me,' said the high priest. And he saluted.

So I saluted back and took myself off and away from the platform at the hurry-up. And up the stairway. But as I didn't have my big torch, it was rather dark on the stairway and I tripped over a few times and got myself in a right old strop.

But eventually I made it to the concourse and from there to the outside world. Which wasn't too easy, as someone had nailed back the timber I had prised away to gain entrance.

But I did some petulant kickings and eventually I was out. And I sniffed once more at the New York air. And the New York air smelled rank. And I glanced up at that great building soaring high above, and I knew that *he* was in that building. The Homunculus, I could feel him. And a hunter's moon swam in the heavens above that building.

And it was night-time in smelly New York. But I didn't have a watch, so I didn't know what time of night-time it was. But it didn't really matter, because in New York, as in all civilized cities, you can always buy a pizza at any time of the day or night.

I glanced across the street to the parade of shops where I'd purchased all my sub-ground paraphernalia. I figured that if Mr Molesworth was still behind his counter, I'd pop in and sing the praises of his torch and braided cord. Not to mention the dynamite.

Which I thought that I probably wouldn't.

But all the shops were boarded up. And the boarding all covered in posters.

'That was a bit quick,' I said to myself. 'I was only in that shop yesterday and now it's closed down, been boarded over and smothered about with posters. They don't waste any time in New York, do they?' And assuring myself that clearly they did *not*, I went off in search of a pizza takeaway. Breathing through my mouth as I did, because New York really ponged.

And I hadn't got too far before I became a bit confused. Surely I was travelling back towards Times Square, back the way I had come yesterday. But all looked somehow different.

More modern, somehow, more futuristic.

More futuristic? I did groanings. I had done *futuristic* before. Back in nineteen seventy-seven. On that terrible day when I had entered the parallel world of the alternative reality and been (partially) responsible for the death of Elvis Presley. I couldn't be having with *futuristic*. *Futuristic* was trouble.

And if I *was* in some alternate reality again, it would be the work of the Homunculus. And it would mean that he knew where I'd been, and had been preparing this to greet me on my re-emergence from the Underworld.

You see, we detectives reason this kind of stuff out. It's what keeps us a cut above the plain and everyday folk.

So I worried about *futuristic*.

And I kept a wary eye out for airships that were powered by the transperambulation of pseudo-cosmic anti-matter. And blokes whizzing by on jet packs.

And I went trudging onward.

And presently I saw neon lights and a great big sign reading 'PIZZA'.

And I said, 'Praise the Lord,' to this and made my way inside.

And it did look rather futuristic. But in a downbeat sort of a way. All mod cons, but all mod cons well knackered. There was plenty of neon and plenty of chrome, and we all know deep down in our Fritz Lang's *Metropolis* hearts that the future will mostly be Art Deco-looking and composed of neon and chrome. And there was a feisty-looking New York girlie behind the counter. But it was a bit difficult to see too much of her because she stood behind a Plexiglas security screen. And it was somewhat grubby and stuck all over with stickers.

I spied out customers awaiting the arrival of their orders, and these numbered two: a tall Jewish-looking man in black, whose looks made me wonder whether Jewish had come back into fashion – retro-Jewish, a very good look, I thought – and a chap who had all the makings of a professional wino. Much like the bum I had encountered the day before, who had been thrown from his office by the Homunculus. But with slightly less hair and rather more smell. And two fine shadows he cast.

So I gave this fellow a bit of a miss, smiled politely at the Jewish-looking one and approached the counter. To have my way barred by the Plexiglas screen.

'Hey,' said the feisty New Yorker. Which I understood to mean, 'Hello'.

'Hey yourself,' I said.

'Hit the road, ya bum,' she said. And she smiled at me when she said it.

'I'd like some pizzas, please,' I said. 'Sufficient for thirty people. And I have the money in cash.'

'Out, ya bum,' she said. And she pointed to the door.

'I'm not a bum,' I said. 'I'm a detective.'

'Ya look like a bum to me.'

'That's not very kind,' I said. And then I caught a glimpse of my reflection in the Plexiglas. And I leaned forward to examine this reflection. And I was horrified by what I saw of this reflection. And I felt at my face. And it was most heavily bearded. With horrible heavy grey beard.

'What is this?' I cried, falling back somewhat and feeling at myself. And I pulled out beard, for much more was tucked all down inside my shirt. And it was a full grey beard I had and a long, full, grey one to boot.

And the feisty woman cried, 'Out!' once again. And then I saw the TV. And there was a rock band playing. And damn me if it wasn't The Sumerian Royalty. And there was my brother, looking well, but rather grey, all bawling into the mic.

'I know that band,' I said to the feisty lady. 'I was in that band many years ago.'

'We've all had a try at that, buddy,' said the wino. ' "Been in a band like that".' And he laughed.

And my knees were going wobbly.

'What's going on here?' I asked. 'Is this some alternative reality where I'm Father Christmas or something?'

And the wino laughed once more. 'Nope, buddy,' he slurred. 'No such luck. Just another day in New York City. Another day in two thousand and seven—'

'Not just any old day,' said the Jewish-looking fellow. 'It is, after all, a special day. The fiftieth anniversary tour of The Sumerian Kynges, original line-up. And it's on in an hour and I have front-row tickets.'

And I took in the date.

Two thousand and seventeen.

And I fell down in a faint.

Which is very much like falling down into a whirling black pit of oblivion.

If not slightly worse.

64

And I awoke in the gutter with my pockets inside out.

And bitterly bewailed my lot and got in a very bad grump.

Two thousand and seventeen! Another ten years of my life had ticked and tocked away without me even being aware of it! I had a great big beard. And when I looked down at my hands, lit by stuttering street lamps, I saw that I had liver spots on the backs of them. Sergeant Bilko looked like a plague victim.

'I'm old,' I said. 'I'm an old man. How could this have happened? Think! Think! Think!'

And I thought. And do you know what? The answer came to me almost at once. It was not a pleasing answer, but it was a logical answer. And once more I had Captain Lynch to thank for supplying it. I recalled a conversation oh so long ago, in our sitting room, with me sitting on the Persian pouffe and Captain Lynch sipping tea in the visitors' chair.

'Do you believe in fairies, Captain?' I had asked him.

'Yes I do,' he said, 'because I have seen them with my own eyes. They dance at night in Gunnersbury Park – the very last of their kind in this country, I believe.'

'So what *are* fairies?' I asked.

'They are of an order halfway between Man and the angels. They existed in great numbers in ancient of days, but as Mankind became the prominent race, they took themselves away to the wild lands, never to return. And Mankind spread throughout the world, encroaching upon these lands, and then they took themselves underground, down to the caves where Mankind had lived when the race of Man was young. And there they remain to this day, growing ever few in number. And soon there will be no more of them. It is sad in a way but life is cruel and only the strongest survive.'

'But fairies have magic, don't they?' I asked.

'Ancient magic, but it's no match for Man's technology. It is subtle magic. But you must beware of fairies, and should you meet with them you must not trust them. You must not enter one of their fairy mounds, no matter what they say to you. And if you are foolish enough to enter, never ever eat their food, or you may never return to this world.'

'Golly!' I said.

'Where?' said Captain Lynch.

'Why must you never enter their fairy mounds and eat their food?' I asked.

'Because fairy time is different from our time,' said Captain Lynch. 'And though you may think that you have only been inside the fairy mound for a few hours, when you return to this world, *if* you return, you will find that years have passed you by.'

And I said, 'Golly,' once more to this.

And Captain Lynch asked, 'Where?'

And once more employing the detective's logic that I most recently alluded to, I concluded that this is what must have happened. The high priest of Begrem and his mum had both made mention of them having no concept of time. It had to be 'fairy' time down there in Begrem, and what had appeared to me to be but a day had in fact been ten years of my own time up here. Which accounted for the beard.

I sniffed at my armpits.

And the really terrible pong.

And I did sorrowful groanings at this, for this was so unfair.

Another ten years of my life all ticked and locked away. Ten years. Bad for me! *Very* bad for me!

But what of this world? Was everyone now just walking dead? Had the Homunculus raised his status to World Leader?

Was the Homunculus the Antichrist?

I did shudderings now.

And anger rose in me once more. And once more this anger was directed towards Mr Ishmael. *He* had told me that Begrem lay beneath New York. It was *his* fault that ten years were missing from my life and I looked like Father Christmas and smelled like the milkman's horse.

And I began to sob.

Well, I'd had enough, hadn't I? I really truly had. There was me getting all enthusiastic about my Army of the Underworld. And I *was* still quite enthusiastic about that, even though there were so few of them. It was still some sort of army. But this! Now this! It wasn't fair. It really wasn't fair. Was there no justice in this world?

Was this world just a dirty, stinking, unfair toilet of a place?

'Why, I'll—' And I really *was* angry now. 'I'll join the baddies,' I cried. 'I will sell out to the Dark Side of the Force. I will, I really will.'

And I just thought that I would. Well, damn it, I *had* had enough.

'Will you be wanting your pizzas, then?' asked a feisty voice.

And I looked up to see the pizza lady.

'What?' I asked her. 'Sorry?' I said.

'We put you out here to give you some fresh air while I made your pizzas. I've done you a selection, enough for thirty people. And thrown in drinks and garlic bread for free. Oh, and here's your change. I took the money from your pocket while you had your little sleep.'

'Can you manage all the pizzas yourself,' asked the wino, 'or would you like me to help carry them for you?'

'Or I could give you a lift in my car,' said the Jewish-looking fellow.

And I just burst into tears. And the feisty lady comforted me, but from a distance, because I did smell awful. And I was pathetically grateful and did *not* go over to the Dark Side of the Force. So that was a bit of a happy-ever-after, in a small way, really.

And I accepted the Jewish-looking fellow's offer of a lift. And he gave me one, although he did insist that we drove with all the windows open.

'Having a party, are you?' he asked as we drove along.

'Not as such,' I told him. 'It's more a sort of council of war kind of thing. But I wouldn't want to bore you with the details.'

'No worries there,' said the fellow. 'We live ones have to look after each other as best we can. I'm sure you agree.'

'I don't know exactly what you mean,' I said.

'Ah,' said the fellow. 'Perhaps I have spoken out of turn. Perhaps you accept the official explanation.'

'I never accept those,' I said, 'as a matter of principle.'

'Splendid. It's a ludicrous explanation anyway.'

'Please tell me all about it,' I said. 'I have been out of circulation for a while and I'm not exactly in tune with what is going on at the present time.'

'But you know about the undead?'

'I know all about them, yes. But does everyone else know?'

'Not the kind of secret you can keep for ever. A man dies in a car accident. The coroner's report says that he's been dead for five years. A murderer is executed. He gets up out of the electric chair and walks away. It's funny how much of it came to light because of crime. A wife murders her husband in the night, but he's down for breakfast the next day. Because he was actually dead for years before. People are alive. Then people are dead. But they're still alive, although clinically they are dead. A great mystery, eh? The greatest mystery, you would think. And the greatest threat to the future of Mankind. So what is the official explanation?'

'Enlighten me,' I said.

'Mass hysteria,' said the fellow, 'symptomatic of the increasingly stressful times that we live in. Word on the street, as it were, is that the CIA controls all the media now and composes all the news items. And it was the CIA that passed the Panic Law.'

'Tell me about the Panic Law,' I said.

'It is a brand-new law designed to "*enforce common sense and right thinking and stop the spread of panic, dead*". To whit, and I also quote, "*Anyone propagating the myth of the walking dead in any manner, way, shape or form will be subject to arrest without trial and immediate execution.*" '

'Nasty,' I said. 'Although I do see a bit of a flaw in this law, walking-dead-wise.'

'Immediate execution by complete incineration,' said the fellow. 'They don't come wandering back after *that* like they used to after they had been secretly interrogated, saying that they'd changed their minds and it was all a mistake.'

'You mean after they had been *secretly killed in custody*? Is that what you're saying?'

'That is what I'm saying. So now everyone lives in a state of total fear, afraid to voice concerns to their closest friend in case that friend might be either dead, or an informer.'

'Surely you're taking a chance speaking to me of these matters,' I said. 'I might be dead, or an informer.'

'Fella,' said my driver, 'I think you're safe enough. Even the dead don't smell as bad as you. And informers always wear suits.'

'Yes they do, don't they,' I said. 'I wonder why that is?'

'I think they just like the suits. But then again, who doesn't?'

'You're wearing a suit,' I observed. 'And a black one – are you Jewish?'

'No,' said the fellow. 'A tree fell on me.'

And oh how we laughed.

Together.

'Are we nearly there yet?' I asked.

And we laughed again.

Such jollity.

For no good reason whatsoever.

But perhaps to lighten the tension.

And tension there certainly was. And when we reached Mornington Crescent East (discontinued usage), I sat in the car for a bit longer, chatting with the fellow, with all the windows open. And I let the fellow choose one of the pizzas and we shared it.

'I hate all this stuff,' said the fellow.

'I think it tastes rather interesting,' I said. 'Cheese and chocolate and chitlings and chips, an alliterative combination.'

'I didn't mean the pizza,' said the fellow. 'I too am enjoying the pizza. I mean *this stuff*. I mean, I suppose, *life*. I never expected that the whole world would fall all to pieces like this. Nuclear war, perhaps. I imagined that when I was young. And later there was AIDS, and everyone thought we'd all die of that. Then it went all ecological and we were all going to die because of global warming and climate change. But *this stuff*, this undead stuff – I wasn't expecting this. No one was expecting this.'

'Some were,' I said. 'Some were planning it. One at least.'

'Ah,' said the fellow. 'I've heard that theory, too – that this is all the work of a single criminal mastermind, an insane evil fiend of the Moriarty or Count Otto Black persuasion.'

'I think he tops both of those,' I said.

'But surely Count Otto Black was the most evil man who ever lived?'

'This fellow's worse,' I said. 'Far worse. And that theory is true. The fellow exists – I have met him.'

My driver stuffed further pizza into his mouth. 'If you really know who he is,' he said, between munchings, 'then you should kill him. You know that? You should, you really should.'

'And I will,' I said. 'It is my reason for being alive. He and another man have blighted my existence. I will have my revenge upon at least one of them.'

'You're surely not thinking to go at it alone?'

'I have, shall we say, a taskforce. Hence the pizzas. And as I have already mentioned to them that an army marches on its stomach, I must deliver my pizzas to them before they all grow cold.'

'Is this your home?' asked the fellow, gazing about.

'We are camped out in the Subway station.' And with this I thanked my driver and climbed from his car, taking my pizzas and drinks and garlic breads. 'Thanks for the ride,' I said. 'And if everything works out, I'm sure you'll learn about it from an uncensored media broadcast.'

'Good luck then,' said the fellow and he drove off.

And I entered Mornington Crescent East (discontinued usage), whistling. And I entered, I noticed, by a rather larger opening than the one I had left by. And as I screwed up my eyes and wandered across the station concourse, I noticed that it was now a somewhat lighted concourse. There were flares all around and about, spitting sparks, dying.

'Oh no!' I cried, and I dropped my pizzas and drinks and garlic breads and took off down the stairway at the hurry-up.

And when I reached the platform I came upon a scene of doom and desolation. Torches still burned and the remnants of flares did also. And there was a bad smell in the air now, a bitter, acrid smell, and it was the smell of CS gas. And there on the platform lay bodies. Two bodies. One of them was a golden girlie. The other was the high priest. And he groaned in a fatally wounded kind of fashion.

And I approached his golden body and I gazed down upon it and all I could think to say was, 'I am so sorry.'

And I kneeled low to catch a word. And touch the dying brow.

'Men came,' the high priest whispered. 'Men from above. With magical weapons. We fought bravely, but they overwhelmed us. We failed you, sire, forgive us.'

'I am so so sorry,' I said. 'And you didn't fail me. You did your best. I am sorry that I brought you here to this evil place. Can *you* forgive *me*?'

The high priest reached out a bloodstained hand to me. It was clear that there was something important that he needed to say.

'The P . . . The P . . .'

'The "P"?' I said. 'The prophecy, do you mean?'

'The p . . . The p . . . The pizza. What flavour did you get?'

And then he died.

65

I had moved to a point beyond anger.

Beyond rage and fury. Beyond all human feeling.

I raised my head upon that platform, threw it back and howled. An atavistic howl, it was. A fearsome howl, a midnight window–rattler. And I am sure that my eyes blazed fire and that I was an ugly sight to behold. But I was done now with everything but revenge. The red mist had descended. All that remained to be done now was for me to enter the high tower above, seek out Mr Papa Keith Crossbar and rend him limb from limb. The rending would be both slow and laboured, one little piece at a time.

And I arose and stood above the body of the high priest, the golden being whose death was surely my fault. And I swore upon his corpse that I would finish the job I had started and that he would not have died in vain upon this dismal platform.

And then I strode from that dismal platform and up the stairway and across the concourse and out into that rancid New York night.

And suddenly bright lights shone upon me. And I heard a voice I recognised, it being that of the Jewish-looking fella with whom I had so recently shared a pizza. And this fella shouted, 'That's him, officers – the assassin who would threaten the life of our dear leader.' Adding, 'Can I have my reward in cash, please?'

And horrible hands were laid upon me. And I was brutally smitten down by truncheons of the electric persuasion. And I descended, once more, into that whirling black pit of oblivion.

Most angrily.

66

And I awoke from that whirling pit equally angry.

Or possibly just a bit more. Although I must admit that in my opinion I had plateaued, regarding the anger. I just couldn't get any more riled up. It simply couldn't be done.

And I was floating. Floating.

And not on some adrenalin high. But simply floating. Face up in something rather odd. Or was I face down? Or was my face anywhere? I couldn't see, for it was black and I couldn't smell or touch anything.

I did blinkings of the eyes and yes, my eyes were open. But I was in absolute blackness. Had I been blinded? And I opened my mouth to cry out, but no sound came from it. And it was as if all my senses had been shut down and *that* was a terrible feeling.

And I did panicking, I can tell you. All alone in the dark.

And then I didn't panic quite so much. Instead, I did risings up. I projected. As I had done at The Stones in the Park gig after taking the Banbury Bloater. And later in my coma, when I found that I had somehow developed the ability to leave my body at will and float off abroad in my astral form. Just like Doctor Strange.

And I arose in that darkness and moved above my physical body and, looking down by means of astral vision, I could now see myself floating there, all hooked up to wires and whatnots all in the dark in a big floatation tank.

'Oh,' I said to my astral self. 'A sensory-deprivation tank. Probably not the best place to be for a fellow such as myself, with rather a lot on my mind. My, a fellow could go mad in one of those if he awoke and didn't know that he was in one.' So to speak.

And *no*! I did *not* get any angrier at this thought. But only, I must stress, because there was no possible way that I could get any angrier.

I really had reached the cut-off point and I'll say no more about it.

And so I floated up upon high, looking down at myself floating down upon low. And I was pleased to note that someone had given me a jolly good wash and a shave and a haircut. Although I did feel that they might have had the decency to slip a pair of swimming trunks onto my naked loins before they deposited me into the floatation tank and switched off the light.

But why was I in the floatation tank? Why hadn't I simply been killed and conscripted into Papa Crossbar's Army of the Dead? Or bunged straight into the incinerator for instant disposal?

And I did some more detective thinking and drew the conclusion that there had to be a very good reason for my captors to keep me alive. And that it probably wasn't one that I was going to be too keen on. And would probably involve torture and torment, and things of that nature, grimly.

So *where* was I? In the big CIA building? I really did hope that I was, because I had, prior to my truncheoning down, given a thought or two as to how I might gain entry to a building that would probably be rather big on security. So if I was in it, it *was* rather handy. Wasn't it?

So, best have a look-see, eh? And I drifted upwards, and my weightless, invisible, non-corporeal, astral, spirity-magical form passed through a ceiling and into a room above. And this was a locker room of some kind, smelling strongly of plimsolls and man-bits. And I drifted through an open doorway and into a big gym hall where chaps in ninja costumes were doing some working out. They were beating each other up and smashing lengths of two-by-four with their bare hands and generally carrying on in an overly macho manner. And I could hear their thoughts, and their thoughts were simple thoughts that encompassed complete dedication to their leader Papa Crossbar, violence and sex. And I made a mental note that once I had escaped from the floatation tank, I must keep clear of these violent zealots.

And I drifted onwards and upwards, through computer rooms manned by men in white coats, who wore thickly lensed spectacles and carried clipboards. The canteen and recreational areas. Offices, offices and more offices. And then rather elegant furnished apartments. And then to the very top floor, where I saw him.

And he sat there at a great Gothic desk of black basalt. On a great Gothic chair carved from similar stuff. And he had piled up a lot of silk cushions onto this chair to get him up to the level of the desk. Because, as well as being the most evil being alive on the planet, he was also something of a short-arsed little git. Although I might not have put too much emphasis before upon the matter of him being somewhat *vertically challenged*, it really can't hurt to mention it now. All things considered.

The short-arsed little thoroughgoing swine.

And please don't get me wrong here. I have nothing against and no axe to grind regarding the shorter in stature. I'm not *that* tall myself and although I'd like to say that some of my very best friends are positively dwarf-like, I regret that I can't. But only because I have no very best friends. Which is rather sad.

And I stood before the desk of Mr Papa Keith Crossbar, vile twentieth-century Homunculus and would-be bringer of death to all Mankind. And I hated him. With every smidgen of my body and my soul. I utterly, utterly hated him. And I cast my mystic eyes all around and about this room that was his headquarters and his sinister lair. And both he and his room were also rather sad. And I knew instantly, instinctively, why both he and his room were rather sad. And it was because both lacked for love. This man was absolutely loveless. The very concept of love was totally alien to him. And I could *feel* this, as I stood invisibly before his desk in my spirit body. There was no love in this room and there could never be.

The room itself was cold and bleak. The walls were of a dull grey cast, the floor unpolished slate. But for the desk and chair there was no other furniture. No pictures hung upon the walls, the windows uncurtained. The views that lay beyond these windows were without doubt panoramic – all the world that was New York spread beyond and below. And it all looked far more wonderful at night.

But the loveless fellow at the desk didn't look upon the city beyond and below. For he'd had frosted glass installed and so the views were blanked.

And then I realised that yes, this room was exactly as it should be. It was the perfect office for such a cold and loveless foul monster as Papa Keith Crossbar. As The Flange had sought to create the perfect lounge room that would facilitate the Second Coming of Jesus, and the native followers of Jon Frum had done years before that, when they built their imitation airstrips to lure down the God from the sky. This *was* the perfect office for such a creature as this. And he simply *had* to be in it.

And curiously *that* gave me an idea. It was a long shot, of course. But it *was* an idea. And what I really needed at this time *was* an idea.

I drifted around to the rear of the desk and had a peep over his shoulder. He had before him on the desk what looked like an ancient tome. And a *really* ancient one, like one of those really ancient and gem-encrusted golden Bibles that they have so many of in St Katherine's Monastery on the slopes of Mount Sinai.

And I recalled that Captain Lynch had told me about how St Katherine's Monastery had and still has the largest and most valuable collection of Christian holy books in the world. They have hand-written pages from the original gospels there and more gem-encrusted Bibles than the Vatican's vaults. Apparently it was the fashion (a fashion that I suspect was started by the monks themselves, as St Katherine's also boasts some of the fattest and best-dressed monks in the world) for Kings to pilgrimage to St Katherine's (which also has the original burning bush in its courtyard, although it no longer burns, of course) and bring the monks a really expensive present to show how sincere and devout they were.

And Kings, who, without advisors, never had a lot of imagination, would go, 'Now what would be a really nice present to give a bunch of monks? I know, a Bible. I'll get a big gem-encrusted golden one knocked up. And in case they've already got one, I'll make sure that the one I give them is even bigger and more gem-encrusted.'

And boy, do they have some great big gem-encrusted golden Bibles.

And the big ancient book open on the desk of Papa Keith Crossbar looked like one of those.

So what did this loveless body have? This hateful horrible man?

And I peered over his shoulder to have a good old look. And I had a good old look. And then I wished I hadn't.

The words on the pages were penned in Latin and I knew not their meaning. But these were no holy words, no words of inspiration. Nor indeed were they the pidgin-tongued lyrics of old George Formby songs. No, these words were those of ancient magic and although I could not understand their meaning, it was as if, as I looked, they tried to raise themselves from the page and force themselves into my head. For surely these were the words of a magic dark and dire and dreadful. And doom-laden. And dirty-doggish.

And I drew hastily back. But Papa Keith Crossbar did not; his eyes were tethered to the pages by invisible bonds. And the words arose to him and entered his brain. And I knew then what these words must be: the words of the most terrible spell that had ever been brought into reality by Man – the spell to create the Homunculus.

And then another revelation came upon me.

That this was the year 2007.

And that we were now in the 21st century.

And so the twentieth-century Homunculus was preparing to use that terrible spell to raise his own magical son. And that had to be super bad because, as far as I knew, *that* had never been tried before. In all the long history of horrible Homunculus-raising, an actual Homunculus had never done the raising of his next in line. I didn't know just then exactly what the consequences of this would be. But, instinctively once more, I reasoned that they would be dire.

And outside thunder rolled across the sky. And lightning flashed beyond the frosted windows. And I knew deep down in my *Look Back in Anger* heart that tonight was going to be the night that he did this evil deed.

And if he succeeded, then it meant—

The End of the World.

Oh dear.

67

I did hoverings all about and wondered what to do next for the best.
Get back into my body at the hurry-up, escape from the floatation tank,
make my way up here and crush the life from this monster's throat before
he could invoke the terrible magic and bring his awful horror into this
world seemed favourite. No – and I gave this matter some thought – I
could *not* think of anything better than *that*. Although the Devil, as they
say, *is* in the detail.

But now a door opened and in walked an evil cat's paw.

I reasoned that he had to be an evil cat's paw because he was, after all,
an employee of the Evil One himself and apparently had permission to
enter without knocking.

And the Evil One looked up from his evil book and gazed evilly at
the evil cat's paw who had entered his evil room, evilly.

'Did you knock?' he asked.

The cat's paw shook his head.

'Did I call "enter"?'

The cat's paw shook his head once more. I noted that the cat's paw
had a rather nifty haircut, rather retro nineteen-fifties. A bit early-Elvis.
And a suit, of course. A black suit. And a black suit is a classic. Unless
it's made out of polyester.

'Well, can you think of any reason at all why I should not kill you for
your insolence?'

'But for the fact that I'm already dead, sir, no.'

'I'm trying to learn a spell here. It might look easy, but it's not.'

'I never suggested that it was, sir.'

'No, but you were thinking it. I can hear you thinking it. And don't
think that if you sing a song in your head as you are now doing that I
won't be able to hear what you're thinking.'

'Sorry,' said the evil cat's paw. 'Naturally, sir, my only wish is to
serve you absolutely.'

'And have sex with the woman in charge of the Filling Room.'

'And that too, sir. But everyone in my department wants that. At least, all the men do. And some of the women, too.'

'She's a bit of a looker, eh?'

'I should say so, sir.'

'Then I wonder, perhaps—'

And *I* could hear *him* thinking. And he was thinking about the woman that he wanted to become the mother of the twenty-first-century Homunculus this very night. At midnight. Which seemed about right. As this sort of stuff generally comes to pass during the witching hour. And he was considering the woman who ran the Filling Room because he had extracted a mental image of what she looked like from the mind of the evil cat's paw. But he was now thinking that no, he wouldn't do that, he would use the golden girlie that his minions (the ninja fellows I'd seen practising) had kept alive. Having killed off all the rest of the golden Begremites. Whose bodies he had then had incinerated.

Killed off? All the rest? Astral tears now came to my astral eyes. He had simply had all the rest of them killed because he had no use for them. And the one that he had kept alive, he had done so only so that she could be inseminated with a being of absolute and unremitting evil.

I stood and shook in my astral body. 'I will kill you,' I said. Though none could hear this but myself.

'Get the golden woman all prepared,' said Papa Keith Crossbar to his evil cat's paw. 'Get her all scrubbed-up and all loved-up. I don't care what you pump into her veins as long as she remains conscious and compliant. And I want her *here* by the stroke of midnight. Do I make myself understood?'

'Absolutely, sir. But first I have a memo from Accounts that I'd like you to have a look at. It's regarding a purchase order for stationery that hasn't been processed properly. Normally I'd have Mr Carapace in Sales Admin give it the once-over, but he's away at a convention in Florida this week, Corporate Cat's Paw Con, and I—'

Papa Keith Crossbar raised his hand. 'Get out of my office,' said he.

And the evil cat's paw left the office and I followed on behind him.

And once he had left the office and closed the door behind him, he turned around and he did that thing that in America is known as 'flipping the bird', but which we more civilised Englishmen call 'giving the finger'.

Which made me laugh.

And certain words came loudly through that door. And these words were shouted by Papa Keith Crossbar. And these words were, 'I heard you thinking *that*. And I'll punish you for doing it.'

Which also made me laugh. Though not, perhaps, quite so much.

And I followed the evil cat's paw as he slouched along a corridor and into an office of his own. A small and poky office, its walls enlivened by photographs of naked women, mostly bound and wearing nothing but shoes. And though I had to applaud his good taste in wall-enlivenment, I didn't think much of his office as a whole. And when he slumped down into his chair and kicked off his shoes, I was not altogether taken with the smell of his feet. And yes, he was one of the walking dead. But is that really an excuse for poor foot hygiene?

And having kicked off his shoes and got his feet polluting the atmosphere, he picked up the receiver of the telephone on his desk, punched buttons and spoke into it.

'Barry,' he said. 'Dave here. I've just been in the old man's office and he wants that golden tart up there by midnight. What? The purchase order? Yes, I did try to chase that up. Yes, I know Carapace in Sales Admin *should* deal with it. Yes, it is a pain in the neck, I know. But what can you do? What? The End? What "The End" are you talking about? Oh, the one tonight, I see. Well, yes, that will be the end of Mankind as anyone understands it to be and also the end of everything else living upon the planet. Yes. But what? Will it affect the processing of orders for stationery? I never thought to ask. I'll ask when I see him later. He'll probably want me to lend a hand in the ceremony. Sacrifice a cat, or a hippopotamus, or something. What? Trevellian in Corporate Holdings did what? Not with that tall woman from Sales Services? No, really?'

And I just shook my head.

So this was how the world would end. With Dave and Barry discussing what Trevellian in Corporate Holdings had been doing with the tall woman from Sales Services. Although, I supposed, it had probably involved a bang *and* a whimper.

'Oh, Barry,' continued Dave, 'before I forget, the old man wants the golden tart all loved-up and compliant. So can you ask Kevin in Pharmaceuticals to load her up with some happy juice? What? Oh, you'll need a green chitty for that? I thought green chitties were strictly inter-departmental. This is Top Priority for the eyes of Mr Crossbar only, surely? Blue chitty? Now don't be silly, blue chitty is Recreational Services. Well, yes, you're right, it might come under Recreational Services. I wouldn't mind servicing that gold tart in a recreational manner myself, would you? What? Yellow chittie? I've never even heard of a yellow chitty.'

And I took my leave.

And I drifted down and all around and about. And I sought out the golden girlie and eventually I found her, locked in a broom cupboard on the third floor. And she was sitting there, all huddled up and sobbing, and I tried like damn to communicate with her but it was impossible, and so I drifted down some more and returned to the floatation tank.

And how *was* I going to get myself out of that? I drifted low and examined myself and the way I was fixed in. And I appeared to be most securely fixed in with many straps, all soft, but very strong.

And I hovered about above myself and I fretted. How *was* I going to get free? There had to be some way. I counted off on my astral fingers my magical capabilities. I could smell people coming from a distance. I could hear what they were thinking. I could see with my eyes closed. And I could leave my body and travel about in the spirit. And that was it, really. Which was a shame, because if I'd just been able to move solid objects around with the power of my mind alone, I could have had myself out of that floatation tank in next to no time at all.

But there had to be a way.

And then it came to me, as if by divine inspiration. I would employ the positive neutral powers of the Tyler Technique. It had never really had a chance to prove its worth. And this was, I felt, because I had never really been able to give it its head. So to speak. Which is to say that, in order to make something happen by doing nothing at all, you really do have to do *nothing* at all.

And how few are the times when we are consciously doing absolutely nothing? I had always been doing *something*. Thinking something. Planning something. Getting involved in something. The entire point of the Tyler Technique was that it functioned on the principle of total non-involvement on the part of the person who sought to employ it. By doing absolutely nothing, the required something would come into being.

And there was I, down below in that tank, doing completely and utterly absolutely nothing. And here was I, up here, observing this and willing the Tyler Technique to function as I had never willed anything so strongly before.

And below me a door opened, gushing light into the room and onto the floatation tank. And two individuals entered. Two individuals who did not look particularly individual. Both wore thickly lensed spectacles, sported white coats and carried clipboards.

'Did you hear about Trevellian in Corporate Holdings?' said one to another as they both approached the floatation tank.

'About him and the tall woman from Sales Services?' said the other to the one.

'Ms Williams? Not her. He's getting engaged to Ms Haywood in Musical Therapy. The dark one with the sweet nose.'

'I didn't know we had a Musical Therapy department.' The other fellow in the thickly lensed spectacles and the white coat tapped at a gauge on the side of the floatation tank and made notes on his clipboard with an official CIA biro.

'It's not a very big Musical Therapy department. There's just Ms Haywood with her steel pan and her sweet nose.' The first fellow in the thickly lensed glasses and the white coat consulted an instrumentation board upon a wall, tapped at a gauge upon *that* and made notes on *his* clip board with an all-but-identical biro. (His had green ink, rather than the other's red. Because he *did* like to think of himself as an individual.)

'Hold on,' said the other fellow. 'Her steel pan *and* her sweet nose? Do you mean that she plays her sweet nose as an instrument?'

'She probably would if you asked her. She's very amenable.'

'Should this valve be in the *on* position, or the *off*?'

'I've no idea. Do you think it matters?'

'Probably not. I'll switch it to the *off* position to be on the safe side. Tell me more about what she might do amenably, possibly even with the involvement of her sweet nose.'

'Why is this bod in this tank in the first place?'

'So he can't interfere. He's very important to the success of the old man's project. But he doesn't know that he is important.'

'Wasn't he once in The Sumerian Kynges? I had a flick through his file, to check out whether psychologically he could survive this treatment.'

'And could he?'

'Absolutely not. He'll be a vegetable by midnight. But that's the old man's intention. He needs him for the ceremony. But he doesn't need him to do any thinking, or cause any trouble, so he's having him bobbing about in here so he'll lose the last of his marbles.'

The other fellow peered in at my naked person through his thickly lensed specs. 'I don't think he was really in The Sumerian Kynges. I had a flick through his file too and it's pretty grim reading, isn't it? He comes off as a fantasist who always believes that he's something special. Funny thing is that he *is* important, but he doesn't know about that. Ironic, eh? Should this lever be in the *up* position, or the *down*? I've never worked with this particular instrument before.'

'Nor me. Push it down – it looks tidier. Let's talk some more about

Ms Haywood and her sweet nose. Actually, do you think she'll still be on duty?'

'Bound to be. Musical Therapy is an evening thing, isn't it?'

'I don't know. I don't think I'd heard of Musical Therapy until you mentioned it. Or did *I* mention it to you?'

'Who can say? But let's go and see her, shall we?'

'Let's do.'

And so, making a note or two more upon their clipboards, they left to seek out Ms Haywood and fawn about her sweet nose. But, and I had a little laugh about this, they would be thwarted in their plans because I had drifted through the Musical Therapy office on my way down from above. And it was empty, as Ms Haywood had already gone home.

Ha ha.

And so I hovered and I waited and I chewed upon my astral fingernails. Was the Tyler Technique going to come up cosmic trumps? Would what I hoped for occur because I had done absolutely nothing whatever to make it occur, but even *less* to stop it? So to speak.

And I hovered and I waited.

And then I heard a little sound.

It was a little hissing sound. As of pressurised steam backing up. And I drifted low and spied that a little needle on a little dial, one that had been most recently tapped, was moving into the red. And smoke was beginning to rise from the vicinity of the valve, which had been switched to the *off* position, rather than having been left on the *on*. And a lever that had been pushed down rather than having been left pushed up was starting to vibrate.

And the hissing and the smoking and the vibrating grew and grew and grew. And instrumentation boards began to pop and fizz and then to burst into flame.

And many red lights began to flash.

And panels lit up with the words—

EMERGENCY PROCEDURE
SUBJECT RELEASE

And the fixings that fixed me clicked and released and the fluid drained from the tank.

And I returned with haste to my body, now sprawled on the floor of the tank. And I stretched my limbs and climbed to my feet. And I praised the Tyler Technique.

68

Tick tock went the clock, counting down to midnight.

Did you know that the average human life lasts less than one thousand months? It doesn't sound like much when you put it like that. And it isn't very much really. And like anything that matters, the less you have of it, the more precious it becomes.

As I rose all wet and bare-bottom naked from the floor of that floatation tank and gave out with another of those great atavistic howls that were finding so much favour with me of late, I really felt the preciousness of life.

That and the need for underpants.

You just can't go into battle in nowt but your bare skuddies. It's not a good look and they'll never put it in the movie version, the one where Ray Harryhausen is doing the animated monsters.

I was in definite need of underpants and I knew just where to find them.

It was going to be tricky getting from the floatation-tank room all the way up to the God-knows-how-many-floors-above top-most lair and loveless office of Papa Keith Crossbar, necromancer, murderer and head of the CIA. I was going to have to make my way up carefully.

And so I got down to a bit of the old Doctor Strange magic mambo. I crept to the door of the room, pressed my ear to it, nipped outside in my spirit-self and had a good look-see. All clear, so back into my body and out into the corridor and so on. It was a damn fine system, and it occurred to me that should I be able to best the horrible Homunculus and save the World in general, a legitimate job might be found for me in the CIA, as a spy or an undercover agent. Now that I was not only a skilled detective, but also a Master of the Mystic Arts.

I upped to the changing rooms above that smelled of plimsolls and man-bits and sought out one of those smart black suits whose style never dates as long as they're not made of polyester. And I eventually found one that fitted rather well, and I decided that in keeping with the mission I was presently engaged upon, I would go 'commando' while wearing this suit. I did put on a white shirt, though, and a black tie. And a pair of socks and shoes. And, probably best of all, a really spiffing pair of Ray-Bans. And I examined my reflection in a changing-room mirror. And as God had done when finished with His big six days of labour, I looked upon all that I had made and beheld it was very good. And *very* cool.

And then I heard voices and I did slippings away.

I noticed that there was no shortage of wall clocks in this building, and that the nearest one that I noticed displayed its hands in the twenty-to-midnight position.

Which meant a number of things to me.

That Kevin in Pharmaceuticals would probably by now have loaded the golden girlie up with happy juice.

That a couple of burly ninja types would probably be heading to the floatation tank to hoik me out to face whatever horrors the Homunculus intended for me.

And that the quicker I could get up to the office of the thorough-going swine and put paid to his eldritch schemes, then *probably* the better.

Outside the thunder crashed and bashed and the lightning did all that could reasonably be expected of it.

This final showdown should, at least, not lack for suitable SFX and noises-off, I thought.

I wondered, perhaps, if I should take the lift.

Lift or stairs?

Stairs or lift?

It would be a lot of floors and a lot of stairs—

And Hell, I looked the part. I could blend in here. Dressed like this I could pass for a CIA man-in-black spook any day of the week.

With the possible exception of Tuesday.

But then today *wasn't* Tuesday.

I took the lift.

I pressed 'Penthouse Office'.

And then I did something rather clever.

I left my body standing in the lift and put my astral mind once more to the application of the Tyler Technique.

I concentrated really hard and then did *nothing* at all.

And I accompanied the rising lift all the way up in the astral, as it were. And I observed all those folk who were about to push the lift button on various floors. I watched them as they missed the button, changed their minds, tripped over, bumped into one another. And on floor thirty-seven, the tall woman from Sales Services, Ms Williams, fell suddenly into a passionate embrace with Trevellian from Corporate Holdings. Much to the shock of his fiancée Ms Hayward of Musical Therapy (the one with the sweet nose who played the steel pan), who had not in fact gone home early, but simply popped out to purchase a new pair of pan sticks. Because she was having a secret affair with Jonny, the manager of the pan-stick shop. Who was the half-brother of Dave, the evil cat's paw of the Homunculus. Who really quite fancied Ms Williams.

Office life, eh?

So, basically I got all the way up to the top floor unmolested, whipped back inside my body and stepped from that lift looking like a million dollars and cool as a mountain stream.

Just in time to hear all the alarms going off.

'That would be them finding me missing from the floatation tank,' I told myself. On the off-chance that I hadn't already figured it out. 'So best get a bit of a move on, eh?'

And then I did one of those duckings aside and divings for cover, which, as I previously mentioned, you have to *know* how to do rather than try and learn. Because the lift beside mine made that dinging noise that lifts do to signify their arrival and my extrasensory nose told me that there were two men in that lift and one golden girlie. So I ducked behind one of those corporate potted plants, the likes of which you can never grow in your own home, which are watered regularly by strange little Japanese men in overalls. Who always whistle old Go West numbers and smell rather strongly of bicycles.

Or was that a dream I once had?

'Hold on there,' I told myself. Quietly and behind the cover of the corporate potted plant. A *Ficus elasticus decora*, I think. 'Keep your mind together. Don't go wandering off on any tangents. This is *neither* the time *nor* the place.' And I tried very very hard to stay focused, which wasn't too easy, I can tell you, because the temptation to go off on one about potted plants and how Captain Lynch had once told me all about a man-eating variety that lived in the Amazon Basin was tempting.

Oh, *so* tempting.

But I stayed focused.

And the two men, young men, Dave being the one and the other, I assumed (for no reason other than convenience), to be Barry, to whom Dave had recently spoken upon the internal telephone about oh so many things, escorted between them a scantily clad golden girlie who had about her now a rolly-eyed-staggery-stumblyness of a kind that is so much favoured by a certain type of young female as a late-night-Saturday-town-centre look.

And as I have stated that I would make no further mention of my anger, I will make no mention of it now.

But I wondered, perhaps should I take my chances and have a pop at Dave and Barry? Perhaps I could take them down, as it were, and rescue the golden lovely. But, of course, there was always the chance that Dave and Barry worked out in the gym with the ninja types and were well heeled in the martial skills department. Which meant that they would beat me up and I'd never get a chance to take my shot at the Homunculus. So to speak. Et cetera.

So I let them pass by and then I followed them.

Discreetly.

And they were not, it appeared, heading to the office of the Awful One. They passed by this office and went up a staircase. Towards the roof.

The roof! I thought and I smiled a little, recalling a certain idea that had come to me in the Awful One's office. The idea that I had considered a long shot, but one that was still in the running.

And so I followed these fellows as they hustled the golden girlie ahead of them up the staircase. And I heard them make lewd remarks regarding her bottom, which were going to cost them dearly when they *got theirs*. Which they would, I felt confident. Somehow.

At the top of the stairs was a door. And here they knocked and entered. And then I heard a voice cry, 'Don't bother to lock it.' And then some mumbled words.

And I parked my physical self on the stairway, vacated it in my astral and poked my head through the door to see what was what.

And wouldn't you just know it? Dave was crouched on one side of the doorway and Barry on the other. And they had electric truncheons in their hands. And were obviously lying in wait for *me*.

Damned cheek!

'Well, let 'em crouch there till they get the cramps,' I told myself. 'I will find another way in.'

But where was *in*?

What was all this up here?

And so I had a little drift about to see what was what and why.

This was not the open roof. It was a great high-domed conservatory kind of a jobbie, in the grand Victorian style, glorifying in each twiddly bit and the unnecessary fussiness of its design. It was lit by flaming torches held within cast-iron embrasures at regular intervals about the single circular and all-encompassing wall of glass and ironwork – rather out of place upon the peak of this bland tower block of a building, but evidently constructed to serve a particular purpose.

And the purpose it was constructed to serve was all too horribly evident. The circular floor was of marble, inlaid with many precious and semi-precious stones: aquamarine, beryl, chrysoberyl, emerald, sark-stone, heliotrope and tourmaline and lapis lazuli. And wrought into it was the infamous pentagram, enclosed within the double circles, which themselves enclosed the words of power too terrible to be named.

And there were many other symbols and sigils wrought into this floor, symbols and sigils from many cultures, ancient and modern – all points covered, as it were. And at the heart of the pentagram, enclosed within another circle, this one composed of amethyst and sapphire, was the circular altar.

And strapped to this, spread-eagled, was the girlie.

And standing before her, big bad gem-encrusted book in his horrid hands, was Papa Keith Crossbar, the heinous Homunculus.

And he had a wicked old grin on his chops.

And the lightning flashed and the thunder crashed and those two men crouched by the doorway.

My attention was also drawn to a number of television monitor screens that were affixed to the upright structures of the great glazed dome – CCTV. And there indeed was me upon one of these screens, standing sentinel upon the stairs outside the door.

And I did shruggings of my astral shoulders. The Homunculus had probably watched me on screen as I came up in the lift. This was, after all, the CIA building. They *did have* security.

And I returned silently to my body and sat down upon one of the stairs and had a bit of a think.

And having had it, I marched up the stairs, kicked open the door, took one step forward, two steps back, invoked the power of the Tyler Technique and watched as Dave and Barry leaped forwards to the spot where I had been standing, struck each other mighty whacks with their electric truncheons and toppled both unconscious to the floor.

And their heads did go *crack* upon that marble, which must have really hurt. Even if they were dead.

And I stepped forward into that great domed wonderful-terrible room. And the Homunculus glared at me big pointy daggers and closed his book and placed it down upon the central altar.

And then he approached me on short stumpy legs and he put out his hand for a shaking.

And he grinned once more and said, 'Welcome, Tyler, you are right on time.'

And I grinned somewhat in return, but I did not shake his hand. Instead I did something I had never done ever before in my life.

I spat in his face.

'I have come to kill you, Mr Crossbar,' I said, in a manner that let him know that I was not kidding around here. 'Prepare yourself for death.'

And I reached out for his throat.

And do you know what? I never even saw them. But then you never do, do you? You never do see them, because they are all stealth and secret martial arts. Ninjas. Damned ninjas.

All in black and looking cool. They came out of nowhere.

And then—

They had *me* by the throat.

69

'Tick tock, kill the clock, said the faerie queen in her flowery frock.'

The Homunculus did a little bit of a jig on his stumpy legs and he wiped my spittle from his chin. 'Do you know that old nursery rhyme, Tyler? "Tick tock, kill the clock"? I can only remember the first two lines. It's funny what you remember and what you don't, isn't it? What sticks with you and stays with you. Because it is those things that stick and stay when we are children that make us what we are when we become adults. Were you loved, as a child, Tyler? Did your mummy love you?'

A ninja loosened his hold on my throat. And I made a gagging, 'Yes.'

'How charming. And has that made you a good person, Tyler? Have you lived a good life? Done good things? Made your mummy proud of you?'

'I'll thank you to leave my mother out of this,' I said. 'This is strictly between you and me. If you'd be so kind as to ask the ninjas to release me, I will carry on with my plan to kill you.'

'Well, that's one possibility. And please don't think that I am simply dismissing it out of hand without giving it due consideration. But I think . . . no. I think we will go along with *my* plan, rather than yours. After all, that clock that has ticked and tocked your life away has just a little bit more ticking and tocking to do before it stops for ever. Before everything stops for ever.'

I made a very grumpy face. As well I might, considering the circumstances. 'Is there nothing I can say?' I said. 'Nothing I can do to dissuade you from this course of action? Everything that you are doing is so utterly, utterly wrong. Can you not understand how wrong it is? Listen, let's go and have a beer. I know a nice little place – Fangio's Bar. We could drink some beer and talk the toot. I'm sure I could explain things better over a few beers.'

'No beers.' The Homunculus turned his back and fluttered his fingers.

'*Perhaps a sweet sherry, then, you old—*'

'What did you say?' The Homunculus turned back.

'Nothing,' I said. *Just testing*, I thought. Because I had not spoken. I just wanted to know whether the Homunculus could hear my thoughts as I could hear his.

And he could.

'Yes,' said he. 'I can. And they do all seem to be rather confused, the past and the present all jumbled up. However, do you ever get anything done with such chaotic patterns of thinking?'

'I get by,' I said. And I tried very hard to think those words convincingly.

'You do *not* get by, Tyler. You have never *got by*. Your entire life has been orchestrated and manipulated, if not by me, then by Mr Ishmael. Tonight is probably the first time in your entire life that you have done any real thinking for yourself and made any decisions that weren't already prearranged for you.'

'Rubbish,' I said. 'I've done tons of independent thinking.'

'And it's never crossed your mind to wonder why things have always been there, right there, exactly when you needed them? You wish to descend into subterranean depths, and there just happens to be a supplier of subterranean appliances and appurtenances right across the street?'

'That was just a happy coincidence.'

'There have been no happy coincidences in your life, Tyler. Everything was put there, for you to "find". And all so that ultimately you would "find" yourself right here. Right now.'

'Lies,' I said, 'all lies.' And I had a bit of a struggle. But that was a waste of time. And one of the ninjas kicked me. Quite hard.

'Ouch,' I said.

'It wasn't *that* hard,' said the ninja.

'For half of your life, Tyler,' the Homunculus continued, 'Mr Ishmael guided you, saw to it that you learned what he felt you needed to learn in order to defeat me.'

'I know *that*,' I said.

'When you were doing your little out-of-body walkabout, Tyler—'

'You know about *that*?'

'I taught you *that*, while you were in your coma. *I* protected you. You would have gone completely gaga if I hadn't. And then you would never have been able to enter Begrem, fulfil their prophecies and bring me the mother-to-be of my magical son. But what I was trying to say was that when you were doing your little out-of-body walkabout tonight, Tyler, you should have popped down to the freezers in the basement. The big padlocked one at the end has Mr Ishmael's head in it.'

And the lightning flashed and the thunder crashed and I was far from happy.

'All right,' I said. 'Say I believe you, that you have kept me alive until this night. Why? What do I matter to you?'

'You really haven't figured it out?' Papa Keith Crossbar stared very hard at me. 'No,' he said, 'you *haven't* figured it out. Why *you* are involved in this. What your part in it is. You really have no idea who you are, do you?'

'I am Tyler,' I said. 'And I will *kill* you. You will die tonight. I make a promise to you of that.'

'Sadly no,' said Papa Keith, rubbing his pudgy hands together and doing a little pace up and down. '*You* will die tonight, Tyler. *You* are the sacrifice, the magical child who must die if another is to be born. You are the virgin sacrifice.'

'I'm *not* a virgin,' I said.

'I think you will find that you are. In order to *not* be a virgin, you do have to have had sex with someone other than yourself.'

'I've had sex with loads of women. I was around in the swinging sixties. I was at The Stones in the Park gig, in the green room with Marianne Faithfull.'

'Tyler, you have never had sex in all of your life with anything other than Miss Hand and her five lovely daughters.' And he waggled his fingers once more.

'How dare you!' I cried. Most loudly.

And the ninjas sniggered.

'I've had loads of sex,' I told them. 'I had sex earlier this evening with Ms Williams, the tall woman from Sales Services.'

And wouldn't you know it, the other ninja kicked me.

'Ouch!' I went. 'That *was* hard.'

'Ms Williams is my girlfriend,' said this other ninja.

'Yeah, well, take it up with Trevellian. He was snogging her by the lift on the thirty-seventh floor only a few minutes ago.'

'He was *what*?'

'In front of a load of people. No shame at all.'

'You're making it up.'

'Wake Dave up and ask *him*.'

'Cease this nonsense!' cried Papa Crossbar.

'I'm not having *this*!' cried the ninja.

'Stay put!' And Papa Crossbar did foldings of the brow. And the ninja did clutchings of the skull. Which loosened the grip upon me by a factor of one. But didn't help my situation too much.

'I've had loads of sex,' I said.

'You've had none,' said Papa Crossbar. 'Both Mr Ishmael and myself saw to that. We both needed a virgin. It's a magical thing. Don't go bothering yourself about it.'

'But I was married.'

'But you never actually *did it* with your wife.'

'This is outrageous,' I said. 'Let go of me,' I told the ninja who wasn't clutching his skull. 'This thoroughgoing swine has stopped me having sex for nearly all of my life and I'm nearly seventy years of age. At least let me punch him once, really hard, in the face.'

The ninja looked towards Papa Crossbar. 'What do you think, Boss?' he asked. 'One punch in the face seems fair.'

Papa Crossbar did further foldings of his brow. Which had my other captor clutching at his skull. Which at least left me with my hands free.

'Don't even think about it,' said Papa Crossbar.

But I was. And I couldn't stop.

'You had to be pure,' said Papa Crossbar. 'Kept pure, to fight on one side or the other. The choice of which side was always ultimately yours. Personally I think you chose the wrong side. You should have thrown your lot in with me.'

'*You?*' I said. '*YOU?* But you are an evil madman who wants to wipe out the entire World. Why in the name of all that's holy, or otherwise, would I want to throw my lot in with *you*?'

And Papa Crossbar stared very hard at me.

'Because you are my brother, you oaf,' said he.

70

'Your brother!' I shouted. And loudly I did so. 'You are no brother of mine.'

And I sprang forward to do wringings of the neck.

And he took a smart step backaways.

'Now, now, now, Tyler,' he said to me. 'There is no need for violence.'

'No need for violence?' I spat as I shouted. 'I have come here to kill you. And you want *me* here so *you* can kill *me*. I do believe that there is bound to be *some* violence involved. But please do correct me if I'm wrong.'

'Well, in essence you're right,' said he. 'But come, before we engage in any fisticuffs, allow me to explain matters to you. There is a long tradition, both literary and now in the medium of film, that the super-villain explains *everything* to the hero before he offs him, as it were.'

'I am aware of this tradition,' I replied. 'And also that within its closely prescribed boundaries, the hero always thwarts the super-villain once the super-villain has had his say.'

'A break with tradition is never a bad thing,' said Papa Crossbar, producing as he did so what looked for all the world to be *my* trusty Smith & Wesson and pointing it at *me*.

'Ah,' I said. 'My pistol.'

'Correct. So, would you like to hear all the details, or shall we break with tradition completely and I'll just shoot you and have done?'

'Let's stick with the tradition for now,' I proposed, 'and we'll see how things pan out after that.'

'Right then, where would you like me to start?'

'Perhaps with the rubbish bit about me being your brother.'

'Ah, that.' And Papa Crossbar did evil grinnings of the ear-to-ear persuasion, and the lightning did flash and the thunder did roll. And up in this great conservatory in the sky, there was more than just a little weirdness about the atmosphere.

'Oh yes indeed,' said the Evil One. 'Your not so humble beginnings.

You see, Tyler, the trouble is that over the years a number of people have told you a number of things, but they haven't always told you the truth. They have just told you what they wanted you to hear, in the manner that you wanted to hear it.'

'So to speak,' I said.

'Pardon?'

'Nothing, please continue.'

'Captain Lynch – your spiritual advisor, Mr Ishmael – our guardian and trainer, and myself, I confess – we've all been a wee bit guilty of not sharing all of the truth with you. But then, in all truth, why would we have? We only wanted you to know the bits that it suited us that you know. But then you *are* a detective. You really should have figured it out for yourself.'

I had already tired of Papa Crossbar's conversation and was thinking about what would be the best way to wrest the pistol from his hands.

'There is no *best way*,' said he, interrupting the flow of both his conversation and my thoughts. 'I can hear you thinking, Tyler. Do you want to listen to what I have to say or not?' And he cocked the trigger of my trusty Smith & Wesson.

'I'll listen,' I said. And I listened.

'The Ministry of Serendipity,' he said, 'below the *other* Mornington Crescent. The department of the most potent of secret affairs during the Second World War, where the *real* business of war was carried out between the white magicians of the West and the black brotherhood of Hitler's Reich, both sides vying to create yours truly.' And he bowed, but he didn't lower the weapon. 'Had my magical father Adolf Hitler, the nineteenth-century Homunculus, been able to achieve the Great Creation, he would have become all-powerful and Germany would have won the war. But the West won that particular battle, with the help of Mr Aleister Crowley. He was the most skilful wizard of his day, greater even than those of Hitler. And at the behest of the Ministry of Serendipity, and a large quantity of the green and folding stuff, he cast the Spell of the Great Creation, the one in that big gem-encrusted golden book that rests there on the altar.

'But the problem for the Ministry was Crowley's vanity. He created six children, as he styled himself the Beast Six-Six-Six.'

'Two died, Tyler, *only two*. Not *three*, as you were told. Four survived: Elvis, Darren McMahon – who grew up in the Ministry and is its present controller, myself – the *true* Homunculus, and *you*, Tyler, boy number four, not really one thing or the other. The dull one of the family. And there's always a dull one, isn't there?'

'I'm not dull,' I complained. 'I'm as interesting as you.'

'As me? I'm nothing less than the frigging Antichrist. One of your brothers runs the most powerful occult organisation in the world and the other one was frigging Elvis Presley. And you're *not* dull, compared to your brothers?'

'Stop with the *frigging*,' I said. 'But I suppose if you put it like that. If it were true that I'm your brother, which it isn't. And I'm *not*.'

'You *are*, Tyler. Mr Ishmael knew it. Captain Lynch knows it. Frig, Tyler, Captain Lynch attended the ceremony that brought you and me into being. He is a disciple of Aleister Crowley's.'

'No,' I said. 'I don't believe it. Captain Lynch is a good man.'

'A good man? He's been humping your mum for decades.'

'Ha!' I said. 'What a giveaway. *My mum*, you said. That's my real mum, not some sacrificial virgin of Crowley's.'

'Same woman,' said Papa Crossbar. 'Has it never occurred to you what a weirdo *your* – I mean *our* – mum is?'

'Which isn't to say—' I began.

But he stopped me. 'It *is* to say,' he said. 'You *are* special, Tyler. And you have some of your brothers' gifts. Elvis got all the charisma, I make no bones about that. I got *all* of the evil, as befits my status. You got your share of magic, though. You're a magical individual, a little bit of a Doctor Strange, aintcha, though?'

'I have one or two mystical tricks up my sleeve,' I said, and I blew onto my fingernails and buffed them upon my lapel. Which is not something you see every day nowadays, is it?

Although it's not particularly mystical.

'You perfected the Tyler Technique,' said Papa Crossbar – or did all this make him *brother* Crossbar to me? I thought I'd just stick with Papa Crossbar.

'Yes, I did,' I said. 'The Tyler Technique. I *did* perfect that. And it was all my very own idea.'

'Well—' went Papa Crossbar.

'What?' I said.

'Never mind. Let's say yes, it was all your own idea. Well done.'

'So is that it?' I asked. 'Is that all, or do you have anything else you wish to share with me?'

Papa Crossbar did scratchings of the head with the barrel of my gun. 'I can't think of anything else,' he said. 'Unless there is anything you'd like to know.'

'*Anything I'd like to know?*' And I shouted this, I know I did. '*Anything I'd like to know?* Well, I wouldn't mind knowing why you want to wipe out all life on Earth. You might try explaining to me just what the point of that would be and what could possibly be in it for you.' And then I took deep breaths to steady myself. Not that deep breaths ever really do. Mostly they just make you dizzy.

'Well,' said Papa Crossbar. And he twirled my pistol on his gun-totin' finger. 'That is the point of all this, after all, isn't it? So yes, allow me to explain.' And he did so.

'You see,' said he, 'Planet Earth is a frightful aberration. It has all this *life* all over it. And I do mean *all over*, down to the tiniest single-celled whatnot. It's all so busy busy busy, everything whirling away and making so much noise. The sound of it all! Have you ever heard of the Music of the Spheres?' I nodded that I had. 'Complete silence, that music. It's more in the nature of mime. The universe is a great big interlinked body, all completely at peace with itself, this thing moving sedately about that thing, in perfect harmony and perfect silence . . . because these things are dead. But here! On *this* planet! Noise noise noise. And fuss and bother. And the smell! You can smell Planet Earth as far away as Saturn, did you know that? So it all has to stop.'

'And so you are intending to exterminate all life on Earth?'

'Yes, because Earth is the pest hole of life. There is no other planet that supports life. And once all life here is gone, then Universal Harmony will return. Look upon me as an ecowarrior, with a far higher calling.'

'Higher calling?' And I laughed. 'You cannot be talking about God. God created life on this planet. What right have you to destroy it?'

'God?' There was laughter from the Homunculus. 'Perhaps it has escaped your notice, Tyler, but God ceased to be *hands-on* at the end of the Old Testament. He lost interest in His little playthings. He gave His Son the run of the New Testament, but did all that poverty and misery and war stuff end? Of course it didn't. Mankind is a mess. A blot on the Universal landscape. You can look upon me also as God's little helper, sorting out the mess that He made of everything. Restoring peace to the Universe.'

'And say you did,' I said. 'Say that you do your terrible magic, and through so doing wipe out every living thing on Earth. What of you? It will be rather dull for you, won't it? And won't *you* be the last living annoyance? Will you be snuffing yourself out to create complete Universal Harmony?'

'I will merge into the blackness, into the Universal Silence. I will become at one with the Universe. I will become the Universe.'

'What a load of old cobblers,' I said.

'I don't expect you to be able to understand. But have no fear, I have given the matter considerable thought. *I* know what I'm doing.'

'Do you?' I said. 'Do you really? Well, I think you have forgotten one thing. God may be hands-off and all that kind of business, but one thing I have learned is that you can trust *some* books of prophecy. And I'll just bet you can trust John's account of the Revelation.'

The Homunculus nodded, thoughtfully.

'Things have to be done in a certain order. The great wild beast coming out of the sea. The woman clothed with the sun. All that Ray Harryhausen stuff. God isn't going to like it if you try to cut straight to the chase and leave out all that prophesied stuff.'

'You have a very good point there, Tyler,' said Papa Crossbar. 'A very good point indeed.'

'Yes,' I said. 'I have you on that one, don't I?'

'Not at all,' said he, amidst much shaking of the head. 'I'm absolutely certain that God wouldn't like it one bit. Which is why we're not going to mention it to Him.'

'No?' And I laughed. 'Well, I'll tell you this, smart alec. If you do manage to kill me, I will be going straight up to Heaven to spill the beans. And when I get there I'll tell Him all about what you've been up to and I'll just bet we'll be seeing *Mankind Two: The Sequel* in no time at all. With lots more noise and smell.'

But the Homunculus shook his head. 'Not going to happen,' he said. 'And I will explain to you why. Have you not asked yourself why, if I wish to turn the Earth into a Necrosphere, I have gone to all the trouble of actually reanimating the corpses of people when they die?'

'I *have* wondered about that,' I said. 'Mr Ishmael suggested that you were raising an Army of the Dead to wage war against the living. Isn't that it?'

The Homunculus did further shakings of the head. 'No,' he said. 'I have gone to all the trouble of keeping the dead up and about so that their souls can't get to Heaven. If no souls get to Heaven, then no soul is going to warn God about what I'm up to. He never checks what's going on down here Himself, so by the time I've done the business, it will all be too late. And as for *Mankind Two: The Sequel*, God already did that, you oaf. Remember Noah's flood? God won't bother with *Mankind Three*. He's too well past it now.'

'You thoroughgoing, thoroughgoing swine,' I said.

'I know,' said the Homunculus. And *he* did the blowing onto finger-nails and the buffing them on his jacket lapel. 'So that about rounds it all up, really. You can probably work out any little details that remain for yourself. Although you'll only have a very few minutes to do so, I regret to say. The end for you is nigh, Tyler. You are the sacrifice that triggers the magical mechanism, the creation of my magical son, Homunculus son of Homunculus, instant bringer of all death—'

'Ah,' I said. 'I was going to ask about *that*.'

'Well, now you don't have to. Goodbye, brother.'

And Papa Crossbar pointed the trusty Smith & Wesson right at my heart and pulled upon the trigger.

71

And *click* went the trusty Smith & Wesson.

And Papa Crossbar squeezed the trigger again and again and again.

'Oh,' I told him. 'I forgot to mention it – the trusty Smith & Wesson doesn't have any bullets in it.'

'What?' Papa Crossbar glanced down at the trusty Smith & Wesson and then up again. At my fist, as it sped towards his face and caught him right upon the snout. Very hard.

He went down and I followed on and I punched him and I kicked him. 'Couldn't read my mind on that one, could you, sucker?' I went as *biff* went my fist. 'I just wanted you to tell me the whole story so I could stick it all in my best-selling autobiography.' And *clump* went my foot. (In his groin.) 'I didn't want there to be any loose ends knocking about to disappoint the reader or have them doubting the truth of my tale.' And *whack* went my elbow, down deep into his left eye-socket. Nasty.

'And,' I continued, 'I am now going to beat you messily to death as a punishment for all the horrible things that you intended to do. And no one is ever going to think any the less of me for doing it. In fact—' And *clump* went my knee in one of those WWE knee-drops on his throat '—they'll probably make a video game about me. And five-year-olds will be pressing handsets, beating *you* up upon screen. So what do you think about that?'

And then the bloomin' ninjas had me over.

Freed, I suppose, from the headaches the Homunculus had been inflicting upon them, because *he* had other things on his mind, like—

And I managed to get one more really decent kick in before they pulled me off him.

'Okay, okay,' I went, 'no need for this. He's dead now and I'm taking over this place. And you can both have thousand-dollar bonuses and two weeks off. I know a barman who's giving away fortnight breaks to Butlins.'

But wouldn't you darn well know it, Papa Crossbar wasn't dead at all. Bloodied, yes. Broken-nosed, yes. With a big plum bruise growing out of where his left eyeball sat, yes also. Somewhat uncomfortable in the throat and groin regions, also yes, too. But not, very sadly not, dead.

And he rose up before me, and my, didn't he look angry.

'You bloodied me,' he cried. And he spat out some of this blood. 'You bloodied the Universal Destroyer.'

And I spat in his face once again.

Two face-spittings in a single night! Gross, I know, but justified.

'I think we'll burn you up again,' said Papa Crossbar, spitting blood and spittle. 'For real this time, rather than for fun.'

'Shall I fetch the flamethrower?' asked one of the ninjas.

'Yes,' said Papa Crossbar. 'Do that.'

'The big one or the small one, sir?'

'The biggest one you have.'

'Right, sir.' The ninja saluted and turned away. And then he stopped and turned back. 'I'll need a requisition form then, sir. To sign out the flamethrower from Ordnance Processing.'

'Just get the flamethrower *now*!' boomed Papa Crossbar.

'But I can't without a requisition form, sir. You'll have to sign the authorisation and then it will have to go through Thompson in Ordnance Admin. And he won't be here at this time of the night, so we'll have to do it tomorrow. And tomorrow is Saturday, so—'

And the ninja paused. Because there had been a bit of a flourish and a swish from Papa Crossbar. And now the ninja had a big golden ceremonial knife sticking out of his forehead.

'I'm glad he didn't pull that on *me*,' I said to the other ninja, who was looking on with what was probably a surprised expression. Because it can be quite tricky to tell with ninjas, as they have those bandana things tied around their gobs, don't they?

'My brother,' said the ninja. 'You've killed my brother, Pete.'

'These things happen,' said Papa Crossbar, and he withdrew the golden blade from Pete's forehead, and Pete toppled sideways.

'He's a thoroughgoing swine,' I said to the bereaved ninja. 'Why don't you punch his lights out and leave the rest to me?'

'I have a damn fine mind to, as it ha—'

And then, wouldn't you just know it—

And down went that ninja also, to lie beside his brother.

'I really thought he'd have you,' I said to Papa Crossbar. Backing away as I said it. 'Seems they were better at blending in and hiding than at the actual fighting side of it, eh?'

'A piece at a time,' said Papa Crossbar, golden weapon in his hand, blood dripping from the blade. 'I will skin you alive. A most painful way to die, I understand. Mr Ishmael certainly put up a right old fuss when I did it to him.'

'You thoroughgoing—' And I ran.

Not dignified, I agree. Not noble, not heroic. But come on – I really *had* given all this my best shot. And if I got away and he couldn't sacrifice me, then perhaps all the horrible stuff wouldn't happen.

Well, that's my story, at least. And I'm sticking to it.

'Come back, *you*!' he cried and gave chase.

And I somehow went out of the wrong door. Not the one that I came in by. And suddenly I found myself outside the conservatory and on the rooftop of the CIA building. In a veritable hurricane, with the thunder booming fit to bust and the lightning forking around and about and much too close for comfort.

And I have to say that once out and upon that storm-swept rooftop, I found myself with few if any places to run to. In fact none at all. So I backed away towards a corner of the roof.

'Nowhere to hide, Tyler,' shouted the Homunculus, his voice somehow rising over the storm. 'Nowhere to run to, nowhere to hide. Nothing to do but die.'

'There always *is* another option,' I shouted back, 'if you are prepared to work at it.'

'Perhaps the Tyler Technique? Or perhaps you might be a wee bit too distracted up here. Too much input, eh?' The blade came swishing towards me.

And I backed away just a little bit more. Then had no more away to back to.

And I glanced down. And it was a long way down. Down and down and down. With the roof of Mornington Crescent East (discontinued usage) so very far below.

And rain lashed me and thunder growled in my ears and I was now most scared.

And the blade swished once and then swished twice. And my left ear came off.

'Oh my God, no!' I howled and I snatched at that ear as it whirled through the air. And I did manage to catch it. But the blade whirled again and took off my right thumb.

And I howled, 'No!' And I howled, 'Help!' And then I just howled and howled. And I sank down to my knees on that roof all bloody and wretched and scared.

And the evil villain loomed over me. And he rose upon his toes and he laughed. And he cried, 'I win, Tyler. I win all.'

And down came the terrible blade.

72

And in that maelstrom, with the very elements lashing all around me, I knew that I was done. That I was lost, that I *had* lost. And now all would be gone. All life, all love, all everything.

And that terrible blade came down. And then fell to the rooftop beside me and bounced down over the edge. And I looked up from my fearful cower and viewed the Homunculus. And he was clutching at his chest.

And blood was flowing from his chest.

From a nice neat hole within it.

And I saw him turn. And then I heard two shots ring out above the fury of the storm. And the Homunculus turned back and gawped at me. And this time he had a hole in his forehead.

And he lurched at me. And then he swayed, right there upon the very edge of the rooftop.

And yes, I confess it – I gave him a little push.

I leaped up and kicked his bum.

73

And down he went and down. Through the elemental turmoil, down and down. And far below he struck the roof of Mornington Crescent East (discontinued usage) and he passed right through that roof and he struck the concourse below. And then bounced down the stairway, onto the platform, off the platform and into the hole that I had dynamited in the tracks.

And down to the City of Begrem.

And that in itself was a long way down.

And if, as is so often the case, there was any chance at all, in the way of super-villains, that he had somehow survived the gunshots to the head and chest and the fall to Mornington Crescent and then down to Begrem, this chance of survival was denied him by the lady in the golden straw hat, who had been awaiting the fulfilment of the prophecy in *The Book of All Knowledge (and Selected Lyrics)* regarding the second being that descends into Begrem.

The bad one.

That this bad one must be hacked all to pieces.

And the lady in the golden straw hat had her big golden knife all sharpened and ready.

And followed that prophecy, gorily, right to the letter.

74

And I looked up at my deliverer.

And I said, 'You took your time.'

And Lazlo Woodbine looked down upon me and said, 'Could you use a hand?'

And he helped me back to the high-domed conservatory. And he slammed shut the door. And he released the golden girlie. And then he set about sewing my left ear back on and also my right thumb, and I do have to say that although it hurt like the very Devil, he made a damn fine job of both.

'As long as no one ever notices that I have a thumb sewn on where my left ear should be, I think we'll be fine,' I said.

And oh how we laughed.

'And thank you,' I said. 'Mr Woodbine, thank you for saving my life.'

'No sweat, kid,' said Lazlo Woodbine. 'And you can call me Laz.'

'Well, Laz,' I said, 'once again, thank you. I just wish that you'd got here a bit earlier.' And I tapped at my resewn parts.

'But I did, kid,' said the great detective. 'I got here a while back. But you had to have your moment. Get the truth out of that thoroughgoing swine. For your autobiography. It will probably be written up a bit differently in the forthcoming Lazlo Woodbine thriller, but no matter about that. Only thing is, I can't figure just how I got here. Last thing I remember is being at Papa Crossbar's Voodoo Pushbike Scullery and then falling into that whirling black pit of oblivion that we nineteen-fifties genre detectives so often do. And then I'm suddenly here.'

'You have *me* to thank for *that*,' I said.

'And how?'

'It's a long story,' I said, 'and it has to do with a theory invented by a man named The Flange that *things are where they should be, because they should be where they are*. He tried to create the perfect sitting room for Jesus in order to bring about the Second Coming, but he failed. Before him, the members of the Cult of Jon Frum tried it. But tonight I achieved it through the Tyler Technique. The theory is that given the absolutely correct circumstances and situation, what is sought will come to pass. And in a situation where the world was at peril from the ultimate super-villain and there was a final rooftop confrontation (with a storm) going on, who could be there to sort things out *other* than Lazlo Woodbine? I just hoped that the magic would work. I figured it out earlier in the super-villain's office. The idea came to me that if I could just get him up onto the rooftop, you would appear. It was a long shot, but I believed in it and it worked.'

'Well, here's looking at you, kid,' said Lazlo.

'And that's not really *your* line, is it?' I said.

'But hey,' said Laz, 'I'm not even working in the first person. How good am I to you?'

And he shook me by the hand.

And I returned this handshake and felt very good about everything.

And then the golden girlie threw her arms about Lazlo Woodbine's neck and started kissing him.

Which I did *not* feel very good about.

'Hold on,' I said. 'I don't have to be a virgin any more.'

'What?' said Lazlo.

'Nothing,' said I.

And Lazlo Woodbine smiled. 'So all's well that ends well,' he said. 'And I suggest we take ourselves off to Fangio's Bar and celebrate this victory. And then you can settle your bill. Remembering, of course, that I am paid by the day. And I'm thinking, how long is it since I fell into that pit of whirling blackness in Fangio's? Because frankly, kid, you don't look quite so young as you once did.'

And he left that rooftop with the golden girlie on his arm.

And I went, 'Oh dear me.'

And followed him.

75

I wrote, at the very beginning of this book, that I *almost* saved Mankind. And, as you can see, I *almost* did.

I'm certainly not going to take all of the credit. Lazlo Woodbine did the actual shooting in the head of my demon brother, Keith. But I played my part, and my part was special.

If you read the final Lazlo Woodbine thriller, you will note that Laz takes *all of the credit*. But I don't mind about that, because in exchange for me agreeing to let him take all of the credit, he agreed to retire.

And so he did, to the Sussex Downs, to keep bees. And of course he did go out on the high point of his career, having saved Mankind and everything. And so, having done his stuff, Lazlo Woodbine moved on into myth.

Leaving me to carry on where he left off and perhaps even prove myself to be the greatest private eye that ever there was.

And as Laz was retiring, and as I *had* already bought the franchise and everything, I moved into his office and put a new sign up on the door—

SOME CALL ME TYLER
PSYCHIC DETECTIVE

I haven't had any cases yet, but hey, it's only been a week and I have had other things to do. Like visit the hospital, for instance, after I discovered that Laz had amusingly sewn my left ear back on upside down.

And then there was last night's reunion, which I mentioned in the first chapter of this book. In truth it was a bit more than just a reunion – it was my stag night.

Because I'm getting married today. To the golden girlie from Begrem (where we will be spending our honeymoon).

I'm rather excited about getting married. I'm particularly excited about the prospect of finally having sex. Even though I'm approaching my seventieth birthday. I reckon I'm still up for it.

Regarding Begrem, I have decided *not* to open it up to the tourist trade, nor to avail myself of the riches therein. It felt rather wrong, somehow, and as there have been sufficient wrongs done, I don't want to add any more of my own.

And, of course, there was the matter of the head of the CIA going missing. And where he might have ended up. Or down. Questions were asked, but answers weren't furnished and that one remains open on the files.

And regarding all those walking-dead folk. What became of them? Well, they'll all die again in their own good time and their souls will go off to wherever they should go.

Which, I suppose, means that this is the end of my tale.

Which seems a bit of a shame, really, but you have to end it somewhere. And I, like Laz, am going out on a high. But it is certainly not over for me. In fact, my career as Some Call Me Tyler, Psychic Detective, is only just beginning.

And if there is any justice in this world, you will soon be reading my exciting adventures and how I solve the most obtuse conundrums and thwart the diabolical plans of criminal masterminds using my extra-special power and the Tyler Technique.

And so, let me leave you with the words of . . . the George:

It's turned out nice again.